Benediction
at the
Savoia

Christine O'Hagan

Benediction
at the
Savoia

Harcourt Brace Jovanovich, Publishers

New York   San Diego   London

Requests for permission to make copies of any part of
the work should be mailed to: Permissions Department,
Harcourt Brace Jovanovich, Publishers,
8th Floor, Orlando, Florida 32887.

Library of Congress Cataloging-in-Publication Data
O'Hagan, Christine.
Benediction at the Savoia/Christine O'Hagan. — 1st ed.
p.   cm.
ISBN 0-15-111810-8
I. Title.
PS3565.H24B46   1992
813'.54 — dc20   91-47991

Designed by Camilla Filancia
Printed in the United States of America
First edition   A B C D E

For Richard Carson Kehl, Jr.,
my brother, with love

. . . God, whose law it is that he who learns must suffer. And even in our sleep, pain that cannot forget falls drop by drop upon the heart, and in our own despair, against our will, comes wisdom to us by the awful grace of God.

AESCHYLUS, *Agamemnon*

With deepest gratitude

to Shelby Hearon for her boundless generosity,

to Ann Rittenberg for her kindness, sensitivity,

and faith,

and to Claire Wachtel for her insightful, keen eye,

and to all three women for their friendship.

They were supposed to have pizza for supper, but Mae Rooney stopped in front of Empire Meats and stared at the display of roasts and steaks bleeding through the sheets of thin brown paper in the window. Delia Delaney, Mae's daughter, turned sharply and went inside the shop, annoyed, her nine-months-pregnant belly brushing heavily against the door. Mae followed quietly, like an obedient child, folding her arms across her chest, dangling a black square purse that was so big it seemed to bang against her knees.

Delia wore a powder-blue maternity dress with a tiny white collar, which was more a smock than a dress. It was hard for her, at this point, to fuss with buttons or zippers. The smock was very full; even so, her belly button was beginning to strain against the thin fabric. She was a week overdue, and her baby hadn't moved in that long.

Mae wore one of her cotton summer dresses, pastel-striped and cool. She carefully washed all her clothes by hand, soaking her dresses in starch and hanging them over the shower rod in the bathroom to dry. She liked to wrap the dresses in plastic and let them sit for a while in the icebox so they'd be easy to iron.

They were returning from their weekly trip to the A & P up on the avenue; Mae insisted on pulling the shopping cart, owing to her daughter's "delicate" condition. Delia, however, felt anything but delicate, maneuvering around with a stomach as big and hard as a watermelon.

She was much taller than Mae, who had small, light-fingered hands that she was proud of and tiny, puffy feet inside her strong black shoes. Mae Rooney was a staunch believer in good shoes and red meat.

The butcher passed by and smiled at Delia, and Delia smiled back, aware of her full breasts and his darting eyes. She doubted that he could see how pregnant she was through the display case. Pregnancy gave Delia a sense of freedom, her ripe woman's body safe under the cover of a little girl's dress. She liked not having to worry about the way men saw her.

"Be right with you, miss," the butcher said from the back of the shop. Delia wondered if he could see Mae, who was so tiny she was nearly invisible from where he stood.

The August day outside was clear and hot, but the store was so cold that the windows were fogged up and the people passing by, in their bright summer clothes, looked like melting candies. Delia shifted from one foot to the other. Her stomach hurt from bumping into the heavy door. She ran her hand over the lines of the baby, thinking miserably that the blow should have stirred the child. When Delia was pregnant with the others, first with Maureen and then with Patty, the slightest touch made the baby roll and stretch. With them, Delia had stared down at herself and wondered which protrusion was an elbow, or a foot or a fanny, but each bump felt the same, like a round, firm knob punching to get free.

Before Maureen was born, she was so active that Delia had dreamed she was carrying an octopus.

Weeks back, when this baby was still kicking wildly, Delia's husband, Maurice, watched her belly gyrate as she cleared the table and he said that this one was probably wearing boxing gloves.

While she waited for the butcher, she looked at herself in the mirror against the back wall. From the shoulders up, she hadn't changed a bit. She was a rather pretty woman of thirty-two, with light-brown hair, teased into a bouffant style, and wide-set blue eyes. Rosaleen Kowalski, her friend, who was expecting too, swore that except for her coloring, Delia looked like the pregnant First Lady, Jackie Kennedy. Every time she said that, Delia got the goose bumps.

"What should I buy, Mama?" she asked Mae impatiently.

Mae looked over the display case, smacked her lips, and pointed to a good-sized sirloin.

"This steak," she said to Delia. "We'll have baked Idaho potatoes with it and fresh peas. Is that the Rooney meal number one or the Rooney meal number two?" she asked brightly.

"One." Delia smiled. "Number two is the meat loaf with stewed tomatoes."

"I'll never understand why your brother Eugene started that stuff, thinking it was funny to tell everyone on the street that we ate the same five meals over and over again. We always ate good, I saw to that. Everyone said that meat was too dear, but I went to the butcher anyway, though we didn't have a cent, not with what your father drank! I cooked just like my mother cooked. Spend it on the table and you won't be spending it on the doctor. That's what I always say."

Put a beggar on horseback (Mae always said) and he'll ride to hell. You never know from where you're sittin' just how far your drawers are hangin'.

Above Mae's head, the butcher winked at Delia and handed her a ticket for the steak, which she was to bring to the cashier who sat in a glass booth on the other side of the store. Gobs of sawdust stuck under her shoes. As she waited to pay (with Mae's money), Delia swayed from side to side, hoping that if she moved enough, she'd start the birth. Any activity was better than the endless waiting. She washed dishes as soon as she put them in the sink, and she vacuumed two and three times a day, moving the coffee table and the couch. Just that morning, she had washed her heavy white bedspread and dragged it, sopping wet, up the stairs to the roof of the apartment building to dry, being careful not to let the wet fabric near the patches of gooey tar under her slippers. Her arms ached with the effort, and still the baby didn't quiver.

When Delia and Mae left Empire, the sun was so strong that the air burned their cheeks. Big cinders, like huge black snowflakes, and trails of fine sticky ashes fell from the train tracks of the el above their heads. Things were always falling from the train tracks onto the street; cinders and ashes were the least of it. During winter storms, giant chunks of ice slammed down onto the sidewalk, and when Delia was small, a suicide threw himself in front of the train and his head rolled along the pavement below.

Mae tried to avoid walking under the el, but Delia didn't. One pastel winter dusk years before, when air and sky and passing pedestrians were tinged with pink, like an open-air nursery just for her baby, Delia pushed the infant Maureen, in her carriage, twenty blocks under the el, from the five-and-ten in Woodside right up to the Heights. Halfway through the journey, the night crashed on top of them, and strange dark people on their way home from work banged into the carriage on the narrow sidewalk. Bright car headlights flashed on the carriage's wheels, their drivers impatient with Delia's foolishness at having a baby out at night.

Each time the carriage was jostled, the baby cried out, and Delia saw her mouth open, a perfect O, through the plastic wind protector that was stretched across the carriage hood, over the baby's face like a caul. Delia stopped suddenly, and people slammed into her, as if they were human dominoes. She opened her coat, took Maureen from the carriage, placed her flat against her breasts, and buttoned her coat around the two of them. With one hand she held the baby's back (that's how tiny Maureen was), and with the other she steered the empty carriage through the menacing throngs. The screeching brakes of the train above made the baby shudder, but Delia held her so close that Maureen sucked on Delia's neck, so close that the baby's tiny wool hat chafed Delia's chin. Halfway up the next block, a workman's hammer dropped from the el and pierced the empty carriage's hood. Delia believed in God's will.

"Saint Gerard," Mae said to Delia. "You want the labor to start, he's the one you oughta pray to. Patron saint of mothers. He'll help you with the birth. I always prayed to Saint Monica myself. Patron saint of runaround husbands — what's the word: 'wayward'? Wayward husbands and wayward children. Your brothers Eugene and Gerald nearly drove me crazy, and your father too."

She sighed and stood the shopping cart on the sidewalk. "Leave me rest a minute," she said. "You know, Delia, you oughta try prayin' to Saint Monica too. Maybe you'd get on better with Maurice."

But "your father" were the words Delia was thinking of: the little red-faced man in the crumpled white shirt, with his glasses always slipping off his nose. Dead and gone. Everyone in the Shamrock Inn or Healey's or any of the other bars seemed to like Denis Rooney, who was always good for an impromptu round or some off-key Irish fight songs or even an extra ten-spot when it was needed, sitting in a pool of water on the bar.

He died suddenly, right on the street, days before Maureen was born.

"But never pray to Saint Jude," Mae reminded Delia. "He's the patron saint of—"

"Impossible causes," Delia said sharply. "I know, Mama. He'll answer your prayers, but he'll take a terrible price. I know."

They passed Pierre's Dry Cleaners, where President Kennedy's picture hung in the window, and the Regina Coeli Shop, where his picture hung on top of the door by the crucifixes. There was even a picture of President Kennedy on top of a calendar hanging in the window of the Ho Lim Laundry. Mr. Ho stood in his doorway and stared at them. Mae stiffened her tiny shoulders and stared straight ahead. Mae didn't trust the Chinese. On Saturday mornings, she followed Maureen and Patty to Mr. Ho's to pick up Maurice's shirts, standing outside the window in her long black coat, her white hair undone and loose around her shoulders. Mr. Ho caught Delia's eye and nodded.

My weight is all in front of me, Delia thought, glancing at their reflection in the laundry's windows, and Mama, dragging that cart, has it all behind her.

If August passed and led into September and she still hadn't had the baby, Delia knew she'd be ready to call on Saint Jude and let him take what he wanted. The wait for the birth was much too long. Every day, after she had cleaned her house, she waddled over to St. Immaculata's to light a candle at the foot of the Blessed Mother statue. Every day, she climbed the stairs to the top-floor apartment at least four times, carrying groceries up or the garbage down, pumping her legs as hard as she could, until she lost her breath. When nobody was looking, in the sunny afternoons, she jumped rope with her girls underneath the thick maple tree in front of the apartment house, yet the baby didn't budge.

Maybe she had miscalculated, she thought. Something had to free her from the pregnancy, but Delia didn't know what that something was. After all, she said to herself, it's practically still the beginning of August. I'm not going to worry. I still have time.

Although she didn't like to do it, Maureen Delaney left her sister Patty on the street, skipping rope, and walked anxiously to the corner, glancing, as was her habit, into Silvio's Shoe Repair, which was nestled into an apartment house near the end of the block. She was glad to see the old man's white head bent over his workbench. Maureen's father, Maurice, swore that Silvio's tiny shop was so cluttered that he could lie dead for weeks under a sea of oxfords and loafers and tins of polish, and nobody would ever know what had happened to him.

Maureen was a tall, solemn girl of thirteen. She was dark-haired compared to her sister, Patty, who was eleven and had hair that was copper-colored. Both girls had serious gray eyes and black eyelashes that were as thick and as straight as the bristles on a whisk broom.

(Maureen never realized that Silvio was so superstitious: when he looked up suddenly and saw her staring at him, he got so nervous that he crossed himself.)

Maureen was worried about Delia, wondering why she was taking so long to come home from the store. Once, under the el, she had seen a crowd gathering around a car that had all four doors open. A woman's bare legs, her feet in pointy spike-heeled shoes, were in the gutter. Somebody said that the lady was having a baby, right there and then, but all that Maureen could see were puddles of gray water around the woman's feet. Maureen got as close to the car as she could, expecting to glimpse a baby in one of those puddles, swimming around like a guppy. She was afraid that the woman would stand up suddenly and spear the infant with her high-heeled shoe.

She hoped that Delia hadn't had the baby in the A & P.

At the corner, the sidewalk was still blocked off and as usual, a straggling handful of people stood aimlessly at the curb, watching workmen in dirty boots clomp in and out of what once had been Hans' Groceries. The store had had a gas explosion months before, the tomatoes and the oranges spilling into the gutter like a juggler gone berserk. The morning it had happened, the sidewalk had been so

6

crowded that Maureen had had to walk in the street, nearly getting hit by the cars and buses whizzing past. She had tripped over the curb, not looking where she was going, worried that Patty might have tried to follow behind. Even then, Maureen had been frightened to leave her sister, although Delia had said Patty was old enough to stay alone for a few minutes (and Patty had sworn she was old enough to take care of herself).

That morning, standing in the gutter, Maureen had seen the whole block stretched out before her. Only one store had been open for business. People casually walked in and out of Cohen's Stationery one door away from Hans', as if the grocery store were still there, though the hole in the pavement was already as dark as a mine.

So long ago, and yet she still missed Hans. He had let her mother charge groceries when she didn't have any money. The morning he lost his store, he came up the stairs to their apartment to collect what was owed him and he had cried and Delia had cried right along with him because he didn't have a cent.

Somebody standing in the gutter had said that Hans' was going to be an Italian restaurant, that the store had been up for sale for over a year anyway. Maureen couldn't imagine that, a fancy restaurant in the damp air under the el, but it seemed to be true. Behind the boarded-up windows, the hammering and sawing could be heard from as far away as the A & P. She just wanted the gaping hole in the street to be gone. The charred brick around the covered windows had sickened her; all through the spring and now into the summer, the kids on the street had been hanging over the rope to look down into the blackened cellar, Patty among them. For months now, Maureen couldn't sleep at night, fearful that her father might stop off after work in one of the bars and stumble past the section where the street sank, his big, heavy policeman shoes dragging along the pavement.

Chunks of sunlight fell through the thick train tracks over Maureen's head, checkerboard squares of cool and warmth around her shoulders. Across the street, on the other side of the avenue, Maureen could see that some of the old stores had changed owners, different-looking people outside sweeping the sidewalks and cleaning the windows, peering up through the wooden track bed as if they hoped for a bit of the sun to touch their faces. The Shamrock Inn, or the other old places in the neighborhood, never cleaned anything. Year in, year out, the same dead flies were stuck to the Shamrock's front window, underneath a muddy green awning striped with dirty white lines, its frame bent so that the canvas was scooped in the center like a melon half. Maureen had seen birds skip along the edge of the awning and fall into the worn fabric. Pictures of former Miss Rheingolds were Scotch-taped to one of the dark windows, wrinkling and aging in the sun.

On windy days, the dirt in the street in front of the Shamrock whirled about in clouds, pricking and stinging at passing ankles like sand flies. Bits of garbage huddled in the Shamrock's doorway. Sometimes old people slipped on ripped sheets of newspaper in front of the place, or they skidded on the loose covers of Spanish-language magazines lying on the sidewalk. Maureen, who sometimes sat at a small table in the Shamrock, waiting for her father to be ready to go home, had heard the regulars complain about the foreigners as if their magazines went searching through the Heights for victims.

She jumped up on the sidewalk as soon as she passed Cohen's Candy Store, and she thought of her uncle Eugene, who was thrown through the window of the place late one night by a stranger. She never passed Cohen's without searching the sidewalk for bits of her uncle, drops of blood or thin strips of fabric from his shirt, although it had happened a long time ago and Eugene was fine now.

At last Maureen spotted her mother and her grandmother, Delia's blue dress swaying from side to side, her belly level with Mae's shoulder.

Grandma looks like an old wrinkled kid, Maureen thought, running down the street to take the shopping cart from Mae's hands.

"I'm okay." Delia touched Maureen's cheek. "Don't look so scared!"

"I'm not scared. . . . You just took a long time." Maureen saw the bag from the butcher's nesting on top of the other groceries. Looks like Grandma won again, she thought, miserable at the loss of the promised pizza, although Mae was treating them to dinner and she knew she shouldn't complain, even when her grandmother would pour the drippings from the meat into a cracked china cup and try to make Maureen and Patty drink it, "good and healthy" for their blood.

She thought she saw her sister near the construction site again, and so Maureen walked quickly ahead of the others. There was such danger in the world for a little kid like Patty; so many things could happen to her. At night, after dinner, while Delia sat in the living room, rubbing her belly in wide circles, Patty opened the door and ran downstairs through the halls to play with the other kids. Maureen was supposed to be washing the dishes, but instead she tiptoed to the front door and opened it just a bit, enough to count Patty's footsteps on the stairs until they faded away.

In the corner of the girls' bedroom, resting on newspapers, was a freshly painted crib, a gleaming white cloud of a bed for the new baby. Maurice went over it again and again with fresh enamel until the surface was like a mirror. Rosaleen, her mother's friend, had tied a dozen or so tiny dolls to the slats of the crib with thin yellow ribbons. Sometimes at night, Maureen or Patty crept out of bed, pretending to get a drink of water or to go to the bathroom, but instead they sat on the floor and stared into the tiny dolls' faces. Maureen's stomach fluttered whenever she thought about their new baby's face.

She wondered what it would be like to be pregnant.

In the last few weeks, her mother had seemed to stop sleeping. Every time Maureen got up, Delia heard her and yelled out in the dark to leave the crib alone. When it was nearly light, Maureen would be awakened by the white glow from the empty screen of the television set, and she'd find her mother just sitting in the chair, the television screen reflected in the summer linoleum floor, shiny as a puddle. She noticed that her mother looked out the window often, although there was nothing to see from the rear of the building but other apartments and the maze of reddish fire escapes dangling from their windows. Maureen thought that being pregnant meant that there might be a lot to worry about.

Delia and Mae walked past the blown-out store; Maureen waited for them to catch up. Burnt bricks were still stacked up near the entrance.

"Hans never dusted anything." Mae shook her head. "All those cans were just filthy, and his prices were too dear."

(The same words, Maureen thought, over and over again.)

"But he was always open," Delia said, stretching her back. She leaned over and pushed Maureen's hair out of her eyes. "He let us charge things when we were broke."

"He was nice to the kids too, Grandma," Maureen said. "He let us have loose pieces of gum or broken pretzels for free."

"Well," Mae said, annoyed with Hans, as if he had purposely ruined the street, "you only liked him because he always had his eye on you, Delia. Even when he was a young fella and his father had the store, he wanted to take you out, you remember?"

"Oh, Ma, stop." Delia looked as if she were about to cry.

"Well, it's a good thing you didn't marry him, Delia. Now where would you be? The store is gone, and I'll bet you anything he didn't have a lick of insurance, he was so careless. If you ask me, he probably brought it on himself. That dirty store with all them dirty cans. You mark my words, something he neglected started that explosion, I'll bet you, some dirty rags or something. Maybe Maurice drinks a bit, but he's got a good steady job and he comes home to you and the girls eventually. Half the time your father didn't even come home, you remember?"

Delia shrugged her shoulders.

"Where would you be now if you'd married Hans? Think about it, Delia," Mae said. "You know what I always say, don't you? 'I cried because I had no shoes, and then I met a man who had no feet. . . .' What in God's *name* are *you* crying about?"

Alarmed, Maureen looked up at her mother, who had her hand over her eyes, as if some bright light were too close to her face. Delia seldom cried, never out on the street! Maureen stared at the sidewalk near her mother's feet, waiting for the baby to fall onto the pavement.

Mae looked frantically up and down the block. Maureen watched her grandmother's nose twitch like a rabbit's.

"Stop crying in the street, Delia Mary! What if somebody were to see you, what then? Get hold of yourself. . . . You're gonna have that baby any minute now, with the help of the Blessed Mother. You'll see, Delia, you'll have a baby big and strong like the others. Have some faith in God, will you? Will you, Delia? Where's your faith in God?" she asked desperately, taking Delia by the arm, wiping her nose with a tissue. Delia's pale skin was blotched, and her eyes were swollen. She pushed her mother's arm away from her and, by herself, started up the street.

In June, before Maureen left school, Sister Francis had told the seventh-grade class that a woman passed through the Valley of Death every time she gave birth. For a brief moment, she had said, each time a baby is born, his mother could die. Maureen had felt sick when she said that. Her desk seemed to sway.

"Did this happen to Mary, God's mother, too?" someone asked.

"Yes," Sister Francis said. "Of course."

"But she knew she wouldn't die!" Maureen blurted, from the back of the room. "She knew she was having a boy and that he would be God! God wouldn't let anything happen to His mother!"

Sister Francis had looked wearily at Maureen.

"Mary had faith, dear. That's what God wants all of us to have. Faith."

But as the days wore on, there was no baby (and no Valley of Death to worry about), only a wide-awake Delia, staring out the window or, in a late-day burst of energy, scrubbing down the kitchen stove, and Maureen remembered what the nun had said. She tried to have faith. All summer long, she had kept a small Blessed Mother statue in the pocket of her shorts, and she touched it constantly, stopping what she was doing to offer a Hail Mary for Delia. She was still convinced that the Blessed Mother had had it easier than her own.

Now, looking up the block, Maureen was relieved to see Patty running toward them, smiling, with her arms outstretched.

The first time she had met her, Kathleen Delaney told the eighteen-year-old Delia Mary Rooney that Maurice was late in being born and that she had had to wait and wait for him, although she was anxious and hungry for a baby again, having buried Terence and William a dozen years before. And then, when he was finally being delivered, they could hardly get him out, and it was no wonder, was it, she asked Delia, "with him nearly twelve pounds heavy and over two feet tall?"

"Torn," she had said, twice, with her lips pursed and her voice soft, Delia imagining a raw gaping hole somewhere in Kathleen's center, bits of rubbery dangling flesh resting on the tops of her scrawny thighs. Delia thought being "torn" was so feminine, as if Maurice's mother had inner parts webbed across with fine lace, as if inside her a flower had exploded and left behind jagged, curling pink-tinged petals.

Delia had sat on the green couch in the Delaneys' living room, listening to the story of Maurice's beginnings, her hands folded politely in her lap, so anxious to be torn like Kathleen Delaney (who was a nurse and therefore knowledgeable about such things) that her stomach fluttered. She wanted so much to be *married*, the word itself hinting of secretive feminine ailments and then masculine soothings, oozes and oils from a married life, profuse enough to force Delia to lie back delicately against the fancy embroidered pillows she intended to buy, gazing wanly at the ceiling. Her mother never catered to the genitals; she didn't believe in them. Even when Delia had cramps with her period, Mae Rooney pulled her out of bed by the pajama top and sent her off to school. Mae Rooney had no patience with "feminine ailments," and those who claimed to suffer from them were, in Mae's own opinion, full of shit.

Yet right in front of Delia was a woman who whispered "torn" to her, a woman who had suffered just as Delia was more than willing to do for the beautiful Maurice Martin Delaney, who was over in the schoolyard playing basketball.

Kathleen's eyes gleamed when she said his name and then repeated it in an uninflected voice, as if she might have forgotten that Delia was in the room. When he was two, his mother said, he was so big that people on the street grabbed chunks of his face and asked him when he was starting school, and when he was five, they wondered if he had a job yet, delivering newspapers, perhaps. Why, when he was seven, some men on a truck asked him to put down his baseball glove and help them carry a new refrigerator five flights up, to the top floor of their apartment house, for a dime, and she couldn't find him for two hours (growing "frantic," she claimed), but when she checked the roof, there he was in the center of muscular grown men, "like the child Jesus surrounded by his elders."

"At eleven," she said, after a second or two had passed, "he was over six feet tall and his father, Sean, who was a little bit of a man to begin with, stood underneath his chin." Delia thought of the young Maurice not as a boy at all but as some sort of wide shade tree, like a maple. According to Kathleen Delaney, two, five, seven, and eleven marked the years of Maurice's amazing growth, as if he had never been nine or three, as if those years might have passed while he slept (although at the rate he was said to have grown, Delia thought he might have needed whole years to rest, two or three years of normal growth compressed into his one).

"When my Maurice was just a kid" — his mother had laughed — "he couldn't even fit into his father's shoes, those feet that wore not shoes but *gunboats*, they were so long," and Delia imagined the grubby hardworking shoes of his parents keeping a respectable distance from Maurice's huge sneakers and knew exactly how they had looked, long and skinny and bent in the middle like a pair of boomerangs.

Kathleen complained that it was always so hard to dress him, buying his clothes in the men's stores in the Heights when he was just a boy, cutting off the long and skinny pants legs with a pair of borrowed pinking shears and sewing a clumsy hem, but by the time she had finished, he had grown some more, and there was never enough fabric to let down. His shirts never closed against his big neck, and the ties she bought always looked too short. He had looked like Oliver Hardy, she claimed, always fiddling with his little tie, and then she laughed again.

She leaned over the green rug, closer to Delia, and said his underpants were so big she was embarrassed by them, folding them in half before she hung them on the roof clothesline, and it struck Delia that they weren't discussing his underwear at all but rather that part of Maurice that had been inside both their bodies, although Kathleen didn't realize that she and Delia had had so much in common. Delia stared at her ankles when Kathleen stopped talking and sat back.

When she was young, Delia had walked out of Queens Shoes with Mae and reached the avenue minutes after Maurice's father was taken away in the city ambulance, his bloody gray jacket in a puddle on the street and the bus that hit him propped up on the curb, tilted like a ship. It was in all the papers. The next day, Mae picked up a copy of the *Press* and recognized his name. "Sean Delaney," she said to Denis and Delia as they ate their dinner, letting the newspaper drop in her lap.

"I wonder if it's them Delaneys that Anna Curley knows, the Delaneys that lost them two baby boys to the consumption." Delia looked up. She knew Maurice Delaney from school. He was a year ahead of her, and she thought he was the handsomest boy in St. Immaculata's.

"Gawd save us, Mae," Denis Rooney said, taking off his glasses to glare at her. "It wasn't the consumption took them boys. Anna said a million times it was the influenza. . . . Don't ye remember a thing about it, the horses dyin' in the streets?" Then he got up, cursing under his breath, and went to bed.

"At any rate"—Mae turned to Delia—"it's two tragedies—no, *three* tragedies—on that poor woman. That ought to be a lesson to you, miss, answerin' your father fresh, not doin' what he says—look at how easy he could be gone! Think of that other son of the Delaneys', no brothers and now no da. Think of that poor boy the next time you're of a mind to fight with your brothers, miss."

But there was never a time Delia could think of when she didn't

14

do what her father said, and she rarely fought with Gerald or Eugene; they were too busy fighting with each other. "Is Maurice Delaney an orphan now?" she had asked Mae, having read the word in a book, anxious to use it.

"An orphan?" Mae asked incredulously. "An orphan's got *no* parents, miss." Mae thought about that for a minute or two. "And how would you like *that*?" she asked Delia, who instantly began to sniffle, thinking there was something wrong with herself, she felt things so much. With no parents, where would she go, who would she live with? She had no answer for Mae.

But she began to notice Maurice Delaney more than she ever had before, imagining that his two baby brothers sat on his strong shoulders, like guardian angels. He was always late when it was his turn to serve Mass, the only altar boy to race through the schoolyard, with his skimpy tie flipping in his face. Delia, waiting in line to sharpen her pencil, watched Maurice from the second-story classroom window. Even from so far away she could see his ruddy cheeks, as he dragged his carefully wrapped cassock along the ground. All the girls knew how blue his eyes were, and behind his back they called him Superman because of the slice of black hair resting like a comma on his forehead.

On Sunday morning, when Maurice Delaney held the paten against Delia's neck at Communion, she noticed that his cassock did not fit him right: too short, scraping against his shins. On Saturdays, when she and Rosaleen sneaked into the back of the church to watch the weddings, the couples on the altar seemed confused, as if they weren't quite sure if Maurice was an altar boy or a priest. It was just like his own mother said: Maurice was awful big.

After the accident, Delia seemed to see Maurice everywhere, in the schoolyard or on the avenue, in heavy wool suits even in the spring. These, too, were too short, as itchy-looking as burlap, with big gold buttons, embossed in the centers, seemingly welded to his jackets, and a carefully pressed linen handkerchief in his breast pocket, too big to be a child's, big as a dinner napkin.

He had a rich-colored burled leather briefcase instead of a schoolbag, and the smell of it preceded him into the classroom. The teaching nuns would look up from the first-day roster and smile, for it was the kind of briefcase a fancy lawyer might carry into a courtroom and slam down on the defense table.

"Every cent I made," Kathleen said proudly, at the end of a long description of an Irish hand-knitted sweater and a camel's hair coat "just sitting" in Maurice's closet, "I put on his back," and then she smiled. Delia remembered the year his teacher, Sister Thomas Aquinas, had died suddenly and they were jammed into the same classroom, half the room seventh grade and the other half eighth. The camel's hair coat was too long for the children's cloakroom, dragging along the dusty floor, the belt snaking around the ankles of the other students, tripping them. He had been sitting two aisles away from her, a moody, thoughtful boy always fiddling with his alligator pencil case or his gold pen or his black shiny rosary beads in a gold-trimmed alligator case. Mae had found out from Anna that Sean Delaney had been a printer, his fingers always stained black, on his way home from work when he was killed, his wife and only child "left comfortable."

To Delia's mind, "comfortable" was hardly the word for Maurice Delaney, the biggest boy in school, carrying the organ for Sister James the Lesser, the music teacher, from one classroom to the next, bringing the troublemakers (even Rosaleen Clancy, who had been chewing gum) down to Mother Superior so often that he began to belong more to the faculty than to the students. None of the children liked him (except Danny Kowalski, who liked everyone), and he would spend his recess by himself in the back of the church in his long beige coat, reading the booklets describing the life of each saint in the racks by the baptismal font or playing with the holy cards in the religious articles store in the church vestibule.

Delia had spotted Maurice and Sister Mary Alice, the youngest nun in St. Immaculata's School, at the end of a corridor, framed in the sunny window. Maurice was carrying a carton of books, and Sister Mary Alice's youthful white hand rested on his sleeve. She was the prettiest woman Delia had ever seen, with a pouty pink mouth and sweeping eyelashes. It was almost as if some people were too fine and too fragile for the world outside, for the grime and bad teeth all around them.

"Of course," Kathleen was saying, "he wasn't that much of a student, you know. Indifferent. I was always up there at the school, talking to his teachers." Delia nodded her head: she had seen Kathleen in the corridors. Her reflection in the shiny gray floor was spindly, her clothes were too warm and somber, and she always wore a hat. You could guess that the stranger outside the classroom was Mrs. Delaney if you saw Maurice leaning back in his seat and shutting his eyes, his feet sticking out into the aisle.

He graduated and went off to St. Edward's Boys' High School in Astoria, and then a year later Delia was off to St. Catherine's Girls' High in Manhattan. Sometimes she saw him on the street or she saw him after school in the A & P, where he worked part time. They smiled and said hello and turned brilliantly red. In her four years at St. Catherine's, Delia had had only a few dates, all brothers of her girlfriends, with faces exactly like their sisters', so that it seemed twice as wrong when they groped at the front of her sweater in the balcony of the Heights Theater — perverted and dirty and odd, all at the same time, their moist and nasty fingers traveling up her thighs so quickly she wasn't always aware of it happening but reacted instinctively just the same, smashing down on their hungry wrists with her pocketbook, marching herself home.

One Sunday in April of her junior year, coming home from church, Delia saw Maurice in front of the Rexall and didn't recognize him at first. He was in the middle of a gang of boys smoking cigarettes and shoving each other against the car fenders. It was his wool jacket that caught her attention, dangling from the antenna of a blue Studebaker nearby. She ducked into the doorway of Hooperman's Notions and brushed her hair, peeking out to watch Maurice roll the sleeves of his white shirt around his elbows, a cigarette in his mouth, and then lean into the flame of a cigarette lighter held by one of the others.

"Remember that Maurice Delaney?" Mae asked at the supper table a few days later. Delia looked up from her baked potato. Her brothers never came home for supper anymore, and Denis was always working overtime or had stopped off in a bar, yet Mae insisted on preparing enough food for what seemed like half the world. Another baked potato was sitting in front of Delia, just waiting for her, shriveling up. Mae was searching through the silverware drawer for a knife.

17

"What about him, Ma?" Delia asked.

"Who?" Mae looked at her.

"Maurice Delaney, Ma. You were just saying something about him," Delia answered irritably.

"Oh, the nurse's son . . . You remember the babies, don't you, and the day we were comin' out of the shoestore . . ."

"Yes, Ma!" Delia threw down her fork. *"For God's sake, what about him?"*

"You mind your mouth, miss, and don't be hollerin' at me. I heard today from Anna Curley that he's gone bad, runnin' around with a bunch of bums on the streets, out all hours of the night, dressing in tight pants and a leather motorcycle jacket, that's what Anna Curley said, his hair all greasy like and combed back. Ah," she said, shaking her head, "the sufferings of his poor mother."

"Maybe Anna Curley had better mind her own business," Delia said, covering the second potato with her napkin and hoping her mother wouldn't notice.

"Eat the rest of yer dinner," her mother said, "and don't be knockin' my friends."

In August, two months after Maurice graduated, Delia saw him in Cushing's Bakery after Mass, buying crullers, his mother at his side. He wore not a motorcycle jacket but another short hot suit, mopping his brow with his generous handkerchief. He smiled at her and nodded. She'd heard he had tried to join the Marines but he'd had some trouble with his ears and instead he'd continued on at the A & P, working full-time hours. Anna Curley, Delia decided, was nuts.

Then, on the first day of her senior year at St. Catherine's, her mother sent her to the A & P after school, and she saw him in the produce aisle. Sneaking around his back to pick up a head of lettuce (her hair was uncombed, she wore no lipstick), she heard an old lady in a dusty black hat ask him to weigh a bunch of carrots, and then she asked him why he had never married, a handsome man like himself, and he muttered something and then dropped a whole carton of onions on his toes. Delia hopped over two rolling onions and forgot about the lettuce, laughing all the way home.

At the St. Catherine's Thanksgiving Dance, on a night so windy that sparse reddish leaves blew into the open auditorium window, Delia saw Maurice Delaney in a black suit that finally fit him, sitting alone on the stairs that led to the stage, an unlit cigarette concealed loosely in his curved hand. He looked up at Delia, and then at Danny Kowalski — much heavier than he'd been in grade school, with the same trusting freckled face — who sat down next to Maurice. Seeing Delia, they smiled. Maurice hadn't changed much since seventh grade, Delia thought, when he sat in the back of the room, handsome and quiet. She smiled back at them and waved, a nervous little flutter to her wrist. Her heart pounding, she ran across the dance floor to find Rosaleen. (She still couldn't understand why Rosaleen had ever wanted to be her friend. They had sat together at one desk when Sister Alberta grew too old to teach and the fifth-grade classes were combined. Delia was always afraid of Rosaleen Clancy, who came to school with her book covers in shreds, without her uniform shoes. Rosaleen never had a hankie, just wiped her nose on her sleeve, until Delia began to ask Mae for an extra. When they were dismissed for lunch, Rosaleen went by herself to the five-and-ten and got a hot dog. She was the only girl to sit through geography with mustard on her collar. "You want to be friends?" she had asked Delia, after borrowing her ruler and her eraser and sheets from her notebook, staring at her steadily. Delia nodded; she had been afraid to say no.) It would have been too brash — her mother's word — to just walk over to talk to the two boys by herself, but when she plucked at her friend's sleeve, Rosaleen swore she didn't remember either one of them from grade school and didn't want to come with Delia; she didn't want to talk to them anyway, she insisted, finally turning her back on Delia's pleas. Then Rosaleen disappeared into the crowd.

The streets those days were full of handsome young men who smiled at Delia, yet they still gave her a bit of a jolt and made her shy. Well, she decided recklessly, let them think that I'm brash. She went back to the stairs, smiled boldly at Danny, and leaned against the stage. She wore a soft pink sweater and a gray wool skirt; she hugged herself and shuddered when Maurice looked up again, his teeth very white and even, a handkerchief, small this time, in his pocket. Only a year out of high school, and already he had a five o'clock shadow; she remembered how that had excited her. He smiled, and she was aware of a warm-fabric flush creeping across her upper chest, spreading to her neck. Two girls from her religion class, Doris and Betty, jitter-bugged in front of them, their skirts flipping (a flash of the top of their tan stockings and their garters), their breasts bouncing in their cotton blouses. Delia, thankful for the refuge of the loud music, watched Maurice watch them. He had such long arms, she thought, such enormous hands.

The music stopped. "So how've you been, Delia?" Danny's reddish-brown hair swept straight back from his big face. Delia hadn't remembered that his brown eyes were so far apart. People looked so different up close.

"Fine, Danny." She smiled, struggling to sound casual. "And you?" But he never answered, seeing someone he knew, patting her shoulder and jumping up, leaving Delia and Maurice staring at the empty dance floor in embarrassed silence. "How's your foot?" she asked at the exact moment he began to say something; they laughed.

"My what?" he asked, the first words he had ever directed at her.

"Your foot," she explained, pointing at his shining shoes. "One day I was in the A & P and you dropped a carton of onions on your foot. Remember?"

"Oh, yeah." He shook his head ruefully. "I was out of work for a week." He looked sideways at her, no doubt wondering, she thought, if she had heard the old lady in the black hat. "We get a lot of nutty people in there," he said, just in case she had. He cleared his throat. He would never go for Delia, she just knew it. She looked like a thousand other girls, with her pale blue eyes and her too small nose. Such white skin: Mae wouldn't let her wear rouge. She had dotted her cheeks in the girls' room with orange Tangee lipstick and blended it in. Her chin was weak, that was what a girl named Ellen had said to her in science class. Well, she had already decided to make up for her plain-pretty face once she was out in the world and had a job. She was going to dress distinctively, in big Grace Kelly hats, a good black handbag, unusual pins on the shoulders of her well-cut dresses.

"Dance?" he was finally forced to ask when the band started up again, fixing Delia with a level blue gaze. She nodded, and he led her out to the floor, Betty and Doris, Rosaleen and that girl Ellen, sliding into whispering knots. He wrapped his warm wide hands around her slender waist like a belt. Maybe old Anna Curley was right, Delia thought dreamily; he smelled of leather, or maybe she was just thinking of his leather-briefcase days. It clung to him, the dangerous smell of the back seats of Checker cabs, cowboys' saddles, she imagined, the holsters in western movies. His hands were strong and persistent, exciting her and protecting her at the same time. He was a smooth dancer. Delia was used to the light touch of Rosaleen when they turned up the radio and danced next to Delia's bed in her narrow bedroom. Maurice smelled of Aqua Velva; she thought she tasted the aftershave in the scraped nape of his neck. He held her so tightly, her forehead against his chin, that she heard the music vibrate in his jaw, their legs welded thigh-to-thigh.

When they sat down, her underarms were soaking wet, a fine line of perspiration stretched across her upper lip. Maurice said something to her, but she didn't hear him, just looked up at the sound of his voice and saw her father, in his stained and greasy work boots, his worn flannel shirt, walking across the dance floor, looking for her, ready to take her home. She jumped up before he spotted her, before he could say anything, ashamed of his boots and his clothes and his brogue. She turned and waved good-bye to Maurice. "I'll call you," he mouthed, but she hadn't given him her telephone number. She never thought that he'd call, and she cried at home in her bed, squeezing her eyes so tight that when she opened them, she saw confetti dancing in the dark. "Dance?" she had whispered to herself, trying to sound like Maurice, until she fell asleep, hoping she'd be able to just put him out of her mind.

On Monday, at school, Rosaleen told Delia that Maurice Delaney was conceited but Danny Kowalski was cute. (She'd suddenly remembered them both, after Delia had gone.) Maurice had ignored her, but Danny had asked her for her number. Delia should forget about that Maurice Delaney. "He thinks he's God's gift," Rosaleen said, counting change in the school cafeteria to pay for a bowl of pea soup.

When Maurice called Delia the following Thursday night, she was shocked. "How'd you get my number?" she asked him.

"I just looked it up in the book," he said, and Delia felt herself grow weak with gratitude. He was the best-looking boy she had ever seen.

"You want to go over to the Boulevard," he asked, "to see *Johnny Belinda*?" The one movie she had seen, with her mother.

"Oh, but I already saw it," she cried, her eyes darting around the kitchen.

"Oh," Maurice said, and then nothing else. Delia wasn't sure if he had hung up.

"Maurice?" she asked. "Maurice?"

"I'm here," he answered.

Her only chance was another show. "How about *Yellow Sky* at the Heights?" she asked, although she hated westerns.

He came to pick her up, in the same black suit he had worn to the dance, and Mae winked at Delia behind his back. Delia didn't think she remembered that he was the same boy Anna Curley had told her about. He had to duck under the doorway in the kitchen: Mae laughed and patted his back.

Delia hoped he'd liked the movie; she was too nervous to watch any of it, staring instead at the side of his face, which lit up suddenly when the screen did and showed his thick eyelashes and his dimples to great advantage. Midway through the show, he had draped his arm around her shoulder. She came to realize, staring at Richard Widmark, that if she'd given in to her shyness at the dance and walked away from the two boys, Maurice wouldn't ever have spoken to her and right at this very moment she'd be at home setting her hair. Boys just didn't remember her very often: Danny Kowalski was the exception.

If she had any complaints about Maurice, it was that he was so quiet. His heavy fingers tapped against her upper arm. She thought she could draw him out, away from whatever it was that held him back. Maybe it was the inexplicable presence of his dead baby brothers sitting on his shoulders like a set of epaulets, or his father's dreadful accident. He had to feel terrible about those things. Delia was full of feelings she could barely control. She was terrified that he would see how *flighty* she was, how *contrary* she could be (her mother's words) and that she might scare him away somehow. She needed to know everything about him, but she had to use a careful approach.

He lived with his mother in a sedate brick apartment house with stone gargoyles at the summit and a belfry, home to a flock of noisy pigeons. They passed the building on their way home from the movies. He had pointed to his windows on the third floor, white sheer curtains pinkish in the lamplight, plants on the windowsills. Her mother hated plants, accused them of "stealing air."

"My room," he had said, looking up and pointing with his index finger, "the living room, the kitchen, my mother's room." Nothing about his brothers or his father. Delia had to stop herself from begging him to describe the apartment.

"Do you have a desk in your room?" she had asked him on their way home from their second date, again at the Heights, this time to see *Paisan*.

"Why do you need to know that?" He had smiled, somewhat testily, grabbing for her hand. She had to be really careful, watching him all the time, even his reflection in the store windows. He was quiet but so handsome: she needed time to figure him out. Maybe it was just that he wasn't good at conversation. When he pressed his big body against hers in the vestibule of her building, bending down to kiss her, smelling this time of soap and cinnamon, like perfumed apple pie, it was almost as if she were drowning in that smell, with all the buzzers ringing underneath the pressure of her back.

After they had been dating for a few weeks, he quit his job at the A & P and became a bartender at the Shamrock Inn (where her father was a regular), while he waited to take the test for the police academy.

On the Saturday nights that followed, Delia sat at her kitchen table, waiting for him to stop by on his way home from work. She wasn't allowed to go there and sit on a stool at the bar; her parents would have had a fit. Instead she spent her Saturday nights writing her name and his name over and over again on the front page of the next morning's *Daily News*. She bought a beat-up box of stationery at Cohen's Candy Store and wrote him little poems ("I see the skies in your blue eyes" and "I love you so if only you'd know" were two of her favorites), licking the envelope flaps over and over, but they were old and wouldn't stay closed, and he usually forgot to take them home

23

with him anyway. She heard her parents snoring in the back bedroom when Maurice, smelling of beer, sneaked into the kitchen and eventually managed to undo her bra and roughly pull her underpants out from underneath her girdle.

She saved her poems to Maurice and kept them — her Maurice mail, she called it — underneath her mattress. After he had left, she pulled her blondish ponytail across her face because it smelled of him. She wondered if it would actually hurt to have sex, not that she ever would. I love you, he sometimes said to her on Saturday nights, the warm bulge in his slacks prodding her hip. The next day she hoped it wasn't just the beer talking, because his words had made her so happy. Some people just opened up when they drank, she thought; maybe Maurice was one of them. He gave her a birthday card on which he had written, "I like you a lot," and on Valentine's Day he gave her a box of chocolates and a card that said, "I love you," but he hadn't signed it.

He was everything she'd ever wanted, silent and strong like her father, as a real man should be. She'd work hard to get him to talk more, ask him plenty of questions, promise him he wouldn't have to give her any answers. She just needed a little more time.

"A wonderful boy," Kathleen Delaney was saying, starting to yawn, "the dear love of my life," and she covered her open mouth with the wrinkled back of her thin hand.

THREE

Nineteen years old and pregnant with Maureen, Delia took a sickday from her operator's job at the telephone company and rode with her mother on the bus to Feinstein's Bridal Wear.

She had a stack of wedding gown samples on the dressing room chair, but she stood against the wall, waiting until the saleslady left to try any of them on. Mae sat patiently on a soiled brocade chair next to the three-paneled mirror. It was hard for Delia to look at Mae in triplicate; it overwhelmed her.

Taking her mother along for a formal dress, even if it was her wedding gown, might have been something of a mistake. Mae Rooney knew nothing about dressing up. She had two "fancy" dresses (cotton with a little embroidery), and she wore them only to church or to the occasional wedding. The rest of the time, she wore simple housedresses, with deep pockets for her pearl rosary beads and her crumpled tissues and the loose change she found lying on the floor. She usually wore an apron on top of her dress and maybe a sweater on top of that, so that her small, chubby body was sliced by a series of hems that made her look as round and wobbly as a toy. Mae was always cooking a meal, serving a meal, or cleaning up after a meal, and if she wasn't at home, she was shopping for groceries or lighting candles at church. A closet rod filled with her sons' ironed white shirts made Mae Rooney smile expansively; Delia had once found her standing quietly in the boys' bedroom with the closet door flung open wide, her little hands folded neatly across her chest. Delia had never seen her mother wear high heels or red lipstick nor even throw back her head and laugh out loud the way Rosaleen's mother sometimes did. Mae's hair net would fall off, for one thing, and for another, Mae

Rooney said she never had any time for "foolishness." She swore she liked a good joke, but she seemed to like to work a lot more, and sometimes when Delia came home from school or from Rosaleen's house, she stood outside the kitchen door and watched her mother scrub the floor on her hands and knees, moving sideways like a crab.

"Do you have any beauty secrets, Ma?" Delia once asked the scrubbing Mae, having seen the cover of a fan magazine captioned "Beauty Secrets of the Stars!"

"Do I have any *what*?" Mae yelped, looking up from the pail of dirty water to stare at Delia, and for once she gave way to gales of laughter, holding on to her sides, sitting cross-legged on the clean side of the floor.

"My darlin' girl," Mae had said, wiping her eyes with the hem of her white sweater, "I have only two of them. I use Crisco shortening to press out the wrinkles in my face, and I use the Sacred Heart Novena to iron out the wrinkles inside my head."

The saleslady left, and Delia slipped out of her print blouse. The whiteness of her cotton bra, so bleached it was nearly blue, highlighted the bruises on her arm. Quickly, without looking at herself, she thrust her arms into a taffeta dress with transparent sleeves that were strewn with organdy petals and bits of Alençon lace.

"You have to find one with room at the waist," Mae whispered loudly. "You never know, maybe you'll show early." Her reddened hands tugged at the seam of every gown as if it had to undergo some tremendous ordeal.

Feinstein's, under the el, on the way into the city, had ten windows, with a different wedding gown in each of them. The shop was dropped, implausibly, in the middle of factories and government buildings, the last bit of Queens before the bridge to New York. The door to the unemployment office was right next to the door to Feinstein's, in a sliver of a gray building painted with pigeon droppings. The bus made its turn for the bridge in front of Feinstein's, and when Delia was young, she never knew which way to look. On her left she could see the skyline, and on her right, the wedding dresses, and she never seemed to make the correct choice. The back of her geography book contained drawings of skyscrapers next to long bridal trains and wide hoop skirts.

Feinstein's dressing room was different than Delia had imagined. Scraps of white tissue paper stuck to her stockings, and she had to be careful of the straight pins in the powder-blue carpeting. The samples were all size eight, some of them so old that the pure-white gowns looked ivory and those that were ivory looked tan. Sweat and makeup stained the collars, zippers were coming loose. Mae thoroughly checked the price tag on each gown.

The saleslady, her arms filled with more gowns, elbowed her way into the small room where Delia was changing, in her slip, from one dress to the next.

"Here, dear," the woman said, dropping the dresses into Mae's waiting arms. Her tortoiseshell eyeglasses hung from her neck by a chain and were smothered in organza. She coughed and seemed to choke when Mae gathered the gowns together. "Some of these are real popular right now." She stared at Delia and then traced the purple welts with her pinkie.

"What on earth happened to you?" she asked.

Delia looked at Mae. "A shot," Mae said brightly. "She had to have a shot, and her arm is all sore from it."

"Poor thing," the woman said, as if Delia weren't even in the room. "Is she going to Mexico or some foreign place for her honeymoon?" she asked Mae.

"That's exactly right." Mae smiled. "She's going off to Mexico right after the ceremony."

"Lucky you." The woman turned to Delia and winked. "Your fiancé must have a fine position."

"Oh, he does." Mae shook her head emphatically. "He really does."

Fiancé, Delia thought. She had never heard the word said as much as she was hearing it today, through the thin partitions of the dressing rooms. Five times already, and she hadn't been in Feinstein's for an hour! "Fiancé" made her anxious to wear a sheer peignoir set and a pair of white satin slippers with little chunky heels and whiskery pom-poms like faded dandelions on the toes.

"Well, I hope you and your fella have tons of fun." The saleslady winked and drew the curtain closed. At least she didn't say "fiancé" again, Delia thought gratefully, shivering in her slip. Mae sniffed under the sleeves of the gowns. "They think the air-conditionin' turned up high will hide the stink of the dresses," she said loudly.

"Please, Ma," Delia said. After a lifetime of anticipation, she was weary of Feinstein's already. The night before, while Delia hid in her bedroom, Mae had broken the news of her pregnancy to Denis at the dinner table. She heard her father's knife bounce off the wall and crack against a glass in the sink. Oh, my God, she thought, hearing the familiar slur in his voice, and then she held her hands against the door and began to cry.

"She's *what!*" Denis screamed, throwing things to the floor. (The loaf of bread, Delia guessed, maybe the butter dish.)

"She's pregnant, Denis," Mae said quietly. "Please don't turn from her. She needs us."

"*Needs us?* Goddamn it, Mae, get the slut out here now!"

"Denis, now I won't have you beatin' her up, not in her condition. I just won't have it!"

"I said to get her out here—and if you don't, I'm goin' in her bedroom and gettin' her out here myself."

"Delia," Mae pleaded softly, crying, "come out here now, like a good girl."

Delia crept through the long hallway leading from her room into the kitchen. She felt she couldn't stand up straight, as if she were missing the middle of her body, so empty inside that she stooped over, hoping she might faint.

Denis threw Mae into the table, out of his way; she sobbed and cried and pulled at his fists.

"Denis, please, please stop. . . ." She began to rock back and forth. "Please. Maurice and her are gettin' married next month. . . . Please, Denis, no!"

"Don't be tellin' me to stop, Mae," he screamed. "If you were any kind of a mother at all, you would have told that girl to stop!" He turned on Delia. "Whore! You fucking bitch!" He kicked her in the backside, and she fell down. He kicked her in the back and kicked her legs until the curly black telephone wire hanging against the wall wrapped itself around his feet somehow, tripping him. He fell and cut his head on the top of the chair, which made him even madder, and he clenched his teeth, pulling Delia through the apartment by the hair, opening her bedroom door, grabbing her by the shoulders, throwing her onto the bed.

"You don't deserve to wear this, goddamn you!" he roared, leaning over to rip her tiny First Communion crucifix from the thin gold chain around her neck, breaking the gold into small pieces and then throwing it in her face. Blood streamed down from his temple. He wiped his chin with his sleeve. "Now see what you did," he screamed, shoving his shirt sleeve under her nose.

She slid to the floor and huddled next to her closet, with her hands over her mouth. She cried until she couldn't breathe anymore, scared that the baby inside her had been hurt, scared that her father would bleed to death from the cut on his head. My God, she thought, what if I've killed him?

"*Whore! Whore! Whore!*" he screamed from the kitchen. "*Goddamn slut!* She's a slut, Mae, your darlin' daughter, doin' this to me! Goddamn it. . . . Goddamn *bitch* couldn't keep her legs closed, could she now, and all them nuns supposed to be teachin' her right from wrong! *Bitch!*" His voice roared through the apartment.

"Denis, you're gonna need stitches. Go inside and get your jacket on, and we'll walk over to the hospital," Mae said quietly.

"Stitches, shit! Don't need no goddamn stitches. Don't be tellin' me about stitches, will ya! Jesus Christ, and here I was puttin' my own mother's name on that *whore* in the back bedroom. Throw her the Christ out, Mae, her things down the front stairs, and be done with her! And let me have a good talk with the bum she's runnin' around with!"

Carrying a soft towel, Mae opened Delia's door. "It's all done with now; it's all over with." She wiped Delia's face. "It's no good for you, this excitement. I've got to get some peroxide on your father's cut and bring him to the hospital. I'll fix you some tea later on, once he's asleep. You just lay there and rest now." Mae turned off the light. Delia hiccuped into the darkness. What if Maurice had walked in just then, she wondered, what if he punched her father and told him to leave her alone? But Maurice would never do that. He wasn't brought up that way, and she couldn't love him if he did.

Denis was her *father*. She was the one who was pregnant; she was the one who had done wrong. She had disgraced them all. But what if

Maurice had walked in and killed Denis? She was ashamed of herself for wishing such a thing, even for an instant. She hoped he wouldn't go out to find Maurice.

Cars passed her window, throwing small intense rectangles of light across the ceiling. She remembered crawling out of bed on the nights her father never came home at all, sick with fear, kneeling on the chilly floor, praying underneath her pink curtains with her forehead pressed against the cold glass. "Please, God," she whispered, "please take care of him, please send him home." She had to be careful that her mother didn't see her. Mae would be pacing up and down the sidewalk in front, clawing at her thinning brown hair, biting her red, weary knuckles, waiting for Denis, looking for Denis, crying for Denis. When the streetlights finally switched off, just about the time Mae fell asleep in the living room chair, Denis would show up and stand in the doorway of Delia's bedroom, swaying and breathing hard, smelling awful, just looking at her; she hid under the sheets and pretended to be asleep. She had learned to cry without moving her shoulders, hot bitter tears of relief so strong that her arms and legs shook afterward and felt numb. She would fall into a sleep so deep that she couldn't get up for school, no matter how hard Mae shook her, a sleep so sound it was almost as if she were drugged.

Hearing a sudden noise in the kitchen, Delia sat up. She thought they had gone over to the hospital. There was a strangled high voice, a liquidy series of garbled words and sobs, and then her mother's firm, soothing, calm replies. Delia was shocked. She had never heard her father cry.

They decided on an A-line gown with a sweetheart neckline and ordered it two sizes larger. Mae stood in the doorway of the dressing room. "Better be sure it can be let out," she whispered, tears forming in her eyes.

The saleslady stopped writing and looked at them over her glasses. "Just when did you say you needed this?" she asked confidentially.

"Three weeks?" Delia asked Mae, who nodded.

"I'll put down 'rush,' just in case," the woman said, her handwriting fat and elegant. Delia's fingers itched to imitate it.

Mae opened her purse and removed her wallet. A clump of bills stuck out of her billfold like a bookmark in a novel. "I'll pay the whole thing now," she said.

"But, Mama," Delia said, feeling guilty.

"Delia Mary, you stop it. All your life I dreamed of the day we'd come in here for your wedding dress. I always wanted to do this for you. And Daddy does too." The saleslady returned with the change, dropping the folded bills into Mae's open change purse, into a nest of rosary beads. "Now, Delia Mary, come on." Mae buried the small purse in her pocket. "Your dress is lovely, and we got to celebrate. We're not dressed for the city. . . . How's about we go to Stahler's for a sandwich and a black-and-white?"

"That's good, Ma. Thanks." Delia turned and gave Mae a hug. Nobody but Mae ever ordered a "black-and-white." Delia wished she'd just order a chocolate and vanilla ice cream soda. Mae blew her nose loudly into a tissue and then dropped it into a brass ashtray near the front door.

"How'd he take it?" Maurice wanted to know, when she called him from the restaurant to tell him her father knew about the baby.

"Not so bad, I guess," she said. "He hit me in the arm." If she shut her eyes, she felt as if she were still on the kitchen floor, the sole of her father's heavy boots near her face.

"Well, he didn't really hurt you, did he?" Maurice asked.

"No, not really," she lied. The last thing she needed was for Maurice to get angry with Denis. "He was just upset."

"Well, I figured he would be. But he'll get used to the idea, don't worry. If he comes in here, I'll try to talk to him. How you feeling today, honey?"

She winced. Honey. He seemed so young when he called her that. She shut her eyes and imagined how he looked right then, over at the Shamrock, with his full lips resting on the receiver, his white bartender's apron tied around his waist. He had tried it on for Delia before he began the job. She thought it made him look like the innkeeper in the St. Immaculata Christmas play.

"Pretty good," she answered. "Today I'm feeling fine. I got my dress." She hoped he wouldn't ask what it was like. It was white. She forgot the rest.

"Great. Look, I gotta go, I got a customer. See you later," he said, in a rush, and hung up.

Delia walked to the booth where her mother was waiting for her. "Daddy isn't mad at you anymore, Delia," Mae said, fussing with her napkin. "He's just worried about your future, that's all, with him workin' over at the Shamrock. A bartender don't make much money, and with the baby coming . . ."

"But Maurice is gonna get on the cops, Ma. He's supposed to take the test at the end of the month. You'll see, Ma, he won't be a bartender for much longer. It's only for now."

"I hope not, Delia Mary, but you know what I always say. 'Don't be swearin' you got the job until you see your hat hangin' on the peg.'"

"Don't worry, Ma. Maurice'll get on the cops. I just know it."

Delia wasn't convinced that her father had forgiven her.

She got up early, before he had left for work, and sat in front of him in her pajamas, talking to Mae about her job at the phone company. She made her mother laugh, imitating the supervisors who cut in on the girls, trying to correct their grammar, as if they were foreigners just learning the language, and she tried to catch Denis smiling, but he seemed to be too intrigued by the crossword puzzle to hear her. Delia's boss, Miss Berry, came to work in knit suits that were tight on her big hips, and she bit down hard on the ends of her words, keeping her false teeth in place. Delia made her mother giggle by wrapping her bathrobe around her backside twice and asking for "toassst." "Please pass the milllk," she said, and then she got up and slithered over to the icebox. When Delia and Denis brushed hands reaching for the sugar bowl, he pulled away as if he had been bitten.

The next morning, she never made it to the breakfast table at all. While washing her face, she suddenly leaned over the toilet and threw up. She was dimly aware of the bathroom door opening and someone coming in. It was her father, and he held her long ponytail back from her neck.

"See," Mae said after Denis had left for work. "And you think your father doesn't love you."

Now that she had her gown, Delia made an appointment with the manager of the Brau House to plan the reception.

Saving carfare, she and Maurice decided to walk the two miles, all through the Heights to Flushing, where the gaps between the stores underneath the el grew increasingly larger and weeds could be seen sprouting from the centers of discarded tires, from underneath beer bottles sprawled in the dirt. The Heights officially ended on a block with two businesses: a surgical supply house and a store selling used bathroom fixtures. A window full of flesh-colored plaster legs with neatly trimmed red toenails led to a window where bile-green toilet tanks with chipped chrome handles leaned against rusty sinks.

They had passed brown men sitting in doorways on dented metal chairs or plastic kitchen chairs with the gray stuffing hanging out, watching children in sneakers and no socks playing in lots dusted with ground glass.

"The Heights is sure changing," Maurice said.

They noticed two stores they had never seen before, a travel agency with live turtles crawling on the gravel between plastic palm trees in a tank, and a fabric shop where bright silk saris hung in the window, pleated and splayed like a handful of peacock tails. Delia stopped dead in her tracks and tugged on Maurice's hand. "Oh, look at the beautiful colors," she said, pointing to a sheer stretch of red gossamer embroidered with golden suns.

"Hey, didn't this place used to be Pfeiffer's Insurance?" he asked, stepping back to look for the name, pulling Delia with him.

"Yeah, I think it did," she said. "I knew something was missing." She peered in Pfeiffer's window whenever she ventured this far from home. Three months before, when she last passed by (on her way to

Flushing to buy a bridesmaid's dress for Rosaleen and Danny's wedding), she had stopped to look at Pfeiffer's perpetual display of sepia photographs taken way back when Mae was a girl, the black letters ("The Changing Scene") stuck to a corkboard with pushpins. Delia always scanned Pfeiffer's pictures, searching for the young Mae, but she never saw her, only the featureless pale faces of women scurrying by in a blur of old-fashioned dresses like Olive Oyl, some in cloche hats. The fenders of the cars in the streets were curved like the 5's on five-dollar bills.

The window of Pfeiffer's Insurance had made Delia homesick for her mother's youth, but today the sari store made her homesick for Pfeiffer's, and that travel agency—well, it was so strange that she couldn't even remember what had been there before. Disoriented, she concentrated on the bright sky. "This is a longer walk than I remembered," she said, looking up at Maurice. He nodded. They had only a few weeks to make their plans. The man on the phone had said to come in right away; he'd see what he could do for them on such short notice.

Delia had butterflies in her stomach, which intermittently became an icy fear that she was about to throw up. The streets seemed to be lengthening, the distance from one curb to the next a mile long. "You want to get a taxi?" Maurice asked, looking concerned.

Delia was touched by the gesture. "No, let's just keep going," she said, afraid of stopping and giving her sickness that edge.

"Well then, the bus?" he suggested, pointing behind them. She couldn't bear the thought of lurching back and forth, and bus fumes, so afraid of vomiting and disgusting Maurice that she trembled. She hoped the Brau House man didn't ask why they needed a place so soon. If she kept walking, she wouldn't have to think.

"Just how far *is* this place, honey?" Maurice asked. Honey: it still made her catch her breath. Nobody had ever called her that. "We've been walking forever," he said, waving his arms. "Jesus, we passed that Indian store back there and I figured we'd walked all the way to Calcutta." He laughed and tugged on her neck. The sidewalk seemed to be shifting to Delia's left.

"It's right over by the hospital," Delia said, trying to talk without opening her mouth. "Maybe you're just getting old."

34

"Not me," he said with a sideways grin. "By the time we get over to the place, we're gonna *need* the hospital." He poked her softly in her middle, not seeming to notice how she flinched. She'd sworn him to secrecy, but he didn't seem to care, proudly rubbing her stomach, patting her belly softly when they sat in the balcony of the Heights Theater. Sometimes when he touched her she looked away and bit her knuckles, but she couldn't stand to say anything, hurt his feelings, although his hands were warm and heavy and made her feel raw, as if she hadn't enough skin to cover her organs. Without her, Delia thought, he seemed such a sad person. Maurice had lost so much that it seemed to Delia that his timing was off with other people, as if he never quite knew when to pull back, yet his trust was so hard-won she hated to interrupt him. When he put his hand on her neck, she turned and kissed his palm, and when he tugged on her thin dark-blond ponytail, she let her head loll back on his shoulder and looked up at him.

She was so glad her father had never yelled at him. She wasn't sure if Maurice could take that; he might have just gotten up and walked out of her life, and then where would she be? It frightened her to think of it. "Humpf," was all Denis had said to him. He walked out of the kitchen whenever Maurice walked in, and Maurice had told Delia that her father turned away whenever he approached him at the Shamrock, not even letting Maurice serve him a beer and a ball. "But don't worry, honey," Maurice had said to her when she apologized for her father's rude behavior. "I know he'll get over it." She hoped so. She never wanted anyone to hurt Maurice again.

Finally, she saw the front of the restaurant. Her nausea had passed again. Thank God she didn't have to face her brothers, Eugene still in the navy and Gerald away in the seminary.

The walls in the Brau House were covered by a thin red satin, so stained with water drops that it looked like silk moiré. Reddish tablecloths spotted with grease (some tomato red, others almost purple) covered a dozen small square card tables. Tiny champagne glasses that proved to be plastic (although they looked a lot like glass), were lined up on a dusty wooden shelf near the bar, and the knives and forks, in a bin on the bar top, looked dull and greasy, so big they seemed too heavy to pick up. At the end of the bar, two heavy middle-aged waitresses, whose bright-yellow braids were gathered in lumpy red rubber bands, sat knee-to-knee on red leatherette stools, smoking cigarettes, staring at them.

One of the women touched her tongue with her finger, flicking bits of tobacco into the stale air. Delia felt her stomach tighten. A pyramid of beer steins with fancy handles was balanced on a shelf wedged into the corner of the room. "Help ya?" a waitress asked. Delia wasn't sure which one had spoken. She looked up at Maurice, her arms crossed over her belly. They know about the baby, Delia thought; she had seen one of them nudge the other.

"Manager?" Maurice asked, the smoke from the cigarettes fogging near the ceiling.

"Back there," one of the women said, tilting her head toward a small room down the hall.

Maurice threw a protective arm around Delia's shoulder, and they followed the gold-flecked linoleum to a splash of sunlight at the end of the corridor. They walked into a wood-paneled office smelling strongly of grated cheese, where a small, bald man in a white shirt, with embroidered red garters on his elbows, sat behind a long wood desk counting stacks of paper. There were plaques scattered among the perfectly rounded knotholes on the wall: The Kiwanis Club, the Sons of Italy, the Knights of Columbus. Delia had seen paneled walls in magazines at the dentist's office. Rumpus rooms, they called them, such a foolish name. Above the room's large solitary window, which was locked by a gate, was a picture of the Pope and a picture of Frank Sinatra (too shiny, with a blurry fake autograph). Behind the man in the garters was a scarred table where a rubber plant drooped two leaves on a stack of magazines.

"Just a sec," the man said, glancing up at them.

Delia sat wearily in front of him on an old leather office chair on wheels and found herself rolling toward the opposite side of the room. She leaned forward on her knees, dizzy now, and dropped her pocketbook on the floor. The sudden motion of the chair was almost too much to bear. "Whoa," she said, looking up and feeling herself blush. Maurice walked over and pulled her back to the man's desk by her shoulder, his fingers pressing against her collarbone. "My roll-away bride," he said, grinning.

"Sit down, folks," the man said. ". . . thirty, thirty-one . . . Be right with you." He licked his finger at forty and began to hum. Finally, he wiped his hands on his brown pants and stood up. "John Brown," he said, offering his hand to Maurice. "Now what could I do you for?" and then he laughed, showing long yellow teeth, his eyes seeming to fill the entire surface of the eyeglasses he hurriedly put on. Delia couldn't stand to look at him; he didn't blink, so she had to.

"She called you about our wedding — our reception," Maurice corrected himself, gesturing foolishly at Delia. "Remember, she called yesterday?" he said, seeming flustered. Delia couldn't help him out, although she wanted to. She dug in her purse for a handkerchief to press to her upper lip.

Jesus, she prayed, don't let me throw up.

"Oh, yeah. . . . Delaney? I wrote the name down here some-where. You're Miss Rooney?" he asked. "The ones with the rush wed-ding, right?" Uh-oh, Delia thought. Her tongue felt as if it was stuck to the roof of her mouth. If he asked why the wedding was rush, what would they say?

"Right." Maurice smiled down at Delia.

"Okay," John Brown said. "Sit down." Maurice sat in a chair against the wall. "Kinda short notice, but like I told Miss Rooney on the phone, I think I could help you out." Maurice rubbed his thighs anxiously. A noise in the hall. Delia looked out, watching the wait-resses from the bar walk past the open door, their thick legs in black stockings, their feet in white nurses' shoes with worn soles. Through the black zigzag parts in their bleached hair, their scalps gleamed like the gristle in beef. They giggled, and Delia felt self-conscious; a door squeaked and then banged closed. The Brau House was so terribly hot that Delia was beginning to sweat, trying so hard not to throw up. She ordered herself to think of something else, tried to read the man's mail upside down, and then she began to say a Hail Mary, reaching up to her neck for her crucifix; that always made her feel better. Her fingers fluttered against the base of her throat; the crucifix was gone. Then she remembered that her father had broken the chain.

Mr. Brown bent over and took a long pad from his bottom drawer; with great ceremony, he wet his finger again to separate the paper, then slid a piece of carbon paper between the two top sheets. It struck Delia that he looked like a cow with those big eyes behind the glasses and that thick tongue. Matter of fact, she thought, almost unable to stop herself, his tongue looked exactly like the tongues Mae so often boiled in a pot on top of the stove, a disgustingly pink lump of meat with little bumps scattered along the top. When they had tongue for dinner, Delia pleaded a headache and went to her room.

She tried to take little breaths.

"Okay, okay," John Brown said, as if they had asked him for a great favor. "I start off by tellin' ya about the booze. First things first, right?" He smiled at Maurice, who smiled back. "First, we put a bottle of Scotch and a bottle of rye on every table. Ice and club soda and ginger ale. Beer and soda on every table. How many we talkin' here?"

Maurice looked at Delia. "Fif-ty," she said through clenched teeth, like Humphrey Bogart.

"Fifty," Mr. Brown repeated, writing it down. "Hot food?" he asked, gazing at both of them. "Cold food? What?" They looked blankly at him. He reached around and handed Delia a menu with the remnants of a dirty gold tassel dangling from the red leatherette cover.

"Delia?" Maurice asked. She was getting annoyed with him. Couldn't he tell how sick she felt?

"Cold," was all she could manage to say.

"Well, then, this ain't the menu for you." John Brown chuckled, pulling the gold tassel, taking the menu from her hands. "That's our fine Bavarian cookin'." He extracted a single sheet from his desk drawer. "Okay, here's what we're talkin'. Roast beef. Ham. Turkey. American cheese. Swiss cheese. Potato salad, macaroni salad."

Oh, my God. Delia felt her shoulders rising around her ears. Tongue, a small voice said, all the bumps.

". . . coleslaw. Pickles and olives . . . black and green. And rye bread, white bread . . . rolls. You want us to get the cake, or you want to get the cake and bring it here that morning?"

They both looked at her. "Delia?" Maurice asked again. What are you, Delia wanted to say to Maurice, angry with him for the first time, some kind of goddamn idiot? "Which one?" Maurice asked her pleasantly. "The cake here or we get it?" John Brown waited, scratching his head with the eraser of his pencil. White flakes of dandruff fell on his desk.

"Here," Delia said, gesturing helplessly with her hand. "You get it for us." Maurice seemed shorter, as if he were sinking slowly into the floor. It crossed Delia's mind that he was too young and too stupid to get married.

"Butter cream," John Brown asked, "or whipped?"

There was just no end to all this talk about food! Delia never wanted to eat again. She looked at her feet. "Okay," John Brown said. "The little lady could think about it for a few minutes. Reception lasts four hours. You leave me some money today. You got a house band, okay? Now, about the cake . . . You all right, doll?" he asked Delia, watching her warily. "You want one of the girls'll give you a drink of water?" Delia leaned on his desk, propping her cheeks with both palms. Tongue in a pot, little bumps across the top. She shut her eyes. *Stop it.* "Butter cream or whipped?" he repeated. "C'mon, doll, you gotta help me out here." He smiled, licking at the corner of his mouth.

Suppose, Delia asked herself, there were mounds of whipped cream on the man's desk and butter cream slathered on the floor. How would you feel then, she asked herself, if he opened his mouth and began to lick . . . She pushed herself away from the desk and rolled out into the linoleum corridor. Maurice and John Brown looked stunned. She saw something red fall. The menu, she realized; she'd caught it with her finger. She saw a door marked "Frauleins" at the end of the corridor, jumped up, and ran toward it, into a blast of blue cigarette smoke and the strong perfumed scent of hair spray, barely making it into the stall. She knelt on the dirty tile floor, over the toilet, and felt awfully sorry for herself. She missed her mother. Here she was, getting married, and she wanted Mae to come hold her head.

"You okay?" one of the waitresses asked, but Delia couldn't

answer. Her throat hurt, her chest was heaving. She was ashamed to come out, her cheeks wet with tears. Maurice might change his mind if he could see her in this condition.

"I think so," she croaked, clearing her throat. She came out of the stall and walked to the sink on shaking legs, the women moving out of her way. One of them cranked open the window, and garlic-smelling air crept in from the alleyway, sucking out the smoke. One waitress gave Delia a brown paper towel from a package on the tile windowsill. "I'm sorry," Delia said, watching the water run over her wrists.

She had made such terrible noises. "What're you sorry for?" the one woman said. Now that Delia actually looked at them, they seemed younger, more her own age. "Everybody gets sick, don't they?"

"Wet another napkin for her, Julie," the other girl said, pointing at the package.

"Jesus," Julie said to Delia, gently stroking her face. "You oughta see the ones pukin' their guts out after eatin' here." Delia laughed weakly.

"That's a nice advertisement for the place," the other one said. "'Puke your guts out at the Brau House.'"

"Yeah, Loretta." Julie laughed, looking at the other waitress. "Why don't we go in and try it out on the old man. You want some gum?" she asked Delia, squinting her eyes. "You want a life saver?"

"I'm all right now," Delia said, taking deep breaths. Even the garlic wasn't bothering her. She found her lipstick in her pocket; relieved to feel better, she sighed deeply.

"Well, good luck to you, then," Julie said, running her cigarette under the faucet, patting Delia's arm. The other waitress, Loretta, held the door open for Delia and smiled. "Yeah, good luck," she said.

The rolling chair was just where she had left it; the seat was dented, and one arm was dramatically lower than the other. She had to push it into the room to get back inside. "And I'm givin' you that chair as a wedding gift." John Brown laughed, looking at Delia.

In front of him was a bottle of whiskey and two drained glasses. Maurice was glowing, his handsome cheeks flushed, his eyes unfocused, seeming to move independently of each other. Her father sometimes had that look about his eyes; in Maurice's face, it was startling.

"We're just toastin' your new arrival," the man said. "Your fella explained everything. Don't worry yourself, doll; we see plenty of situations just like your own." He chuckled, as Delia stared at Maurice, his unfamiliar goofy expression. "Plenty of girls throwin' up, plenty of fellas sittin' here havin' a drink with me." John Brown filled the glasses again.

How could Maurice have told him? she wondered.

"We're the hurry-up weddin'-day pros" — John Brown handed a glass to Maurice — "and don't ya forget it." He laughed, slapping Maurice on his back, sloshing whiskey over his desk.

Sacred Heart, Delia said to herself, sounding just like Mae. What the *hell* am I getting myself into?

FIVE

Just for getting married, the telephone company gave Delia two days off, and it seemed to her so generous a thing to do that she answered the switchboard with an especially prompt, polite air on the day that she was to leave, hurried the other operators when they lingered over coffee and apple pie after a lunch in her honor.

In a cafeteria on Third Avenue, Delia sat with her co-workers around a square table, all of them in cheap skirts with uneven hems and blouses stretched tight across their breasts, all of them engaged to be married "soon," not, like Delia, in three days. Platinum-haired Veronica, who sat next to Delia at the switchboard, wore a tarnished-looking diamond ring on her nicotine-stained finger. From every paycheck, Veronica folded half her salary into a small flowered wallet, which she dropped into her purse; she was paying on time for a set of pots. A responsible, grown-up thing to do, Delia decided, guilty at not having thought as far ahead as Veronica, saving for pots or buying the dish towels her mother often said were on sale. She had never done anything about the insurance Mae was always telling her to buy from the Prudential man in the office around the corner, never opened a savings account, but she and Maurice had enough to pay for most of the wedding; the rest would come from Mae and Denis's savings. Afterward was time enough, Delia thought, to worry about the boring details, the electric bills and saving for the doctor. All Delia wanted to do was sleep naked with Maurice.

As soon as they cleared the table of their sandwich plates and pie plates (flakes of rubbery pastrami and bits of tan crust) and the coffee cups, Delia's co-workers reached under their seats and pulled gifts from shopping bags. After quitting time, they wouldn't see Delia again until after she was married; she hadn't invited any of them to her wedding, and she didn't expect to be invited to theirs. None of them could afford extra guests, and Delia had an additional reason: she didn't want her telephone company friends to see her father fall in a heap on the slippery Brau House floor.

From her own collection (Delia had seen it before), Veronica gave her a shiny teakettle with a bright copper bottom. "It's guaranteed for life," Veronica said, running her hand lovingly over the handle, sitting back so the light above their heads made the kettle gleam. "Made out of two kinds of steel and two coatings of copper." She took the kettle from Delia's hands and turned it over. "You could clean this with a mild soap and a sponge, you know," she said, while Delia listened and shook her head eagerly. "Then if it gets too dull, you can always use some of that pink paste they sell for copper in the five-and-ten." Veronica pushed the kettle away, as if she couldn't bear to look at it any longer.

Delia hesitated and then put it back in the box. "I'll take care of it, I promise."

Lois, a tiny black-haired girl, whom Delia sometimes met on the train, twisted her engagement ring, a red ruby that made her pale hands look beaten and weak. "I didn't know what to get you for your house and all," she said in a trembling voice, "so instead I got you something for the baby." She handed Delia a white box tied with a big white bow and wriggled back in her chair. Lois had slim hips and no discernible backside; it seemed hard for her to sit for any length of time, and she had a nervous habit of jumping up and walking in tiny circles. Before Delia had finished digging through the first layer of tissue paper, it struck her that her friend Lois would never have any children. She had no real reason to think this, but the minute Delia saw the tiny silver rattle with its yellow bow in the bottom of the box, she could see Lois with an entire collection of silver rattles at home, as if she gave them away for every occasion, and then Delia felt angry at herself and ungrateful. At their coffee break, it was Lois who had been carrying Delia's coffee to the sturdiest chair in the company cafeteria, Lois who put on her raincoat and skittered over to the deli when Delia had a yen for rice pudding.

"Next week," Veronica said, watching Delia bend over and kiss Lois, "after we get paid, I'm getting the double boiler."

43

"Ohhh," Delia said, hoping for an appropriate expression, not quite sure what a double boiler was. She looked at Barbara, who was older than the others and seemed to know more: at least twenty-five, Delia had thought, the first time she had seen her. With her short-cropped light hair and high Slavic cheekbones and her dignified posture, she appeared as if she might have suffered some great soul-wrenching tragedy. She claimed to be engaged but lacked a ring; "Unnecessary," she simply said. Delia had no ring either, but it was only a matter of time. Maurice had promised her Kathleen Delaney's small engagement ring just as soon as she died. All Delia had to do was wait.

Barbara said nothing about the double boiler, just handed Delia a heavy wooden box with a warped top, something that looked like an instrument case. Delia stared at it. "Well, open it up," Barbara ordered, and Delia pulled at the ends. It slid apart like the crucifix that hung above her mother's bed, with the candles and the holy oil for the last rites inside, only this box contained a set of pearl-handled carving knives on a red velvet bed.

Delia stared at them. Mama will hate this, she thought; with all her sophistication, didn't Barbara realize that knives would always cut a friendship? "Oh, Barbara, thanks," she said, turning the box over to look foolishly at its underside, just as Veronica had done with the kettle.

"Well, take one out," Barbara ordered. "Make sure you like them."

What was there to like about knives? The other girls had opinions about things that Delia had never even considered. She had never looked twice at pots or rattles or knives. She liked to browse at silk slippers and lacy nightgowns and pretty sheets.

"Oh, they're just fine," she said carefully. "Yeah, these are good knives. Now I gotta learn to cook." She smiled, put the knives back into the box (not too quickly, she hoped), and set it next to her, patting all her gifts and smiling at her friends.

"I started a collection of recipes," Veronica said proudly.

"From where?" Delia asked. How would she ever learn to cook? They'd starve. Her mother would have to show her how.

"From the newspaper. I just cut out the ones I like, and I paste

44

them on index cards, and then I put the cards into a metal box I bought in the stationery store."

"What a good idea!" Delia said, deciding to stop in Cohen's Candy Store on the way home. He must have index cards and metal boxes, she thought; he had everything else. Maybe she should read the newspaper. All she ever glanced at were the funnies.

Just then, Barbara stood up and patted Delia's shoulder. "I just saw a friend," she explained, pushing her hair behind her ears, waving at a heavyset man, much older than herself, who stood at the cafeteria door. "I'll see you girls back at the office," Barbara said over her shoulder, and then she was gone.

They stared after her, and they all shrugged. "Barbara's life is different," Delia said, and everyone agreed.

"You know what I've been doing?" Lois leaned back, crossing her thin arms over her childish chest. "I've been buying children's books whenever they're on sale. I got sick of buying towels and pillowcases and tablecloths. Al says we really got time. Every time I bought any linens, they made me sad, the way they smelled too new, like the wedding's too far away. I like the books a lot better. I even read them myself." She laughed.

Smelled too new. Delia liked that. She knew exactly what Lois meant, her own nostrils burning from the scent of some homely new curtains Mae had hung in her bedroom. She'd miss Lois, she thought sadly, though she'd never really known her. Another month or so of work, and she'd probably never see any of these girls again. Delia had no children's books and not a single tablecloth or towel. She was the one who was getting married Saturday and all the others had months yet, and she was the only one who was having a baby. . . . She didn't have any dishes or glasses or spoons or forks and not an iron or a garbage pail, no insurance and not one pot. Not a pot to piss in, she had heard her father say of her mother's poor relations. She didn't even have that. She had pearl-handled knives and a good kettle and a silver rattle. And she had handsome Maurice, whom she loved with all her heart. Maurice (she even loved his name), knives, a kettle, and a rattle.

Well, nobody said it was going to be easy.

They were married in November, on a day so warm and sunny that fat, stunned bees lumbered across her white-rose-and-baby's-breath bouquet, drifting about Maurice's white carnation boutonniere.

Delia didn't show; not a bit, she thought proudly, as if it were her finest accomplishment. She checked herself from the side that morning in Mae's bedroom mirror, her heavy taffeta gown brushing past her trim stomach like a flat rock skimming the surface of a lake.

Maurice stood at the altar in his gray suit with Danny Kowalski, who wore brown, and they waited for her, both of them looking sick and pale. Like Delia and her matron of honor, Rosaleen, the men had to receive Communion, and they hadn't eaten since the day before. They had skipped Mae's rib-roast dinner and shared five pitchers of beer with Denis at the Shamrock Inn. Maurice looked so white that Delia tried to concentrate on his shoes as she glided past the guests, staring at the bow on the back of Rosaleen's pink gown.

Delia was clinging to her father's thin arm, trying to decipher the whispers in the pews. They had to know she was pregnant. For weeks, Mae Rooney had been going to morning Mass, sitting with the women who had cancer in their families or whose husbands had run out on them. Delia hadn't even had to tell Mae about the pregnancy; she just knew—although Delia did leave the unopened box of sanitary napkins close to the edge of her closet shelf, where her mother couldn't possibly miss it. There was something odd in the iris of Delia's eye, Mae said later, and it was the strangest thing, Mae herself getting odd cravings for salt, something she hadn't felt since she was pregnant with Delia.

As Delia came closer to the altar rail, where Father McKenna waited patiently, she saw that Maurice's gray pants were hemmed just right. She had sewn them the day before, and she knew by the way they barely kissed the shiny black tips of his shoes that she would make Maurice very happy. She turned to Maurice, who was smiling down at her from the front of the church. Denis was befuddled, overcome by the crowds, and he tried to sit down without kissing her, but she wouldn't let him go, and then she remembered to lift her veil, her tears clinging to the net. "I'm sorry," she whispered, holding on to his sleeve.

"Today is no time for tears," Father McKenna said softly, taking her hand from her father and putting it on top of Maurice's. Denis slumped in the pew next to Mae.

Danny smiled at Delia, but when she smiled back, she saw he wasn't looking at her at all but at Rosaleen next to her. They were practically newlyweds themselves, radiating a misty look. Danny drummed his fingers on his leg, and Rosaleen fussed with her flowers. It was hard for them to be together without touching each other.

To the side of the altar, on the scarred wooden kneeler, Delia saw a tiny blue-and-white nosegay of tea roses and more baby's breath, the long white ribbons curling along the marble floor. Her mother had seen to that, she thought. In the middle of the wedding Mass, Delia and Rosaleen stepped away from the altar and walked slowly to lay the nosegay at the feet of the Our Lady statue. Mae wanted her only daughter's wedding to have a special blessing, just as she had wanted her to be a special child, consecrating her to the Blessed Virgin when she was small, dressing her only in white or pale blue until she was seven years old, the age of reason. Standing in front of the statue, Delia heard her mother's sobs.

She wanted her baby so much, but she wished she weren't pregnant just yet, hating the shame. She wished the white dress and the white veil and the nosegay were all for real. She wasn't consecrated anymore, she wasn't even a virgin; she was getting married in sin, and yet she had been ashamed to admit her pregnancy in the confessional a few days before, fearing that the sacrament of marriage might not take.

It was one thing to tell the girls at work — they weren't even Catholic — but the people she had known all her life: that was something else. At the altar, she held the Sacred Host in her mouth and waited

47

to be struck dead, remembering her grade-school catechism illustrations of mortal and venial sin: the first was a bottle filled with black ink; in the second, the bottle was half filled. Standing before Father McKenna in her white gown, she wondered what he saw in her soul.

She had gotten pregnant so easily — it was over so quickly, and it had hurt. They were supposed to be checking the Kowalskis' apartment (Rosaleen and Danny were on their honeymoon, in Asbury Park) and getting their mail, but somehow they found themselves on the brown secondhand sofa in the living room. It was the first time she had let Maurice go all the way inside.

No matter how delicately she balanced the nosegay, it wouldn't stay at the statue's feet, sliding instead to the floor.

"Too bad we can't stick the flowers between her toes," Rosaleen whispered as Father McKenna smiled indulgently at them, "or in her teeth, like a flamenco dancer." Finally, the nosegay seemed to balance itself, and Delia turned around to smile at her mother and father, trying to fix them just like that in her mind.

(For months after the wedding, especially after Denis died, while she scrubbed the kitchen floor on her hands and knees like her mother, moving sideways like a crab, she remembered exactly how they had looked, and in her mind's eye she dressed them again, putting Mae back into her pale-blue gown, adding the pale-blue hat with the blue veiling and then the elbow-length blue gloves, repinning the blue carnations onto the blue netting of her "bosom"; she chuckled at the thought of the tiny blue hankie Mae had arranged to have in her tiny blue purse. She lingered over Denis, clothing him carefully in his navy-blue suit — the one he would also be buried in — and then she sat back on her heels, holding the scrub brush, missing his scent of newsprint, tobacco, and beer. She shut her eyes and pretended to close his cuff links, the image so real that she found herself flexing her fingers, wondering for a moment if his death had been a dream.

Kathleen Delaney, Maurice's mother, had worn a beige tweed suit and a small, serious brown hat. "It's obvious the woman has no taste," Mae had hissed to Delia at the head of the receiving line. But when Delia thought of Kathleen sitting in the first row at St. Immaculata's, her yellow corsage brushing her chin, she was easiest of all to dress:

two tan pieces and Delia was done. When she had kissed Kathleen in the back of the church, her cheeks were as dry as paper, her lined face flattened against Delia's flushed cheek.)

Outside the church, as the new Delaneys and the nearly new Kowalskis ran down the steps, through the hail of rice, into Danny's old black Ford, women in housedresses, pulling shopping carts, stopped to watch, standing so close to the bridal party that they looked stunned by the rice pellets bouncing from their foreheads. A few miles away, as if they were part of a club, more women in housedresses with shopping carts stood in front of the Brau House and watched the bridal party leap out of the car and into the reception, parade music floating out onto the street, so loud that young boys playing stickball stopped the game and put down their bats to listen.

Somehow, after a lot of beer, Danny lost his brown jacket, and his tie slid underneath the table, and when he picked it up, it was covered with gray footprints. He danced a frantic polka with Rosaleen, his open brown vest flapping underneath his arms like wings. The other guests, seeing the size and girth of Danny Kowalski coming at them in the wrong direction, turned quickly and followed in his wake. When the music was slow, Delia danced with Maurice (biting her lip and trying not to cry when he whispered that he loved her), everyone hooting and stomping their feet when she pressed her lips against his neck, as much to show her affection as to quell her nausea. Rosaleen fox-trotted with her older sister, Sheila. Delia didn't recognize her at first, with her newly dyed black hair and heavy reddish pancake makeup. Sheila wore a sheer yellow dress with a cape and yellow spike-heeled shoes. The sight of them dancing in each other's arms made Delia miss her own brothers, Eugene somewhere on a ship in the Mediterranean and Gerald in the seminary out West. Sheila caught the bouquet — she had never been married — and although her son Junie was only six, he was the one to run out to catch Delia's garter as soon as Maurice tossed it to the men, but when the time came for Junie to slide the garter on his mother's leg, he ran and hid in the men's room and wouldn't come out. Maurice had to go and get him, carrying him over his shoulder, Junie beating against his back with harsh flailing little fists.

In John Brown's chilly back office, that room smelling of grated cheese, Delia changed into a stiff new white suit from Lerner's, threads dangling at her knees. She bent over, plucking the threads away from the skirt, and making pulls in the fabric, but she didn't care a bit. She was married, and feeling brazen, she slipped into her heels and walked over and winked at the picture of Frank Sinatra hanging on the wall.

She told Maurice to wait while she said good-bye to Mae, even though she and Maurice were only going back to their new apartment in the next building, three flights above her mother's. (There was no money for a honeymoon; maybe after the baby they'd take a trip.)

Mae was standing over Denis, pressing a cup of black coffee to his lips, although his eyes were shut and he appeared to be asleep. "We're leaving now, Mama," Delia said, staring at Denis.

"Oh, darlin'." Mae put the cup down and turned to hug Delia. "You were a beautiful bride, and Maurice, I have to say it, is as handsome as Clark Gable. Sleep tight, my married girl, and I'll see you tomorrow." She kissed Delia loudly, a wet spot on Delia's carefully applied face powder.

Kathleen Delaney was sitting alone, staring at the dance floor. When Delia stepped toward her, Kathleen looked up, and Delia lost her nerve and turned around, almost falling over Eileen Riordan, in a print dress, dancing past in the generous red-chiffoned arms of Alice Branigan. "Canned gravy," Mrs. Riordan said to her, in a husky voice. "You buy enough canned gravy, Delia, and he won't know what the hell he's eatin'." She laughed.

"And, Delia," Mrs. Branigan leaned closely into Delia's face, "don't ever be sayin' no to him. I made it a point never to say no to Leo all these many years. Sweet Jesus," she said, looking around her, "by the time you finish fightin' over it, you cryin' and him punchin' the wall, you could have it all done with and be fast asleep. Take my advice, Delia, you'll be a happy woman."

Anna Curley, walking past with two highballs and a pack of cigarettes, somehow managed to poke Delia in the ribs. "Never fight about the money, Delia," she said, not even noticing Rosaleen and Sheila, who bounced by and nearly knocked her down. "You just get yourself some envelopes," and then Anna stared at Delia and waited.

"Envelopes," Delia repeated, watching her carefully. Envelopes of what? she wondered.

"One envelope for the rent," Anna Curley said, "and then one for the electric and one for the gas and one for the telephone and one for the insurance. You take them all and put the money inside and hide em under the rug until they're due. D'you have a rug?" she asked, and laughed uproariously when Delia shook her head no.

Delia opened her arms to the three women and hugged them. Over the tops of their crimped heads, she saw Maurice staring at her from the doorway, his tie off and his collar loosened, a flush on his cheeks. In another week, he was starting at the police academy. She was the luckiest girl in the world.

"I'll try to remember everything," she said solemnly to the women in her arms. "Thank you so much, everybody." She was filling up with tears, wanting to tell them that she loved them, but she caught herself. What a foolish thing that would be!

On her way out, she turned back in the doorway, trying to fix her reception in her mind exactly as she had done with her wedding, and her eyes fell on her father, his head down on the table, Mae nowhere in sight. Although Maurice had turned impatiently and gone outside to hail a taxi, Delia walked quickly to Denis and put her hand on his. "Good night, Daddy," she said, bending down low to be sure he heard her over the music.

"Good night, Delia Mary," he answered clearly, turning his head to kiss her knuckles.

She spent Sunday in bed, too nauseated to even talk to Mae on the telephone, and on Monday morning she wasn't much better. Maurice stayed home from work at the Shamrock (although he wouldn't get paid) just to take care of her, and Delia had to use up her sick time. Maurice brought her warm ginger ale and a Ritz cracker after calling his mother and asking her what to do, but Delia couldn't hold any of it down.

Even sleeping naked with Maurice, her bare belly pressed up against his bare backside, was no help, his warm skin failing to soothe her trembling flesh. She huddled by herself on her bed, one of two pushed together in the nearly empty apartment with the bright white walls. Although she was pregnant, their marriage wasn't consummated yet, and Delia worried that they weren't off to a very good start. In the early hours of their first days, she lay next to him, enraptured by the enormous amount of light in their top-floor apartment, right in the sun's face, she thought. Her mother's place was so dark. Delia didn't want to use the shades they had bought, letting them stand in the corners of each room, leaning against each other like miniature tepees.

But on Monday, in the afternoon, she felt better, and she and Maurice finally made love, and although it had hurt as much as the first time, it was a worry off Delia's mind. While Maurice slept, Delia was well enough to get up, shower, and bring her wedding gown around to Pierre's French Dry Cleaners on the avenue. After he'd cleaned the gown, Pierre would hang it in the front window, the sleeves and bodice packed with pale-pink tissue paper and a small card attached to the sleeve with her married name on it, Mrs. Maurice Martin Delaney, right where everyone in the Heights would see it, almost as if Delia were getting married again.

After a week as a married woman, Delia decided that marriage agreed with her. She wasn't sick at all anymore and was glad to go back to her job. She'd stare at her wedding ring on the subway, moving her hand so that the sun would fall across her lap—such a meager bit of sun to light up her finger—although the heavy ring felt peculiar and itchy and made her aware of sudden veins springing up below her fingers, the interesting shapes her hands were taking. If her ring wasn't quite so new, she reasoned, it wouldn't make her hands look so old. She was eager to dunk her ring into a bowlful of chopped meat, to stare at it inside a basin of ammonia and hot water. She wondered if she'd ever throw her ring in Maurice's face or drop it into a dirty ashtray, as she had once seen a woman do in a gangster movie. Her new wedding ring gave intent and purpose to everything Delia did, like a mold to somehow harden and set her soft edges, gathering her new grown-up life into a single gold focus. She held her head up and settled her purse evenly in her lap when she sat down: Delia Delaney, married lady.

But she scarcely had time to get used to being married before she began to think about the baby. The little rattle that Lois had given her was still in its box, underneath her bed, and when she was alone she looked at it and quietly put it back, almost as if she were teasing herself. At lunchtime, she watched the other operators bite into their sandwiches, the crumbs or the caraway seeds from their rye bread falling onto the table, and she wondered how big her baby was. When she went into the five-and-ten to get the pink paste for the kettle, she couldn't stop herself from staring at the goldfish, wondering when a baby became that size, that real.

On Saturdays, after her weekly visit to the butcher, Delia went to the library and looked through the medical books in the reference section, at the pictures of the unborn babies, although they looked like monsters and not like anything she and Maurice could have created.

She gave up her lunch hour (Lois sneaked cookies and small containers of milk to her) so that she could leave work an hour early, when the subway was nearly empty. She walked through the cars and stood by the conductor's small booth at the head of the train, looking out at the miles of serpentine tracks in front of her, the frame houses joined together like paper dolls on her left, the teeming cemetery on her right. When she touched her stomach, she felt as if she had been alone all her life. She was standing there, listening to the conductor's bad cough through the metal door, on the afternoon when she first felt life, as if she were lying underwater and a starfish were creeping across her belly. She looked around herself, shocked, but nothing had changed, the frame houses looking exactly the same and the cemetery still there, the conductor announcing the next stop in a hoarse voice, but everything in Delia's life was different; everything that had gone before this moving baby now belonged to someone else.

Her pocketbook was on the floor, but she didn't remember dropping it. She wished she had some way to tap out "I love you" to someone the size of a goldfish. She didn't know what to do, looking around the subway car, whom to tell how much the quickening meant to her, so she got on her knees on the dirty speckled floor, on top of the twisted gum wrappers and the flattened cigarette butts, and said a Hail Mary. Then she stayed very still, waiting for something else to happen, but nothing did. At her stop, she bounced out the door to tell Mae and then Maurice. When she passed the five-and-ten, she ran inside to look at the bright hard baby clothes, and there at the counter, sipping hot chocolate, was a little blond-haired girl in a pinafore, with her mother just staring at her. It struck Delia that the small girl would leave that woman just as surely as the baby inside her would leave her, that the parting of their flesh would be as unavoidable as midnight on New Year's Eve.

When she was young, she had read a story in the *Daily News* about a girl strangled and molested in an alley only a few miles from their own apartment, and remembered how Mae wouldn't let her step a foot out of the house alone.

She waited in line to pay for a pair of fire-engine-red baby booties to take home and tuck under her pillow. She hoped her baby wasn't a girl. She didn't think she had the courage a daughter demanded.

When the infant Maureen finally stopped crying, her small face pink and round rather than red and distorted, Delia found that she could get dressed again and wash her face instead of staggering blindly through the day from one feeding to the next in a soiled night-gown and with a bad taste in her mouth.

In the first two months of Maureen's life, Delia was never sure at first if she was looking at A.M. or P.M. hours when she glanced at the clock. Maurice had finally graduated from the police academy, and she never got his hours straight—his tours, she kept reminding her-self—in her sleep-deprived state. She was never sure what should appear on the table, whether she was supposed to cook breakfast, lunch, or dinner, and so the Delaneys floated around for two months, eating hot dogs in the early morning and cornflakes at suppertime, and it seemed as if they lived in a tunnel of infant cries, its walls the inside of the baby's mouth. They marveled clinically at how her tongue vibrated with her screams.

Mae tried to help out, climbing the four flights of stairs to Delia's apartment with two dinners wrapped in waxed paper, but she said she was too nervous to stay. When the baby, in her rage, tried to climb her grandmother's chest on weak and wiry legs, Mae made up an excuse to leave. Now that Denis had died and the boys were home again, they needed their dinners, so she threw the plates on Delia's table, peeked in at the baby, and fled.

Although it seemed they spoke on the phone a dozen or more times a day, Delia, for the first time in her life, saw very little of her mother.

"What's she doing now?" Mae liked to ask, from the safe distance of her kitchen, the second Delia answered the phone. Delia, who walked in circles while the baby screamed in her arms, would run to the phone gratefully before the first ring was complete, but she could barely hear and barely be heard, as she pulled the heavy black receiver away from the baby's bobbing, screaming head.

"She's crying, what else?" Delia shouted, and began to cry herself. Her breasts ached, and every time she showered, a thin stream of greenish milk flowed along her belly. The pediatrician, Dr. Carroll, assured Delia that breast-feeding was "archaic," a thing of the past. "I'm tired," she whined. "I've been up all night long."

"Maybe you should have nursed her," Mae suggested. "D'ya think?"

"The doctor said —"

"Oh, never mind what that young boy said." Mae made a clucking sound. "You must be doing something wrong, Delia Mary. A baby don't cry this much. Are you making sure her formula fills up the whole nipple, that there aren't any bubbles in it? I don't think you burp her long enough. Do you burp her at all?"

Delia threw the phone receiver in the silverware drawer and slammed it shut. Guilty, she instantly retrieved it. Not burp her enough . . . Leaning on her shoulder, the baby tore at Delia's hair all day long and spit up down her back. Her nightgowns were streaked with yellow formula, even the backs of some of Maurice's undershirts.

"Of course I burp her!" Delia cried. "Do you think I'm stupid or something?" But her mother had already hung up, probably sensing the presence of the knives with the pearl handles and Delia's four forks. At night, or in the day, whenever Maurice happened to come home, the first thing he encountered was Delia and Maureen wailing together on the sofa.

Mrs. Gallagher downstairs began complaining about the noise, rapping smartly on the ceiling with a broom handle just as Maureen finally dropped off to sleep. When she began crying again, Delia banged her feet and threw a kitchen chair across the bare living room floor, approximately on top of Mrs. Gallagher's blue easy chair. Then she flung open the window and screamed, "You bitch!" and was instantly horrified, hiding behind the curtains with her knuckles pressed firmly to her lips. My God, she thought, Mrs. Gallagher had made her First Holy Communion dress. This baby was driving her nuts!

In the middle of a terrible afternoon, Mae called and told Delia to give the baby a bath; that was certain to calm her down. "Never mind that she had a bath already this morning," Mae said when Delia protested. "Do you want to make the child stop crying, or do you want to worry about too many baths?"

"But the place is so cold!" Delia said, bouncing the baby on her hipbone so that she made a bleating sound, like a young animal; but at least it wasn't crying, not unless Delia stood still or put Maureen down in her crib.

"Being clean never hurt anyone, Delia Mary," Mae chided her daughter. "You're worried about the cold, go and warm up the bathroom first, like I used to do for you." Her mother was getting disgusted with her stupidity. She had no idea how to raise this baby the right way, the way she had been raised. She just didn't know what she was doing.

She closed the bathroom door behind her just as Mae once did and then ran the bathwater in the tub so the room would warm up with the steam. Then she spread the baby's comforter on the tiles to warm up the floor. The floor, Mae always said, was much colder than the rest of the place, especially in Delia's second bedroom, which had nothing in it but the ironing board and enough of a draft to move the curtains.

Mae called back. "Don't give her a cold," she admonished. "Put her in a draft, she might get pneumonia! And make sure that your tub is spotless. You can't go bathing a new baby with that delicate skin in a dirty tub. Warm and clean — that much you can do, Delia Mary, can't you?"

So Delia hung up and put the screaming baby in her crib, and she went into the bathroom and shut the door; kneeling on top of the comforter, she scrubbed the tub with scouring powder. The phone rang and rang, a tiny weak sound that Delia ignored, working as fast as she could, but then she remembered that Mae had said scouring powder would leave a worse film than dirt and that film would really hurt Maureen's skin, so she rinsed and rinsed the tub and then dried it with an old terry-cloth towel, and it still didn't look clean enough for Maureen, so Delia ran out into the kitchen, the phone beginning to ring anew, to get her steel washtub, and she rinsed that and wiped it down with a sponge and set it inside the big tub in the bathroom. (She didn't want Mae to know she had been filling the kitchen sink with warm water and dunking Maureen inside: maybe a proper bath would relax her, and she should have done it more carefully from the beginning.) She ran to get the baby and then put her down on the warm comforter, right next to her. She rubbed the baby's back with her less tired left arm while the washtub filled, but by the time she had taken off Maureen's clothes, the water turned lukewarm, so she left the naked screaming baby on the floor and ran into the kitchen to set her one pot on the stove to heat. When the little bubbles began to rise, she carried the pot carefully into the bathroom and poured some of the water into the steel tub and tested the water with her elbow and then tried to add cold, but the baby was screaming and writhing across the floor, bunching up the comforter, so she put the pot of hot water on the sink, bent over to pick up Maureen and hit the pot with her backside, the water spilling over everything but the baby. Delia reached for a towel and almost slipped, the naked baby in her arms.

Enough was enough, she thought, wrapping Maureen in a towel and carrying her into the bedroom. As she laid her on the bed on top of a receiving blanket, there was a tremendous banging on the door. It was Mae. Hearing the baby's shrieks, she tossed a platter of hot lamb chops on Delia's table and ran down the hallway into the bedroom. Delia reluctantly followed.

"Naked!" Mae roared. "Delia, are you *mad*? I told you *never* to let her catch cold, and here you are leaving this poor child *naked* in the middle of this bed"—Maureen had somehow crawled out of the towel—"in this freezing room! You must want to see her get sick. You must want to see her get hurt! I called and I called to see if you want these chops I cooked for you, and there was no answer! What else was I to think but that you had drowned her in the tub?" Mae grabbed up the baby and the receiving blanket.

"But she was covered. . . . I spilled the water for her bath. . . . I only had her there for a second!"

"A second is too long! You *never, never* leave a baby, a *naked* baby, no less, on a bed alone, no blanket. What's wrong with you? Suppose she fell off and got a concussion? What then? Then would you be happy?"

"But, Ma . . . she can't even turn over yet!"

"Delia, you can never be sure of that. . . . Gerald turned over a few days after he was born! Why are you takin' such a chance with your baby? Don't you love her? Don't you care about her at all?" For at least the tenth time that day, Delia cried, throwing back her head so that her hot tears filled her ears. Maureen seemed to be listening intently to the two of them, her face snuggled into Mae's collarbone, her little back quivering with the hiccups. Disgusted with Delia, waving her away, Mae sat down on the bed. "Aw, your gramma's here now," she crooned. "Poor little baby, what's your foolish mother doin' to you?" Mae laid the baby across her thighs and rocked her back and forth. Then she picked her up and marched into the bathroom. "Delia Mary," her voice echoed, "you go outside and eat that supper I brought up. There's enough warm water left in the little tub there to bathe her. You go outside; I'll take care of this child."

"But she stopped crying, Ma," Delia insisted, wiping her cheeks with her palms.

"Well, she may start up again! Don't be arguin' with me, miss. Now I told you to do something. Go outside and have some supper. Lamb is dear. I didn't cook those chops for you to be throwin' them out." Then Mae shut the door. Delia stood outside helplessly. She couldn't get in the bathroom without opening the door and letting a draft in, and the baby would surely get sick. Instead she got the baby's clothes from the closet shelf and laid them in a neat pile right outside the bathroom door, on the floor. "Her things are right out here, Ma," Delia called, a chilly breeze running over her bare feet.

Outside, in the living room, the winter afternoon had suddenly turned into black evening. She switched on the lamp and then, in the kitchen, the overhead light. She was hungry; her mother was right. She didn't even know when to eat. This baby she had wanted so very much had an idiot for a mother. Mae was probably right. Delia *was* careless enough to drown her child. She could clearly see her baby floating facedown in the bathtub, the back of her yellow kimono puffed up with water. She had had a dream that she had taken the baby for a walk in her carriage and dropped her, in slow motion, onto the Brooklyn-Queens Expressway.

She got a fork and dropped a chop onto a plate, but it was fatty and too cold to eat. Maybe later, she thought, when Maurice comes home, we'll have toast. She filled her kettle for tea. She needed a nap more than anything.

"Delia Mary, come in here," Mae shouted through the cracked-open door. "I absolutely *refuse* to be puttin' these on her."

"You won't put what on her?" Delia asked, pushing at the door, but Mae had her foot wedged behind it. All that Delia could see was her nose.

"Don't be comin' in here now — what's the matter with you? You'll be gettin' her sick. These rubber diapers. They're bad for her skin, don't you know that? I never put rubber on you children, and none of you ever had as much as a rash. Maybe that's why the child cries so much, from the rubber you're pressin' against her skin."

"They're not rubber diapers, Ma; they're rubber pants. If I don't use them, she'll wet the sheet."

"So what? All you children wet the sheet. I didn't have no washing machine. I just kept washing the sheets, and I hung them in the kitchen to dry. Do you want a happy baby or a dry sheet? What's your priorities, miss?" she fumed, closing the door. When she came out, Maureen was asleep in Mae's arms. "Mama," Delia asked, "can you stay awhile, just in case she gets up?" She hovered over tiny Mae, walking behind her into the bedroom. "She does that sometimes, Ma. I think she's going to sleep, and then she gets up in a second." Delia whispered rapidly. "I'd like to change and take a bath. I'm not sure; I think Maurice is on his way home." Some wife she was, not even knowing when her husband was due back.

"No, Delia. I'm tired now. You have to learn to do these things for yourself. You can't be expectin' me to help you all the time; I'm not a young woman. When Maurice comes home he can listen for her. After all, he's her father, isn't he?" She laid the limp baby back in her crib. "She'll sleep now." Mae kissed Delia brusquely on the cheek. "I'll call you later."

Maybe her mother was right. The baby seemed to be exhausted.

Delia picked up the wet towels and ran a bath and brushed her teeth. She tied her hair back with a clean ribbon. By the time she had lowered herself into the steaming tub, Maureen was screaming and Maurice had his hand on the doorknob.

"Well," Mae said later on the phone, "you probably don't give her enough stimulation. Maybe you need to play with her. Have you tried to play with her?" she demanded. Mae sounded so far away. Delia didn't have the strength to answer. Her tongue felt as if it had fallen asleep in her mouth. Delia said nothing. "I never see you give her any water," Mae continued. "She's probably just awful thirsty."

"I do," Delia found the strength to insist. "I do give her water!" It was the worst part of her day, the water running out through the bottle so quickly that the baby choked and coughed. Delia had to pull her arms up over her head to get her breathing again. She finally confessed this to Mae.

"Ah, Delia, Delia, don't you know that you mustn't give her water from a regular bottle? You need to buy her whole nipples for water and pierce them yourself. Are you trying to make that baby choke to death?"

The next morning, Delia dumped Maureen in Mae's lap and ran to the drugstore. When she got home, she held a match to one of Mae's sewing needles over by the kitchen window, where the light was strong, and pierced each of the new nipples she had bought with a tiny hole, yet the baby still choked and screamed. "She's crying because she's probably cutting early teeth and you don't even know it," Mae said, pushing the baby in Delia's face. "Look in her mouth; I can't see with my bad eyes. Are there any white lumps, any points trying to break through?"

"No, Ma, I don't see anything."

"Ah, Sacred Heart, I feel so sorry for little babies like this one." Mae shook her head ruefully. "They're at the mercy of the whole foolish world."

There began to be brief periods of quiet, when the baby turned her head on her crib mattress and made soft questioning sounds into her sheet. Delia wondered what she was looking for.

"You have to always *be* the baby," Mae insisted, "and then you'll always know what she needs." But Delia couldn't be the baby, or anyone else, and she didn't know what she was doing wrong. She could only be Delia Delaney, the unfit mother. When the baby finally began to sleep, in fits and starts, Delia was terrified that she would die. She kept the crib close to her side of the bed and watched Maureen sleep, one hand resting on the baby's chest.

At three months old, Maureen stopped crying, and everyone was surprised by her features.

Maurice nicknamed her "Moodles."

This new child, "Moodles" Delaney, slept twelve hours at night and four during the day, taking two-hour naps after breakfast and lunch.

"That child sleeps too much," Mae said, looking anxiously into her crib. "D'ya think that maybe she's got a bad heart?"

EIGHT

Delia had no money for a playpen, so she carried Maureen with her from room to room and laid her in each doorway on a blanket. The baby, on her stomach, stared at Delia intently while she cleaned the apartment, and sometimes she became so excited, kicking her feet and flailing her fists about, that Delia stopped what she was doing and flopped down on the baby's blanket next to her to see the world as it might appear to Maureen Mary Delaney.

Whenever he came home, Maurice planted raspberry kisses on his Moodles's cheeks, while she shrieked in delight. Delia stood next to them with her arms out and ready, like a baseball catcher.

She soaked the tons of diapers in a yellow pail by the tub and washed them by hand in the sink, and on nice days, she carried them upstairs to the roof to dry: on bad days, the diapers hung over the stove, dripping from a rack that was mounted on the kitchen ceiling. All winter long, Maurice complained that his dinner tasted of soap flakes and baby pee.

Around the time that Maureen stopped crying, Delia's stitches disappeared, and she was aware of a ripening deep inside herself, some sense of depth that wasn't there before. Her waist seemed lowered and her backside fuller, more sensitive to the touch. Something in the birth process had raised her ribs, she swore it, and she noticed a new dark line from her crotch to her navel, which wouldn't wash off no matter how hard she scrubbed. Rosaleen told her that the line was painted on her belly in the hospital, that she had noticed it herself after she came home with Kevin, who was a month older than Maureen. "It's routine," she had assured Delia, who hated to hear it, as if her belly belonged to the hospital, like a towel.

The bruises on her ankles and wrists from the delivery room restraints began to fade to a dull yellow, and her breasts had become very round, brown and tough near the nipples. Even her skin felt different; she was softer now than before, and her flesh seemed warm, as if she were always running a slight fever. It was as if she had come home from the hospital with a new body and with senses keener than before. She never heard the blasting television or Maurice's snores once the baby began to cry, and she could clearly see in Maureen's face Maurice's nose and his chin and her brother Eugene's gray eyes; she would hold on to the infant's feet and kiss what looked like Mae's miniature toes. She had never thought much about how connected they all were, such unlikely couplings as Mae with Maurice and Maurice with Eugene in one tiny seven-pound baby girl.

At nineteen years old, Delia thought that she might have been born along with her child, and she wanted to say that out loud to someone but there was nobody for her to tell, nobody to trust with such a crazy thought. At night, she lay in bed and listened for the baby's breath and wondered about her new self. If Maurice moved against her in his sleep, sometimes she wanted him very much, and it made her feel ashamed. What would he think of her?

She couldn't fit into any of her old clothes yet or even her shoes. Her wedding pom-pom slippers, gray and stained, were the only things that felt comfortable. Before Maurice was due home, she took a bath and sprayed perfume on her arms and slipped into an old lace slip that had been her mother's. She pummeled her soft belly into a tight girdle and put on dark stockings and then a housecoat — nothing else would button yet — and tugged at the straps of her slip until her new rounded breasts threatened to spill out. She leaned back against the door when he rang the downstairs buzzer, hoping she looked like the sexy star of some Italian movie.

It thrilled her to see Maurice's face light up at the bottom of the stairs, the way he looked uneasily at the closed doors on the landing. He rushed at her, burying his scratchy face in her neck, and sometimes she kicked her pom-pom slippers aside and stood on his feet, and he walked her inside stiff-legged, as if he were on stilts. Delia told herself that their young marriage was a success; his quietness no longer bothered her. In fact, she thought, she had turned the long silences into a sort of joke. "Penny for your thoughts," she often said to him over two mugs of tea. "Yeah, well, I don't have no change," he'd reply, and that made everything all right. They smiled at each other. He's a good man, Delia thought.

Maureen began to roll against the bars of her crib at dawn, wet, hungry, and noisy, waking them up. "It's time for her own room," Maurice said, and a wave of sadness washed over Delia. They bundled the baby and went out to buy pink paint for the second small bedroom; they collapsed the ironing board and stashed it in the hall closet. Delia put the two cans of Petal Pink in front of the second-bedroom door like a pair of wet shoes, hoping to buy a little more time, but it didn't work: Maureen gulped down applesauce and oatmeal and grew strong enough to lean on one elbow and smile at them when the alarm rang, and sometimes they woke the baby when they coughed or kissed or even turned over. As if to assert herself, Maureen grew a little black cowlick, and in the morning, when the baby shook the crib with her kicks, Delia stared over at her bit of pointy dark hair vibrating in the air like the needle of a compass and grew sad. She couldn't help but remember that Maureen had been born without a single hair, her head as bald and sore-looking as a bitten-down thumbnail. Most of all it bothered Delia that Maureen was old enough to be remembered as someone else.

It was bad luck, Mae had said, to take a baby out before she was christened. (What with bills and all, it had taken Delia three months to save enough money for a christening dress. Rosaleen, the baby's godmother, offered to buy one, but Rosaleen was pregnant again, and Delia just didn't think it was right.) After the ceremony (which Delia didn't attend — Mae having told her it was bad luck for the mother to go), when she could finally take the baby for a walk, she felt as if she had won a huge sum of money in some contest. She put Maureen in an old plaid carriage Rosaleen had given her, which was now too small for Kevin and, she felt, too worn for her expected baby. Delia considered it better than nothing, though she envied the other young mothers she passed on the avenue, with their shiny dark-blue English prams, their silver-plated blanket clips glinting in the sun. Coverlets of pink or blue lace cascaded over the sides of the prams like waves of frothy water on the shore, so generously cut that the lace was practically touching the gleaming white wheels.

Delia studied the faces of the babies who rode in the English prams, propped up on lace pillows embroidered with their names, Scott Michael or Karen Marie, and she decided that none of them were as pretty as her Maureen. "Maureen Mary" might have looked nice like that, she thought, all those trailing letters in a name that was as close to Maurice as Delia could get.

The babies on the pillows would probably grow up to ride through the streets of the Heights in sleek black Cadillacs, and Maureen would chug along in an aging Plymouth.

Maybe they'd ride in Cadillacs, Delia thought smugly, but they all had faces (even the girls) that cried out for fat cigars.

"Beggars can't be choosers," Mae had said, watching Delia seal the thinning spots with fabric tape from the five-and-ten; the papery carriage hood and the plastic wind protector offered no real shelter from the blustery winds which gave Maureen gas. Delia had only one sheet for the carriage, so often, when it was soiled or wet, she would take one of her own sheets and fold it in such a way that Maureen was raised up like a queen and everybody passing by could see her beautiful face framed in her small lace bonnet. If her own sheet was also in the wash, she would use one of Mae's old white damask tablecloths, embroidered with silk and stained pink in spots with cranberry sauce.

On nice afternoons, Delia and Maureen met Rosaleen and Kevin in front of the A & P, and the two women wheeled their babies to the park. Rosaleen had colored her hair, and some of it was black and some of it auburn. She bent over to wipe Kevin's face with hands that were rough and scaly and reminded Delia of the legs of turtles. She's aging, Delia thought. Am I?

Kevin Kowalski's nose was always running, and though he was only a bit older than Maureen, he stood early, placing himself at the end of his new carriage, looking out at the street. He would have appeared just like the shining horse on a Packard's hood if he hadn't had a tiny prizefighter's face, with droopy eyes and a slightly flattened nose. When Rosaleen and Delia went for walks with their babies, the same strangers who stopped to admire Maureen's pink cheeks then laughed at Kevin's defiant chin.

"You're so lucky you had a girl." Rosaleen put her hand on top of Maureen's head. "I could really make her a beautiful blanket. . . . I even have some pink wool at home," then she looked miserably at her son's delicate blue blanket, which was balled up under his stockinged feet. He had thrown both his little white shoes onto the sidewalk. When Rosaleen grabbed Kevin by his shoulders, forcing him to sit down, he leaned over and gummed her knuckles. A week or so later, Rosaleen met Delia by the playground swings and handed her a lumpy white box from Mays. When Delia opened it, turning the sheets of tissue paper carefully, she found a pale-pink crocheted blanket with a creamy-white scalloped edge and a set of plastic blanket clips covered with white lace. Underneath the blanket, Delia found a matching pink bonnet and a tiny pink sweater with long trailing ribbons. "Mittens to match." Rosaleen smiled, digging in her voluminous purse for a pair of small pink mittens, waving them in Delia's surprised face.

"Aw, Rosaleen." Delia hugged her friend and kissed her. Maureen was asleep, but Delia picked her up anyway and handed her to Rosaleen. She slipped the new bonnet over her head, straightened it and tied it under Maureen's chin, the baby mewing like a kitten. Then Delia draped the new blanket over the old one on the carriage and smiled at the snap of the new blanket clips. She walked quickly to the sandbox and turned around for the full effect. Rosaleen was balancing the baby and waving something pink at her, and when Delia moved closer, she saw that Rosaleen had made the baby a pink satin pillow and embroidered her name across the front in the flowing script Delia had often envied in school.

"Aw, c'mon, Delia." Rosaleen looked embarrassed. "Don't start crying all over the place. It'll be for her first birthday, when it gets here, okay?"

Overcome, Delia squeezed Rosaleen's hand.

"But where do you get the money?" Delia asked.

"What money?" Rosaleen hunched her shoulders, opening and closing her hands. "I don't have any money. How much you think

Danny the Mailman makes? Probably no more than Maurice, probably less. The stuff to crochet with, the hooks and the knitting needles I sometimes use, they were in my mother's house. Hell" — she laughed — "Judge Crater could have hidden in my mother's house, Delia; you know the mess of that place," and Delia smiled. "You should have seen us when she moved." Rosaleen rolled her eyes. "I had a lot of pink yarn, just in case Kevin was a girl" — they both looked at Kevin, who was pulling off his socks — "and the satin and the lace — well, you'd be surprised. None of that stuff costs as much as hamburgers, and I gotta tell you, I like to sew and crochet a lot more than I like to cook. So one night we have spaghetti with butter. No big deal."

There were other women at the park who looked like Rosaleen did now, with her straggly, badly colored hair and busy grubby fingers, and Delia had seen them sitting in the sunshine, knitting with a furious energy, yanking the sweet pastel yarns from brown paper bags between their legs, their long knitting needles or their sharp crochet hooks stabbing like daggers through butter. They seemed to be driven with a hunger and a yearning that was too great for Delia to understand, and yet the results of their ferocious labors were tiny soft sweaters and airy delicate hats that offered them no relief, for when the projects were finished and the babies all dressed up, propped on their fancy pillows, the women were restlessly tapping their feet on the cold, hard pavement, rocking the babies so violently they threatened to fall out, smoking their cigarettes down to the end, mashing the butts with the heels of their shoes until the filters split open and shredded on the concrete. Delia was always relieved to see the women in the park tear the wrappers from new skeins of soft yarn, and she often walked over to admire their work.

"Well, then, where do you find the time?" Delia asked, turning to Rosaleen on the bench. She seemed to feed Maureen breakfast, and then, before she knew it, the baby needed her lunch, and then there was the laundry and the shopping for dinner, and as soon as Maureen went to bed in the early evenings, Delia did the dishes and sometimes fell asleep on the sofa with the *Daily News* still folded across her chest.

"I just love to do it." Rosaleen shrugged. "It's no big deal. I get a kick out of making something that wasn't there before. When I sew or knit or crochet, it's something I can look at and hold on to, something that stays the same even when I don't do it for a while or pay no attention to it. Housework's different. It goes to hell the minute you turn your back."

The thought of the apartment Rosaleen had lived in, above the Greenleaf, her parents' bar, gave Delia a sharp pain between her eyes. Sheila Clancy's stockings had hung from her headboard with stiff and dirty feet, and Spooky, their cat, slept on the kitchen table. Delia had once seen Geraldine Clancy wipe cat urine with the dishcloth.

Even so, Delia thought, it would be nice to have something she had made that stayed the same. "Maybe you could show me how to do that stuff," she said.

"We tried that already, remember? I tried to show you how to do a cat's cradle when we were in grade school." Rosaleen opened her eyes wide and laughed. Delia had forgotten; she had panicked, feeling strangled with the bright-green yarn, and Rosaleen had laughed up-roariously while Delia ripped the yarn away in terror. "Besides" — Rosaleen put her hand on Delia's sleeve — "you would never find the time. You work much too hard in the house, Delia, you really do."

"I have to do it, Rosaleen. I can't rest till it's all done, the house-work, and it never seems to be all done."

"And Mae, Queen of Saints Herself would have a fit if it wasn't."

Mae, Queen of Saints . . . Geraldine, Saint of Queens . . . Rosa-leen had made up those names, and she used them in a thick brogue to make fun of their Irish-born parents, whose accents were different and yet somehow the same. It was a way the girls had had of reassur-ing each other and moving away from their backgrounds all at once, not "foreigners" like their parents, yet not quite ready to leave them behind. In Rosaleen's parody, Liam Clancy had sounded English, but Mae Rooney had a voice that rolled from Delia's cheeks like cool, soft rain. Mae had a way of asking Delia to bring out the garbage, please, or hang up her jacket like a good girl, and the sound of her voice was so beautiful that tears sometimes came to Delia's eyes, her mother having traveled such a distance to America to live, so many had died on the boat coming over. What if Mae had stayed in Ireland and never met Delia's father? It was almost as if Mae had risked her very life so that Delia could hear her brogue in the living room of their apartment in Queens, and Delia felt obliged to listen to every word. She stood still in doorways until she was sure that her mother had stopped talking. "What?" Mae often asked. "Why do you *look* at me so much?" but Delia just shrugged. It was easier than trying to explain.

"My mother doesn't care if I do my housework or not," Delia said lightly, looking across the street.

"The hell she doesn't!" Rosaleen propped a half-filled bottle on Kevin's pillow, half in, half out of his mouth. She had an annoying habit of being right, and they both knew it. They had known even when she and Delia were two of seventy children in Sister Alberta's fifth-grade classroom, the beads of early body odor misting the windows, dew on the desks in steamy hot air smelling of yeast and grass and chalk and of something stronger if the radiator was on and the classroom door was shut. A good if unruly student, Rosaleen always knew what to study for the tests. When Sister Alberta nodded off in that warm-bread classroom, Rosaleen always caught the first eraser that the boys threw to the girls' side, and when Sister began to snore, she threw it back.

It was true that Mae called every morning to see if Delia had fed the baby and with what, asking in a suspicious voice if Delia had done the wash; when they shopped together, she always told Delia what to cook, throwing some packages into her cart and taking others out. She put back soaps that she thought were too expensive, and she never let her daughter waste her money on nonsense. In the spring, she made Delia buy white vinegar to wash her windows and camphor flakes for her closets. Delia told herself she should be grateful for her mother's plentiful advice, even if she did want Glass Wax and Ivory Snow. Delia's home was clean, thanks to Mae, and she was learning how to run a good table. Left to her own devices, Delia knew, she'd never clean up but just sit on the couch and play with the baby or watch television and read the old movie magazines she found piled up on the street next to the garbage cans.

Maybe she could crochet, but Rosaleen had never learned to run a proper household, with her mother in the Greenleaf all day long. She had sold the bar after Rosaleen's father died, and she opened another one (a *lounge*, Rosaleen had said disdainfully) in Atlantic City.

Rosaleen, Delia decided, might be a little bit jealous.

On the way home, Delia thought about stopping in at Mae's to show her Maureen's new things, but she knew her mother wouldn't like them. She never liked anything she hadn't given Delia herself. Whenever Mae met Delia and Rosaleen on the street, she touched Kevin's bare head and asked where, in God's name, the child's hat was. "At home," Rosaleen always answered cheerfully, "in his dresser drawer," although Delia had seen Kevin pull his hat from his head and throw it on the ground, had watched Rosaleen pick it up and stuff the hat in her purse.

"Humpf," Mae always said later to Delia on the phone. "That one, with them magic knittin' needles, can't even keep her poor child's head warm."

In the early evenings, when Maurice, working days, was due home soon and the infant Maureen was asleep in her crib, the fuzz of her new, lighter hair hovering above the thin sheet like a faded dandelion, Delia left the barely furnished apartment and climbed the stairs to the roof to take her clothes down from the clothesline and look at the city, *her* city, the sky streaked with red.

She didn't know anybody who lived in Manhattan.

She knew people who merely worked there, but they were all home by now, or on their way, like Maurice. Her neighbors were proud enough of themselves, having passed successfully through the subway tunnels or having endured the bumpy ride of the jowly buses lumbering over the rusting bridge twice a day, although it took everything out of them. There seemed to be nothing much for people from the Heights to do in the city but go to work and then come back home again; nothing to buy there and bring home to the others, nothing they could afford. The crowds on New York streets dangled cameras from their necks and, in their enthusiasm, carried people from Queens past the lavish windows of stores on Fifth Avenue, and when

71

they came home, the people from the Heights laughed at the dressed-up window dummies in the city, like creatures from outer space.

The restaurants in New York made Heights people hide in doorways to peek into their wallets and then keep going, and the New York churches were intimidating. Individuals who dripped with thick furs and shone with old jewelry seemed to be of a different faith than Delia's, one that deserved plush velvet kneelers and crystal-clear fonts of holy water. People visiting New York churches from the Heights seemed to hate denting the kneelers or sullying the holy water with their fingers, and so they just blessed themselves, dry, near the back door, anxious to go back to their own broken-in faith and their familiar bulky priests, to the sins that fit them comfortably and were free.

When she was younger, Delia rubbed the head of one of the stone lions outside the New York Public Library, hoping to get enough courage to go in, and when she finally did, she didn't see a single book, and her cheap shoes made loud sounds on the floor and she had to leave.

Everyone she knew in the Heights, even her Aunt Margaret, Denis's sister, who had arthritis and could hardly walk, claimed to have been in Times Square on V-J day, watching a sailor kissing a nurse, and although Delia was only a kid, she felt overlooked and uninvited whenever the subject came up. Years later, when Delia saw the picture of the sailor and the nurse in *Life* magazine, she was disappointed and yet somehow relieved not to recognize a single person standing on the sidelines.

From the roof, Delia stared down at dark, flat Queens, held back by the water from hurling itself under Manhattan's feet, the flashing lights of the airport close enough to the cemeteries so that the landing planes seemed to scrape against the tops of the mausoleums. The New York skyline was just beyond the roof of Delia's kitchen, heart-stoppingly beautiful, and she imagined a hundred young Queens mothers like herself tying their aprons around their waists in a frilly embrace and standing behind their bright, clean kitchen curtains frying pork chops and finding it, as Delia was, about as easy as turning their backs on the sun: everything in front of them glowed, and, eventually, blisters stung their backs.

At dusk, the tall buildings twinkling over her head in the lavender air, Delia pulled her wash from the clothesline, startled to see the long frozen arms of Maurice's shirts slap against each other in clumsy applause.

If Delia moved to the edge of the building she could lean over and look down into her own apartment through her sparkling clean windows; the starched white curtains stood at pristine attention, yet she knew they were like curtains on a movie set. If she had left them open just a bit or if a draft in the old apartment blew the curtains aside, then it was clear to Delia that the home she worked so hard at was practically empty, that what she was seeing, her table set for dinner and her clean bedrooms, Maureen gurgling in her crib, were simply the contents of her entire life, preserved under glass like butterflies in a collector's case. She knew that she loved her baby and she loved Maurice, but the towering buildings, big and bright, made her own choices dim and small. Some nights she waited for King Kong to snatch her away.

But as Delia grew older, after Patty had been born (that surprising, bright-red hair, in the hospital nursery like a lit match) she was up on the roof a lot less. She had become more organized, she told herself, and she worked now with a schedule and she rarely forgot about her wash or anything else. After all, there were two children downstairs that she was leaving alone, and even if she found herself up there again in the evenings, she was so busy she didn't have a minute to think. With the new baby's laundry, the basket was heavier, and it seemed to take her much longer to walk up and down the stairs. In her own apartment, there was more furniture to walk around than there had been before. She bought a clothes rack made of wooden dowels, a skeleton of a frame, and she stood it in the corner of her bedroom, where the things dried but didn't smell as nice. Still, if the girls got sick in the night, she hung their sheets up on the line to dry, and often the wind seemed to cooperate, blowing them into a puddle right by the roof door so she didn't even have to step out on the tar to pick them up, which was a relief. She had lost her curiosity, no longer anxious to look down into her own house. She had tangerine-colored drapes drawn over the living room windows, and they didn't blow open the way the white curtains had. Behind the drapes there was now enough furniture to make a home, and two beautiful little girls in printed flannel pajamas, fresh from their baths, their plump feet in warm slippers with fur trim around the ankles and little white pearls dancing across the toes. Their shiny faces, looking up at Delia, made the Delaney apartment a holy place, a church that smelled of steam heat, hot soup, and brushed damp hair.

First, Delia had bleached her light shoulder-length hair champagne blond, then she dyed it golden blond, and waited for something in her life to change, and when nothing did, she colored her hair medium brown and then, rather desperately, henna red. She would arrange it in a new style, teasing the top of her unfamiliar hair into a full strong crest, tucking the back into a French twist with a handful of long black bobby pins. Sometimes she let the back down, combing it straight over her shoulders, walking the length of the avenue with her children after school, aware of the shopkeepers standing in front of their family-owned stores, watching her.

She bought a gray eye pencil and lined her lids, both top and bottom, although the beauty books she bought in the five-and-ten advised against this, hinting that it would make her look cheap. Not that she minded: in otherwise static afternoons, she liked having the shopkeepers look at her, although she couldn't help but notice that their faces were hardening into the shrinking faces of their fathers, and sadly she would realize how seldom she left the Heights.

Every autumn, she watched Mr. Shine's back as he delicately pinned red leaves to the hems of his corduroy slacks and cardigan sweaters in Shine's Men's window, and then she noticed his granddaughter, leaning on the faceless dummies, waiting to help him clamber out. Every summer, Delia saw old Miss McKee climb into the window of the five-and-ten and stick yellow shovels into shiny tin pails, and her white floppy sneakers had somehow turned into black open-toed orthopedic shoes. Often, when Delia came home from her shopping, she stood at her bathroom sink for a long time, looking in the mirror for Mae's wrinkles in her own flesh.

She liked her early mornings best, waking up to cook breakfast for the girls, meals that she remembered, eggs and thick Irish bacon from Sullivan's, or oatmeal with heavy cream pooled into the center of the bowl. Sometimes she squeezed fresh oranges for their juice, straining it into two tall glasses, drinking what the girls left behind. She liked to sit and watch them eat, although they seldom looked up from their plates. Perhaps Delia made them nervous, staring at them like that, but she had worked so hard on the breakfast that she wanted something back; a glimmer of appreciation might have been enough. She was aware of that, the wanting something back, and she didn't know where it came from, nor why it was so important to her. Her mother had made breakfasts like hers all of Delia's life, and then she went inside to scrub the bathroom floor. The only thing she had wanted back from Delia was the empty dish.

When the girls were finished, she waited at the door until their footsteps drifted down the stairs and out onto the street, then she stood quietly, listening for echoes. The sunny mornings were the worst, after the girls had left for school, when there were bright, empty gaps of time, while cool fresh air from the open windows filled the apartment. There was the vacuuming and then a gap of time when Delia couldn't decide what she wanted, whether it was a cup of tea or someone to talk to, and she stood by the kettle with one hand on the telephone. The lemon furniture polish she used smelled like candy from her youth and made her long for the summer, which she ordinarily hated, all that noise and busyness and heat. When she looked in the polished end table at her own reflection, her chin wiggled.

Midmorning, she put cold cream on her face and ran a hot bath. She sat in the tub and watched beads of water trickle down the tile walls. It made her feel very efficient to use the steam for softening her skin and cleaning her bathroom at the same time. She dried her body, then used the towel to wipe down the walls. She climbed out of the tub and stepped into a small nest of Maurice's underwear that was headed for the washing machine: there were plenty of ways Delia found to combine her tasks.

Before getting dressed, she wrapped a towel around herself and ran into the girls' bedroom to play an Elvis record, and then, as she did her hair, she'd jitterbug naked, catching hold of the bathroom doorknob. After the record stopped, there was a gap of time when Delia looked in the mirror, out of breath, breasts jiggling, feeling like a fool.

She watched *I Love Lucy* and saw the episode where Ricky devised a tight schedule for Lucy, and Delia tried to do that, writing down everything she had to do, taping the list to the refrigerator door. After two days on her tight schedule, Delia received a flurry of unexpected telephone calls. She ripped the list to shreds, understanding why Lucy had wailed like a banshee.

Next, she created the once-a-week plan. Once a week, she scrubbed and waxed the kitchen floor, refilled the tiny holy water bowls above the light switches in the bedrooms, wiped down the insides of the windows with a rag dipped in cider vinegar and warm water, polishing them with bits of torn newspaper. Once a week, she put fresh sheets on the beds and went over everyone's closet, rearranging the clothes according to size and color. She bought a spool of red ribbon in Hooperman's Notions and tied small red bows on top of the hangers where a stitch or a button was needed; two red bows indicated a major repair, like a hem. She allotted an hour of sewing in front of the television screen once a week and put her sewing box, which had a picture of the Eiffel Tower on its padded satin cover, next to her on the couch, but the picture depressed her. The Eiffel Tower was something she was sure she'd never see, so she kept the sewing box open. She found herself sorting pins and buttons and colored threads in the order of her preference, and before she knew it, the hour was gone, so she put her sewing box away and shut off the television.

Sometimes, after Mae had made her daily phone call, Delia took a nap, only to wake up with her face mottled from the spread. At other times, she dragged a kitchen chair into the bedroom and pulled her wedding pictures down from the closet shelf. On her dresser, she had one big picture of herself and Maurice sitting at the table on the dais at the Brau House, but often she needed to remember more of the day than that, and besides, the picture on their dresser always struck her as funny: she was so pale, sitting behind a big jar of mayonnaise, and Maurice was beet red, sitting behind the ketchup.

In a manila envelope stashed in her underwear drawer, Delia kept wedding pictures of Jackie Kennedy that she had cut from a magazine. She loved to look at Jackie, so beautiful in a lace mantilla, married on a farm, of all places, in Rhode Island: the bright sunshine, the thick grass rising on everyone's shoes, handsome Kennedys all around her. (Delia always asked herself how Jackie knew which handsome Kennedy to choose.) When she looked at Jackie's pictures, she told herself that *she* was a pretty bride and Maurice just as handsome, and then she smiled slightly as she imagined Jackie might, glancing at herself across the room, in her bedroom mirror.

Sometimes Delia set the ironing board in the middle of the living room and dumped a pile of wood hangers on the white leatherette chair like a pile of kindling. She would pull the basket of wrinkled clothes from the hall closet and begin to press a piece at a time, starting to think that Jackie was so lucky to have such a wonderful husband and such gorgeous children, especially little John-John. Maurice, she thought (sprinkling a handful of water from the sink on his shirt), might be a different man if he had a son.

Unlike her daughters, unlike John-John, Delia thought her son, if she had one, would be white-blond, as she was when she was small. Unlike the others, he'd be breast-fed, lying quietly in her arms, his jagged newborn fingernails resting on her breast, staring intently into her eyes, and when he got a little older, he'd sit quietly in front of Mae's kitchen window, out on the steps, and play with his toy trucks, a collection started by Maurice. Delia knew exactly how her son, if she had one, would look, the way his head would tilt to one side and she could clearly see the shine of his blond hair. The back of his neck would always be clear for her kisses, and she'd stare at his small hands and wonder who would lie in them someday and what would slip through those pudgy fingers.

She thought about it all through the summer, staring at the cool straw rug in her living room, which hurt their bare feet, how rough it would feel on a crawling baby's knees. (She was overjoyed to throw the rug away after Maurice burned a hole in it with a cigarette.) She thought, while she was cutting the plastic slipcovers from her sofa with scissors, how uncomfortable she would be if she had to sit on the sofa in a diaper, with her bare calves stuck to the furniture. (When the girls came home, they knelt on the bare floor and traced the metallic thread that ran through the sofa with their fingers and their noses, like blind children.)

The bare sofa, Delia thought, was better in the warm weather, the bare floor actually much cooler than the straw rug.

It would do until the winter came and the brown rug, soft enough for a baby to crawl on, came home from the cleaners, as it always did, with a deep crease in the middle. Every fall, Delia laid the set of encyclopedias she had bought at the A & P right across the crease and watched the girls tiptoe across the books with their arms flung out, like circus performers. She imagined the little boy following his sisters, with gold wings attached to his back and a halo floating above his head like a cherub on a Christmas card.

She had to stop thinking about babies, and so she started a project.

She borrowed Sally Malloney's sewing machine to make new drapes for the living room, hoping that the gray-and-orange fabric she had selected would be fun to work with and keep her occupied, like construction paper glued with bits of felt. But it didn't work; she pumped her foot up and down on the sewing machine pedal and thought and thought. Her children were too big for her to go through it all again, she told herself; she was thirty-two already; her oldest was nearly thirteen. It wouldn't matter a bit to Maurice, either way; it wouldn't change his life at all. Actually, a new baby might improve it. They'd go on just the way they always had, with Delia taking care of the children and the apartment and Maurice working shifts and overtime, when he could get it. In fact, she thought, it might be the best thing for them. With a new baby to occupy her time, she'd expect less from Maurice, and he'd be so happy, he'd come home straight from work and not stop at any of the neighborhood bars. He'd probably think it was a wonderful idea, but Delia didn't want to even mention it to him, not yet, until she had it all sorted out in her head. She knew it would be her decision, anyway, in the end.

She'd be nearly forty by the time he was in school, she thought, trying not to swallow the straight pins in her mouth. She'd be almost forty all too soon even if she didn't have another child. She'd worry about forty when it came. The baby would be only eight and still need her for at least ten more years. She loved being a mother; it was the only thing she knew how to do. Still, she remembered how Maureen had cried, and she just couldn't be sure. There was no guarantee she'd have another one like Patty, a child who seemed determined to raise herself. She just didn't know.

For a few weeks, when she walked along the avenue she stayed away from Schwartz's Infant Wear and far from the goldfish tank in the five-and-ten. She let herself go into Moderne Home Decor, where she bought a bright centerpiece of orange and red plastic flowers for the top of the television set, and then she put a deposit on two shiny black-panther lamps with white parchment shades for the old scarred end tables. When she finished the new drapes (too quickly, she told herself), she bought colorful magazines, ones that she never read, and she laid them out on the coffee table, spine to edge. She became very angry when the girls made stray ink marks on the covers with their pens or when Maurice left an imprint of his coffee cup. After a while, a page or two would loosen and stick out at Delia like a tongue.

In the kitchen (her busiest room), she lined her shelves with plain white paper from a roll and stacked the boxes according to size and use, the salt in the front, the bay leaves in the back, against the wall. Everything in the refrigerator was assigned a specific place. She hated to open the door and see the short, fat mustard, its top not quite attached, right next to the gummy bottle of jelly, or congealed milk drops scattered on the glass shelves. She set the meat far away from the carrots and the onions, and to keep the potatoes fresh, she assigned them a section of their own. In the morning, she cautiously opened the refrigerator door as if, overnight, the foods might have intermingled and turned into stew.

She said she was tired, but she didn't want any help. Her daughters washed the dishes carelessly, and it was easier to do it right the first time herself. The girls skidded across the slippery kitchen floor in their socks and crashed, giggling, into the dish cupboard. In their closets, they knocked the red bows on the hangers down onto the floor, or used them to tie back their hair, and Delia was forever retrieving red ribbons from underneath the sofa or the bottom of their closets or inside their shoes; when the freshly ironed blouses somehow fell to the closet floor, on top of the red bows, Delia roared like a woman gone berserk. She found a long chain made of the small gold safety pins in her Eiffel Tower sewing box, and she shook her fist in Patty's face and threw the box on the floor, the buttons inside bouncing like castanets. She just couldn't keep it all neat, no matter how hard she tried.

As long as she still had the sewing machine (she reasoned), she'd buy patterns for throw pillows, and quickly she turned out a dozen tiny, severely edged squares in gold and avocado and white. She stood them stiffly along the back of the black sofa, but the seams kept splitting from the pressure of the girls' heads, and in a temper, Delia ripped the pillows apart, stuffing everywhere, and threw them out. She still hadn't decided about the baby. She saw a picture of John-John in the newspaper and forced herself to think of other things to do to the apartment, putting a sheet of loose-leaf paper right on top of his picture and numbering her ideas.

"New bedspreads for the girls," she wrote, number one, and imagined that she'd buy fabric of light green, with enough material left over for doll dresses, but Maureen didn't have any more dolls, and Patty would rather run around outside with the boys, chasing them among the garbage cans, whooping through the alleys. She moved on to the next project on her list, number two, a new bedspread and curtains for their bedroom. Maurice liked yellow, and she liked the fabric plissé, because of the sound of it, like water shining over rocks. She tucked away money for a yellow plissé spread and curtains, hiding it in an old bank envelope in her underwear drawer, under the Jackie pictures.

She nearly had enough, when the television set began to act funny: the picture faded in and out, the screen became covered with bright dots like measles, and then, one Saturday, it went black.

Maurice had wanted to watch the baseball game, on a rare day off.

He turned the buttons and moved the dials carefully and stared at the blank screen, and then he opened the window and stuck the rabbit-ear antenna outside, but the picture couldn't be retrieved, not even when Maurice, in his desperation, knelt down and appeared to be praying into the tuner.

"What's wrong with the TV, Daddy?" Patty asked, looking up from the coffee table, where she knelt, drawing mustaches on the faces of the women on the new magazine covers.

"I'll be goddammed if I know," he said, exasperated, moving the orange and red flowers to the side, bending over to look in the back of the set. He stared at the plug, tugging on it, and then he scratched his head. "Goddamn it," he said. "Everything looks okay. . . . What the hell is wrong with it?" He jammed the plug into the wall and set the rabbit ears on the floor. He picked up the whole set and shook it and then put it back down. "Now . . . ," he said, pushing the knob in and out, and then he did it again, but the set stayed as dead as a fire hydrant. Delia looked up from the newspaper ads for a bedspread sale at Macy's. "Son of a *bitch*!" Maurice yelled, banging his fist on the top of the set again and again until finally it collapsed, Delia's plastic flowers bouncing inside the set, smashing the picture tube to smithereens.

"Are you satisfied now?" Delia screamed, standing up to stomp across the floor and run down to Mae's kitchen to complain about them all — the mustaches on the pretty magazines, the red bows on the dusty closet floor. She cried and said she wished she lived by herself. Now they didn't even have a television set! It seemed to have happened in slow motion, toothpicks of wood bouncing on the bare floor, Maurice's surprised expression, the toes of his white socks knobby and rounded so that she had felt strangely sorry for him. Now she had no more money for any more projects, she cried; she'd have to save up the money for a new television set. Mae stood suddenly, grabbed her pocketbook from the closet doorknob, and pulled Delia by the hand to the five-and-ten. She bought her two yards of mahogany-colored adhesive paper, which Delia took home and stretched across the television top, handing Maurice the bedspread money for a new picture tube. He was able to slip it through the back, careful of

the top where Delia had repaired it, pressing down hard on the edges of the adhesive paper so it wouldn't peel away. They threw out all the inky magazines, and they put the plastic flowers, none the worse for the ordeal, over on the coffee table, and the living room looked fine, but after a while, when the television set was turned on, the heat from inside softened the adhesive paper and it sagged down into the set.

And then Delia found it hard to concentrate on any television programs. She was mesmerized by the way the top of the set pulsed and sank, like the soft spot on the top of a newborn baby's head.

TEN

After Maurice's hours had changed again, he came home early in the morning, right after the children had left for school, pulling Delia into the bedroom with him and down onto the bed, getting angry if she wriggled away to pull the old white spread from underneath him, folding it and laying it gently on the floor.

They made love, ignoring the ringing phone, knowing it was Mae who would not hang up. Maurice stopped Delia from answering by kissing her so fiercely that her head fell back and her neck ached. When they were done, it changed Delia's whole day, left her weak in the knees, with her hair flattened against one side of her head and the apartment not quite as clean as she usually liked it. She worried that the children might notice the breakfast dishes still in the sink and the garbage pail filled to the top with the remnants of last night's dinner. But on those days she left the apartment just as it was, grabbing onto Maurice's hand, parading him through the streets of the Heights in the sunshine, her handsome husband, a prize that she kept winning. Sometimes they met Mae on the avenue, and she stood too close, almost as if she were sniffing at the very air around them. She pressed her flattened fingertips against the faint bruises on Delia's neck and asked her how on earth she could have gotten them there, in such a funny place; but Delia just shrugged and pulled on her collar.

"I wondered if something was wrong," Mae often said, "when I couldn't get you on the phone. Where were you all that time?" she demanded. "In the tub?"

She continued, without waiting for an answer. "How could you be in the tub for so long? What if the school nurse was trying to reach you? What then?"

"Well, then they would have given up eventually and called *you*."
Maurice laughed. "C'mon, Mae, the kids are fine." He patted her
shoulder, and she glared at him. Delia knew her mother didn't like
seeing grown men on the streets in the daytime; she thought they
looked like sissies. Except Gerald and Eugene, who also worked
shifts and were sometimes home during the day, but she had never
thought of them as men anyway. It was almost as if neither one of
them had ever left home; they were Mae's boys, just as they had
always been.

"I'll talk to you later, miss," Mae said, turning away from them.

Delia looked up at Maurice, but he wasn't paying attention; he
was looking at some point over Delia's head, as he always did when
they were out together. "Where'd your mother go?" he asked finally,
but by then Mae was practically out of sight, a tiny figure in a long
black coat.

The days Delia spent with Maurice always turned out so much
differently than she had imagined in the mornings, covered with his
cinnamon scent, sure they were making a new start. His whole face
seemed somehow to break apart after sex, his lips pinker and broader,
his rosy skin almost feminine-looking, with his long black eyelashes.
He would lie on his side, watching her, his hand propping up his
cheek. It was so nice to look directly into his shining eyes. Maurice
was twelve inches taller than Delia, and it was difficult to look up into
his face and know what he was thinking. Sometimes he said something over his shoulder as he was walking out the door, and Delia had
to practically stand on her toes to grab at the end of it.

At picnics or parties, when Delia met the wives of the other cops,
they all told her how lucky she was to have such a handsome man,
smiling longingly at him. Their men really thought the world of
Maurice: "He always gets the job done," was what they always said.
"Thank you," she always replied, but it sounded foolish, accepting a
compliment for someone else, even if it was her own husband, and
sometimes the other wives looked embarrassed for her. Delia promised herself to look closer at Maurice, to pay more attention to him.
She must have been missing a lot of his good qualities in his silences.

She began to stare at Maurice when he was home, wondering

what she had missed. She watched him read the paper, and she watched him sit in front of the television set, and the girls began to watch him too, trying to see how to make him happy, but as Maurice grew older, that seemed to be harder and harder to do. Patty ran to buy him the newspaper as soon as he woke up on the weekends when he was home, and Maureen pored over the daily baseball scores, to have them memorized as soon as her father walked in the door. With his hours, he often didn't get to see his children for days, so that his being home had an air of ceremony about it, times when Delia didn't clean the apartment or run the vacuum cleaner or iron. She gave herself the time to just sit next to him on the couch, her hand on his knee, and she cooked him big dinners, roast turkey in the middle of the week, with sausage stuffing, or a leg of lamb with purple numbers stamped in the flesh.

After they ate, Delia threw the dishes in the sink, to wash after Maurice had gone to bed. The wives of the other cops sometimes asked her how he had the nerve to jump from one apartment house roof in the city to an adjoining one or how he had really felt about finding that baby's body underneath an old couch in the tenement backyard, but Delia knew nothing about those things and just made a silly face, rolling her eyes, as if each story were something she was hearing for the hundredth time.

Right before their tenth anniversary, they had had a terrible fight — Delia didn't remember later what it was about — but she heard him say she was lucky he'd married her, pregnant and all, and the shame of it made her weak like a fever. He apologized the next morning. Sometimes when Maurice drank his shot of whiskey and glass of beer, the liquor fell inside him like something solid dropped into a lake, his thoughts finally bubbling to the surface, and for a few minutes, Delia was often overjoyed, as if she had cracked open a rock and found it filled with golden honey.

"*In vino veritas*," Mae liked to whisper to her at parties when one of Denis's shy nieces took off her shoes and danced on the table. Delia knew exactly what her mother meant. When Maurice drank, at least at first, he longed for her; it was written all over him, the way he reached out from the white chair to grab at her skirt when she passed by, and it wasn't always Delia he reached for, grabbing at the girls' hands when they walked past. He liked it when they sat down in the living room and listened to his stories, about how his father moved Maurice's pictures from the end tables to make room for his cups of hot tea, while his mother had to take more pictures of Maurice to hide the white rings in the wood. He would laugh and shake his head at his parents' foolishness, but then, after he had had more to drink and the girls had gone to bed, he confided to Delia that Sean Delaney had had a cold heart, had harbored anger at Maurice's surviving when the little brothers, dead before Maurice was born, had not. Sean Delaney had insisted that those other children were saints. "I was never good enough for my father," was how Maurice put it, his eyes filling with tears, and Delia had to turn away, busying herself in the kitchen with scouring the sink or straightening the shelves in the refrigerator, bent over her tasks as if she had been punched in the stomach with her husband's young life. The story continued through the rooms, how he came home from playing basketball and would hear his bickering parents just as he reached the top of the stairs, and when he walked in the door, they were suddenly silent, his mother making no more dignified calm responses to his father's angry mumble.

"It took me a long time," Maurice said, "to figure out they weren't fighting over me at all; it was my brothers they were missing. It had nothing to do with me. I lost my brothers, and it made me stronger. End of story," he said, and then he fell asleep in the chair. Delia stared at him, pressing each of his words into herself like a fossil. Although she had hated alcohol (the way the smell sucked away her breath, the ruined faces she passed on the street, the swollen bellies of aging women pregnant with dying livers), it bored through the center of her husband as she never could, and that was where she would find the Maurice that she loved and pitied so, but then that Maurice would disappear in an instant, bogged down in a gray and sullen quiet.

She had to be quicker. She had to pay more attention.

If she had raised him, she thought, she would have loved him so much he wouldn't need to drink. He needed a son of his own, Delia was becoming sure of it, and he didn't even know it. She wanted to give him that son. She lay in bed tracing his bare shoulder, imagining exactly how he had looked to Kathleen Delaney when he was two.

"Maurice, what about another baby?" she asked, pulling the sheet up to her chin. The phone was ringing again, and they were ignoring it. He sat up and leaned forward on his arms. "Well, what about one?" he asked glumly, shaking out his socks.

"You think we should have one more?"

"I don't know, Delia. I never really thought about it. All these years, and it never happened." He turned to face her, resting his hand on her hip.

"Maybe you should stop pulling out," she said. "You know, just see what happens."

"Lots of couples pull out, Delia," he said, standing up suddenly. He picked up his pants, which were puddled next to the bed. "Of course, they have more kids anyway. Funny, isn't it, how it took just one time for Maureen?" He zipped his fly, came over to the bed, and held out his hand. "C'mon," he said, "get up. Your mother'll be breaking down the door."

Delia paused and pulled herself back against the pillows. She wasn't going to let him get away that easily, not after her constant thoughts about another child. It was something he was good at, changing the subject. "Yeah," she said, while he watched her quizzically, "but we were young and stupid." She tossed the covers back.

"You know," Maurice said, pinching her bare breasts, "I kind of had it figured out that we weren't supposed to have any more, like fate or something." He pushed her hair back from her forehead. "The girls are getting kind of big to start again, don't you think?"

"Well, yes and no," she said, getting up and walking to the closet to find her bathrobe. "I don't have all that much to do anymore with them, you know, and I think they'd love to help me with a new baby." She spoke lightly, as if the thought had just occurred to her, and tried to gauge his reaction. "Maurice, don't you even *want* a son?" she asked, slipping on her robe, turning to face him.

He stopped in the doorway and looked at her. "Truthfully, Delia, I don't," he said softly. "Sometimes I wonder what it would have been like if one of the girls had been a boy, but then I think about my father. You know what he used to say to me when I got a good mark in school, which I did here and there, believe it or not." Delia laughed.

"'That's all well and good,' he'd say, 'but can ye do a fair day's work with them big hands?'" Maurice shook his head. "I tell you, Delia, I never said it, but sometimes I'm glad we had girls. It's just so much easier. . . . Nobody expects much from them, you know? Come on, woman," he sang, in an exaggerated baritone. "Get out in that kitchen and rattle them pots and pans."

But later, apropos of nothing, Maurice looked up from his chicken soup and said, "If that's what you really want, Delia, another kid, well, I guess it's okay with me."

After lunch, she rinsed out the soup pot and stacked their two bowls and dishes in the sink and put the dirty silverware in a smudged glass on the drainboard. They held hands and walked the three blocks to St. Immaculata to meet the girls, and Delia squeezed his arm and felt so lucky, after all these years, to be dizzy with love for him, wondering how she could hold on to the feeling. She watched him dance the steps of her day, shopping with her at the A & P, popping into Farone's Candy for a half pound of chocolate nut clusters, struggling to keep the children's schoolbags tucked underneath his arm, and as they got to their corner, while they waited for the light to change, Delia giggled and hugged Maurice. He saw someone he knew across the street and called out to him, looking down at Delia and the girls, promising he'd be right along, and before she knew what had happened, she was sitting in her mother's kitchen, drinking tea, smelling strongly of cinnamon herself, watching the girls devour the nut clusters, their delicate mouths smeared with chocolate. Mae complained about ruining their dinners, and Delia felt that she was starving, her own hunger for her husband making her ache.

One morning, she jumped up to fold the bedspread, Maurice watching her, and she made the decision, just like that, and climbed on top of him with her eyes shut, riding him back and forth, not letting go, thinking of the little boy with the blond hair, tightening herself around him as firmly as a fist.

A few weeks later, Maurice was back on the day shift.

ELEVEN

She knew she was pregnant even before she was a week late, with stomach butterflies of intense excitement like hunger pains, so strong she couldn't sleep at night, or eat whole meals in one sitting, or even concentrate on a single thought. Like a little kid, she was happy with the simplest of things: fresh pretzels from a stand on the street and the crisp new winter air and a new roll of Scotch tape. For no good reason, she found herself in Hooperman's Notions, poring over the bright cards of buttons. (Later, when she merrily spread the cards over Mae's table, her mother looked at her as if she had gone mad, accusing her of wasting money, pulling the food from her children's mouths.)

When she was pregnant, everything Delia touched seemed to vibrate under her fingertips; the smell of a new box of soap made her sick to her stomach and positively giddy at the same time. At St. Immaculata's Church, where Delia had begun to pay a daily visit, the wavy heat from the votive candles distorted the faces of the statues. Each saint seemed to be whispering urgently, but Delia had no idea what they might be trying to tell her.

When she was two weeks late, she decided she had to tell someone. She called Rosaleen and asked her to lunch at the five-and-ten. Rosaleen had known her so well that although Delia rarely saw her anymore, she was sure to guess just by looking into Delia's face. She didn't want to say a thing to Maurice or the girls until she was sure, and she didn't want to tell Mae. ("Gawd save us!" her mother would cry. "Again?" and Delia certainly didn't want to hear *that*.)

On the day she was to meet Rosaleen, she was up before dawn, setting the breakfast table. A thin tube of sunshine filled with bits of dust began to touch the rose pattern on a dish, and Delia was struck by its beauty. ("The beauty," she had read in one poem or another in school, "of commonplace things.")

Delia was grateful to be alive.

She heard the girls get up, the scrape of their dresser drawers, Maurice running the water to shave. He patted his face when he was finished, a sound that always made Delia smile. She loved it when he worked regular hours, like everybody else. For another short time, they would eat dinner together and watch television together and go to bed around the same time. The day tours centered her and shaped her life. She had to have breakfast on the table by seven and the housework done by noon if she wanted to get to the store and have dinner ready by five-thirty. She hated for Maurice to come home to an empty table. If dinner wasn't ready, sometimes she fooled him with pots of water boiling on the stove.

"Come on, everybody," Delia called happily. "Breakfast time," and she broke four eggs into a steel bowl.

"Not me." Maurice came into the kitchen, holding his hand up as if he were stopping traffic. "I'll get something downtown," he said, walking to the stove to kiss her forehead.

"Careful," she always said, and then, "God bless," although that was something Mae said often, and it annoyed Delia; what made Mae think God would hear her?

"You bet," Maurice always answered, winking, and then he was gone.

Maureen and Patty sat glumly at the table, staring at their eggs. Delia couldn't wait to close the door behind them and get on with her day. Impatiently, she began to scrub the top of the stove as she waited for them to finish, pulling the burners away, dunking them under the running water. They were heavy, made of cast iron, and Delia held on to them tightly, as though she were afraid of letting go and soaring around the ceiling.

She was sure it was a boy. She'd be so grateful that she might call him Jesus, as the Spanish people did. A mute boy in the neighborhood was named Blaise, after the saint whose feast day was celebrated with the blessings of the throat, and there had been a boy Jude in class with Maureen who'd nearly died at birth and was sickly. Saint Jude always took back. Jesus Delaney. No, that would never work.

She'd never be able to stand on the roof and call him to dinner without sounding like a crazy woman, making people look up. She wanted to call her son Rick or Todd, a change from the Irish names she was used to and sometimes resented, names with too much of a past, like her mother's yellowed lace doilies. She was named for her father's mother, Maurice was named for his mother's father. She felt about Irish names the same way she felt about museums, as if everything she looked at was coated with memories she didn't necessarily want.

"I said we're *going*, Ma." Maureen tugged on the sleeve of Delia's robe. Delia blinked and stared at her. "Where?" she asked. "To *school*," Maureen said, exasperated. Patty had already left, her "Good-bye . . ." echoing through the halls, the front door not quite closed.

"Oh, okay," Delia said, drying her hands on the towel, smoothing the top of Maureen's collar, something she was never able to do to Patty. God, Delia thought, Maureen looks so much like Maurice, with his sharp nose and strong bones. "God bless," she said again, and Maureen nodded. Somehow, Patty was always gone before Delia had a chance to say anything.

She had four hours before she was to meet Rosaleen. She cleared the table, trying to think of things to do, and then Mae called. "Is Patty sick?" she asked breathlessly.

"She didn't seem to be, Ma. Why?" If Patty was sick, Delia thought miserably, then she would never get out. The school would send her home, and Delia would have to keep her secret another day.

"It's her color, Delia," Mae said. "Her color's so awful. She just now ran past the window here without so much's a wave, her hair flying all over the place, the schoolbag open. Don't you give her anything to eat? Don't you close up her books? Are you asleep when they leave, is that it? You children always ate before you went off to school, you know that, Delia. Eggs and juice and oatmeal. The most important meal of the day. You, of all people, should know that; I said it to you enough. You know the table I ran, Delia."

"But, Ma," Delia whined. Thirty-one years old, her third baby, still whining.

"I think that maybe it's her hair," Mae said.

"Her hair?"

"She's too thin, Delia, and that hair's not helpin'. If you are feedin' her right, then the hair's sappin' all her strength."

"Oh, Ma." Delia tried to laugh; instead she made a snorting sound. "That's an old wives' tale."

"Okay, miss, you know so much. Plenty of the 'old wives' tales' run true, you know."

"Well, maybe." Delia hedged. It was too nice a day to have a fight. "But I don't think that one does."

"Suit yourself, Delia, but that child of yours is not thrivin'; that much I can see. But you're her mother, and I'm not. What I think now doesn't seem to matter to you." Delia rolled her eyes. "Besides," Mae said abruptly, "I need you to come here today and take down my curtains."

"Oh, I can't today, Ma," Delia said, walking back and forth through the kitchen, looking for things to clean. The phone wire wouldn't stretch to the window. Delia began to clean the receiver.

"I can't *hear* you, Delia. Come closer to the phone."

"*I said I can't, Ma,*" Delia shouted. "*I'm meeting Rosaleen.*"

"Sacred Heart, don't scream at me," Mae said. "I'm not deaf yet. . . . Rosaleen? What're you meeting her for?"

"For lunch. Not for anything. In the five-and-ten." Hadn't Delia told her?

"Well, when did you make these plans? You never said nothin' about going out today," Mae said accusingly.

"I'm not really 'going out,' Ma. It's just Rosaleen." Delia felt guilty and didn't know quite why. "Can't you have Eugene take down the curtains when he gets up? Or Gerald? Couldn't he do it?"

"I guess he could, either of them, but they aren't careful like you are. They're liable to rip them." She sighed.

"Well, I guess I could call Rosaleen," Delia said slowly, "and meet her some other time."

"No, no, never mind that. You went ahead and made plans with your friend, now you go ahead and keep them. If I'd known you had something to do, I wouldn't have bothered you."

"Ma," Delia said, "it's no bother. . . ."

"But I'm a different sort." Mae kept talking. "I never had any time to meet any friends when I was a young woman like yourself. Even though I left her when I was small, I was the type to worry about my mother. Always. I think you're very smart and modern not to concern yourself with me. Times were very different when I was young."

"I'll come in when the girls come home from school, and then we'll take them down together, Ma. How's that?" Delia asked. Her poor mother, nobody to help her. She was so good to Delia and the children.

"No, Delia Mary, that's no good to me. I don't ever take down my curtains late in the day. Only in the morning. I'm not leavin' a whole evening with bare windows, only the shades for coverin', like Gypsies. You don't worry yourself about me. Go meet your friend and have a nice lunch." And she hung up. Frustrated, Delia banged the receiver against the doorframe. It'd be just like Mae to climb on a chair and pull the curtains down herself. What if she fell and broke her hip? Well, I'll make it up to her. First thing tomorrow morning. Angry for no good reason, she vacuumed the rug in a rush.

Rosaleen was sitting at the lunch counter, trying to keep her eleven-month-old son in her lap. Robert, who wore a soiled blue sweater, was trying to grab the salt and pepper shakers Rosaleen had pushed in front of the old lady sitting next to her. Delia noticed the old woman and thought of Mae, who at that exact moment could be writhing in pain on her oilcloth floor with a broken hip. With the way Eugene snored, if he was home at all, it'd be a miracle if he'd hear a thing. She tried to remember what time her brother Gerald came home.

Rosaleen and Robert looked up; Delia smiled and sat down, and the baby grabbed onto her finger. An omen, she thought. "Boy, Delia, you look great." Rosaleen smiled and bounced the baby on her lap, gray hairs springing out around her head, dark circles underneath her eyes. After Danny began to work for the post office, he and Rosaleen (they only had Kevin then) bought a frame house around the corner from the Greenleaf; the house drooped in the middle and had a misshapen brick chimney sitting on the roof like a dowager's hump.

Delia and Maurice had visited them every few months, walking through a front porch littered with toys and broken furniture, the old piano from the Greenleaf standing in the corner with its keys yellowed and stiff, its top scarred and dented. As the boys grew older, the porch took on their salty leather smell; baseball mitts and pronged cleats were piled under baseball bats, everything arranged as if for some religious rite. Inside, the old brown couch where Maureen had been conceived sagged underneath a flowered slipcover.

"Thanks, Rosaleen. So do you," she said politely, even though it wasn't true. Rosaleen looked as if she could sleep for a week. I hope I'm sure about this, Delia thought. Infant Maureen had kept her awake for three months. "Boy, Robert's getting big." Delia smiled at him. His two baby teeth looked too big for his face.

"I'll have apple pie and coffee," Rosaleen said to the waitress, looking at Delia expectantly.

"The same," Delia said, not the least bit hungry.

"Big and fresh, just like the others," Rosaleen said, standing Robert on her knees, jabbing her nose into his belly. The baby laughed and swayed backward.

"How're the girls?" Rosaleen asked.

"Oh, fine," Delia answered. "Doing good in school. How're the others and Danny?"

"Good. Getting older. You know." Rosaleen looked at her. Delia wondered if Rosaleen could tell and was just teasing. "The kids, I mean. I haven't seen Danny since the summer, I don't think." Rosaleen stopped Robert from hitting her face. He yanked on her hair.

"Aw, Rosaleen." Delia laughed. "Come on. Since the summer?"

"Okay, okay, you're right." Rosaleen tried to extricate the baby's fingers from her hair. "But it really seems like that, you know? It's like he's been working for about forty years straight. Maurice too?"

Delia nodded. "The same thing; not home enough." Did she imagine it, or was Rosaleen stealing glances at her middle.

Rosaleen held the baby's fists, and he began to scream. "Danny told me he hasn't seen Maurice in months," she said loudly. Delia nodded, but she was glad they missed each other on the streets.

Before the children came along, Danny and Maurice sometimes disappeared together for hours and came home drunk. The four of them had been close, going to the movies together and out to dinner, taking the bus into the city to gawk at the people there, but that had all changed. After all, Delia told herself, whenever she started to miss her friend, she and Danny had had boys, and Delia and Maurice the girls, and the children had no interests in common. When they made a rare visit, the children sat on that dirty porch looking at their hands. It made Delia sad to see how easily women's friendships fell apart. All it took was two husbands who got along too well or children who had nothing in common (or even a mother who needed a lot of attention), and the months would fly by.

"Well, what've you been doing all day by yourself?" Rosaleen asked, plopping Robert into his carriage, feeding him crumbs of pie.

Delia hadn't touched hers; she pushed it to the side. "Well, let's see. This morning I made them a big breakfast, and then I vacuumed the rug, and I washed down the kitchen stove." As Delia spoke, she tried to center herself squarely in the middle of her seat, hands over her purse. Rosaleen was bound to notice *that*. She sighed often and loudly, but Rosaleen watched the baby throw his yellow bottle over the side of the carriage, straight into a bin of hard candies, and then laugh. The woman next to Rosaleen glared at her, and Rosaleen glared back. Embarrassed, Delia jumped up and ran to get the bottle, and when she stood next to Rosaleen she noticed a thick ladderlike run at her ankle and her badly scuffed shoes, the heels run down and close to the ground.

"Thanks." Rosaleen put the empty bottle in her purse. "And how's the Queen of Saints?"

"Fine." Delia smiled. "And the Saint of Queens?" Although Rosaleen's mother lived near the beach now, Delia couldn't picture her in a bathing suit. She was the sort of woman who always wore a stiff girdle, and earrings to match her necklace. Delia wasn't even sure if Geraldine Clancy possessed bare feet, as if underneath her shoes she might have another pair, her high heels leaving tracks in the sand like those of some extinct bird. "And how's your sister Sheila?" Delia asked uncomfortably. Maureen had come only seven months after

Delia's own wedding, but asking about Sheila—whose illegitimate son, Junie, was now old enough to be in the army—seemed somehow poor manners.

"She's okay." Rosaleen jiggled her keys in Robert's face. "She still lives with that same guy, Arnold, on Soundview Avenue in the Bronx. She says they're gonna get married. I hope so."

"And Junie?" Delia swallowed the last of her coffee.

"Still in South Carolina." Robert was falling asleep in his carriage. Rosaleen laid him down. Rosaleen was the only person Delia could think of who would take a big carriage like that into the small five-and-ten.

"And Fiona?" Delia asked brightly, fond of Rosaleen's younger sister, relieved that Sheila was still around, and Junie too.

Whenever Delia polished Maureen's or Patty's little-girl finger-nails, she thought of bedraggled Fiona.

"She's gonna graduate college in June." Rosaleen smiled. "Can you imagine little Fiona, that snot-nosed kid, a social worker?" She shook her head.

"That's just great." Delia wondered what it was exactly that social workers did. It sounded vaguely threatening, as if it had something to do with communism. "If I ever need any social work, at least I'll know who to call." She grinned.

"Yeah, I know what you mean." Rosaleen stood up. "I don't know what the hell it is either," and they both burst out laughing.

Delia wondered if she could have become anything. She was a good mother; what was more important than that? Even Jackie Kennedy had said that being a good mother was important.

Outside on the street, Rosaleen turned to her. Now, Delia thought. She's going to say she noticed a difference in me now. "You know, Delia," Rosaleen said, her hand on Delia's sleeve, "there's more to life than having tea with your mother. I really wish you would come over and have lunch with me or just drop in. I never see you. You'd almost be better off changing the altar linens over at church with the old farts in the Rosary Society than washing the light bulbs and ironing all your towels—which I'm pretty sure you do." Then she laughed and slapped Delia's upper arm, and it hurt.

Tears came to Delia's eyes. She kept smiling, but her arm stung. It must be all those boys, Delia thought. They must all do things like that to each other, all the Kowalskis chasing each other up and down their narrow, dark staircase. Delia hadn't been hit by anyone since her father died, and for an instant she forgot how old she was.

"Why don't you try to have a boy?" Rosaleen was asking over Robert's sudden screams. People passing by slowed down to look at him. Rosaleen dug in her pocket and handed him a shriveled-looking pretzel.

"Maybe I will," Delia said, not looking at her. Being poked at, being angry, made her uncomfortable. Her sweater felt too tight.

"I'm trying for a girl," Rosaleen said coyly, "and I think maybe I've succeeded."

"Again?" Delia asked, louder than she had intended.

"Yep, afraid so." Rosaleen caught the pretzel Robert had hurled at her. "I'm only a couple of months along."

"Congratulations," Delia said, disappointed, as if there were only a few pregnancies available, as if Rosaleen might have stolen one from underneath her nose. "What did Danny say?"

"Oh, I'm going to tell him in another day or two." She laughed. "Poor guy, he doesn't remember Robert's name as it is." The baby stopped crying and looked up expectantly. "It'd be nice if you got pregnant and gave Maurice a son. Every man wants one, even if they don't always admit it," Rosaleen said, turning the carriage in the opposite direction. Delia kept her distance; she half expected Rosaleen to push her or pull her hair. "Call me when you have a minute, okay?" Rosaleen asked, and crossed the street.

Delia ducked into the doorway of the library to watch her until she was out of sight. She could see little Robert's white shoes kicking about in his carriage, and if she had been a stranger, she would have assumed that Rosaleen Clancy Kowalski was a happy person just by the tilt of her head and the way she looked strangers in the eye, as if she didn't have a thing in the world she owed to anyone.

"I got to the top of the chair," Mae said, standing perfectly still in front of the sink, holding the kettle in midair, "and I took a dizzy spell and nearly fell through the glass."

"Rosaleen's pregnant," Delia said.

"What, again?" Mae shook her head, turning on the faucet. "She's a breeder, that one is. She don't even take proper care of the ones she has. None of them children have any hats."

"Did you call Eugene to help you?" Delia looked down the hall to see if her brother's door was closed.

"To help me with what?" Mae asked distractedly, fussing with the hem of her newly ironed curtains.

"When you almost fell through the glass, Ma, like you just said." Delia rolled her eyes.

"Don't be rollin' your eyes, and don't be fresh to me, Delia Mary. I told you this mornin' Eugene and Gerald are useless to help me, and anyway, Eugene sleeps like the dead."

"I would have helped you tomorrow, Ma. I said I would." That was the trouble with Mae: she could never wait.

"Well, what's done is done. The windows are clean. The curtains are up. Thank God I didn't fall and hurt myself; that's the main thing. Thank God I don't need help much. I'd be waitin' a long time for it."

Delia sighed and looked up at the ceiling.

She wanted somehow to be more than Rosaleen, but what made Delia think she could ever be another kind of person? She was still walking the same streets she had walked when she was five years old, still looking into the windows of the shops, still drooling at the crullers in Cushing's window.

She wanted so badly to be pregnant the way Rosaleen was pregnant, not looking to save herself from loneliness or looking to fill the hole inside herself that her husband knew nothing about. She had wanted a baby to bridge the gap between herself and her growing-up girls; they would hand her the pins and the diapers and the powder and know how much they were wanted. Rosaleen didn't want a new baby to do any of these things; her baby would simply exist. Rosaleen had no expectations, and Delia thought that maybe that was as it should be.

Mae stared at the kettle, and Delia thought of Rosaleen's skirt, dotted with fine lint: how jaunty it had looked!

"I don't like that Rosaleen Clancy" — Mae shook the kettle by the handle — "and I never did. She's dirty, and she's got too many children. Her mother was dirty too, from what I hear, and they say she never paid proper attention to her own. The apple don't fall far from the tree, Delia Mary."

Thick-headed, Delia thought, feeling vaguely disappointed and sad, that was the word to describe Rosaleen. Too wrapped up in herself to notice the changes in anyone else. Delia didn't think she liked Rosaleen anymore, either.

TWELVE

By the time they all got ready and rode the subway into the city, the Thanksgiving Day parade was over. A few curled brown leaves rolled across the pavement: Delia thought they looked like lizards.

The Delaney women wore felt hats in autumn colors to complement their old spring coats; gold to set off Delia's hair (dyed golden again), forest green for Maureen, and red for Patty — a mistake, Delia realized too late, on top of her reddish hair. It reminded Delia of the tablecloths in the banquet room of the Brau House.

Maurice, bareheaded, wore his new navy-blue suit. It had only two buttons and was baggy, just like the suits President Kennedy wore, and Delia had talked him into a new pair of pointy-toed shoes. He walked in front of Delia, holding Patty's hand. In her gold-toned high heels, Delia had to run to keep up, watching the wind blow through Maurice's hair, making it look thick and wavy, just like the President's. She wasn't watching where she was going and stumbled over the curb.

"Did you have a nice trip?" Maurice turned around to smile at her. "See you next fall!" He laughed, and so did she, proud of his even white teeth, which emphasized his dimples (or perhaps it was the other way around). She wondered if people passing by asked themselves what he had seen in her. Oh, she guessed she was pretty enough, but she looked like a lot of people. Jackie Kennedy, Rosaleen had said, but Delia didn't believe that. Jackie was so beautiful, and Delia knew she didn't have much of a chin and her skin was rather sallow. Maurice, in Delia's opinion, was spectacular-looking. Everyone he met said something about his startling blue eyes. In a roomful of people, Maurice was the one they remembered, the strapping

101

black Irishman, although if he had been drinking, his eyes didn't seem to have any backs to them, a matched set of keyholes into a dark room. Delia hated his drinking eyes.

"Where're we gonna go now, Ma?" Maureen's breath smelled of milk and powder. Young men on the street were starting to stare at Maureen, who was oblivious of their attentions. Delia wished she could take her by the shoulders and shake away her innocence; she worried about Maureen being loose in the world.

"Well, maybe we'll just walk around a bit. We don't have to be at Grandma's for dinner till four." If Delia could have had her way, she would have turned around right there and gone back home. It was different when they planned to go to the parade, but in New York without a goal, Delia felt as loose and light as a balloon. Her legs were shaking. She was used to walking under the el on the avenue in the Heights, in semidarkness, shoulder-to-shoulder with people she had known all her life.

Up on the subway platform that morning, in all that air and space, Delia grew dizzy, and she had had to hold Maurice's arm. When she looked over the edge of the platform, something in her thighs stretched, and she was tempted to jump in front of the speeding train. She thought of the man who jumped so many years before from the very platform she was standing on, and she wondered what went through his mind before he leapt to the tracks, before his head rolled down onto the street. Maurice stood close to the edge of the platform, holding Patty's hand, and Delia watched them carefully. Once they boarded the train, Delia sat snuggled between Maureen and Maurice, pulling their arms over hers like a blanket. Patty insisted on standing up. She clung to the pole in the middle of the car. When the train went underneath the river, Delia stared at their faces in the blackened windows across from them, like photo negatives, and realized that her shoulder was level with Maureen's. She wished Maureen could be a baby again. She wished she were sure enough to tell one of them about the baby inside. She wished she could know for sure.

"Maurice, you want to go back home?" Delia tugged at his sleeve. He stopped dead in the middle of the street, people stopping short, trying not to bang into him. "I don't care," he said absently, scratching at his ear. "If you want to go back, let's go back. We might as well. We missed the parade, and there's nothing else to do."

"But, Ma, we just got here," Patty whined.

"Listen to me, Patty." Delia tried to grab for her hand, but the child was angry and hid it behind her back. "We'll come back next month. There'll be all the Christmas windows and the big tree in Rockefeller Center. I promise. Now how's that?"

You don't *ask* them, Mae would say, you *tell* them.

You have to be the child.

"Tell you what, Patty." Maurice put his hands on Patty's shoulder and bent over. Delia positioned herself behind him so nobody would knock him down. "Next month, on payday, Mommy and Maureen and you'll come into the city and meet me after work, and we'll all go shopping together and see all the sights. What d'ya think about that now, huh?"

Patty shrugged.

"Want to do that, Delia?" Maurice asked. It was the first time he had looked directly at her all day. The cold air reddened his cheeks.

"Sure, sure," she said eagerly. "That'll be real good. I'd love it. There's the subway across the street," she said hurriedly. "C'mon, everybody. Let's go back home."

The train going back was crowded. Delia, Maurice, and Maureen were lucky to slide into an empty seat as soon as they boarded, and Patty balanced reluctantly on the edge of her father's knee. Delia saw two Negro women sitting across the aisle, one dressed entirely in kelly green and the other in a brilliant shade of blue. She rarely saw Negro people anywhere. They looked so finished and dignified, Delia thought, with their dark eyes matching their dark skin and hair, rather than the light eyes in the freckled faces that she was so accustomed to, faces easily stung by heat or cold. The pink undersides of the women's hands looked tender and kind and plump, like small pillows. The first time she had ever seen a colored person, she was on the subway with her father on one of their Sunday trips into New York. A Negro man sat across from her, wearing black galoshes with open buckles that jingled like Christmas bells.

"Stop yer starin' at the man, miss," Denis had whispered, and although she was a grown woman now, she still felt ashamed. She wasn't supposed to stare at people; she wasn't brought up that way. When she was small, Delia often wished for X-ray vision, to see people straight through from their bare toes to their underwear; that was as far as she wished to see. She smiled to think of Rosaleen, swearing that she had seen Sister Alberta's iron underpants from underneath the stall in the girls' room, assuring Delia that Sister wore an iron chestplate rather than a bra, but Delia didn't buy it, for the nun floated silently through the school corridors, seeming never to touch the floor.

She thought of the way the dark-green sleeves of her father's coat had touched his wrists, and the black hairs on the backs of his hands, sparse and unruly. Maurice was asleep, his head thrown back against the wall of the subway car, and she remembered how her father had held his hat loosely in his hands, staring morosely out the window of the train at the tops of row houses and into the apartments butting against the curving el.

She used to ask Denis what time it was, just to have something to say, the silence between them so deep that Delia feared the people around them might think that they were strangers, a little girl traveling by herself, a grown man all alone in the world.

"Half after." He would give her the time and nothing else, but she looked up at him for a long time afterward, hoping that people had noticed.

He took her to the Statue of Liberty and the top of the Empire State Building, but he disappeared when her back was turned, and she found herself in clusters of tourists with odd ways of talking. She hated them just because they were there, especially the women, who had nudged her in the arm, asking, "Isn't that pretty?" "Isn't that nice?" as if she were visiting, too, and had nobody to care for her.

Her old Sunday shoes had been so tight they pinched like sand crabs and left jellyfish-like welts on her heels.

In her unlined wool skirt on a cold marble bench, she sat once for two hours at the Cloisters with a friendly guard, and when her father finally came for her, he said he had had to go to the bathroom but on the way he had stopped for cigarettes and met a guy he knew. "Pretty girl you got there, mister," the guard had said, tipping his hat.

"I know," her father had answered, "and she's able to take care of herself," but when they came home, she never told the beaming Mae about the guard, she only told her how much fun she had had, how her father had made her laugh and the beauty of what she had seen, and from the corner of her eye she saw Denis shift his weight slightly and lean forward to listen to what she was saying, as if he wanted to know everything about the other father Delia was inventing, as if he were anxious to learn how to do it right.

When the train stopped, Delia poked Maurice in the ribs. "C'mon," she said. "Our stop."

"Let's go, Patty." Maurice yawned and rubbed his eyes. Patty almost pulled him down the stairs. She got to the third step and jumped ahead, out onto the station floor. Together, in front of the token booth, they began to skip, Delia wondering why Maurice's spirits had suddenly risen. Patty led him along the street by the tips of his fingers, and he had his tongue over his teeth so that his upper lip bulged like a gorilla's. He bent his knees and slapped his free hand against his thigh and grunted.

"Mommy" — Patty smiled — "I found this monkey on the street, and now I'm takin' him back to the zoo!" Maurice pawed at her hair and the nubby collar of her light coat. Patty giggled. People passing by started to look at them. Maureen (mortified, Delia thought) lagged behind. Delia looked at the clock in the bank and saw that it was only three: they had an hour to spare. She wished it weren't so early. There were three bars they had to pass: Shanahan's, Healey's, and the Shamrock Inn. Maurice was sure to stop in one of them. Delia always forgot about the bars until she was right in front of one. She should have remembered, she told herself, she should have made some excuse to walk another way. In midgrunt, Maurice looked up at her, and her mouth tightened. She grabbed for Patty's shoulder, but the child resisted and ran around to the other side of Maurice.

"No, Ma, c'mon — let me take the monkey back to the zoo!"

"Never mind the playing, Patty. You're all dressed up, and people are staring at us." Delia tried to catch her but failed again. Patty was so quick.

In front of the Shamrock, Maurice simply straightened up and pushed Patty's hand away. "Delia, listen," he said, not looking at her. "Why don't you go ahead to Mae's and I'll see you there in a few minutes. Really, I gotta go to the bathroom."

"But we're only three blocks from home!" she cried. "Can't you wait another five minutes?" She tried to smile, anxious to hold on to their pleasant family outing.

"No, I really can't," he said defensively. "Why do you always have to give me such a hard time?" He stepped back from them. "Didn't I take you all out today? Didn't we have a nice time? What more do you want?"

Delia rubbed at her forehead until it was sore. Every outing had its price. He'd go on a picnic if they had brought plenty of beer, and he loved a party as long as a bottle of Scotch was on the table in front of him. Delia would be mad at him before they even got where they were going. She could never seem to get used to it, so angry at Maurice so much of the time that she thought her heart was growing callused. She grabbed Patty's hand and knocked her off her feet, and Patty began to whimper.

"Well, you know it's Thanksgiving Day, Maurice, and *if* you decide you want to spend it with us instead of those damn *bums* inside there, then you know where we'll be. God knows the Shamrock's the only bathroom for miles around. I guess this marks the official ending of today's good time."

They watched him turn on his heel, wordlessly, stared at the back of his President Kennedy navy-blue suit, followed it through the bar's front door. She stood right in front of the place so that he could look out the dirty dark window and see what he had left, his dressed-up family in front of such a seedy place. She wanted people passing by to ask themselves who that woman and those children could be waiting for, and she stared at them as they dropped their eyes and nervously shifted their white boxes of Cushings's apple and pumpkin pie from one hand to the other. A skinny man in a worn gray suit came out and looked at them dully and blew his nose, and while the door was open, Delia was aware of someone standing at the bar waving at her. She turned her head.

"C'mon, Ma," Maureen pleaded, tugging on Delia's arm. "Just let's go to Grandma's, okay? Please just let's forget about this."

"Yeah, sure." Delia put her arms around their thin shoulders just in time to walk smack into the Malloneys, who were turning the corner. They lived directly across the courtyard from the Delaneys, and sometimes, late at night, Delia stood sipping water by the sink in her dark kitchen and looked over into the Malloneys' living room and considered living Sally Malloney's life.

Bill Malloney held on to the sleeve of Sally's jacket. A yellow chrysanthemum corsage, so big the blooms brushed against Sally's neck, was pinned on her shoulder. She was short and energetic, with prematurely gray hair — salt and pepper, some people called it — and already her three children, two sons and a daughter, towered over her, even Joannie, the youngest, who was a few months older than Maureen. Bill junior and Tom had bored, vacant expressions. "Happy Thanksgiving, girls." Bill, clean-shaven, smooth-cheeked, leaned over to kiss Delia's cheek. He smelled of aftershave and cough drops, double doses of clean and sober menthol.

"Where's the man of the family?" he asked. "Don't tell me that the poor guy had to work? What's the matter with the cops — don't they have a heart?" When he smiled, which was often, Bill looked so terribly nice, his small teeth unobtrusive and well tended.

"No, I guess they don't," Delia said lightly, hugging her daughters, "but he'll be home pretty soon." Maureen and Patty looked up at her, ignoring the Malloney children. Bill smiled. He has such a thin mouth, Delia thought, and a blunted, harsh nose: he looks like Dick Tracy, but with no jaw.

"You spending the day with Mae and the boys?" Sally asked, shaking her head to get her hair out of her eyes. The day had turned windy, and from time to time, big black clouds smothered the sun in a fierce tug-of-war. November was so strange: before Delia could answer, the day had turned brilliantly sunny.

"Yes, we always see them on holidays," Delia said. "Where are *you* going?" They might think a holiday scavenger hunt would be fun, she thought, or a family basketball game: anything they might all do together.

"We're going out to eat, and then we're going over to Idlewild to watch the planes land." Bill smiled. "We promised the kids."

"*You* promised the kids!" Sally laughed. "He's always taking the kids and me one crazy place or another! I don't think the man's got enough to do at work, fixing leaks or tightening faucets, so he thinks all the time of the next fun thing we could do. Like last week, he took us all down to the Village to an Indian restaurant. You ever eat curry?" she asked Delia, sticking out her small pink tongue.

"Yeah." Bill looked down at Sally, pulling her under his arm. "But you had fun, didn't you?"

Sally shrugged. "Once I drank a gallon of water, I felt fine."

"Look, Delia," Bill said, pushing Sally along the sidewalk a bit. "We gotta run. Reservations. Tell Mae we wish her a happy holiday, and the boys too. And the old man when he comes home from the salt mines. Would you do that?"

"I will, Bill. Thanks. You have a nice holiday too."

"Mrs. Delaney," Bill junior nodded as they passed. Tom just stared. "Bye, Maureen," Joannie said, lumbering behind the rest.

"I hate them," Maureen said when they had passed.

"Shh, Maureen, they might hear you." But for that minute, Delia had hated them too, wondering in the next breath what her life would have been like if she had been the one who married Bill Malloney. A month ago, she and Sally chatted on the street, complaining about their piles of ironing, and Sally suggested switching — she thought it might be fun to iron some different clothes — but after a week of ironing Bill Malloney's boxer shorts, Delia brought Sally's clothes back and told her Maurice was dead set against the idea. He had never even known she was doing it; it was Delia who couldn't look Bill Malloney in the face. Sally didn't mind at all, taking her laundry basket back with a grin; everybody said she was such a good sport.

In Mae's lobby, Delia looked at her reflection in the mirror. She wished she'd gotten a corsage, and then the sudden wish that Maurice would die stabbed her and she said a quick Act of Contrition. What sane woman would hate the man she usually loved? But at least, she reasoned, trying to think it all out, if he died right now, she'd remember him as handsome and young, and so would the girls. She knew what the drink would eventually do to him. God, she had seen it in her father! Red lines would run through his clear cheeks and overlap on his straight nose. The whites of his eyes would turn yellow, and then he'd stop eating, and those beautiful eyes would grow too big for his purple face, and his hands, with those strong white fingernails, would shake horribly, and he'd blame it, as her father had, on his nerves.

Of course she didn't want him to die—she loved him; she loved him.

But she was still so young: she might have another chance. The world was full of men. All those lights in all those windows in New York: hadn't she wondered about a different life beyond her own roof? She and her girls were never enough for Maurice, no matter how nice they looked or how much they wanted him. Maybe after it was all over, an older man, a "hard-boiled" detective (as the pulp magazines described such men), a widower, would drop by to console her. Instantly, Delia could see herself in a different apartment, throwing out the first wife's furniture, taking her picture from the mantel, packing up her lace doilies.

She leaned on Mae's doorbell and shut her eyes, trying to push back the picture of Maurice, peeling Patty's fingers away from his, as if her hand had been a glove.

Rather than cheer Delia, Mae's apartment, smelling of boiled turnips, made her feel sick.

"Ma, why are you still in your nightgown?" Delia asked, kicking off her shoes and tossing them in the corner of the kitchen. The kitchen window was covered with steam. The dampness and the smell of boiled onions seemed to settle on Delia's flesh. Mae stood at the stove in a pink flannel gown, her hair in pin curls; she was stirring two pots at the same time.

"I been cookin' since six this morning, miss." Mae didn't look up. "Why ain't I dressed, she wants to know," she said to nobody in particular. "Where is he?" she asked, taking short breaths, as if she had been running.

"He" was Maurice. Usually, "he" was "him"—never "himself"; that had been Denis—and "her" was Kathleen, Maurice's mother. Mae didn't like her.

"He stopped at the Shamrock. Said he had to go to the bathroom." Delia was more hurt than angry.

"Well, that's as good an excuse as any," Mae said, shaking the spoons into the sink. She turned to Patty, who had wandered in. "Patty, did you get to wave to Santa Claus?"

"No, Mama," Delia answered for her. "The whole parade was gone by the time we got into the city."

"Oh, what a shame!" She rested her short, pudgy arms on Patty's shoulders. "Tell me, Patty," she asked, "d'ya like turkey with giblet gravy, creamed onions, and sweet potatoes?" Patty smiled and nodded her head. "And do you like mashed potatoes and string beans and stuffing?" Patty began to cheer. "Oh, what a shame!" Mae cried. "I wish I'da known that! All I've got this year is calves' liver and peas."

Patty pretended to look crestfallen, and Mae burst out laughing. "Oh, go on, I'm only kidding you. Now you go inside and tell Maureen we're havin' liver!"

"You know, Mama," Delia said, watching Patty skip through the kitchen, "I wish you wouldn't say things like that in front of the kids — that going to the bathroom was just an excuse." She had tried to keep her voice down in front of the Shamrock. She wasn't even sure the kids knew what she had said to him.

"And why not?" Mae asked, poking a long fork into a steaming pot on the stove.

"I don't want them to know that he drinks too much."

"Well, that's the truth, isn't it? Why don't you just tell the children the truth?"

"Why didn't you ever tell us the truth about Daddy? You were always telling us he was working late when he didn't come home, and you said he was sick when he couldn't get up for work."

"Why did I have to?" Mae asked, with her own sort of logic. "Was I raisin' blind children; didn't see him layin' on the floors or passed out in the chair? Look, I'm not about to be ruinin' the holiday arguin' with you over your husband. He's a rummy, just like your da was a rummy. Now you go over to the stove and start heatin' the cream for the potatoes, and take the butter from the icebox to soften as well. Leave me go inside and get dressed. Nearly dinnertime on Thanksgiving Day, and I'm not yet dressed!"

Maybe things weren't so bad, Delia thought, pouring cream into the saucepan, placing the butter dish on the windowsill. They did have a nice time going into the city, after all, and Maurice wasn't the one who had wanted to come home. He might have been willing to walk around New York all day long with them; how did she know he wouldn't have? She was the one who was ruining it, making his few minutes at the Shamrock into a federal case—one of his favorite expressions.

In Mae's living room, the big mahogany table was opened, empty of the First Communion pictures and Delia's wedding picture, which were piled on one of the red brocade chairs, next to a tall brass floor lamp with a yellowed silk shade.

"I set the table," Eugene said proudly, perched at the head of the table. He wore a starched white shirt; his drooping sleeves seemed to be attached to strings, like a puppet's. He had a long thin colorless face and pale hair, and the skin on his throat was covered with thick red blotches that practically matched his purple tie and suspenders. Underneath his left ear was a thick scar, which ran down along his neck and, as Delia knew, continued along his arm. She hated the summer, Eugene in his short-sleeved shirts, that scar creeping around his arm, twisted and jagged like an aerial view of a river.

"Looks like you did a good job." Delia smiled, gently touching a dish with her finger. On one side of the plate was a fork and on the other a knife. No spoons were in sight, and the napkins were under the dishes. "Ma's been cookin' since she got up," he said, drumming his fingers on the worn tablecloth. "Nothing like smelling onions the minute you open your eyes. Where's Maurice?"

"He stopped at the Shamrock. He'll be here soon," Delia said lightly, ignoring the girls, who suddenly looked up.

"Uh-oh." Eugene shook his head from side to side.

"No, it's okay, really. He just had to go to the bathroom; he really did."

Eugene shrugged, began to fiddle with his knife. Gerald, her older brother, came out of the bathroom in his undershirt. He was heavy and rounded, as wide as Eugene was thin, with the same light hair, only Gerald was balding on top of his full face and thick neck. Delia often wished she had seen him just once in his priest's clothes, the loose flesh of his jowls dignified by the tight white collar. He had come home right after she was married; she was pregnant with Maureen and so excited by her new life that she hardly noticed Gerald. He gave no real explanation, simply dragged his worn suitcase down the street and back into his bedroom. "I just wasn't cut out for it," he had said simply, and that was the end of it.

Gerald looked at them, nodded, and threw his damp newspaper on the white tablecloth.

"Gerald!" Delia cried. "Don't do that. You'll get Ma's cloth all dirty!" She snatched the paper, folded it, and put it on the floor.

"What I want to know," Gerald said, leaning on the table to stare closely at Eugene, "is why the hell you're sitting at the head?"

"The hell's the difference?" Eugene asked, rubbing his eyebrow nonchalantly.

"The difference, jerk, is that you're younger than me! If anybody's the head of this house, supposed to be sittin' there, it sure as hell isn't *you*."

"Yeah? Well, I'll tell ya what, Monsignor. I ain't movin'! How d'ya like that? I'm stayin' right where I am."

"Then you can eat by yourself, you goddamn moron. I ain't eatin' here! Happy Thanksgiving, your ass!" He roared, stomped into his room, and slammed the door.

Eugene stood up. "Good!" he screamed. "Who the hell needs ya?"

Mae flung open her bedroom door and stood there a minute, in her slip, hands on her hips, the flesh hanging from her shoulders in thin, worn pleats. She marched over to Gerald's bedroom door and banged on it with her tiny fist. "You," she said, twisting the doorknob, kicking the door with her tiny stockinged feet. "You, Gerald Aloysius Rooney, are gonna come out of there right this minute, nice and clean, in a pressed shirt, and then you're gonna sit down and eat this goddamn nice Thanksgiving dinner and shut your goddamn mouth." (She said "mout'," because she was angry, and Maureen giggled.) "You're a pair of imbeciles, the both of you." (She said "bot'," and Maureen giggled again.) "I'm the one sittin' at the head, not either of you. Do you hear me, Gerald? Do you hear me, Eugene?" she asked, in the direction of the living room. When she turned around, Mae seemed to remember she was only half dressed. She passed the table, picked up a plate to hold over her bosom, and went back to her own room. "Scuse me," she said, as the front door opened.

"Gobble, gobble," Maurice sang out, letting the door slam behind him. He went straight into the kitchen, and Delia got up and followed him. He had two wilted red carnations in his hand. Delia brushed past him and grabbed the pot of string beans from the stove, the boiling water sloshing over. "I'm here," he said foolishly.

"So I noticed." She wouldn't look at him. He was sorry; Delia could tell by the way he held the flowers, waving them softly in the air like a white flag. Now she had his full attention, at least until he fell asleep. There'd be no more looking past her head or over his own shoulder, no more one-word replies to whatever she asked him. He'd spend the rest of the night trying to gauge exactly how angry she was, and then he'd try to get her to forgive him, and Delia knew by now exactly how to keep him guessing. She could travel a long distance on his air of apology. Her wrists felt strong and powerful as she leaned over the sink and drained the string beans. Why, she was willing to bet she could take one of the carving knives right off the table and frighten Maurice into a corner.

"Hi, Dad." Maureen came into the kitchen hesitantly, holding a glass bowl out for Delia to fill.

"Hey, Moodles," he said enthusiastically. "You cook those beans?" He weaved a little as he spoke.

"No." She smiled. "Grandma did. She cooked everything. I'm just helping."

"And you're a good helper too. I ever tell you that?" He touched her shoulder, and Maureen blushed.

"You want me to do anything else, Ma?" she asked, looking uncomfortable.

"No, that's enough. You just go inside and sit down now, okay?" Then Delia stared at Maurice until he appeared ashamed. He put the flowers into his other hand. He had no idea what to do with them. Good, she thought. Let him stand there looking like an idiot.

"Where's Mae?" he asked finally, looking around the room as if perhaps she had been hiding underneath the table or standing with the pots in the sink. "I got these for her. Guy says they're fresh. You got some water for them?"

"Well, not on me," she said, wanting to punch him. "There's a vase in the closet behind you, on the top shelf. Rinse it and then fill it with water. I have an idea. Maybe you could go back to the Shamrock and use some of their water, from their own special bathroom. I know how fond you are of the place."

"Ah, c'mon, Delia. Don't be like this, please," he begged sheepishly. "Not today, okay?"

"Maurice, give me the goddamn flowers," she said, holding out her hand. "You go sit inside with the boys." What was the use?

"Delia." Mae hustled into the kitchen, looking neat in a flowered dress, her gray hair pulled back smoothly in a small bun. "Do you have the carving knives in here?" she asked.

"Hi, there," Maurice crooned. "I got these flowers for my favorite mother-in-law, Mary Rooney." He nearly hit her in the face with the carnations.

"Oh," Mae said, taking the flowers from his hand. "Well, wasn't that thoughtful of you."

"Oh, you're welcome." He grinned. His open suit jacket was rumpled and creased.

"I didn't say thank you, Maurice," she carefully enunciated. "I merely said it was thoughtful. Now why don't you go inside and sit down with the boys and the children?"

Maurice nodded vigorously. "Good," he said. "Good idea."

When Mae cut into the breast of the bird, golden drops spurted over the front of her dress. She'd expected it; she sighed, tugging on one drumstick to loosen it, and then she did the same thing on the other side. The misted kitchen window was flung wide open to let out the cooking heat, and the slices of turkey on the platter were beginning to chill. Delia touched them with the back of her hand. The kitchen looked so empty — all the chairs had been moved to the mahogany table in the living room — and the winter night's air tickled Delia's legs. She thought that if she were alone, she might try to tapdance across the floor. Instead she bounced up and down on her heels. Mae dropped a piece of freshly cut turkey on Delia's hand.

"You're not payin' attention to the way I'm cuttin' this, miss. I won't be around forever to do it, and then what'll you do?"

"I don't know, Ma." She smiled. "I guess for Thanksgiving we'll have hot dogs. Come on, Ma, the turkey's getting cold."

"I know, I know. You're so smart. Just hold your horses, and let me fix this on the platter nice, okay? It's the one day a year when I use some of these things that were my mother's and came shoved in my trunk, all the way from the other side. These cups were hers and this small pitcher for the gravy and the cloth on the table, all hers. When I'm gone they'll be yours, and then you'll pass them on to Maureen."

Delia stared at the crack in the small pitcher, like a long black hair. The tablecloth had dime-sized holes. She had seen Eugene stick his knife through one of them. "You know, Delia Mary, when I'm out here in the kitchen like this, on a holiday" — she sounded tired and wiped her forehead with her wrist — "fixin' everything up nice, I make believe Denis is outside and that I have you children small again. When I'm fixin' these fancy dinners, I think of my own mother, and I know that wherever she is, she's smilin' down at me, happy with the way I turned out, and sometimes when the window is all steamy, like it is now, I think I can nearly see her face in the glass. And when I'm carryin' the bird down the hall, I make believe she's out there, at the other end, just waitin', and for a second there I start to believe it. Every holiday, Christmas too, I think like that. Now I guess you'll be thinkin' I'm gettin' old."

"Oh no, I won't, Ma," Delia said softly, trying to hug Mae, who shrugged her away.

"Ah, never mind that stuff." Mae blushed. "Come on; let's go out with the others and eat."

Patty was sitting on a telephone book to be closer to the table. She was toasting Maureen with a bit of beer in a small glass that Delia recognized: Mae had served shrimp cocktail in that glass to Maurice's mother on the night they had planned the wedding. Kathleen was still in her nurse's uniform, having come to the Rooneys' straight from work. She ate none of the shrimp and barely picked at the standing rib roast it had taken Mae all day to prepare. Delia had walked around the table that night like a waitress, with the platters of food

115

and vegetables in the crook of her arm, and when she saw Kathleen's slender fingers resting on Maurice's hand, she accidentally splashed his cuff with the juice of some pickled beets.

"Don't worry, Delia," Kathleen said, in the tone of someone used to calming others. "I'll soak that tonight and have it out in no time."

Maurice didn't quite know what to do. He smiled uncomfortably at his mother and at Delia and rolled his sleeve above his elbow. Kathleen looked either at her plate or at Maurice.

"For Christ's sake, Kathy," Denis had yelled, as if she were three blocks away. "You haven't swalleyed a bite!"

Kathleen smiled tightly, showing none of her teeth.

"I'm afraid I haven't much of an appetite, Mr. Rooney," she had said, but Denis certainly did. Delia remembered the sucking noises he had made with his ill-fitting false teeth. Delia watched Maurice's mother stare at the stains in the cloth, no doubt the same one that was on Mae's table now.

"With what's happened," Kathleen Delaney said, finally, "I think we'd better keep the wedding quite small." Her voice was so low that everything she had said sounded like a secret.

"You mean the baby," Delia had said clearly. "Our baby."

"Yes, dear, of course." Kathleen turned to her. "I mean the baby and all."

"So, Kathy," Denis had said suddenly, "how long you been a widow now?"

"Since my Maurice was twelve. His father, my husband, was run over by a city bus. An accident. A long time ago, Mr. Rooney."

"The city do right by you?" he had asked. Delia sprang up to clear the table, nudging her mother's back as she passed with a stack of plates.

"Denis." Mae had pointed at Kathleen. "Why don't you just let Mrs. Delaney finish her meal now."

"Oh, I'm finished, Mrs. Rooney. Everything was just splendid. Yes, Mr. Rooney, there was a settlement, if that's what you mean."

"Good, good," Denis said heartily. "It's only right, after all, you with a boy to raise."

"Shame," he had added as an afterthought, the table cleared now, crumbs scattered in front of him. He ran his fingers through his straight gray hair.

"Ma, can I say grace?" Patty asked, rocking from side to side on Mae's telephone book.

"Well, of course you can say grace." Mae leaned forward, with her wrinkled hands folded on the table. "You're the littlest one, aren't you?"

"Grace!" Patty screamed, and then almost fell off the chair, laughing.

"No, Patty, you got to do it right." Eugene stood up and cleared his throat, waving his fork like the conductor of a symphony orchestra. "Look out, tonsils, look out, tongue," he sang, "look out, belly, here it comes! Amen, alleluia!"

"Eugene!" Mae grabbed a roll and seemed ready to throw it at him.

"Goddamn asshole," Gerald said, looking up at the ceiling and laughing in spite of himself.

THIRTEEN

On nights when Maurice was working late, Delia and her girls often ate dinner with Mae and whichever of the boys happened to be home.

Delia would sit at the table, watching her mother pile giant-sized musty potatoes in the oven like an Indian woman piling rocks for a fire. In the late afternoon, when the sun seemed to fall behind the tall buildings across the river, Mae's kitchen turned dark quickly. The blue oilcloth floor felt thick underfoot and was somehow hard to walk across. Eugene might be about ready to get up and go to the watch factory where he was a guard, Gerald on his way home from his token clerk's job with the transit authority. Delia hated the thought of Mae all by herself most of the time, with nobody to talk to (although she swore that Denis, from wherever he was, heard her every word). There was nobody in Delia's house to make a mess while she sipped tea with her mother, thinking happily of her spotless home upstairs, pressing her toe into the soft blue floor, a yielding sensation, as if she were probing her organs, her heart or her uterus. She looked forward to opening her own apartment door in the evenings, the sweet smell floating about her face.

She could see the glitter of the vacuum cleaner in the corner of her bedroom as soon as she stepped through the door. It seemed as though Delia's clean apartment led its own special life, as if, in Delia's absence, the sofa might have stood up and fluffed its cushions or the black panther lamps dusted each other's noses.

She had a recurring nightmare: What if they came home one night and they were already there? Where would Delia and her girls go? Who would believe that they were actually themselves and the people living in their apartment the impostors? She wondered what it would be like to have two husbands to pick up after, two paychecks to cash, two men to sleep with.

One night late in November, Eugene came out and sat at the white table, his hair bent in a thousand directions. Delia liked to be at Mae's when he woke up and her mother put on a pot of coffee, although she had an unreal sensation as she drank tea in that deep-brown chocolaty smell. In deference to Delia, he wore a rumpled shirt, unbuttoned except for the collar and the cuffs, snug around that scar. Delia couldn't bear to look at it. Everything about Eugene was jagged and raw-looking, from his bony limbs to his bitten-down fingernails and his inflamed red skin. Right after he woke up, his skin was clear, as if his ever-present flush hadn't caught up with the rest of him, and he looked briefly rested and cared for. Delia wondered about women, if he had ever been with anyone. There was only that brief explosion when he was thrown through Cohen's window and ruined the holiday display, smashing into the cardboard Christmas fireplace, breaking the plastic menorah.

Mae and Delia had sat with him in the emergency room of the city hospital, where he seemed to be quite proud of himself, swinging his legs from side to side on the examining table as a young doctor with thick eyeglasses sewed his neck and arm back together.

For the next few weeks, Mae sighed and raised her eyebrows whenever anyone asked her how Eugene was doing and, anyway, what the hell happened to him? A woman, she had said, shrugging her shoulders. Ah, you know how it is, she sometimes added, and as if passion was something people in the Heights were accustomed to, they nodded gravely. They had thought he was a nancy boy, and his "incident" seemed to put an end to all that talk, although they never found the stranger who had tossed him and Eugene didn't remember a thing about the night, only that his wound seemed to be less painful to him than all the innuendo had been. As his neck healed and the scar hardened, he appeared free of some burden, and he walked through the Heights with a new swagger. People seemed to treat Eugene with something close to respect, even his mother, newly in awe of him.

Mae confided to Delia that her son had gotten his strong "desire" from his father, and she had looked down and admitted that Denis was "quite a physical type," which made Delia want to hide her head underneath her blouse. When he was young, Eugene had had a voice that was clear and strong and beautiful. It rang out from the choir at St. Immaculata's, making everyone turn to look at him, smiling, proud that someone they knew could sing like that, as if they had discovered his talent in themselves. But he never did much with his voice, and Denis, his father, often told him not to let it go to his head. His voice echoed so because his head was so empty, that was easy to see.

The night before Gerald left for the seminary, at his going-away party in the back room of the Democratic Club, Eugene had stood on a chair and sung "Danny Boy" into the yellow, cigarette-filled air. The women, in flowered cotton dresses, put down their highballs, and the men, with their bright noses, their sweaty, twisted ties undone, hanging loose underneath open collars, with the ends resting on their puffy breasts, held paper cups of flat beer between their knees to applaud. Someone looked at Denis and pointed out that Eugene's voice had made his father cry, but Denis said, no, no, it wasn't that at all, it was all the beer, and his kidneys right there behind his eyes, and everyone had laughed.

Mae brought the dishes down from the closet and began to set the table. Delia was sitting at the head of the table, Denis's old place, and she sat just as he had, crossing her legs to the side, looking up at the clock with narrowed eyes. Her mother stared at her as if she were someone Mae couldn't quite place. "Delia Mary," she said finally, "you look just like your father, sittin' there like that," and then she started to peel carrots with a tiny sharp knife. Maureen and Patty were due home from school, and every noise on the street was making Delia jump.

"I see they're finally starting to fix up Hans's store down the corner." Eugene wet his finger, as his mother always did, and turned the pages of the newspaper. "'Bout time, don't you think?" he asked of nobody in particular.

"I saw them doing work on it," Delia said, trying not to stare at his scarred finger. "I heard that it's going to be a restaurant."

"Yeah, I heard that too. An Italian restaurant."

"Eyetalian?" Mae asked, letting the last dish fall heavily. "Nobody said nothin' to me about no Eyetalian restaurant. I hate that Eyetalian food. All that spaghetti don't fill nobody up; all those tomatoes ruin perfectly good meat, if it is good meat they've got underneath it, but then who'd know? They could be slicin' up alley cats and puttin' them on the plates, for all you know. You won't be catchin' me there, that's for sure."

"Ah, c'mon, Ma. It won't be so bad. You and me and Gerald'll go there some night, and we'll have some scungilli and a dish of manicotti and a pizza. What d'ya think, huh?"

"You and Gerald can go by yourself, thank you very much. I'll stay home, where I can see what I'm eatin'. Don't blame me if one of you comes home sick to your stomach, all that oil and grease, all those tomatoes."

"No adventure in your soul, Mae Rooney, none whatsoever." Eugene winked at Delia.

"Don't you 'Mae Rooney' me, Eugene Dermot. I'm still your mother, no matter how big you think you are. Don't you forget that."

Eugene rolled wide, frightened eyes at Delia and walked to the window. "Here they come now," he said softly, "poor little ragamuffins."

Maureen and Patty burst through the door into the kitchen and headed right for the windowsill behind the curtains, where Mae hid their treats, orange cupcakes with bits of orange peel sunk in the white frosting like coarse hairs, or the furry pink and red coconut cakes from Cushing's under the el. Sometimes, when Delia and Mae were out shopping, Maureen and Patty came home to Eugene, alone in the house, and they found the windowsill empty except for a folded bit of paper that might say "Oven" in thick, blurry print. And when Maureen and Patty ran to the oven and opened it, they found another bit of folded paper in the roasting pan, which said "Sink," and they whirled around to find yet another piece of paper in a teacup, wet and nearly transparent, which said "Dish closet." But when they got there, they couldn't find a thing but dishes, until they looked in the creamer, where they found a note that said "Icebox," and when they opened the Frigidaire, they found two small silver cups of chocolate pudding with whipped cream from the German bakery ten blocks away. They would try to thank him, Maureen claimed, but he didn't even look up, just kept working his crossword with his stub of a pencil. "What notes?" he asked them. "What pudding? I didn't go near no German bakery today. Christ, I got better things to do than *that*." He tried to go back to his puzzle, but the girls hugged him hard and made him laugh and kissed his sad, thin face.

Delia hoped that Eugene sang out through the empty corridors of the watch factory, that his voice bounced from the iron gates that stretched across the elevator down through the elevator shaft that frightened her the one time she saw it, that the factory, all seven empty floors, was full of the sound of her brother, that maybe it might take some of the emptiness out of him. And then she worried that nobody would hear if, instead of the singing, Eugene wailed and screamed and banged his skinny head against the walls.

Today Mae had a plate of brownies hidden behind the curtain. The girls hugged her and ran inside to do their homework. "I don't know what time to be expectin' Gerald." Mae sighed, looking up at the clock. He was working days this week, again the opposite hours from Eugene's. Their shifts kept Mae busy with unmade beds and meals at odd hours. Like Eugene, Gerald liked his job, selling tokens underneath the ground at subway stations around the city. When Gerald smiled, he had a gap between his front teeth, and as he got older, there was less and less light hair on top of his round head. In another time, Delia had thought, Gerald would have made a perfect hayseed farmer; she could see him wearing a straw hat, chewing on a blade of grass, with rippling stalks of wheat swallowing his dungarees. Eugene at least had that singing voice to balance him somehow, but Gerald had no special features. There was nothing about Gerald to remember. Delia had thought Gerald tried to become somebody by becoming a priest, but the vocation "didn't take," Gerald's words, as if his vocation were an inoculation. When he had gone away to the seminary, the clasp on his suitcase had sprung open, and Gerald had had to close it with one of his going-away presents, a sober black belt.

His presents were all black, Delia remembered, black and serious: a new watchband, a leather-trimmed blotter for his desk, a black missal, a black diary. Her parents had had such high hopes for Gerald. Delia remembered the cake at his party, a white plastic collar propped in the center amid a pile of chocolate-chip rosary beads. "'*Congratulations Gerald*,'" Mae had shouted, reading from the cake, beaming up at her son like a bride, and with her hand resting on top of his, they cut the rippling cake into small, pineapple-filled chunks.

After he came home and offered no real explanation, Denis had stopped speaking to Gerald, so angry with him that he walked out of the room the minute Gerald came in. And then, soon after, when Delia was pregnant with Maureen, Denis had died on the street of a sudden heart attack, right in front of Healey's pub. Everyone said the shock of Gerald's coming home was what had killed him. Gerald never mentioned a friend, and he had never seemed to date, just went off to work and came back home again, and yet from time to time he stayed out all night, just like his father, and Mae would grow frantic all over again, calling hospitals and the police until the sun rose. He never said where he was, just came home and immediately went to bed. He seldom laughed, and he rarely said much. When they needed him to, he worked the shifts down in the subway that nobody else wanted. The graveyard shift, he had said, suited him just fine.

But at 4:00 A.M., if Delia happened to wake up and look at the clock next to her bed, she might think of her older brother, by himself in that tiny booth, and wonder if he was frightened, as she herself would surely be, hearing the moans of ghosts or the dragging of chains through those subway tunnels. Unlike Eugene, Gerald made Delia nervous; whenever she happened to meet him on the street, he just stood in front of her without saying a word, as if he had no idea what to do next. She'd have to tell him where she was going, just to make it clear that she was awfully rushed and he couldn't possibly come with her. Sometimes she didn't even give him the chance to say hello before she told him she was on her way to Feldman's to buy a new dress, which was rarely true. She felt relieved to see him shrug, touch her arm, and stroll away. People looked at Gerald in a funny way, trying to see if they might be the ones who'd be able to figure out why he came back home, what was wrong, studying his face as if he were one of those drawings in Patty's school magazine that hid monkeys and firemen in the branches of ordinary trees.

Once, Delia saw Gerald across the street, standing in front of the

123

bank, in the middle of a line of older men underneath the gloomy shadows of the el, the glint of the gold night-deposit wheel matching the glimmer of their gold retirement belt buckles. Delia recognized her brother's dark coat; Gerald himself was hidden behind the newspaper he was holding in front of his face, and she thought about calling over to him, just to be friendly. She'd say she was on her way to the A & P, with only a minute to chat, but Gerald was engrossed in *The New York Times*, a much longer, more substantial newspaper than the others on the stand, one that marked Gerald as an intellectual, and Delia hated to disturb his concentration. (At the newsstands in the Heights, whole stacks of the *Times* stood alone and gathered dust.)

As she watched him, Delia realized that she was proud of Gerald still, he was so bright and knowledgeable, so much more than he seemed. He would have made a good priest, she thought, just by the way he pored over that difficult, tall newspaper. Maybe he'll go back, she often prayed, and become that fine priest, an excellent teacher. And then a woman came down the el stairs, holding on to the banister and walking sideways in her high-heeled shoes, and Delia watched Gerald lower the paper and saw the other men stop talking, and all at once, every man in front of the bank looked up the woman's skirt, their heads rising with the precision of the Rockettes. Delia wasn't sure what she should do, and so she resumed walking, hoping Gerald hadn't seen her watching him. It could have been worse, she thought; it could have been her coming down those stairs. Rather than bright, Delia admitted to herself, Gerald was merely clever, having found a disguise in his used-up vocation.

When Gerald finally came home, he was over an hour late.

The girls had brought their homework to Mae's dinner table. Mae was pacing back and forth from the window to the stove, and to distract the girls from her mother's anxiety, Delia opened Patty's English book to the page where she was learning to diagram sentences, the sheet of paper so shiny and the print so dark that it made Delia hungry, the words of the sentences resting on a thick black line that looked like a table, the sturdy breadlike nouns in boxes between the spicy verbs, and then the objects, round and pearly at the ends of the tables, like eggs. (In her pregnant state, she felt an unusual appeal in common and ordinary things.)

"Adjectives and adverbs are like pickles and olives," Delia said to Patty. "They aren't necessary to the grammar meal, but they're nice to have. Look." She pointed. "See the way they hang down from this thick black line, like pieces of old spaghetti?"

"Uh huh." Patty scratched at her head with the eraser end of her pencil. "Can I have a new bike?" and Delia tapped her on the head with Maureen's ruler.

Mae stood at the stove, poking the platter of drying meat and the bowl of shriveling vegetables with a fork, everything set neatly atop pots of simmering water. "Ma," Delia said quietly, "why don't we just eat? Gerald's a grown man. He's probably fine."

"Well, things can happen to grown men too, Delia. Anyway, he might be a grown man to you, but to me, he's still my child, you know. What if this is one of them nights he don't come home at all?"

"I think I hear him." Delia had heard the lobby door slam.

"Gerald?" Mae called, staring at Delia with her eyes wide. "That you?"

"Yeah, it's me, Ma." He stood in the doorway and smiled. "Why? You expectin' a date? Hey, Delia," he said, and patted the top of her hair.

"Hi," Delia said, embarrassed. Gerald had never done anything like that before, and although her hair was probably out of place now, she didn't want to fix it. She felt warmer toward Gerald than she had since they were kids. Maurice always called Gerald the Invisible Man. (He should talk, she thought.)

"What in heaven's name kept you so long?" Mae pointed toward the stove. "I been keepin' your dinner."

"Ah, Ma, you shouldn't have done that. Don't ever wait dinner for me. Don't make these lovely ladies wait for their supper." He tugged on Patty's braids. She smiled and flicked her head, surprised by his sudden attention, and began to kick her leg against the table.

"Patty, stop that!" Mae said harshly. "Gerald, I'm askin' you once again, where *were* you?"

"I was at Cushing's Bakery," he said, rubbing his hands together as if he were cold.

"Doing *what?*" Mae asked. "Did you bring somethin' home for me?"

"No," he said. "I, ah, I met this girl."

Mae's mouth dropped open; the ladle she held began to droop. "What girl? What girl did you meet?"

"Well, all this week?" he asked, unsure of himself. "Working days? I've been seeing this same girl getting off the subway in the mornings, just when I've been getting on. I noticed her the other day on the subway stairs."

Delia looked at him steadily, but he didn't flinch.

"Yeah." He laughed uneasily. "I've been going up, and she's been coming down. We laughed about that. Anyway, today she dropped a quarter right in front of me, and I picked it up, and we started talking."

"A *stranger?*" Mae glared at him.

"Well, not anymore," he said brightly. "Not now. Her name is Bernadetta LaBriola. Berni, they call her. She works behind the counter at Cushing's. She just started there. Used to work in the other Cushing's, in Forest Hills."

"Oh," Mae said sarcastically, "and isn't that nice! Here I am, not knowing what happened to you, the kids starving and your poor sister too, and you're right around the corner, talkin' to some strange girl you just met, a girl from the *subway* of all places, and sounds like a *foreigner* to boot!"

"Aw, for Christ's sake, Ma," Gerald said, leaning on the table. "I'm not a kid, and I'm not a priest anymore — not that I ever was, I know. But I'm thirty-five years old, and I'm tired of being alone. If I don't come home right away, don't worry about me. Just go ahead and do what you want."

"Do what I *want?*" Mae said, spacing each word. "And then who'll fix your meals when your crazy hours change? Who'll clean and press your clothes? Who'll care where you are, huh? Your new Eyetalian girlfriend? Huh?"

Patty and Maureen, holding their notebooks, looked from Mae to

Gerald and then gazed at Mae again. "Are you girls finished with your homework?" Delia asked quietly. "If you are, then go inside and put the books away. We're going to eat now, Mama, isn't that right?" Mae simply looked at her. "Now you girls go and do what you're told."

"Ma, why don't you leave him alone?" Delia whispered, as soon as the children had left.

"Why don't I leave him alone?" she spat. "He makes us wait for dinner, without even a phone call to let me know he's all right, and then I find out he's right around the corner with some girl, some *pickup* he meets on a subway platform, and he just forgets about his family. That's a fine bit of gratitude for you! That's real nice, Gerald. I want to tell you thanks a lot!"

"I don't need this goddamn bullshit!" Gerald screamed, and stomped out of the kitchen. He slammed the door to the apartment and left.

Mae ran to the window. "Don't you curse at me, Gerald Aloysius!" she yelled, trying to open the window. "And don't be comin' back until you're sorry!"

Delia shook her head. "What're you gonna do, Ma, hit him? Punish him?"

"Never mind your smart answers, miss, and don't you think you can interfere! I don't interfere with you and your children; what gives you the right to be doin' it with mine?"

"I'm not tryin' to interfere, Ma! It's just that maybe it'll be good for him to meet some girl, some woman. Maybe it's time he got married, don't you think?"

"Some girl, some nice girl, sure. He goes over to one of the church dances and meets up with some nice girl from the neighborhood, that's fine with me. Sure I'd like to see him married and settled, I'd like to see the two of them with families of their own. Don't you think I would? Just not like this—foreigners on the subway, of all things. It's just not right!" And she began to cry. "Delia, let me ask you," she said, leaning forward to look in Delia's face, her thin gray mustache illuminated by the overhead light. "Who knows what kind of disease this girl from the subway might be carryin'. You're a married woman; you know what I'm thinkin' about."

"But, Ma, why don't you just let Gerald worry about that stuff?"

"And who's the one takin' care of him if he gets sick? You, Delia? What do you do for him—or any of us?"

"Nothing, I guess," Delia said, shrugging her shoulders and standing up. What did her mother want from her, with two children of her own (and one she was carrying, that nobody knew anything about). "What am I supposed to do for him?" she asked, pushing her chair into the table harder than she intended to. "Maureen," she called, "Patty. Come on, we're going home."

"*What?*" Mae was incredulous. "And you're leavin' me with all this food?" Her hands were flung open wide. "I'll have to throw everything out!"

"I'm taking the girls home, Ma. I don't think it's a good night for us to stay. Come *on*, girls, let's go."

"Well, suit yourself Delia. Maybe you shouldn't stay here for dinner anymore anyway. After all, you've got your own place, whether your husband is home or not! Stay where you belong," she said, her pale nostrils flaring. She took the hot plates from the stove and dumped everything directly into the garbage pail, the meat sizzling as if it were continuing to cook.

"G'night, Grandma." Maureen tried to kiss Mae's cheek, but she had turned her back.

"Don't forget your books," Mae said, throwing the silverware from the table across the room and into the sink.

The air outside was so cold it made them gasp.

Delia was relieved to be away from Mae (getting so *old*, Delia thought, so *unreasonable*). The girls were still in their school uniforms, dragging their schoolbags as if they didn't have a home. Maureen was upset, her gray eyes fixed straight in front of her. Nothing seemed to faze Patty, who ran ahead, past the dingy alleyways that so frightened Delia. "We don't have a thing for dinner," she said to Maureen.

"Never mind about dinner, Ma." Maureen nudged her elbow. "Let's just get dessert. Let's go to Cohen's and get ice cream—please?"

"Ice cream?" Delia smiled. "What kind of a dinner is that?"

"Come on, Ma," Maureen pleaded. "Just for tonight?"

Mr. Cohen carefully packed their brown paper bag with two pints of ice cream and two bottles of cola. Ever since Eugene's accident, Mr. Cohen had seemed wary of Delia or any of the Rooneys if they came into his shop. Sometimes he had seemed to be angry if he had to turn his back on her to get change from the register. Delia hated to see that, anger or fear directed at her, so when Mr. Cohen was searching in his pockets, she walked over to the magazine rack and selected *Screen Stars* and *Hairstyles of Today* and tossed them into the bag so she wouldn't need change. "Thank you," Mr. Cohen said, surprised. He handed the bag to Maureen, wiping his hands across the front of his spotted white apron and smiling slightly. "You should let this big girl work a little," he said. Behind him, Delia saw the cola syrup bottles lined up on a drooping shelf. When the girls got sick and couldn't stop throwing up, she bought containers of Mr. Cohen's syrup and fed it to them, their pink mouths open to her like little birds, that terrible trust of children so wrenching that Delia always swallowed a double dose of their medicine before she gave it to them.

Outside Cohen's, the cold air froze the inside of her nose and made her sneeze so forcefully she became dizzy. She looked up at the full moon from underneath the tracks of the el and for some reason thought of her brothers' bedroom, Gerald's half with hardly a thing in it — a chair, a dresser, and a small lamp next to a table by the bed — and Eugene's half a wreck, his skinny black socks all twisted around his dirty underwear, and his wrinkled pay stubs piled high on the unmade bed.

Last July, coming home late one night from a church dance, she and Maurice followed a handful of chattering women all the way down their block, and when they passed Mae's apartment, where Maureen and Patty were asleep in her tall feather bed, they saw Gerald sitting attentively at his bedroom window, as if he was hungry for the clatter of high heels on the pavement or was trying to sniff the perfume in the air through the wire-mesh screen. Solemnly he raised his hand at them. "Poor bastard," Maurice had said, the minute they passed.

Delia couldn't understand her mother. The image of Gerald on that straight-back chair had haunted her for weeks. If Gerald was seeing a girl, especially one who was working in a bakery, with sweet stains on her apron, like Mr. Cohen's, and colored sugar grains underneath her fingernails, well, that'd be just fine — although she'd have to go around and get a look at her, just in case, peering through the window, looking beyond the dusty plaster wedding cakes that held up the faceless brides and grooms, to see this "Berni."

Turning her corner, she said a quick prayer for Gerald and hoped that Berni was pretty, with a kind manner and a pleasant face, and wanted him too, and that she had breasts as round and as sweet as the linzertortes in Cushing's window. As Mr. Cohen might say, they couldn't hurt.

FOURTEEN

She decided she would tell Maurice and the girls about the baby when they met him in front of the skating rink at Rockefeller Center.

In her underwear, Delia stood in front of her bathroom mirror, her cosmetics strewn all over: topless lipstick tubes, the pancake compact spotted with a few drops of water, the sponge she had used to apply it dripping a thin pinkish line into the basin.

She wanted to look special, although it seemed harder and harder to do. The more she tried, the more her face seemed to resist. It was the same way with her apartment: the more perfectly she had tried to vacuum, the more the tiny snowflakes of paper had seemed to show up on the rug. Delia worked on her hair, teasing it and smoothing it, but new jagged pieces kept jabbing out near her temples. She ripped open a tiny bag from the five-and-ten with her new eyebrow "stencil" sheet and brown eyebrow pencil. It was a new idea: under each cut-out pattern was the name of a famous Hollywood actress, and if Delia held the sheet at arm's length, she recognized the eyebrows layered on top of each other like apartments in a high-rise. Choosing between Elizabeth Taylor and Bette Davis was hard. She stuck her head out of the bathroom door. "Maureen, can you come in here for a minute?" she called, pulling her half-slip over her head. Maureen came in and stared at the stencils. She seemed to be trying hard to understand the whole idea of makeup, looking from the sheet of famous eyebrows to her mother as if she wanted to laugh.

It was exactly the way Delia had felt watching Maureen lurch along the street in her high-heeled shoes, taking shallow breaths in her new "training" bra. It hurt her so much to see her young daughter get accustomed to discomfort that Delia thought it funny, this looking at each other through artifice, under props, when they knew each other so well. Yet actually to come right out and laugh, well, where would that leave Maureen, or Patty, with so many years of it ahead of them?

With the new pregnancy, her clothes were starting to get tight. There was so much thick, warm flesh to be restrained. Her tight bra turned her naturally rounded breasts into a pair of dunce caps, shooting out from her chest in the strong cotton fabric with a new strength, so fiercely independent and powerful-looking that the skin on Delia's neck seemed crepey and weak. Breasts in armor, like mine, Delia thought, seemed capable of anything. Why, they could practically shoot ammunition into the air! The cups of the bra were pointed like the toes of her shoes, which were shaped exactly like wedges of pie. After a day of high heels, Delia's feet might lose their feeling entirely, as if they had turned to blocks of wood.

Someone, Delia didn't know who, had decided that she should have hard lines where she was soft, so she wore a rubber panty girdle with lace edging to hide the tight elastic that turned her thighs purple. The girdle had a smooth satin crotch that shone and gleamed like a half-moon between her legs, and the garters cut into her thighs and left imprints like tattoos, but she was still better off than Mae, who wore a pink corset laced across the front, though slightly less fortunate than Maureen, with her thin white garter belt sprigged with blue flowers. Little Patty had the best deal of all in her flesh-colored tights, which were all the rage. (Delia wished they were made for adults too — none of her stockings were ever long enough, leaving a band of soft skin exposed to the chafing winter air, a piercing feeling like caramel candy stuck in the cavity of a tooth.) But, Delia figured, all other women were in the same boat, and that consoled her. On Sunday, waiting for the Mass to begin, Delia watched the others in girdles and bras so tight that their flesh bubbled up around their waists and around their shoulder blades as if they were wearing padding. The trimmest women, Delia couldn't help but notice, in the long-line girdles and long-line bras, had the fattest calves and the thickest necks and were the first to faint. At night, when Delia got undressed for bed, there were marks in her soft stomach as if she had been run over by a tractor.

"Whose eyebrows do I want?" she asked Maureen.

"Elizabeth Taylor's, I guess, Ma. Now come on, we don't want to make Daddy wait." The girls stood in front of the bathroom and sighed loudly. They had stayed home from school as a special treat, to make up for the ill-fated trip to the Thanksgiving Day parade. They would meet Maurice and see the Christmas windows and buy new winter coats. It was payday, and they wanted to have dinner at the Automat, to stand at the change booths and wait for the surly clerks to convert their dollars into nickels and dimes for the machines.

Delia was delighted every time the little glass doors sprang open. She would reach in for her macaroni and cheese, and then, if she happened to see people in white uniforms washing the tile floors behind the stacks of plates, she was disappointed, wanting to think that the Automat fare floated through walls like magic.

The girls looked nice, all dressed up, with their white gloves from the summer on their hands and their old patent-leather shoes, buffed to a shine with Vaseline, on their feet, although they wouldn't be warm enough in old spring coats on a bitterly cold day. Maureen's shoes, her first pair of heels, tended to buckle under her feet and make her twist her ankles, and her garter belt seemed to be too big, Delia realized, by the way she was tugging on it, evidently causing the back garters to fly open. Maureen kept pulling up her skirt and her coat to fix her garters, and when she walked, she took little mincing steps in her old heels, with her hands fluttering nervously at her thighs. "Can we buy pretzels from the pretzel man?" Maureen asked.

"Sure we can." Delia leaned closely into the mirror to blot her lipstick. "Pretzels from the pretzel man and chestnuts from the chestnut man. We'll light a candle in Saint Pat's, and then we'll meet Daddy and go down to Macy's for the coats."

"And *then* the Automat?" Patty asked, the crotch of her tights dangling a little below her short spring coat.

"And then the Automat. With Daddy," Delia said, lifting Patty's coat to fix her tights. As if he were the dessert, she thought.

"Is Grandma coming with us?" Patty asked, rubbing her nose with her gloves.

"Get a tissue. No, Patty, not today," Delia said, guilt washing over her, leaving a bad taste in her mouth. Mae always sulked when they left her home alone.

"But we'll stop in just as soon as we get home tonight," Delia had promised Mae that morning, on the telephone. "We'll save you a pretzel, and when we come home we'll fix some hot chocolate in your kitchen, okay?" And then I can tell you about the new baby, Delia thought. "Look, Mama," she had said soothingly, when Mae didn't answer. "We'll go in to New York together at Christmastime next year. Or if you want, we can even go in during Easter-time."

"Ah, Delia," Mae said, "that's if I'm still here next year. Or even next week," she added.

Delia stepped back from the mirror to study the effect, although she could only see her reflection as far as her waist. The light pink coat she wore had just come back from the cleaners, and it felt a bit too short, the sleeves barely skimming her wristbones. She wore elbow-length beige gloves, which draped her forearms in soft fabric. Her shoes matched her gloves. (She had read in a magazine that Jackie Kennedy always wore beige shoes, with gloves to match: the magazine didn't say anything about the First Lady's pocketbook, but Delia figured that Jackie would match everything, and so she bought a beige purse and tucked it under her arm because it had no handle, like an evening bag. Delia knew from the newspapers that Jackie carried evening bags.)

She turned her head, happy to see that her bouffant hair looked rounded and full; she had made it springy and lush in the back. Her new pale lipstick called attention to her eyes, made them look bluer, and she liked the dark dramatic curve of Elizabeth Taylor's eyebrows better than her own, the way they swept toward the temple. Her face finally looked fine. She had wanted to wear a pillbox hat, but they never stayed on Delia's head, so she wore only a stiff piece of pink netting on top of her hair, pulling it over her eyes to rest on the bridge of her nose. She thought the veiling made her look mysterious, even if everything she looked at seemed to be hidden behind a fence. She hadn't even left the house, and her girdle hurt already and pulled on her buttocks. It had been Rosaleen's girdle, and it smelled like a bathing cap and took forever to dry. She'd get rid of it after today, she decided, and buy a new one; today she wanted to look perfect. She wondered how surprised Maurice and the girls would be by her news.

"Let me have a look at both of you," Delia said, putting Patty's new pink velvet hat on her head and stretching the elastic so it wouldn't scrape her chin. She fastened Maureen's white wool beret with a pearl hatpin. Such pretty children, she thought; nobody will even notice those pastel spring coats.

"You both look so beautiful," Delia said. "Just wait till Daddy sees you." She noticed fine lines around Maureen's mouth that she hadn't had before, and hips and breasts changing the shape of her yellow coat, carrying her away as if she were being kidnapped. Maureen wasn't ready for any of it, not the shopkeepers looking at her suddenly or the men on the subway who might press their thighs to hers or grope at her backside when the lights blinked off. Today she was wearing her training bra underneath her sweater; a light coat of orange lipstick made her face look bruised. Patty was jealous of the lipstick and the bra: Delia had sewed a bit of ribbon on her undershirt, and she let her shine her mouth with a tissue dipped in Vaseline.

She herded them out the door, holding her pocketbook painfully against her full chest, sensing that her body was humming along like a tightly wound motor she knew nothing about.

As soon as she saw in Maurice's eyes how nice they all looked and how he really loved them all, she'd just come right out and say it. Pregnant, expecting, another baby on the way. Something in the oven: she had heard Eugene say that; or in the family way: Mae's expression. She had an hour at least to decide how to put it.

A son would change things, she thought; he'd know Maurice in a way that the girls could not. He had nothing in common with girls, but did any father, really? Her father had had nothing in common with her (but for that matter, he'd had nothing in common with her brothers). But that was Denis, she told herself, and not Maurice.

On their way to the bus, Delia was more hopeful than she had been in a long time, the new baby inside her and Christmas just ahead, and now her girls were getting new coats to keep them warm. Tomorrow they would go to Joannie Malloney's birthday party, and Delia was looking forward to both things, the coats and the party, as if she were getting one and attending the other. She thought she had finally taken her mother's advice and learned how to *be* the baby, although her daughters weren't babies anymore. She couldn't wait to turn their new soft coat collars up against their pretty cheeks; she looked forward to ironing their party dresses. Mae warned her that she was fussing with them too much, but she thought she was trying to make up for their father's frequent absences. Even when he was home, he watched television or he fell asleep on the couch, more silent than he had ever been.

But not today, she told herself. Today she'd have his full attention. She walked as quickly as her girdle would allow, the girls struggling to keep up. She didn't want to be late or let Maurice grow impatient, drumming his fingers against his thighs or, worse, stalking away. Not today, when she was about to change their whole life.

Patty had taps on her shoes that Eugene had bought for her from Silvio the shoemaker, and her shoes made a smacking boys' noise on the sidewalk. Maureen kept turning her ankles and catching her heels in the street gratings, so that by the time they got to the bus stop, Maureen lagging behind, her heels looked whittled and raw, like wood. The bus, when it came, was so crowded that they had to stand. Maureen held on to the strap above her head, her feet folding over on themselves like the flaps of an envelope. How her feet must be hurting, Delia thought, noticing the white edging of Maureen's bra, which was showing underneath the V neckline of her sweater. Delia remembered how easily bras moved around when there was little to anchor them. The more she looked at her child's sweater, the more she pitied her, those burgeoning nipples like cloves of garlic exposed to that scratchy wool.

Delia kept slipping and grabbing onto Maureen's shoulders to steady herself, unable to see very well through the veiling that covered her eyes like an awning, and she dropped her gloves when the bus turned corners, right onto the taut laps of tired shoppers. When she went to pick up her gloves, she banged the people standing behind her with her clutch purse. She felt too tall in her shoes, too close to the ceiling. The bus rolled and pitched like a ship, and Delia thought of her nine-year-old immigrant mother (who she imagined came to America in braids and a starched white apron), determined to plant herself in the new country like a sturdy little tree, prepared to walk through the Valley of Death the nuns were always warning Delia about, that perilous stretch of childbirth, for Delia and her two brothers. Mae said she wasn't seasick a bit, unlike the others, and there was an impertinence to the nine-year-old Mae that Delia admired, a spunkiness that made Delia feel like a sissy, somehow resenting her own cushioned early life, the child Mae somehow a tougher, better Delia. Sometimes the debt Delia owed to the young Mae seemed too great to repay, and Delia resented her, dreaming she had grabbed one of her mother's childhood braids and had strangled her.

As the bus approached the bridge into New York, in front of Feinstein's Bridal Wear, Patty threw up in her pink velvet hat, and three seats opened up to them.

They got off the bus on Fifth Avenue, across the street from St. Patrick's, Delia holding Patty's hat closed in a neat bundle. She dropped it into the first trash can they passed, along with Patty's soiled gloves. The biting wind made Delia's net veil stick to her eyelashes, so heavily mascaraed that her eyes stayed painfully open. She pulled the veil off her head, and as she shoved it in her purse, she noticed that Patty's bare fingers were bright red with the cold, her reddish hair stuck to her forehead in straggling bangs, her face ghastly pale. Delia took off one of her own long gloves and pushed it onto Patty's hand, rolling the top into a cuff and turning it over on itself. The one beige glove on Patty's hand made her look stunted, like a midget; Delia's bare hand and lower arm were freezing.

"Put your hands in your pockets, Patty," Delia said, in a patient tone she didn't feel.

"But I have no pockets," Patty whined, pulling on the satin flaps of her powder-blue coat. Not believing her (she had warned Patty so many times about ruining the shape of her coat) now Delia tugged on the flaps, the bits of blue satin material like blanket edging, but Patty was right, so Delia gave her the other glove too and angrily watched the child study her own reflection in the glass storefront behind them. Patty rested her index finger on her cheek, the fingers of the glove long and wilted and funny-looking, and cupped her elbow in her palm like a woman in a soap commercial.

"Patty!" Delia shouted, with no feeling in her blanched fingers. "Stop playing with the goddamn gloves!"

"Oh, my God," Maureen whispered dramatically, standing as wooden as a marionette. "I have only one garter left on my right leg!" and then she began to cry.

"What?" Delia asked, angered some more by Maureen's reddening eyes and running nose. "Where's the other one?"

"It popped open," she sobbed, her hands pressing on the hem of her coat.

"Oh, for Christ's sake!" Delia grabbed both the girls' hands and dragged them across the avenue and into an empty corner of St. Pat's. They hid behind a pillar; Delia knelt down, soiling her coat, to hook Maureen's garter back in place, a few tourists looking in at them, cameras banging against the pews. "If they take a picture of me like this"— Maureen shut her eyes —"I'll just die!"

"Oh, nobody is taking a picture of you at all. Come on now. I don't want to make Daddy wait," Delia said, and they dashed back across the avenue.

She left the church thinking that she should have combed her hair, but St. Pat's didn't seem to be the place for it. Only underwear in an emergency, she thought, laughing to herself. They walked quickly to the skating rink to meet Maurice, but he wasn't there yet. Delia was uneasy; he was twenty minutes late.

Not that I'm not used to it, she thought, he's always late, but today she had no money in her wallet, not even enough to get them back home, only a few nickels in the bottom of her purse. She had asked him for money before he left the house that morning, but he claimed he didn't have a cent to spare.

"What the hell are you so worried about?" he had asked. "I'll have money when I meet you. All you gotta do is get into New York, and I'll take care of the rest."

"I just get nervous going out with nothing," she had said, on her toes to search the top of the refrigerator for coins she had stashed in a small jar, but the jar was empty.

"I borrowed that already." Maurice smiled sheepishly. "Look, why don't you just borrow a few bucks from Mae? I'll see you later," and then he was gone. She shook her head; it wasn't fair, not including her mother and then asking her for money. Delia couldn't do it.

Her legs ached with the cold, and her nose was running, and she knew, with her face so stiff, that her cheeks and chin were red. Free from the veil, her hair blew over her eyes and was flat as a board from the hot bus and then the icy wind. She took a small brush from her purse and ran it through her hair and then Patty's. Patty was slumped into Delia's belly; she had had to push the child away to look into her face.

"Patty, are you okay?" she asked. God, what would she do, without a cent, if the child was really sick?

"My stomach hurts again," she said sadly.

"Well, maybe you need to eat something. As soon as Daddy gets here, we'll go and buy you a pretzel and a drink. Would you like that?"

Momentarily satisfied, Patty nodded.

Delia looked into her compact and put on fresh pinkish-white lipstick. Her Elizabeth Taylor eyebrows had faded; only her own thin tan ones were left. She powdered her red cheeks and tried to tuck her hair behind her ears. Leaning on the railing behind her, the skaters twirling merrily below, she arched her back and pushed her pelvis forward like a model in a magazine. He had to be along any second; she at least had to try to look good. Elegantly, she crossed one frozen foot over the other. She had seen pictures of Jackie Kennedy standing like that, the wind blowing her hair, her chin held up. She wanted Maurice to remember how she looked today, eyebrows or not, but Patty kept tucking herself between Delia and the fence, holding her stomach, sheltered from the wind.

Just a few more minutes, Delia said to herself when her face began to lose feeling, the wind bringing tears to her eyes. Maureen pretended to watch the skaters, biting down hard on her bluish lips. Delia strained to see Maurice's powerful dark head, his habit of bursting through crowds like an actor jumping through the curtains on a stage, but he was nowhere to be seen, so she gave up posing and tucked her chin down into her thin collar and watched every single pair of passing shoes.

Maurice was already an hour late.

Damn, Maureen thought, freezing with the cold, he's got to be dead.

There'd be a funeral Mass for him at St. Immaculata's, and all the kids in her class would have to come, just as she had had to go to the Mass for Mr. Cullen, Dorothy's father. Maureen had tried to see Dorothy's face as she followed her father's casket down the aisle of the church, as if she were a bride and Maureen was trying to see underneath her veil.

Maureen would have to follow her father's casket in her short spring coat; there'd be no time for a new one now. She looked out onto Fifth Avenue and was ashamed of herself.

Maybe they'd have the Mass over at St. Pat's.

Maureen couldn't imagine that, her father's casket lying there, their cries dwarfed by the soaring height of the place, their sobs falling into the hundreds of nooks and crannies inside, lost forever. She wondered if the other policemen would wear white gloves (just like hers and like Patty's, sitting in the trash can on the corner), if they would line the sidewalk as though there were a parade.

The day after Mr. Cullen's funeral Mass, Dorothy came back to school wearing red nail polish, although she wasn't allowed to, but the nuns didn't seem to notice. Dorothy had folded her hands across the tops of her brown-paper-covered books, as if she had become someone else entirely.

That must be what happens when people die, Maureen thought. The people left behind had a sort of new start. The incense at Mr. Cullen's funeral had smelled like black pepper and made Maureen's eyes burn and tear, and for weeks, every time Dorothy went up to the blackboard, the smell of black pepper had followed her. Maureen had tried to move as far away from Dorothy Cullen as she could, searching her own desk for a scattering of tiny black specks. She was happy to see Dorothy leave class early on Tuesday afternoons for her piano lesson.

Maureen looked out to the avenue and watched the horses pull hansom cabs along the street. No book did justice to a horse, she thought, trying to distract herself. They always seemed so much bigger than they were supposed to, looking as though they could barely support their weight on those skinny legs. Some of them appeared impatient, throwing back their strong heads as if angry, and some of the others looked drugged, their breath mixing with the clouds of exhaust from the backs of buses.

If there were animals in heaven, Maureen knew they'd be horses, their manes flowing behind them like the long white hair of God.

In heaven, the horses couldn't hurt anyone, but here on Fifth Avenue, if a man with drink in him fell in front of a horse, he might split his skull.

She looked over at her sister Patty, standing by herself now, not saying a word to Maureen or to Delia, who kept pushing her hair down or touching her pale and angry face. Delia had paid a lot of money for Patty's hat, walking back and forth in the millinery aisle of Feldman's Department Store, trying to talk herself out of spending so much on such a luxury, but in the end, Delia had seen how Patty looked in one of the rounded mirrors on top of a hat-covered table, turning the pink hat this way and that, as if Patty just couldn't wear a hat straight on her head the way Maureen did. Her grandmother had yelled at Delia. Did she think her name was Rockefeller, Mae had asked her, with a nasty sneer, although she had reached into her own wallet to lend Delia ten dollars until payday, complaining all the while about her own small pension check. "Put a beggar on horseback," Mae had said (too loudly for Maureen) when the saleslady handed Delia the hatbox, "and watch him ride to hell."

She wondered if there were beggars in heaven and if her father was there yet.

There was nothing she could do but watch her mother chew on her pale bottom lip and look desperately through the crowd. He was nearly two hours late now. Maureen wanted to ask Delia if they could go down to the Automat anyway, but she didn't dare. When Delia was worried about Maurice, any wrong word could make her blow up and start screaming. She hoped they wouldn't fight, if her father did show up and was still alive. She hated it when they argued. Sometimes it seemed to Maureen as if her mother was not very loyal to her father. She often told Mae on the telephone that Maurice was always short of money, claiming he had lent it to some other cops at work or to one of his friends in a bar somewhere, or simply that he had lost it or Hans, when he'd had the store, had given him the wrong change, or maybe it was that Cohen, stiffing him in the candy store. "People are always giving Maurice the wrong change," Delia had said sarcastically to Mae. "'How do you know who gives you the wrong change,' I asked him, 'when you're usually too drunk to count it?'"

Maureen, sitting at the table doing homework, had shut her eyes against the triumph in Delia's voice.

If Maurice didn't have any money, then Maureen believed that somebody had taken it, or somebody *had* given him the wrong change. She had seen him often enough standing between barstools with a pile of wet dollars and shiny wet coins in front of him. It would be easy for a stranger's arm to just reach around him and steal everything her father had.

She wished that her mother would believe him and that he would just come along, that she could have a regular father like Joannie Malloney did, a man who came home on time and met them on time and could be depended on. And one who wasn't dead.

Delia was about ready to stop waiting; Maureen could see it. Her worry over her husband was turning to rage. While Maureen stared at her, she crossed and uncrossed her arms over her chest, swinging her tight fists near the girls' heads. The cold breeze was pulling Maureen's stiff crinoline slip away from the soft flesh of her legs. She wished she could look down at the windowpane checks that she knew the crinoline had made on her thighs and just scratch them; then she'd feel better. She wished she were wearing her flannel pajamas. Joannie Malloney's birthday party was tomorrow; she'd have to wear the same dress and this same hard slip again. She tried to concentrate on the Automat. There was no way to get out of the party; it was useless to try. Delia would never let her stay home, not when Patty liked to go and all the neighborhood girls would be there, standing stiffly in the Malloney living room, pink streamers and pink balloons everywhere, the whole room suddenly unfamiliar and not at all the same apartment Maureen could see so clearly from her bedroom window across the court as she polished her shoes night after night, staring into the Malloneys'. (At one time or another, she had seen all of them in their underwear.)

She had seen Billy and Tommy fighting, their arms and legs bobbing up and down above the windowsill and their mother, Sally, ignoring them, sitting on a kitchen chair ironing shirts and watching television, or ironing shirts and chewing on her fingernails, or ironing shirts and eating something that looked like a cupcake from a saucer on the ironing board. Delia would never have done that.

The Malloneys never pulled down their shades and they seemed to have no secrets and they laughed a lot, throwing things at each other across the living room. Maureen had borrowed Tommy's geography book once and had found an English composition tucked inside, all about their summer trip to Cape Cod, and it had made Maureen want to cry. One night when Maureen was supposed to be sleeping, she had peeked out her bedroom blinds just in time to see Bill Malloney, in his khaki jacket, hold his hand out to Sally, who was ironing in her pajamas, and just like in the movies, she had seen them dance gracefully across the messy living room floor. She had never seen her parents do that. She wondered if they ever had.

Sally Malloney was different from Delia. She didn't mind too much about mess. At Joannie's parties, the girls got down on the rug, heated and flushed, and pushed marbles with their noses from one end of the room to the other, for prizes that Joannie usually won, for she was bigger and stronger than the others. Sally made her put them down — they were for her *guests*, she explained, every year the same words. Maureen liked the pink balloons and the streamers and the dolls propped up on the couch like company, looking practically brand-new. Sometimes Joannie gave them their presents back a day or two later (she always wanted a new football), and the girls who were asked to Joannie's parties knew they were possibly shopping for themselves and convinced their mothers that Joannie had specifically asked for Young Miss makeup kits or red, white, and blue strands of pop pearls.

It was in between the games that Maureen hated Joannie's parties, when she remembered that Maurice was supposed to be home by now and how mad her mother was bound to be if he wasn't. And then, during the games — which weren't fun if Maureen thought of Maurice — she would move herself again and again over to the Malloneys' living room window, peering out from underneath her blindfold with the donkey's tail in her hand, trying to see over into her own kitchen, where her father might be asleep with his head down on the kitchen table, the curtains open wide for everyone to see the can of beer or the whiskey bottle in front of him. Maureen groped her way over to the window and pretended to be lost and confused, without anybody knowing where she was actually looking; they hooted and screamed with laughter at her stupidity — how could anyone have such a terrible sense of direction? — and she played along with them so that they'd laugh even harder, and she pinned the donkey's tail to the Malloneys' open drapes, Joannie laughing so hard she rolled across the floor in her light-blue party dress.

She was a good actress during pin the tail on the donkey. It was her only chance to see how things were at home.

But if she somehow hadn't had her turn, and the game was over quickly, and Sally saw her standing by the window when they were having ice cream and cake, she led her gently by the elbow back to the others at the table, wondering softly what the matter was, wasn't she having a nice time?

Maureen couldn't tell her that her own kitchen window, black and shiny in the crisp December air — or, worse, lit up and bare — kept calling her name, that she was compelled to look over at it, it was so empty and foreboding and bleak.

FIFTEEN

Come on, girls, we've got to go. We can't wait here all day long. We've waited too long already." Delia started to walk away. "I don't know where your father could be."

"But where," Maureen asked, "where will we go?"

"Well, I don't have enough money to get us back home, and I don't even have money to get us something warm to drink, but I think that your uncle Gerald is on days now. Your grandma told me he's down at Herald Square. We'll have to walk down there and see if he can lend us money to go home." She was aware of a panic rising inside her, a fearful thickness to her tongue, her breathing so labored she was beginning to sweat, despite the cold, worried that she might lose the baby. At the corner, she stood perfectly still to see if she was having any sort of pains. I never worried about losing the others, she thought. The girls were staring at every man who passed, and she remembered Patty once standing up in the A & P and yelling "Daddy!" at one of the stockboys.

She was growing tired of always worrying about Maurice, of the chances of his falling on the subway tracks, in front of a train; how simple it would be, if he was unsteady on his feet, to be pushed. There was always the fear of the gun: when he drank he was careless, and when he didn't drink, he sometimes got the shakes, but Delia tried hard to discount all that and concentrate on things that were pleasant. It was especially important right now, with the new baby, to hold her stomach muscles in, to move carefully, to treat her own body tenderly. This pregnancy meant so much to her, almost more than the others, she admitted to herself.

Her life needed more of something — she didn't know what — and much less of Maurice. She had to telephone the neighborhood bars when she couldn't stand it anymore. "Is Maurice Delaney at the bar, please?" she'd ask of strangers, the background noise deafening, and then she'd have to ask for him again, but they never seemed to get his name right and she'd have to repeat it, again and again, until it was a ridiculous name, and they never seemed to be quite sure who he was anyway, and Delia could barely stand the agonizing minutes she spent holding on while they polled the place.

If he wasn't there, she hung up calmly as if nothing were wrong, telling the children, hovering in the doorway, to go back to bed, but the minute she thought they were asleep, she ran up to the roof to watch for him, just as her mother had done for her father, tearing at her hair, nearly sobbing in her fear until she finally saw him turning the corner. While he walked unsteadily up the block, her grief was turning into a rock-hard anger, her heart beating so erratically that she'd have to sit down hard on the tar, afraid to move, a sickly-sweet taste in her mouth, unable to trust her wobbly legs. She was afraid of the dark, and yet she was unable to move, the shadows flitting around her, strange shapes, eerie noises. She thought she might have a heart attack, and thought of the people Mae was always telling her about, fine one minute and then gone the next, never sick a day in their lives.

Her new baby was depending on her old heart, she thought as she put one frozen foot in front of the other, and she had to take care of it. "Just think," Delia said, turning back to look at her daughters, trying to force herself to smile, "tomorrow's Joannie Malloney's birthday party." At the moment, it was all she had to give them, something to look forward to, and it worked, at least for Patty, who began to perk up, skipping ahead of them on the sidewalk. (Patty had helped her choose Joannie's gift, grown-up earrings, which Patty swore Joannie collected, though Delia had her doubts.)

Maureen had no reaction to the party at all, just stared straight ahead. It must be that she's getting older, Delia thought. She wondered how Sally did it, the wonderful parties for so many girls in her small apartment. Every year Delia looked over at the Malloneys' living room and watched the pastel blur of party dresses whirl past the window. She tried to spot one of her girls, but all the dresses looked alike, pink or blue or yellow, and it was hard to tell them apart. It was always a bad time for Delia, Christmastime, with Maurice and the drink. She worried about him so much on the day of the party, it being so close to Christmas Day. What a terrible thing it would be if he never came home at all. When she shut the door behind Maureen and Patty, on their way to Joannie's house, she always envied them their peace of mind. She could barely remember being young.

As they began to walk down the subway stairs to the Herald Square station, Delia was practically knocked over by the smell of flowers from the florist's shop near the token booth. She was starting to have the feeling back in her hands. She leaned against the black iron gate that was split in the middle and drawn back against the florist's window like a curtain. The flowers were too big, as if they had been bred to grow despite the dirt and the darkness with special vitamins, but then Delia noticed that everything seemed bigger down below the street. The chocolate candies in some windows were as big as her fist, and the chocolate chip cookies she couldn't buy for Patty to eat were nearly as big as tires.

Maureen seemed to be miles behind Delia and Patty, barely able to walk in her heels, shuffling past the dreary men who loitered against the walls, slipping in the dirt and grit underneath her feet. Delia found that she was growing angry with Maureen, who was having such trouble with her clothes: the garters popping open and the stockings falling down and the brassiere riding up around her neck and her ankles twisting over in her whittled-looking shoes. Maureen always looked haphazard these days, as if her clothes had been beating her. It bothered Delia that her daughter hadn't even begun to menstruate, as if she were holding back on purpose. Holding on to the florist's gate to wait for Maureen, Delia ran the sole of her tingling foot across the stiff back of her shoe. The cold metal under her fingers made her think of the missing Maurice and his gun, and she let go and shut her eyes. "For God's sake, Maureen," Delia shouted, "do you have to walk around like some little old lady? My shoes hurt me too, you know, and I have no idea where your father is! Now if you could just hurry up a little bit, maybe we could get ahold of Gerald so's we can get home." Her face had begun to tingle, and so had her scalp.

"But, Ma." Maureen took her shoes off and stepped right into the dirt on the concrete floor of the subway passage.

"Never mind your 'But, Ma,'" Delia said, starting to feel sick to her stomach, asking herself what else could go wrong. "Put your shoes back on; you'll get some kind of disease, doing that with your stocking feet. You both stay right here; I'm going to phone Grandma. Maybe she heard something from Daddy." She walked to a telephone booth and sat down on the bench and immediately felt a wet spot spreading beneath her coat. *Damn*, she thought, standing up to feel a sticky substance hardening across her seat. Now she'd have to buy herself another coat, and she certainly couldn't afford *that*, unless she somehow came across some large sum of money, like life insurance. No, she thought, dialing Mae's number, stop it. She couldn't understand how she could be so contrary, worrying about Maurice half the time and, the other half, just wanting him gone away.

The phone rang once. "Delia?" Mae answered, as if she were the only one who ever called the house. Somebody else had to call Mae from time to time, Delia thought; how else would she find out about all those heart attacks?

"Ma, did Maurice ever call you?" Delia asked.

"No. Why would he? Where are you?"

"At the subway down at Herald Square."

"Are the children okay?"

"Yes, they're fine. It's just that Maurice never met us. We waited over two hours, and he never showed up. Ma, Gerald is working down at this station today, isn't he?"

"I think he is, Delia. Yes, he said that this morning—Herald Square. You're lucky he's workin' days today. Do you need money—is that why you're askin' me about your brother?"

"Yeah, sort of." Delia wondered how Mae knew.

"Delia Mary, now you listen to me," Mae said sternly. "Get some money from your brother, and then you stop into one of those stands and get the girls something to tide them over, and then come straight home, to me, and I'll have your supper on the table, all ready for you. That rummy didn't show up, did he? Well, plenty's the time your father did that to us, don't you remember? Don't be worryin' about him. God protects them, Delia Mary, the rummies and the fools. Just

148

think about it — Maurice is both, so he's twice as safe. Why are you so quiet? Tell me, Delia, are you sick?"

Yes, Delia thought, sick and pregnant. The thought of what might be drying on her coat made her shudder.

"I'm just worried about him, Ma, that's all. He told me he'd be at Rockefeller Center. He knew I had no money. Something might have happened to him; he's got his whole paycheck. He knew how excited the girls were to meet him and go shopping. If something's happened to him . . ."

"Your father knew we were waiting for him, time and time again, but it never stopped him. You know what I always say about 'if': if your aunt had testicles, she'd be your uncle! Now what else is wrong? Don't be tellin' me it's nothin'. I can tell."

"Oh, Ma, it's just I'm scared."

"Delia Mary, you've nothin' to be scared of. Your brother is there for you. As long as one of us is alive, you've no reason to be afraid. Now you do as I say and go down to your brother."

From the top of the stairs, Delia stared down at her brother Gerald, who was losing his hair in a perfect circle around the crown. Eugene was right; he always claimed Gerald still looked like a monk, or a priest, the way he was sitting there, a paperback book open in his hands like a missal, a white woolen scarf hanging around his neck like an alb.

Delia wondered what it might have been like if he had gone through with it, how it might have been to kneel before him in the confessional and get absolution, what it might have been like to smell his aftershave through the dusty screen of that box. They had had such hopes for Gerald, as if he might redeem them all.

"Delia." Gerald looked up, turning his book over on the counter, folding his hands across the title. "What're *you* doing here? Where's the kids?"

"We were supposed to meet Maurice," Delia said wearily, running her hand over the little worn bowl where the tokens and the money were exchanged. She tried to peek down and see what he had been reading. "The girls are back there." She nodded her head toward the staircase, where they were sitting. "He never showed up, Gerald,

149

and I'm worried sick. I don't know how I'm going to get the girls home. I don't have a cent." People were lining up behind Delia. A woman in a fur coat pressed against her back.

"Ah, Delia, c'mon, you know he's okay!" Gerald seemed to be in much better spirits than Delia could ever remember. He stood up eagerly and reached into the pockets of his brown pants, tossing his book into a drawer. "Everyone knows it when something happens to a cop. How much you need, De? Ten? Twenty?"

"Five, Gerald. Five dollars is fine." She thought she might throw up. Dear God, she prayed, just get us home.

"Come on. Take ten. Here's a few tokens. You know Maurice — probably bending the elbow somewhere. Holiday spirit and all that stuff. Keep worrying and you'll turn into Ma, God help us all." He smiled down at her, one of his front teeth discolored.

She wondered if he was still seeing that girl from the bakery, that Berni. Mae complained that he came home with cheap lipstick all over his white shirts. "I hate to take that much money." Delia fluttered the bill nervously. The woman in the fur coat coughed and tapped her foot.

"Never mind about running the kids home right away, Delia. Take them for an ice cream soda, why don't you?" He waved at the girls. "You gotta go, De," he whispered. "The line's building."

"Thanks," Delia said, pushing her fingers inside the bowl and wiggling them. Gerald tapped her hand. "See you home," she said, turning to give the woman in the fur coat a nasty look.

When the girls were little more than babies, Gerald climbed to the roof of the apartment building on Christmas Eve and ran, stamped, and jumped right on top of the Delaneys' apartment, making neighing sounds and plenty of ho-ho-hos, and then he "just happened" to drop in on them while they were trimming the tree, listening with feigned astonishment when the girls hurled themselves into his lap, chattering excitedly about Santa, right upstairs, over their heads. Some Christmas Eves, thanks to "Santa," they never slept at all and the next day fell sound asleep in church, but Delia never had the heart to ask Gerald to stop.

Waiting for the train, Delia thought about Maurice again, and grew tired of her own obsessional ruminations. She sat down on an empty bench, a blast of sandy air making her eyes tear. A train roared down the center tracks, tearing past the pillars so that the passengers seemed to move with the same foolish, jerky motions of actors in silent films. Her eyes hurt to look at them, her stomach suddenly sicker than it had felt before. She convinced herself that she needed to eat, like Patty, forgetting all about the cookies and the chocolate upstairs. Patty sat down next to her, leaning her head on Delia's shoulder, and the pressure made her feel worse.

"Patty, don't lay on me, please. C'mon, sit up like a big girl, okay?" Delia shoved her away. Patty slumped on Maureen instead. Maureen ignored her.

Maybe he was run over, like his father, by a bus.

The train blew into the station, stirring up the stale air, which reeked somehow of urine and vanilla extract. She sat on the train, holding her stomach, trying not to upset the children, thinking about the black dresses she would need for the three days of the wake and the funeral Mass.

By the time they had reached their stop, Delia had herself so upset she staggered out the door and threw up into a trash can.

"Oh, why does everybody keep *doing* this!" Maureen cried, digging in her purse for a tissue.

"Are you sick, Ma?" Patty grabbed onto her arm. "You threw up like me."

"I'm okay, girls. I'm okay now. Relax." Delia put the back of her hand to her mouth. She felt a little better.

"What happened, Mom? How come you didn't say you didn't feel good?" Maureen asked, close to tears.

"I thought I'd start to feel okay, that's why. I didn't want you to get worried about me too. I'm not sick. I think I'm pregnant. Sometimes pregnant women throw up," she said bluntly. It wasn't what she had planned, telling them like that, by herself, before she had even told Maurice, but what did it matter anyway?

"When?" Maureen asked, pursing her lips as if she were blowing out a candle.

"In the summer. I think around August. We'll have to see what the doctor says." She sat down for a minute before venturing out onto the street.

"Maybe it's gonna be a boy." Patty grinned. "Does Daddy know?"

"I was going to tell him when we saw him today."

"Will he be surprised?" Patty asked. "Can I tell him?"

"Well, we'll see. I guess he'll be surprised."

If we ever see him again, Delia thought.

They went straight upstairs and not to Mae's. Delia felt weak and tired, and she wanted to lie down. She called Mae. "We're home, Mama. We won't be downstairs tonight. The kids are frozen stiff. I'm going to make them take baths and go to bed. Did Maurice ever call?"

"Not a word. I been keepin' you some soup."

"They'll have cereal or something. I don't feel good myself. I just have to wait and see what happened to Maurice." A strange calmness fell over her, as if she were somehow prepared to accept his fate. It was the uncertainty that was so hard to deal with, the waiting and the not knowing.

"Well, it's no wonder you don't feel good, out there this whole bitter day in the cold. That rummy you married," Mae fumed.

"It wasn't the cold so much. . . . Ma, I'm pregnant."

"Sacred Heart, no!" Mae cried out.

"That's a fine way to wish me luck," Delia said miserably.

"Well, that's a fine way you're tellin' me, isn't it? Of course I wish you luck. What else would I be wishin' my own daughter? Go and lie down, Delia, and rest yourself. You know what I always say: Bad news travels fast."

Not fast enough, she thought.

The girls sat at the table after their baths and ate cornflakes.

Delia didn't bother calling any bars: as far as she knew, Maurice was still in the city, and she wouldn't even know where to begin. While waiting for the kettle to boil for tea, she looked over at the Malloneys' apartment, across the black courtyard, watching Sally hang pink streamers from the ceilings and blow up pink balloons, carrying dolls into the living room underneath her arms like footballs, setting them up on the couch.

It was so depressing to watch perky Sally that Delia stared at the night sky until the kettle nearly flew off the stove. She let the tea steep and sent the girls to bed, listening to their beds roll back and forth on the bare wooden floor, and she remembered what it had been like to fall asleep waiting for footsteps. She put herself on the couch and instantly fell asleep.

Around midnight, the downstairs buzzer rang, a scratchy sound like radio static. The small foyer of their apartment echoed with the sound, it was that empty (Delia had never figured out what to do with it, white walls and a dumbwaiter that she hated to think about), and she was disoriented; the buzzer seemed to sound inside her teeth. She jumped up from the couch and clung to the wall and, after a few seconds, made her way slowly to the door. She opened it, keeping the chain on, and rested her forehead against the cold metal. Hearing muffled voices, she stared out at the tiny black and white tiles on the floor near the landing. If it were daylight, a rectangle of white light would be falling in front of her door, down through the skylight mounted on the roof, resting on the tiles like a crooked rug. Footsteps on the stairs: cops and the chaplain, she was sure of it. "Who's there?" she called out. She heard other doors opening on the landing and quickly shut the door for a few seconds, standing perfectly still, scarcely daring to breathe.

She saw Danny Kowalski's head first, the rusty-colored hair and a gray jacket she seemed to recognize from years before, and for a minute she thought he was dragging a piece of furniture up the stairs, but the furniture turned out to be Maurice, his arms hanging limply at his sides, his head bobbing up and down on his chest. Danny had one arm around Maurice's back and one arm across his chest. In the middle of the staircase, Maurice stopped dead and leaned backward over the railing.

"Whoa!" Danny sang out. "Sum bitch gonna fall on me!"

"Shit," Maurice growled, lurching against the staircase wall. "Not gon' fall anywhere," and he grabbed for the banister.

He was alive! Delia felt dizzy with relief. Now, she prayed, just let me get him inside, where nobody can see him.

They climbed the last few steps, and Delia saw that Danny was nearly as drunk as Maurice. His eyes weren't focusing very well, and his hair was slicked back from his face, showing the pink skin of his face like meat done rare; the collar of his woolen coat was stained dark. Inches from the last step, right in front of her, they almost fell down together.

"Special delivery, lady!" Danny laughed. "Where you want him?" She stepped out barefoot into the hallway and grabbed Maurice by the elbow and pulled him inside. Behind Danny, who stood swaying on the landing, people were double-locking their doors for the night. (Disappointed that it was only Maurice, Delia thought, they went off to bed.)

"Hey, Della?" Maurice asked, suddenly coming to, trying to stand up straight, weaving from side to side. His forehead was cut, a scrape the size of a quarter, a scratch branching across the side of his nose. "I love you, Della," he said, and she thought of herself as someone else entirely, Della, with a tight red dress drawn against her new expanding belly, teetering on blood-red high heels. "Let's try for the couch, Danny," she said, and they started into the room but made it only as far as one of the two chairs. Maurice fell into it; his head bounced back and hit the wall. Maurice had something stiff spilled across the front of his jacket. There were stains everywhere she had looked to-day—her own coat, Maurice's, Danny's—and she and Patty had thrown up, hardly usual events: Delia hadn't been sick at all with the second pregnancy, and Patty wasn't prone to car sickness.

"Ouch," Danny said, hearing the crack of Maurice's head on the wall. He grinned, looking like a carved Halloween pumpkin. "You want me to take his clothes off and get him into bed?" Danny asked, a goofy smile on his red face. Delia stared at Maurice. There was a bulge in his jacket. Good God, she thought, his gun.

"No, no, Danny, he'll be fine. I can take care of him, don't worry." She stared at the door, willing him to leave.

"I never seen anything like it," Danny said, taking his hand-kerchief from his pocket and waving it in the air like a magician. "I leave the post office, I'm stoppin' into the bar on the corner for a Christmas drink with a couple of pals, and then right next to me, who do I see standing there but Maurice, havin' a beer, and the next thing I know, it's dark outside and bang, he's on the floor, passed out."

"I know, Danny," she said, dimly aware that she was not wanting to hear what he was saying. "But don't worry, he'll be fine." She was glad Danny was drunk — she didn't have to make sense. She kept her hand on Maurice's shoulder, trying to feel the bulge in his jacket. "Thank you very much for bringing him home."

Danny's brown eyes filled with tears. Oh, no, she thought.

"'Thank you'? Like I'm a stranger or something?"

"No, no," she said. "I didn't mean that."

"He's my best friend, Delia!" he cried passionately. "Always was, always will be."

"Oh, of course, Danny, I know that."

"Me and him and you and Rosie. Funny, huh, how it all turned out?" He lurched toward the empty chair. Delia didn't move. She heard one of the girls get up and go into the bathroom. "Shit," Maurice moaned, turning his head from side to side. "Shit, shit, shit."

Delia and Danny stared at him. "You want me to get him un-dressed for you?" Danny repeated. He made wide circles with his scruffy hands, not knowing quite what to do.

"No, no, Danny, it's late. You go on home. I can take care of him, don't worry." I've been doing it long enough, she thought. Danny looked longingly at the chair.

"You sure now?" he asked.

"Sure I'm sure." She tried to smile. "You go ahead."

"Geez, he's like a brother to me, you know? I forgot the way we used to be, until tonight. He's just like a brother, just like you — a sister. I mean. . . . Jesus, from when we were both this big!" He slapped his knee. "From this big," he said again. "You know he had no brothers or sisters," he said sadly, shaking his head.

"Oh, I know." She shook her head along with him. Maurice began to snore loudly. "You go ahead, Danny," Delia said, her hand on his arm. "You want me to call Rosaleen and tell her you're on the way? In case she's worried about you?"

"Would ya?" he asked gratefully. "Tell her I'm on the way, so I don't catch hell." He grinned.

Catch hell? she asked herself. Rosaleen?

"Sure I will. Thanks, Danny."

"You're sure?" he asked again, for no reason she could think of.

"Oh, positive," she answered, for no reason either.

Maurice began to moan.

"Okay, okay." Danny turned to leave, Delia trying to stifle a sigh of relief. "Well, g'd-bye, then."

"Go ahead." Delia steered him to the door, her hand on his back. "I'll call her in a few minutes."

"She's a wunnerful girl, that Rosie, y'know?" he asked, turning to lean on the doorframe. "A wunnerful girl." He sighed deeply.

Delia forced herself to smile. "Oh, I know that." She began to open the door, forcing him to move. "Go ahead now; Rosaleen'll be waiting up for you. Go ahead home to her."

"Yeah, you're right, y'know? She is a wunnerful girl," he said, as if Delia had mentioned it. "Waits for me, you know? Like you for Maurice. Poor bastard," he said, looking past her shoulder into the living room.

"I know, Dan, thanks. Good-bye."

"You're sure now?"

"Good night, Dan."

He kissed the top of her head and was gone.

She locked the door, put on the chain, and waited for a tremendous noise, Danny falling down the stairs, but the hallway was quiet.

After a few minutes, she went to Maurice and opened his jacket. It struck her as just so sad, his body trying to save itself, shutting down like that with too much alcohol. She could have cried, not for Maurice, but for his body, wanting so much to live. It reminded her somehow of a picture she had seen in one of her magazines, flowers and tufts of grass springing up on the grounds of a concentration camp. Maurice slapped at her hands. "Get lost," he spit out at her. Carefully, she plucked at the front of his shirt. It wasn't a gun bulging from underneath his jacket; it was a tall beer glass. She pulled the glass out carefully and stood it on the end table. His jacket was full of beer and so was his shirt. The smell of so much of it made her breathless.

But he was home, she told herself, and he was safe, and for now nothing else mattered.

"*Son of a bitch!*" he screamed, his eyes shut.

"Maurice, it's me. Sit up!" She tried to pull him forward, so he'd lean on his knees. She slid his arms from his jacket and threw it on the floor, not letting go of him, scared he'd fall on his face. She began to unbutton his wet shirt. "Come on, Maurice, you got to sit up. I've got to get off your shirt," but he fell asleep again and resumed snoring. She took off his shirt, his head against the chair, sound asleep. She was afraid he might sprain his neck; she ran inside and got a pillow from her bed, rolled it, and propped it on top of his shoulders. He felt cold and clammy: she ran back inside, pulling the blanket from their bed to cover him. She knelt down on the floor to take his shoes off. He must have stepped in a puddle, she realized; his socks were soaked, and his toes were icy and bluish. She rubbed his toes to get his circulation going: a friend of Denis's fell asleep in a snowstorm and lost his whole foot from frostbite. Maurice kicked at her. "Maurice, stop it," she said sternly. "I've got to get these wet socks off you."

"Ter-*ence*," he screamed. "Will-*yum!*"

She was shocked, sitting back on her heels, looking at him. She had never heard him say his brothers' names. "Such beautiful children," Kathleen Delaney had told her, "heads full of curls," and she had often wondered how her mother-in-law ever got over such a loss — it seemed too great to imagine.

The tears streamed down his face and into his open mouth.

"It's okay," she said huskily, drying his face with the hem of her nightgown, her own eyes filling. "It's okay, Maurice."

"What's wrong with Daddy?" Maureen asked from the bedroom doorway. "Why is he crying like that?"

"He's sick, Maureen," she said. It seemed the easiest explanation; she hoped to spare Maureen the knowledge she herself had had as a girl. "That's why he never met us. Danny Kowalski brought him home. He got sick on his way home from work."

"I know. Me and Patty heard you talking to him." Maureen seemed planted in the doorway.

"Yeah, well, you go back to bed, Maureen. Daddy'll be fine." Why couldn't everyone just leave them alone?

"Did you tell him?" Maureen asked suddenly.

"Tell him?" Delia asked. "Tell him what?"

"You know," Maureen said. "About the new baby." Maurice was still crying, silent tears streaming down his face.

"No, Maureen, no," Delia said, exasperated. "I didn't tell him.

For God's sake, will you *please* go to sleep, sweetie?" She had sounded sarcastic, not what she intended.

"Mom?" Patty called out, as Maureen went into the bedroom.

"Jesus Christ, it's o*kay*." Delia tried not to scream. "Daddy's home now, and I want you both to go to sleep! Now I don't want to hear another word, understood?"

He kept kicking the blanket away, but Delia kept wrapping it around him. Going into his dresser, she came out with a pair of warm socks, rolled them onto his feet. Crushed bills from his pockets fell to the floor. He had only a few dollars. She opened the front door and looked out on the landing for the rest of his money, but there was nothing there. Mae would give them money if she had to, or one of the boys. Mae wouldn't let the girls go without warm coats or without a Christmas.

When he seemed to be sleeping soundly, she shut off the light and went to bed. Their bedroom was freezing; she looked at the rumpled sheets and remembered the blanket, outside, on Maurice. Her pink coat was hanging on the door. It seemed so long since she had taken the coat out from underneath the dry cleaners' bag, so careful not to stain it with her makeup, so excited about the baby and the city and meeting Maurice. Taking it down, she folded herself into a neat bundle and slipped under the coat and lay on the bed, but he coughed outside and she jumped up to cover him again and then lay back down. Her eyes sprang open: what if he got up to go to the bathroom and fell on the tile floor and cracked his head? She thought about that for a long while, listening for him until her eyes started to cross. She finally turned over on the icy sheet, pulling her knees up to her chest, saying a decade of Hail Marys. She wasn't so sure a new baby would do anything for Maurice, even if it was a boy.

He cried out again for his brothers in the pitch-dark apartment, and she began to weep for him, for them all, and then she prayed some more to fall asleep. Patty came into her bed, huddling underneath her arm. Delia fell asleep and then woke up, again and again, until nearly daybreak, when a pale light crept through the venetian blinds and seemed to cover her with a soft blanket of gray fleece, and she fell into a sleep that was soft on her back and her legs, a sleep made of felt.

Terence William, she thought, William Terence. Fine names for sons.

Late in the morning, when she and Patty awoke, her coat was balled up on the floor and they were covered with the blanket, tucked neatly under their chins. Maurice's pants hung on the closet door-knob, the door open as if he were looking for a clean shirt. Delia went into the living room, where Maureen was sitting cross-legged in front of the television. "Where's your father?" Delia asked her.

"I'm out here, Delia," he called from the kitchen, before Maureen had a chance to answer.

He had two frying pans heating on the stove and a big bowl of pancake batter next to his elbow, a coffeepot bubbling on the back burner. His hair was sticking up like a row of miniature picket fencing. "Making pancakes." He smiled. "Coffee?"

"Maurice . . ."

"I *know*, Delia," he said. "I'm really sorry. Never, I mean, never happen again. Got outta hand, that's all. I stopped for a drink with Jack Kelly, one drink, I said, that's it, I gotta meet my wife and the kids, I said, you could ask him. I can't stay, I kept saying, then the next thing I know, Danny's coming through the door, and then all of a sudden it's eleven o'clock at night, and the next thing I know, I'm waking up in the living room chair. Strangest goddamn thing I ever saw." He shook his head and shut his eyes.

"We waited and waited for you in the city. You remember I didn't have a cent? I had to go find my brother down at his job, so's we could get home. God almighty, Maurice, it's getting worse and worse. Used to be you were late when I was to meet you, but at least you'd show up. Yesterday I didn't know where the hell you were at all!"

He nodded his head and walked over to her, holding out his arms. "It's over, Delia, swear to Christ. It's over! Never again. I'm just so sorry, sorry a million times over."

"The kids were disappointed," she said accusingly. "They never got the coats they need so bad."

"Maureen didn't seem to be so mad at me when she woke up," he said, looking down at Delia. "She saw me sitting at the table, and she asked me to make some pancakes. Remember when I used to do that every day I had off?" Delia remembered his pancakes. It was the one food Delia could never prepare correctly; her pancakes burned and stuck to the bottom of the frying pan, as if pancakes had a hum to them, a rhythm she couldn't make out, and she flipped one shredded pancake after another into the garbage. Delia couldn't help but smile at Maurice. He scratched at the stubble on his chin. "I swear to God, Delia, no more," he said earnestly. "I'm off it, I promise you, I mean it. Look, I called in sick today. We'll take the kids to Flushing. We'll buy them the new coats at Carter's, and then we'll take them out to lunch, kind of to make up for yesterday. Okay?"

"But do you have any money?" she asked.

A dark look came over his face. "Danny!" he said after a few minutes. "Danny's got my pay. I gave it to him to hold. We'll grab a cab over to his house, and then we'll be off."

"I'm pregnant, Maurice," she said levelly. "At least I think I am," and for a second or two she caught the thrill that ran through his face, just as she had known it would, and then he got hold of himself, his expression reverting to his somber usual one. She thought of the other times when Maurice's face was pure open feeling. After sex. The day she had come back from the hospital after Denis had collapsed and she said to him, "My father's dead." The time she had taken Maureen to the emergency room with a blazing fever; she met him in the lobby and told him that the baby would be fine, an ear infection.

She savored the moments when she had seen the real Maurice.

"No kidding?" he asked. The girls must have been listening from the living room, for they ran into the kitchen and stood with their arms around Delia, giggling.

"Nope," she said, "no kidding. Of course, I didn't go to Mullaney yet, but I just know."

Delia knew very little about the world outside the Heights, but she was an expert at the workings of her own body and the bodies of those she loved, recognizing a fever by the press of her lips to a child's forehead or the brightness of her eyes, and there was a sort of alchemy to it, the aspirin for the fever, lemon and honey for a cough, fish-oil salve for a rash. For Delia, the world was manifested in the rounded bodies of her daughters and herself and the long, strong form of her husband. She was so aware of their bodies that she could feel them if she just shut her eyes, having kissed them all so much that she could taste their flesh.

"Geez," Maurice said, "that's great," and he kissed the three of them and went back to the stove to start his pancakes. Delia ran her hands up and down her daughters' backs. Maurice hugged her shoulder and kissed her again when he leaned over and poured her coffee, and she tried not to be disappointed with his scant reaction. She couldn't show him how she felt; one wrong word and he'd be gone again, for another six or seven hours.

Right after breakfast, in order to be home in time for Joannie's birthday party, they took a taxi to the Kowalski house, Delia and the girls waiting outside for Maurice to get his pay. Rosaleen came to the door and nodded; Delia tried to wave, but Rosaleen was gone, and she sat back, puzzled. The cab was a Checker, and the girls sat on the small fold-down seats in the middle. The back of the car felt too big, like the foyer of their apartment, with its unfilled floor space, and when the taxi left the Kowalskis', it seemed to be flying through the streets, leaving the Delaneys nothing to hold on to but each other.

In Carter's Department Store on Main Street in Flushing, they walked straight through to the coat department, and Maurice picked out two coats for them to try on. He had never gone shopping with them before; the girls laughed with delight. For Maureen, he brought over a woman's red coat with a mink collar, which dragged on the floor (Delia thought of the camel's hair beige coat he used to wear), and then, for Patty, a rose pink, totally unsuitable, in Delia's opinion, but the girls tried them on anyway and hesitated in taking them off, watching their father's face in the triple mirror. Delia shook her head, and when she put the coats back on the rack, he appeared to pout, leaving them to go upstairs and look at the appliances. The girls seemed angry with her when she selected two coats, big and little sister, that fit them, in a sedate-looking, dressed-up navy blue, and while waiting in line to pay, she remembered that she had never called Rosaleen to tell her that Danny was on his way. Perhaps that was why Rosaleen only waved.

In her new navy-blue coat, her old party dress on underneath, Maureen waited at the door for her sister. Patty held the box with Joannie's birthday earrings, waiting for Delia to finish brushing her hair.

Her father was sitting in the living room, looking at the newspaper, and her mother had a chicken baking in the oven, the whole apartment smelling of some spice Delia called rosemary. Maurice had promised them they'd go buy a Christmas tree after the party. It was the first year Maureen had gone to Joannie's party with her father safely at home and her mother not worried about him.

She finally won the prize for pin the tail on the donkey.

SIXTEEN

August, Dr. Vincent F. X. Mullaney told her, sometime in the beginning of the month.

"You're in good company." He'd smiled, standing in the doorway of the examining room, holding her chart. "I read in the morning paper that Jackie Kennedy is expecting again."

On the bus ride home from his office, Delia looked out the window and remembered Jackie's beautiful smocks from her pregnancy with John-John, and her flattering coats (although in her pictures she had always looked so startled, as if she were dreaming of being anyplace else). Delia made a mental note to go shopping for pretty smocks with Mae, and then maybe she'd go over to Hooperman's Notions for matching ribbons for her hair. She sat in the bus seat and tried to look refined, arching her back to improve her posture, wondering where her white cotton gloves could possibly be, wanting to wear them to church, as Jackie did. Delia promised herself to keep her fingernails filed neatly and to add all the r's and g's to the ends of her words, and when she went to Dr. Mullaney for her checkups, she'd wear a new full slip with delicate modest embroidery across her bosom, as Mae called it.

Maurice, thinking he was amusing, called Dr. Mullaney "Vinnie the Thumb," as if he were some kind of gangster. Delia would make him stop that. She wanted more dignity in her life. Bad enough that he disgraced them all with the drink—although things might change: she was back to thinking that the new baby might be a beginning for all of them. Wasn't she much wiser now than she had ever been before? Maybe Maurice would just stop drinking. It happens, she told herself, as the bus neared her corner. She had walked through the tail end of stories, hearing ". . . and then I never touched another drop," although it was usually someone else who made that promise so urgent — the dying mother who recovered, the sickly child who was suddenly cured. Some near tragedy always spurred the sobriety, and it frightened Delia to think that was what it might take, a huge price, like a prayer to Saint Jude.

Standing up as the bus approached her stop, she practiced crossing her legs demurely at the ankle, trying to look startled herself and shy.

"President Kennedy," Maurice said, half a grin on his face, "is a nincompoop. An Irish donkey nincompoop harp," and then he looked over at Mae, who began and ended her day with a decade of the rosary devoted to the President's well-being.

The Delaneys were sitting in the Rooney living room on Sunday afternoon after Mass, eating bologna and liverwurst sandwiches and watching television, when the President's handsome face flashed across the screen. Delia had the newspaper open on her rapidly diminishing lap, studying an ad for baby clothes. She didn't hear what Maurice was saying, at least not at first, only that he had sounded exactly like Denis.

Delia could still see him, sitting in front of the television set, his cigarette stubs in the big white Copacabana ashtray and his can of beer in front of him. Toward the end of his life he bathed infrequently, and Mae told Delia that when he came to bed, he smelled like a goat. Delia could see for herself the grayish cast his skin took on, and when she passed him, she distinctly smelled his hair.

He argued with the newscasters on television, and he shook his fist at the snow-covered screen and the game-show hosts, who drove him crazy. "Balls!" he yelled at them in disgust, at their "foolish ways" and their "simperin' jokes," telling anyone who'd listen that he hated the news and he hated the game shows and he hated the comedians on Ed Sullivan and especially the singers. He hated the ads, the dancing tubes of toothpaste and the pairs of cigarette packs linking arms and marching across the screen, and occasionally he'd throw his own pack at the singing bars of soap, particularly the flirts with barbed-wire eyelashes.

Denis hated the boy who delivered the newspaper (especially after he had retired from construction work, when the afternoon paper was the highlight of his day), although all Delia could see was that the newspaper boy had a lot of brownish freckles — which could be construed as irritating, if she wanted to give her father the benefit of the doubt — and he didn't always collect his money on Thursday afternoons, when Denis thought he should. On Friday or Saturday afternoons, he refused to answer the door when the boy came around (just as he refused to shut off the television when the ads came on), glaring at him from his chair when Mae left the front door open to go and find her purse. The paper boy stepped off to the side, outside Denis's line of vision, and Denis said that proved he was a sneak.

He hated the Palladinos on the third floor because they were Italian. If he looked out into the hallway and saw Mae talking with Lena Palladino by the mailbox, he opened and shut the door half a dozen times, and when she finally came inside, he yelled at the top of his lungs that Mike Palladino was just a dirty guinea bastard and ordered Mae to cross the street whenever she saw Lena walking her way. Delia began to notice that the children on the street hid in the alleys when they saw Denis.

"Why don't you like the paper boy?" the newly married Delia once asked him, feeling herself to be somewhat adult and perhaps capable of understanding him.

"If you're too stupid to know," he said, dragging on his cigarette, "then don't be expectin' me to tell you."

She thought she probably hadn't been an adult long enough; that must have been it. Six months later, when she was just about to deliver Maureen, she started to think about passing through the Valley of Death — what if she didn't have many more opportunities to discover the truth? — and she asked her father why he hated Mike Palladino, who had danced with her at her wedding and was always polite in his sparkling-clean shirts.

"He's a *son of a whore!*" Denis had screamed, and then slammed the bathroom door.

"Delia," Mae said wearily, sticking her head into the living room, "why do you always need to start with him?" and Delia couldn't answer. She thought the pregnancy was making her even more contrary.

Then he stopped talking to anyone he thought had English blood.

He said he had to do it for his father, Seamus, who came to America hidden in the belly of a boat, not once but twice, with the English police searching Ireland for him, wanting to put him in jail for his "political activities," so when Denis passed Anne Edwards, the music teacher, who lived on the fourth floor, he didn't even nod, although she offered him a polite hello; he merely looked the other way, having heard that Miss Edwards had a picture of King George VI over her sofa.

Mae sent him to Hans's Groceries to pick up milk, and he threw a box of English water biscuits at the cash register. "You have my sympathies, Mrs. Delaney," Hans said to Delia that afternoon, shaking his head from side to side.

Denis began to hate the rich, whose faces were sometimes in the newspaper. When he skimmed the pages, looking for the crossword or the word-jumble puzzle, he stopped at the society pages to ink out the jowls of the Rockefellers, drawing beards on the Whitney women. "Was he always like this, Ma?" Delia asked Mae, as Denis's life ebbed away in a bitter puddle and none of them knew it was happening. She couldn't imagine her mother marrying such an angry and terrible man.

"It's the drink, Delia Mary," Mae sighed. "The drink's got him crazy."

When she waited endlessly for Maureen to be born, Delia left her apartment in the early morning, while Maurice slept, and went downstairs to have breakfast with her parents, but by that time, Denis was ignoring the oatmeal and eggs in front of him and swallowing a shot of whiskey, snorting like a horse. One morning, while Mae was fussing in the bedroom, Denis asked Delia if she knew why it was that the nuns always traveled in pairs. "No, Daddy," she said, relieved by his tender, calm tone. "Why is it?"

"'Tis so that one nun could make sure that the other nun don't get none." He guffawed, as Mae looked anxiously into the room.

Delia could barely believe it that Sunday afternoon so many years later, listening to Maurice ask Gerald if he knew why the sisters were called nuns.

"I don't know," Gerald said, turning to face Maurice. "Why?"

"They don't get nun of this, and they don't get nun of that." Maurice had laughed, and Delia looked up as Gerald walked out of the apartment, his face angry and tight. It reminded her of the night she and Gerald were laughing at the supper table, seven and ten years old, and Denis bounced two red-hot potatoes off their foreheads. That night, Gerald had sworn he was going to kill his father.

"I will," he cried from his bed at the end of the bedroom the three children had shared. "Someday, Delia, I'll kill him. I don't care if I go to jail for a million years."

"And what'll we do then?" Delia had asked into the darkness, starting to cry. "Where will we go, me and Ma and Eugene?"

"I don't care, Delia, I'm gonna do it." He hiccuped and turned his face to the wall.

As he got older, Denis couldn't stand to wait in line at Hans's to buy his beer, seething when someone ahead of him ordered an eighth of a pound of Swiss cheese, wishing them death under his breath or, at the very least, an accident of the most terrible kind. Often he went into the store and just helped himself to two cans of beer and walked home. Hans watched him, writing it down in his black-and-white marbled notebook, and simply told Mae, who just as simply paid it. "It's easier that way," Hans had said to Delia once after she and her mother paid Denis's bill. "He leaves everyone else alone."

"I know," Delia had replied, shaking her head in humiliation.

Then he began to walk in and out of the other stores in the Heights as easily as Hans's. He didn't get enough soy sauce in the Hong Kong China Kitchen with his take-out shrimp chow mein, so he stole the whole decanter, hiding it underneath his coat, screaming at the employees that they were cat-eating Chink bastards.

The Chinese waiter, a very old man, ran out the next time he saw Delia pass and plucked at her sleeve. "Your father take soy sauce," he had said.

"I'm sorry." Delia had tried to pass by. "I'll tell him." But he wouldn't let her pass, and she grew afraid, remembering Mae's version of the Tong Wars in New York City, where she'd first lived, and so Delia gave him her last five-dollar bill and ran home. She had been on her way to the Ho Lim Laundry for Maurice's shirts, and now she was embarrassed. What if the Hong Kong China Kitchen warned the Ho Lim Laundry about the Rooneys?

"No ticket." Mr. Ho shook his head at Mae when she and Delia came in later that same day for the shirts. Tearing the pink slip Mae had held, he threw it in the trash. "You no need ticket. I know you," Mr. Ho said accusingly, and then he began to send their things, Maurice's shirts and Mae's sheets, back dirty and wrinkled. The first time it happened, Delia redid the shirts herself, but Denis stripped the sheets from the bed and took them back to the laundry, where he ripped the calendar from the door, tore the picture of the woman on its cover right through the slash of red lipstick on her chalk-white face, halving her ornate headdress, and threw the pieces of paper, along with the sheets, across the marble counter. He tried to tear up the pad of months, but it was too thick, so he pulled the pages off one by one and threw them on the floor and spit on them. Johnny Devane, Eugene's friend, had seen the whole thing and told Eugene, and then Eugene had told Delia, but they didn't want Mae to know what Denis had done; she'd only get upset. (He'd told her only that he'd "complained.")

"I don't know what's wrong with the Chinaman," Mae said, coming right back home with the dirty sheets piled up in her shopping cart. "I got as far as the door of the laundry, and he ran around and shook his head and then slammed the door in my face, quick pullin' down the shade and then turnin' over the sign to 'closed.' He wouldn't even let me say a word." (Delia and Eugene, in the living room, refused to look at each other.)

When Mae told Denis the story, he said she wasn't allowed to bring any more sheets around to the Chinks, nor to do any more business with Hans, on the corner: he didn't like Hans's sneer, and while she was at it, she was to cancel that paper and write to the editor and tell him of the paper boy's insolence.

He stopped going to church, and he forbade Mae to go, what with all the foreigners moving in all over the place, not wanting "them" to rub against her wool coat, those men with their greasy unwashed hands, so she would come home smelling of garlic bulbs. At which point Mae tightened her mouth and squared her tiny shoulders and said nobody was about to tell *her* what to do, and after she had left, Denis turned to Delia, crying drunkenly that he had loved his mother, and Delia didn't know quite what to do with him but listen, for after all, she had been named for her grandmother and therefore she had some responsibility, but she didn't know what it was, other than to pretend that her father made sense and it was everyone else who was crazy.

Then he forbade Mae and Delia to go to his niece Bridget's wedding to Henry Goldblum, because Henry was Jewish. "It's the principle of the thing, Margaret," he had said to his sister on the telephone. "The sparrows don't marry the blue jays and the lions don't marry the lambs, if you know what I'm sayin'. It's not right, and we won't be in attendance."

Yet on the morning of the wedding, Mae asked Delia to zip the back of her good yellow dress. Delia then slipped into her own black and white checkered skirt and white blouse, and they went to Bridget's wedding by train and home by taxi, and they had to duck Denis's Copacabana ashtray, which he pitched at them through the darkened living room as soon as they opened the door. Bridget gave Delia a piece of wedding cake to slip under her pillow, but Denis threw the small white box into the soggy garbage bag. Delia had expected it and hidden a small net bag of sugar almonds in the palm of her glove, and she slept on that instead.

He began to mutter to himself when he was alone in the living room. "What did you say, Dad?" Delia always asked, standing in the doorway to be sure she would hear his reply.

"Anyone who asks 'what' can hear," he always answered, and Delia was sure there was some clue she was missing to solve the riddle of her father, some explanation she wasn't quite smart enough to understand. She was too *dense*, she told herself, to know what she'd done wrong in her relationship with him. He was the only father she had, and she knew so little about him, besides his temper and his rage. She thought of Gerald's vow to kill him, especially afterward, when someone might mention the shock of her father's death, especially the way it had happened, mere days after Gerald came home from the seminary. She didn't truly believe Gerald had killed him; it had more likely been his mean old heart, just shriveling up and falling apart.

Maureen was born a few days after he had died, and any grief Delia had felt, she merely shoved under some sort of mental cushions and sat down hard.

And now here was Maurice, carrying on in Mae's living room about those immigrants from the other side with their "potato faces" and their "brogues you could cut with a knife," the "harps" and the "donkeys" and the "micks," he called them, while Delia closed the paper carefully, watching Mae's back stiffen against the red brocade chair. She didn't know why he was doing it; his people were as Irish as hers. He was sitting in her mother's house, carrying on about his own blood!

"If you don't get that man out of my house, Delia Mary," Mae said pleasantly, "then I'm goin' to go out in the kitchen and get crockery to bang down on the top of his head."

"Well, what do you want, Ma?" Delia said defensively, staring at Eugene, who smirked as he passed through the room. "Eugene encourages him," but when they were outside, she made a fist and poked Maurice in the belly.

"Why do you *do* that?" she asked him.

"Ah, c'mon, Delia." He hugged her. "I'm not doing any harm. I'm just trying to get Mae's goat. What're you doing, losing your sense of humor?"

"I don't think it's funny, that's all. All that Irish stuff makes my mother furious."

He hugged her again. "If you can't laugh at yourself, then who can you laugh at?"

She didn't know why anyone had to be laughed at. She loved peaceful times and kind people and soft words, but she had had a father who hated everyone and a husband who seemed to be going in the same direction. It was hard for Delia to hate anyone; it took a lot of effort and concentration, especially when it was directed at her own people, whom she saw as brave and funny and strong. Teasing, she had often thought, was a sort of watered-down hate: she tried not to hate, and she tried not to tease, because she herself could not bear being the butt of a joke that was so sharp she didn't always know she had been cut. It was only after the laughter had stopped that the joke throbbed and pulsed inside her, and then she felt herself puff up in indignation, like the tender skin that surrounds a wound.

She had to think of some way to excuse Maurice: she had to make it up to Mae.

SEVENTEEN

Delia sat at the kitchen table, her expanding belly pressèd against the edge, and watched Maurice drink his coffee. She asked him what he was thinking on the morning of his daughter's thirteenth birthday.

"Nothing," he said, his hand wrapped around the cup. "Why do there always have to be all these *thoughts* about things?"

He seemed so strong and rational at times, so much more controlled than Delia, with her messy love for all of them, love that leaked from her pores and seemed to stain their clothes.

No child was ever her Maureen at thirteen; Maureen would never be a child again.

"Maureen's thirteen, which means she's not twelve anymore. I guess that's what I'm thinking about, okay? Why do I always have to say everything I think?"

"I don't know," she admitted. "Maybe so's I could hear your thoughts too, for a change."

"And what if I want to keep my thoughts to myself?"

"Go keep them!" she said angrily, wishing to storm from the room but struggling to get out of the chair. She had become very pregnant very quickly, and it was hard to get up and leave in a huff. She had to plan arguments for them to be effective.

"And shove them up your backside!" she shouted from the doorway.

She wanted to hear that he remembered the early days when Maureen, so small, waited in Mae's bedroom for him to come home from work, staring out the window, her nose pressed against the glass and her curly baby hair making fine brush strokes against the frost, her fat little elbows propped on the peeling windowsill. Delia hid behind the curtains for a glimpse of Maurice's face when he looked up suddenly and saw his Moodles waving in the window, on the cusp of two.

Maureen's "terrible twos" were hard on Delia. The baby was active and might climb into the toilet bowl when Delia had turned her back. Delia, newly pregnant with Patty, was very tired. When Delia took Maureen for walks, the baby was so exhausted from her active mornings that she seemed to collapse in her stroller, and she slept for hours. Delia didn't believe in waking her, and she walked the streets long after the lights had been turned on, often noticing old fathers and grown-up daughters like herself with babies like Maureen strolling along the avenue, the grandfathers usually pushing the babies energetically, pretending to listen to the young women, who punctuated the air with their index fingers as if they were telling them things "for your own good," glancing at their fathers' profiles once or twice, the fathers nodding.

Some of the old men needed a shave — Delia thought from their somewhat seedy appearances that they were widowers — their cheeks glistening with a faint silver stubble like sleet falling under a streetlight, and some of them, fresh from their wives, wore neat jackets, their sparse white hair clipped short on the neck, their tweed hats worn back from their smooth rubbery faces, the high naked foreheads making them look like cherubs.

Although it was two years since his death, Delia thought a lot about her father, and it struck her that she had never known him and never would.

Maureen was born so soon after Denis had died, everyone had said it was just like trading one life for another, and there was something strange about watching her father's casket being lowered into the warm, late-spring earth while the baby inside kicked Delia's pocketbook, forcing her to hold her coat closed with both hands.

Each year, as Maureen grew bigger, Delia's memory of her father grew smaller, and it seemed, sometimes, as if a hundred years had gone by since she had last seen him. The mean, terrible things he used to yell played through her head in small, bitter whispers.

Maureen was now a teenager, and Delia's separation from her father was in its adolescence. As if that meant something, she thought.

Now that Maureen was no longer a child, Delia wanted to celebrate her birthday by bringing a group of her friends to Stahler's Luncheonette for sundaes. It was a relief for Delia not to have to compete with Sally Malloney (not that she ever did), for surely Maureen was finally too old to push marbles through the rug in anyone's apartment, too old for kiddie prizes. It was hard to see Maureen grow up, Delia thought, but there were compensations.

Delia had invited Joannie Malloney to come along with them and she had grudgingly agreed, but Delia had to watch her, lumbering along in her long black Mary Janes, in case she sprinted up one of the side streets to the schoolyard for a quick game of half-court.

Maureen's friends were polite to Delia, smiling at her simple jokes, lowering their eyes against her pregnancy to answer her pleasant questions, bumping against her sides, they were walking so closely.

Delia realized that Maureen was jealous when she saw her slink away from the group and look with interest at a miniature chair in the window of an upholstery shop. Delia tried then to be quiet and walk alongside Joannie, who was lagging at the rear of the group. They had to pass Conlon's Funeral Home, and Delia automatically looked up at the steel bars covering the small window on the top floor of the two-story brick building. She could never understand why those bars were there, and when she was young, her mother had laughed and said they were to keep the dead from climbing out.

Whenever she passed Conlon's, Delia felt sure she would see Rosaleen's crazy grandmother still inside, her hair splayed all over like a picture Delia had once seen of Poseidon, god of the sea, or Richard Reilly, a boy in her eighth-grade class who'd been struck by a car, up at the window in his confirmation suit, a stiff white bow on his arm.

She was especially leery of seeing Denis there, even now, so many years later. Before he died, she had had dreams that he was already laid out in Conlon's, in his navy-blue suit, and they had to hit him with a broom to keep him in his coffin and not in one of the gin mills, with Mae screaming at him to get back where he belonged. Delia woke up sweating, the idea of her parents fighting again more terrifying than the idea of her father being gone.

At least if he was dead, Mae used to say, peering out the window, I'd know where he was at night.

But when the time came, Mae collapsed in a quivering ball, and it was Delia who stood in front of his closet, staring at the navy-blue suit, hating the thought of Denis at Conlon's by himself, without any shoes. The day before the wake, she had ironed his white shirt on the kitchen table, on top of a thick Turkish towel, Mae keening on the chair by the window. Delia ran her fingers over the stiff creases she had made near the shoulders, trying to leave something of herself on the cloth that would touch her father forever, the collar of the shirt frayed and yellowed from the oil of Denis's hair. She held it against her cheek, while Mae watched and screamed even louder, until finally Delia started to cry and pushed the shirt she had so carefully pressed into Gerald's hands, piling Denis's folded suit and his tie and his clean underwear and socks on top, forcing Gerald out the door, slamming it on his pale, fat, teary face.

The next day, at Conlon's, she couldn't see the worn collar around her father's neck, only the white satin pillow underneath his head, and she thought about telling the nice man who worked in the office that they really should put something under her father, or their nice pillow would be ruined, and despite herself she laughed.

Funeral parlor giggles, people in Conlon's said, smiling uncomfortably at Delia, and her so pregnant!

Conlon's had given them the biggest room because theirs was the only wake that day, and Delia sat on a worn tapestry sofa off to the side, looking at the rows and rows of empty purple leather seats facing the coffin. Her brothers stood outside on the street, chain-smoking cigarettes: through the slitted venetian blinds above her father's body, she watched Eugene and Gerald pace back and forth, while Mae fussed with Denis's tie.

A wild-eyed man in a rumpled beige shirt and dirty shoes stood in the doorway, waving a yellow sheet of paper around his head, and for a minute Delia prepared herself to be ashamed, thinking the man was her father's friend, but he was only from the florist, looking for a signature. Maurice was late in getting to the funeral home; he offered his hand to the deliveryman and introduced himself, and Delia saw that Maurice had made the same mistake. He signed the yellow paper with his face beet red, then he sat down next to Delia, rubbing her back. A few minutes later, the deliveryman dragged a giant-sized green shamrock made of carnations across the faded Persian carpet and stood it by Denis's head, and she *was* ashamed and guilty, embarrassed by her father, who was so newly dead.

"From the Shamrock Inn," Mae said quietly, just as Eugene and Gerald stepped into the room, and all of them noticed the gold and white ribbons interwoven around the shamrock's stem. "Dear friend," it read, and Eugene recited the names from the small attached card, pausing between them for emphasis, as if each name were more important than the one that had gone before, as if a signature might have belonged to a head of state or a club president, as if their father's drinking was a noble calling or, at worst, some harmless affectionate hobby that might have called for amusing clothes—stubby black hip boots and a tackle-filled hat, or a whistle and the sweet striped cap of a toy-railroad engineer.

Later on, a man without a foot (the friend who lost his foot to frostbite, Delia realized, with a start) hopped over to the casket, tears pouring down the gouges in his face, his empty pant leg gathered together with a trailing piece of yellowed string, and then a woman without teeth followed him, a red veil drawn carefully over her thin hair; turning to kiss Delia, she left lipstick on the white collar of her full black dress, so that Delia had felt tainted that whole first day.

Denis knew a man whose bluish toes stuck out of the front of cut-open carpet slippers and the fat bald man in a shiny brown suit who reeked of urine, and Delia smiled politely at all of them, pretending to herself to be the daughter of a man with unusual tastes and a million little quirks, someone who enjoyed people who were different. The fat man might have been a struggling artist, the man in the carpet slippers an eccentric millionaire; her father a man who loved people. It helped her get through it, watching Denis's friends borrow her brothers' cigarettes and then haggle over them, hanging on to Mae until Delia struggled to her feet and pried her mother loose, and then they hung on to Delia, until she ran into the bathroom, sitting down hard on a tiny black boudoir chair studded with nailheads, staring at herself in the mirror. The woman in the red veil followed, and Delia found herself holding her comb as if it were a weapon, but the woman flopped down on the black sofa in the room and let out a sigh. The more Delia looked around, the more she realized that the bathroom could easily serve as another "chapel"—there was even a screen in the corner, folded and thick with dust, like the one around Denis.

"Ho," the woman said, staring at Delia, who pretended to comb her hair. "Ho." She tapped her open-toed green sandal on the linty rug.

Delia smiled slightly, still gazing at herself in the mirror. She didn't dare face the woman; she couldn't look any of these people full in the face.

"When you due?" the woman asked, pointing weakly at Delia's middle. She opened her purse and removed a compact.

"This week," Delia said. She had had to raise her voice, the woman was so far away. White pipes crossed over each other on the ceiling, Delia noticed, trying not to watch herself speak. Even at the hairdresser, when Delia said anything, forced to watch herself in the mirror there, she felt like a liar and a fake, becoming a self so diluted she wasn't even real.

The woman nodded. "I had five myself," she said, unscrewing the top from a worn-looking tube of lipstick. The lipstick was purple and seemed to have been bitten in half.

"Oh, isn't that nice," Delia said, relieved. "How old are they all now?"

"They're all dead," the woman said bluntly, rubbing her pinkie over her lower lip. "They all died in the womb."

"Oh, my." Delia touched her belly, looking at the door, willing Mae to come in and rescue her. "What was wrong?" she asked, not wanting to but somehow compelled to continue.

"Wrong?" the woman asked. "What was wrong was that I carried them all in my ass."

Delia never remembered what she said next. She never passed

Conlon's without thinking of the red-veiled woman in there along with the rest, and she never passed a woman with a big backside without a fleeting thought of babies inside, punching to get free.

She opened the door of Stahler's, and the smell of ice-cold sweet vanilla drew them inside. While they waited for a table, Maureen and her friends squatted down in front of the cashier to look into a glass display case full of dolls from different nations. The waitress, a tall woman with frizzy hair, seated the girls in a high-backed booth underneath a round mirror etched with a lily.

Delia stood off to the side, intending to sit at the counter. She wanted Maureen to feel grown up, and besides, she knew she wouldn't be comfortable with her belly flush against the table. She tried not to look at the girls, in their dark wraparound skirts and their cotton blouses, but stared instead at a couple of abandoned spoons, dropped haphazardly on top of the silver bins of ice cream, dull metal with a milky film on the handles.

The kitchen was at the end of the counter, separated from the rest of the store by a short burlap drape held on a narrow gold curtain rod by thin gold rings. If she looked underneath, Delia could see only arms: thin ones, muscular ones, arms with tattoos underneath the rolled-up cuffs of white T-shirts. The strangers, seeming to sense her interest, bent down and stared back at her from under the drape, and it was hard for Delia to keep her eyes steady. She was reminded of prisoners or patients in a hospital, and she felt guilty, for she could get up and go elsewhere.

She ordered a coffee ice cream soda, watching the counterman drop a gob of whipped cream on the top, idly wondering how she might someday break into Stahler's late at night when it was closed, eating every bit of whipped cream in the place.

Waiting for her soda, she watched her daughter's face in the mirror on the wall, a sudden sharp angle to her chin, shadows where she once had full cheeks, a widow's peak that Delia had never noticed before. She looks just like her father, Delia thought again. These days, the resemblance was startling.

She wasn't sure she liked the change in Maureen: it was too much like watching her dive underneath the waves out at Rockaway and then stand up, her hair slicked back, some replacement child Delia didn't quite recognize. She was never certain the child in the familiar bathing suit was her Maureen; sometimes Delia asked the child a senseless question that didn't really need an answer, only the reassurance of Maureen's voice.

It was hard to think of being thirteen. Delia watched the girls play with their charm bracelets, tear their paper napkins into tiny pills, pushing them into neat piles and blowing them through their straws.

Across from the girls, against the wall, was a line of tall, narrow booths meant for one diner, each seat facing the back of the one in front of it, with nothing at all to look at but a sort of wall and, rather like an afterthought, a tiny lamp affixed to the wall, with a tulip-shaped glass shade. Delia had been in Stahler's in the early-evening hours and watched solitary lady diners in navy-blue dresses pick at baby lamb chops and baby peas and little dishes of macaroni and cheese, bits of things that wouldn't fill a bird, saucer foods too scant to appease even the tiniest appetite. The lady diners patiently read paperback books in plastic brocade covers so that Delia couldn't see the titles, or they cleaned out their purses while they waited for their suppers, filling the tops of the small tables with plastic eyeglass cases and cigarette cases and the plastic paperback covers and, sometimes, plastic pillboxes, as if they were barricading themselves against the pitiful glances of strangers with a wall of containers.

The men who ate alone were different, spreading out the newspaper, the serrated edges hanging down, tending to get caught in the waitresses' short nylon aprons before sliding to the floor past the men's knees, which stuck out into the aisle. The men who ate alone in Stahler's ordered hearty plates of mushy spaghetti flecked with bits of green pepper, laden with chunks of tomato, so that they appeared to be celebrating, merry dinners covered with confetti.

Maureen raised her straw to her mouth, and Delia observed that the child's wrists were slimming down and her fingers taking on peculiar strength. She had begun to hold her hands in a fluted way rather than the wide-splayed way of a child, with hands that seemed outlined on construction paper. Her white blouse was covered with fat pastel bows dangling thin ribbons of lifesavers.

Delia didn't want Maureen to wind up in a navy-blue dress in one of those lonesome booths. Jesus, she thought, it was better to be in the thick of it, struggling from one paycheck to the next, hiding dollar bills in the underwear drawer so you could go ahead and buy shoes — better to be married at any cost, even if the men drank or they turned out to be mean or cheap; there were ways around that. No man was perfect, none of them were without fault. She had listened to the snippets of conversations in the playground, whose husband was easy and who was lucky because of that, whose man didn't care what he ate and whose husband handed over the whole pay envelope. And the overtime.

A woman with wiry graying hair had bragged that all "he" wanted from her was a decent meal on the table and a decent nightgown in the bed, but the next time Delia had seen her, she was lumbering through the sandbox, pretending to scratch at her crotch and spit on the street the way her husband did, her friends laughing and jumping up from the benches, taking turns pretending to be their husbands, swaggering through the sand where the little ones played with empty milk cartons, the last woman topping all the others by belching loudly and scaring a tiny girl into tears — but that was better, oh, yes, than those itty-bitty meals and the wall of plastic cases and the secret paperbacks held carefully by the well-manicured, self-pleasuring fingertips.

By now she knew what she had in Maurice and she knew what he was sorely lacking, yet she was grateful that her appetite for figuring him out had never been satisfied. Besides, once the babies came along, the men weren't even that important anymore, as long as they worked steady and eventually found their way home. There were many ways around men; you just had to figure out your own: nice dinners or pretty nighties, the little things that paid off in the end so the worst of them became bearable and then went to sleep, and even if they weren't and they didn't, as long as they didn't hit you or didn't hit you too much, you were doing okay. Even if a woman married an out-and-out rummy, people still respected her, but Delia thought there was no respect for the women in the blue suits; they were just left behind. The waitresses knew it, paying little attention to the lone women while they fluttered around the men, picking up their newspapers, bringing them fresh pats of butter.

She hoped that Maureen found a good man, but she knew, deep inside, that all she needed was a man good enough.

Finally, the girls finished, and Maureen ran to Delia with the check. "Thanks, Ma," and she smiled, rushing through the door with her friends, whirling about in their loose skirts, the sun forcing itself through the rotting tracks, making them bow their heads, as if they were being knighted.

She paid the check and, on impulse, bought Maureen a red-haired doll in a green velvet dress and a stiff white pinafore embroidered with a green shamrock and the word "Eire." There was a tiny white card attached to the doll's wrist, and Delia bent over the table in am empty booth, digging in her pocketbook for her eyebrow pencil, writing carefully: "To My Darling Maureen, Happy Birthday, With All My Love, From Mom," and the date, although she didn't know why she had to do that, why she needed to formally put an end to Maureen's childhood, closing it up so neatly, questioning her own sense of the day as an event, something she had to fix in time, something difficult and final.

EIGHTEEN

August, finally. Delia smiled to herself, touching the date just above the headlines of the *Daily News*.

Soon, she whispered to herself, it'll be all over. She was looking forward to being busy, not having a spare minute to look at the newspaper or anything else. She leaned back on the couch and took a deep breath. I'm ready, she thought, deciding that the first day of August was something to celebrate, and so she took the girls to the Rexall after lunch and let them buy the new baby a tin of talcum and a bottle of baby lotion and a package of safety pins with ducks on the ends, a silky yellow-and-green hairbrush, a tiny yellow comb, and a bag of diapers. When they came home, Maureen arranged the baby things in the white crib like a store display. "You can't leave the baby's things inside the crib like that," Delia said, patting Maureen's shoulder. "All the stuff might fall on the baby's head."

Then Maureen cleaned off the top of the dresser she shared with Patty. Her old Nancy Drew books went under her bed, along with the statue of Saint Joseph, and she even unplugged her tan radio and stashed it in her closet. She arranged the baby things again, on her half of the dresser top. "No fair!" Patty cried, grabbing for the talcum, a thin spray of powder rising up to make her sneeze.

Later in the week, the heat so bad that she seemed to move in slow motion, Delia and the girls boarded the bus to Arthur's Discounts in Sunnyside for some more baby things, undershirts and plastic pants (she had learned enough about wet sheets with Maureen), a blue kimono and a pink one, a tiny blue-and-white-striped sweater and a blue cap with a peak and a tiny pink bonnet. Delia bought the pink things — the cheapest she could find — just to satisfy fate. It wasn't a girl; Delia just knew it.

"But what if it is?" Maureen asked, leaning on Delia's shoulder as the bus turned.

"You can name her if it's a girl, Maureen, how's that?" Delia promised, vaguely annoyed. "What's your favorite girl's name?"

(Terence, William, or Todd, Delia would choose among them, but she wanted to humor the child.)

"Oh-h-h-h." Maureen's eyes lit up. "Sherry. Just like on the radio, Sherry Baby."

"Okay," Delia said, trying to be patient. It was so *hot*, after all. "Then Sherry Baby it is."

"No fair!" Patty cried, from behind them. She reached over and pulled Maureen's hair.

The frame houses in Sunnyside, which was a neighborhood or so closer to New York than the Heights, were pressed together over tiny fences. They were the kinds of houses where garbage from the street blew into the corners by the stairs, so near the sidewalks that Delia had to look away from the wet underwear dripping onto the cement in the communal backyards. Sunnyside life seemed too public for Delia, the houses no doubt full of the smell of car exhaust pushing at the curtains, although she thought it might be nice to live in a neighborhood where the Blessed Mother statues in the front yards were practically close enough to hold hands.

Arthur's Discounts stood directly underneath the old section of Holy Sepulchre Cemetery, where Denis and Maurice's brothers were buried, the crooked tombstones jutting toward the sky like loose teeth. Although the baby clothes were cheap, she was pleased to see that they were wrapped carefully in plastic, unlike the dusty appliances and the toys smudged with soot. Everything else that Delia had ever bought in Arthur's seemed to be preowned, which was a relief; the bright chattering newness of things held Delia in an uncomfortable suspense.

Besides the baby things, she bought herself two pretty nightgowns and a fresh lipstick, and when they came home, the children helped pack her suitcase, standing it against the living room wall. It wasn't until Maurice prodded the suitcase with his shoe and said, "Here we go again, huh?" that she remembered having placed the suitcase in that exact spot with each of the girls. "Yup, here we go again." She smiled, rubbing her middle. "I can't wait!"

And then on August 7, she put Maureen's radio on the kitchen table and she heard that Jackie Kennedy had delivered early, a baby boy, whose name was Patrick, and Delia thought that was a good sign, first Jackie and then herself, but two days later, Jackie's baby Patrick had died, and Delia felt as upset as she would have if the baby were a relative, taking to her bed and sobbing. For the next two days, Delia drifted in and out of sleep, stuck to the hot sheets, and all she could remember later about that time was that it was so hot and it was the last time she had felt the baby kicking, a weak trembling high underneath her breastbone.

On the third day, she had to get up: she had an appointment with Dr. Mullaney.

She got dressed in what she thought of as her doctor underwear, a big serious white cotton bra, heavy and thick as a strip of tapestry, hard and unyielding on her full breasts, and a snowy-white lace slip that fell below her knees, pure and pretty as a postulant's veil. She hadn't a speck of hair left under her arms or on her legs, and she wore no cosmetics on her face, only lipstick and her best maternity dress, tailored and brown.

Ready for her appointment, she clomped into Mae's kitchen in her sturdy tan doctor shoes, and her mother, who was going with her as always, stared at her feet. "You look like you're from the Visiting Nurses, Delia Mary," Mae said, her usual joke, but Delia pretended that she didn't hear a thing. She wanted Dr. Mullaney to know that she was serious about the baby, so on the mornings of her appointments, she laced her tan shoes and kicked her thin-strapped sandals underneath her bed.

"Shame about the President's son, huh?" Dr. Mullaney asked her, suddenly looking too young to Delia to know anything.

Delia couldn't answer; it hurt her too much.

She wished Maurice were with her. He was supposed to stand between Delia and awful things like that baby Patrick's death. Delia tried not to cry. She was afraid, suddenly, of what might happen to her.

"Everything's fine," Dr. Mullaney said, and left the room. Delia was so grateful she didn't ask him a single question. She thought of Jackie and hurried to get out of his office before he changed his mind. If she were to hang around, she'd be tempting fate. Mae was always warning her about that, tempting fate. Mae put her hands over her ears when Delia said she loved her girls so much, and if she said the girls were beautiful, her mother's neck blotched and she covered Delia's mouth with her own hand.

"We'll see you next week, Mrs. Delaney?" the doctor's red-haired nurse asked, looking up at Delia through her tortoiseshell glasses. She was also Dr. Vincent F. X. Mullaney's wife, the mother of seven redheaded children, two girls and five boys. Dr. Mullaney's office was a small white building attached to the side of the family's large white house like an ear, but if someone were to look at the grounds quickly, they might reasonably mistake the office for a playhouse, especially after seeing so many children rolling on the dense green lawn. Delia couldn't explain it, but the children everywhere seemed to make some kind of promise to the doctor's patients, even to the older women whose children were grown, some sort of red-cheeked testimony to a plentiful Catholic life, and he was very popular, plenty of women bunching together on those hard green sofas waiting their turn, staring at the framed Norman Rockwell paintings on the walls.

"Yes, next week," Delia answered, turning, only to have her big belly brushed by a small red-haired boy who had burst into the reception area, into his mother's arms.

She'd be trying to fill the tiny cups for a urine specimen, ever so carefully moving her big serious tan shoes out of the way in the tiny "lavatory," and she'd hear Mrs. Mullaney push open one of the windows with the green shutters and call out: "Bridget, where is John Martin? Siobhan, watch what Kiernan is doing over there. Sean, be a good boy, won't you, and find Seamus's other shoe, and please, someone, make Timothy wear his sweater!"

Their rich poetic names lulled Delia into a kind of stupor: she had never heard the children whine or cry, and when she came out of the lavatory, holding her still-warm cup, Mrs. Mullaney always looked quite satisfied, filling the appointment book, making notations on a chart.

In the waiting room outside, Mae sat on one of the sofas. She wore a fresh cotton dress, with her hair neatly curled. Once the baby was born, Delia thought Mae would miss coming to the office. She had seemed to like the sense of ceremony that went with the visits. She deferred her nightly bath to the morning of Delia's checkup, and she had dinner ready before she left the house.

Mae wore her nicest dresses to go to Delia's doctor, as if she were the one with the appointments rather than her daughter, who would have preferred to make these trips by herself or with Maureen but just couldn't bring herself to disappoint Mae, who sat with her feet tucked neatly underneath her chair, browsing through the current magazines.

As August oozed on, Delia grew certain that her baby had stopped moving.

The tenth, her due date, was circled in angry red marker on the church calendar hanging inside the broom closet. Delia began to pamper herself, taking long naps, getting up a few times a day to stare reproachfully at the calendar, holding on to the broken strap of her old wristwatch, which she carried around with her just in case her pains started, which of course they never did.

"A watched pot never boils," Mae singsonged to Delia over and over again.

Lying on her bed in the late afternoon (if she had rested more with the others, she told herself, Patty might have done better in school, Maureen might have been less *sad* a child, always closer to tears than Delia liked to see), she remembered some cousin of Mae's who had suffered a single labor pain and then delivered a twelve-pound son in the elevator on her way to the dentist. Although she didn't remember ever meeting the cousin, Delia began to cultivate an intense hatred toward her. Perversely, getting angry felt good, tiring her out and helping her to sleep, though her head pounded when she woke up and she was disappointed not to be in labor, and then she felt worse.

"The baby isn't moving, Ma," she said to her mother on the telephone one night.

"Good," Mae said emphatically. "They never move before they're born. It's the calm before the storm, Delia. Don't you remember nothin'?" she asked loudly.

One afternoon, Patty crept to the side of the bed and stared into Delia's face, her child's adenoidal breath teasing the blond hairs on Delia's upper lip. "Ma, can I take one of the sheets?" she whispered. "The kids downstairs are making a tent in the garden, and they told me to ask." Delia nodded, not caring what Patty took from the house. They could play jump rope with my wedding veil, Delia thought, dreaming vaguely of falling elevators and dentists' chairs and tiny men. Maureen, amazed, stared at Patty sauntering through the living room with Delia's best sheet tucked under her arm. She looked in on her mother.

Poor Maureen, Delia thought. She was so attentive, bringing Delia ice water and cold cloths for her head, running up and down the four flights of stairs to check on Patty and then on Delia, running errands for Mae, fixing supper at night for her sister and her father (when he came home), who stood in the doorway of the bedroom and stared at Delia. "Don't worry about it," he said to her. "Nature takes her own sweet time, Delia," and she worried that he might have been talking to Mae, he had sounded so much like her then. Maurice went out into the kitchen to eat one of Maureen's hamburgers (big and round and red and gummy in the middle, just like a jelly doughnut, he had said kiddingly).

At first it was only one day that Delia was convinced her baby didn't move, and then it was two days, and then it was nearly a week, but she thought that she might have forgotten how quiet a baby was before birth; after all, she told herself, I haven't had a baby in eleven years. For a while, Delia thought that the baby might have kicked while she was asleep and she just didn't remember it.

Maurice said that made sense; why not?

At the end of the fifth day without a sign of life, Delia got up, not giving herself a second to brood, went into the kitchen, and defrosted the refrigerator. When she passed through the living room, she noticed that her suitcase, still against the wall, needed to be dusted. On the sixth still and silent day, Delia bent down and cleaned underneath the sofa, remembering that the night before she was born, Patty had kicked Delia's pocketbook from the balcony of the movie theater down to the rows below.

She called Rosaleen, just to talk.

"Oh, you're just looking for trouble," Rosaleen assured her. "You're thinking of poor Jackie again." Besides, she asked, didn't Delia have a doctor's appointment soon? Delia said she did, feeling rude that she hadn't inquired about Rosaleen's own pregnancy.

"Tell Mullaney you're worried," Maurice had said, shrugging his shoulders. "But I'm telling you, Delia, you always worry too much. The kid is fine."

Every time he said that, on his way out the door, Delia felt better.

She went to see Dr. Mullaney the next morning on the subway, rather than the hot bus, on a day so muggy that the heat clung to her bare legs like plastic wrap and the door of the subway car malfunctioned somehow, closing itself on her stomach as she held hands with Maureen, who was inside the car, and Mae, standing outside on the platform, both of them screaming so much that at first Delia wasn't sure what had happened. She accepted the whole thing calmly; somehow it seemed entirely appropriate to be sandwiched like that between her mother and her daughter, hit squarely in the middle as if it were the most natural thing in the world.

Almost detached, Delia watched an old man throw down his newspaper and run toward her, and from the other end of the car a teenage student dropped his book on the floor, leaping gracefully to her side, and it was almost as if she were watching a movie from the ceiling, feeling rather happy despite the circumstances. It wasn't that she was happy to be stuck between the doors like that, watching her beloved Maureen hysterically clawing at the subway car or her mother beating on the glass, but if the baby really was dead, now it wouldn't be entirely Delia's fault.

The door was to blame, they would say (surely they would never forget the day such a thing had happened), and while the old man and the boy struggled to free her, their knuckles white and trembling,

Delia felt a great sense of peace and a calm she hadn't known in a long time. It flashed through her mind that the man from her youth who had flung himself from the same platform where Mae now stood crying might have felt a certain relief, a decision that wasn't his, after all, to make.

It was rather like a dream, holding on to her old mother and her young daughter while the door was inched away from her, Delia trying to let go of Mae, afraid that the train might start moving and her mother be dragged along the platform, but the old woman held on with a surprising strength, and when Delia was freed, the train did start to move and the men pulled tiny Mae into the car, Delia's wrists bearing the deep red indentations of her mother's fingers, and the baby didn't budge.

"My darlin'!" Mae sobbed. "My darlin', darlin' girl," and she threw her arms around Delia's neck and kissed her fiercely on the cheek. "Thank you," she gasped to the two men, patting their sleeves. "You've saved my girl's life," and then she sobbed again and collapsed in the seat.

"You all right?" the older man asked Delia. "I mean"—he gestured at her middle—"everything okay?"

She could only nod. The young man stood in front of her with his hands spread as if she might fall. "You're sure?" he asked, and she nodded again, Maureen burying her face in the brown dress, butting against Delia like a baby goat.

"Shhh." Delia stroked her hair. "I'm fine, sweetie. See?"

"But, Mommy," Maureen rasped. "The baby!"

"Ah, sweet girl," Mae said, reaching across Delia to hold Maureen's hand. "Don't be worryin' about that. Babies are protected well. God sees to that."

Just like drunks and fools, Delia thought. Maybe not this baby, she wanted to say.

And why not? Delia knew her mother would ask her. God has something against you? and then she'd stare at her, the same image in both their minds, the sealed box of sanitary napkins on the shelf of Delia's closet. Although so many years had passed and the children had been perfect, the idea of God's retribution for her sin had never really left Delia's mind.

She looked at her mother's profile, her tight-knit mouth and thinning eyebrows, and said nothing. The men who had helped her seemed embarrassed, now the older man staring at his feet, the teenager drumming his fingers on top of his closed book.

In Flushing, on their way to Dr. Mullaney's office, Mae was walking much too slowly to suit Delia, insisting on looking into every shop window they passed, stretching out the day. Delia would see the same miserable reflection every time they stopped, except in the window of a drugstore, which was covered with a blue transparent paper that cast an eerie light on a mortar-and-pestle display. She looked the worst in that one, like a shapeless cloud with a head.

"Come on, Ma." Delia nudged Mae's shoulder with her elbow.

"We got time, Delia Mary. Hold your horses." She was staring at a collection of dishes in a gift shop. Maureen tugged on Mae's purse and nervously ran her red fingernails through her bangs.

Delia looked down at her own hands, the bitten-down fingernails and fleshy thumbs reminding her of a newborn's bald head. She was distracted by a balloon floating in the gift shop window, and when she looked closer, she realized she was watching her own belly, becoming embarrassed at how pregnant she really was.

The baby was probably fine.

Her middle came to a point, and everyone said that meant she was carrying a boy — no doubt a big one, from the way she seemed to be dragged through the streets by her belly, although boys were less active than girls. (She wasn't sure if someone had told her that or if she had made it up. She tried to picture the way Rosaleen's mouth might look if she had said it.) Or was it the other way around, girls were less active? Rosaleen had had only boys, so how would she know?

She didn't want to think about the baby. She wondered if she was going crazy.

Maureen broke away from Delia and Mae and ran to the corner. Delia tried to remember moving that quickly, but she couldn't. She felt as if she had been born pregnant. Maureen ran so fast she seemed to be able to leave the earth, and Delia felt a quick flash of envy at her own daughter, at her own mother, at the slender women she passed in the street, at anybody who belonged to herself. Everyone she encountered seemed to look at Delia's belly and then away, and she thought about her too-tight wedding ring, at home, in her drawer. She tried intermittently to hide her hand, but two young girls passing by seemed to look for it and poke each other when they realized that her swollen fingers were bare.

At the corner, Delia saw an empty bench underneath a shady tree, and while Mae scanned the window of a shoe store, Delia sat down to wait, and her arms, feeling as if they were filled with water, fell asleep. She had never paid much attention to her arms before this pregnancy, but lately they became numb all the time and felt like the huge skin-colored bolognas hanging in the window of Empire Meats. She shook her arms to wake them, folding her hands in her lap.

I shouldn't feel funny because I have no fingernails, Delia told herself. Sweet Jesus, I don't even have any fingers! From her bologna-like arms dangled what appeared to be ten swollen frankfurters, and Delia began to worry about her preoccupation with meats, remembering that the slight smell of blood in the butcher's always made her shudder.

"Do you think my fingers look like hot dogs?" she asked Mae, who strolled up to her.

"Oh, that's just the cravings, Delia Mary. You must be hungry. We'll see what the doctor says, and then I'll treat you to lunch."

Delia put her thumb to her nose and wiggled four of her frankfurter fingers at her mother.

"Well" — Mae laughed, trying to pull Delia to her feet by the elbow — "and that's a fine thing you're doin' to me. Come on, you're in such a hurry. Let's go."

"In a second." Delia was trying to force her midsection in and out, just in case that might wake the baby, but she had to pee too much to keep it up. She wedged her purse into the space that was once her lap.

Delia wanted to be able to say to Rosaleen on the way to the doctor that the baby began to kick again. But nothing happened, and Delia felt like shoving her fist down her throat and shaking him by the shoulders. There was nothing else she could think of to do. Maurice's sperm, such a weak and puny-looking substance, had unsettled her whole life.

She wished that she had Patty with her. Patty just *looked* at her so much less than Maureen did, Patty tended to calm Delia, but she was at home, with Eugene. As they were leaving Mae's apartment, Patty had waved good-bye, a bowl of wet bread in her lap to feed the birds outside in the garden, and Eugene was tugging on the old green window screen to pull it up, and Delia wondered, as she passed their street, if Patty was still frightened, as she always had been, by a bird's sudden movements.

"Okay, Ma." Delia stood up. "I'm ready."

As they neared the office, Delia saw the Mullaneys' dog, an Irish setter. One of the little boys started down the white stone steps to the street, and one of the bigger ones, his sister, quickly followed, bringing him back to the fold.

The Mullaney children seemed to have everything, Delia thought. They had plenty of air and sun and space and shade in the big white house, ready-made playmates, and even a dog who looked like the rest of them. Delia wanted to protest to someone that she and Maurice loved their children very much even if they couldn't give them everything they wanted to.

"If only we had a house like that one," Delia sighed.

"Yeah," Mae said crossly, flushed and obviously uncomfortable, wiping the perspiration from her upper lip. "And if wishes were horses, beggars would ride."

The baby was probably fine.

"Hullo, hullo," Mrs. Mullaney said to them when they opened the door. She seemed cheerier than usual, wearing a green pleated dress with a thick belt around her small waist, like a giant bug ready to drop larvae on a leaf. "Doctor will be with you in a bit," she said merrily, a musical quality to her voice, as if she were about to burst into song. Mae sat by the door, her usual spot, and Delia sat next to her. There was a woman across the room who seemed twice as pregnant as Delia, and she managed to take up the whole other couch. Maureen sat in one of the tiny maple rocking chairs scattered around the room for the young children, her knees at her chin, her face on top of the children's Golden Book she was pretending to read. Mae stared at the other pregnant woman, and then she turned to Delia.

"I cried because I had no shoes, Delia Mary," she said, raising a skimpy eyebrow, "and then I met a man who had no feet. Do you get what I'm sayin'?"

"Ma, please," Delia said quietly, staring at the back of Mrs. Mullaney's head as she stood at the filing cabinet. "Doctor, would you like the turnips?" she imagined the woman saying to Vincent F. X. (as Delia was beginning to think of him) on a holiday, waltzing through a set of white double doors in their elegant dining room, carrying a shiny golden turkey on a silver platter to a polished wood table set with real crystal and real china, the red-haired children in flattering red-and-green plaids and black velvet sitting quietly in Windsor bow-back chairs, the ones she had seen in a magazine, with their heads bent and their hands clasped in prayer. Then Delia thought of her mother's phony marble kitchen table with the red plastic chairs that were ripped near the seams and one holiday when she was a kid, she didn't know which one it was, only that Denis had come home drunk and Mae, in a blind rage, flipped the table over onto the floor, and the turkey landed on its back, on top of a hemorrhage of cranberry sauce, and had seemed to twitch its legs, as if it were trying to stand. She smiled to herself, turning the page of the magazine she held, which smelled somehow of disinfectant.

Mrs. Mullaney's thin, pale leg flashed by the doorway, and then her husband's broad, thick hand rested on the frame, and Delia thought of them in their big airy bedroom, the doctor's broad, sober erection winking from between the starched flaps of his white coat, and his wife's eyeglasses, the chain snaked around her bare breasts. She wondered idly if they ever climbed on top of the examining table together, crushing the stiff white paper underneath them: she wondered if their bed had white paper sheets. She was starting to blush, and she turned her attention to "Quik'n' E-Z Recipes for Busy Days," feeling foolish.

"Doctor will see you now, Mrs. Delaney," Mrs. Mullaney said, and just by her name, it had seemed as if Delia had come so close to real success. Delia Mullaney, the doctor's wife, with the seven red-haired kids.

The woman handed Delia a gown to slip into, and Delia just knew somehow that Mrs. Mullaney had a dressing room with a small round table and a bouffant skirt, as full as if it were wearing a crinoline, and that one of the red-haired little boys liked to hide underneath it.

She undressed in the bathroom, and slipped into the green gown hanging on the back of the door. She looked at herself in the mirror, her breasts swollen and bulging, with blue veins crisscrossing each other in her white skin, the nipples dark and brownish, the very tips rude and thick. If she forced the issue, her belly would fit perfectly into the basin. The fluorescent lighting made her hair dull, her skin mottled and pitted.

Dear God, she thought, I look just like Eugene.

No matter how carefully Delia prepared, no matter how many showers she took or how clean her clothes were, in Dr. Mullaney's office she felt unclean, uneducated, unworthy, and clumsy, guilty of something unpure, so full of juices and smells and sounds that after she had left, the doctor might have to wash his walls.

You wouldn't move at all toward the end, she imagined she'd say one day to Terence or Todd, as he sat with her at the dreadful marble table on a rainy afternoon, holding a cream-cheese-and-jelly sandwich in his knoblike little fists, watching her solemnly with serious three-year-old eyes.

You really had me scared, she'd tell him, just as soon as he was old enough to understand. She folded her clothes and held them tightly against her chest to keep the gown closed as she left the bathroom and walked barefoot down the hall. Pigs in a blanket, that's what she thought when she looked down at her toes. Stop all this bologna, she said to herself, trying to smile.

She climbed onto the table and then lay down, the paper crunching loudly. The venetian blinds right next to her were open only a sliver, yet the sun was strong and striped her arm and her belly through the sheer white curtains. She was tempted, as usual, to peek out onto the street while she waited for Vincent F. X., but she never recognized anything out there anyway. Everything beyond that window looked fake, like a street scene in a painting. When she got outside, Delia was never sure which window she had been looking through, they all looked so much the same.

"How are you?" the doctor asked. She had never really looked at him before. He was a colorless man, with thinning brown hair brushed back from a high and shiny forehead. Somebody in that family had to be colorless, Delia thought; someone had to absorb the others' rays.

"I'm okay, but the baby is kind of quiet." There, she thought, she got it out.

"Late, are we?" he asked, glancing at her chart. "Let's have a look."

Gently, he placed each of her legs into the stirrups, and then he put the stethoscope on her belly and leaned forward, his face intense. He moved the instrument and listened again. He rolled her onto her side and listened even harder, and while he was listening, he stared at the window. He put his hands in his pockets and stood up, biting the inside of his mouth. He sat down and examined her inside, and then he put the stethoscope back on top of her belly and listened for a long time, until his wife knocked discreetly on the door. "Come in, Mary," he said, sounding relieved. He looked at Delia quickly and walked over to the door and opened it. Delia didn't want to know his wife's name: she felt as if it were one more thing she had to carry.

Vincent F. X. stood in the doorway for the longest time. When she could stand it no longer, she asked him, her voice shaking and her heart pounding in her ears, if something was wrong. Mrs. Mullaney was standing close to her, her hand on Delia's shoulder. Her wedding band was slender and white-gold, like the wedding band of a nun.

"Well, there might be," he said, looking not at Delia but at Mary. The woman's hand began to burn Delia's shoulder, and she shrugged it away. Delia somehow felt sorry for them both. They already knew: the doctor's pointed look at his wife, the wife standing so close to her. Delia knew it herself. The baby wouldn't move, the baby was dead. Simple. She couldn't bring herself to say a word about the subway door. Her face felt hot, and she thought she might throw up, as she held the sheet to her chest, struggling to sit up. They both offered Delia their hands, but she refused them, looking directly into their eyes until they looked away. Her legs had fallen asleep, and she wasn't sure she could stand, although she wanted to run.

"I can't seem to hear the baby's heartbeat," he said, his arms folded defiantly over his chest, as if Delia were about to argue with him. Delia couldn't speak; she forced herself to her feet, and Mary busied herself tidying the paper on the examining table. "Sometimes this happens near the end," Dr. Mullaney said. "Why don't you come in tomorrow morning, early, and we'll try again?"

"But tomorrow's Sunday," Delia said, holding her robe closed. She wanted to get away from these people, grab her belly and her purse and her mother and her daughter before they took anything else away.

"I know it's Sunday, but I'll be here for a while in the morning. Come in around ten, and don't worry. Like I said, sometimes this happens and it doesn't mean a thing."

Sometimes this happens: doesn't mean a thing.

Delia held on to the two phrases as if they were crutches, and she would have held on to them a lot longer if she hadn't forgotten her slip and gone back inside and seen the doctor and his wife whispering together behind the door.

After she was dressed, she stopped at Mary Mullaney's desk with her checkbook in her hand. She wanted to have another little white card, the same one she was given after every appointment, and she wanted to see her name wedged in with the others who had to come back on Sunday, but she was the only one.

She looked down at the appointment book, and Sunday's page was empty.

"No, no, no," Mrs. Mullaney called from the end of the hall. "You can leave a check tomorrow if you want, Mrs. Delaney. You don't need an appointment. We'll be here for you."

She refused to think about anything, going into the lavatory to wash her face with scooping handfuls of cold water. She wouldn't look at herself in the mirror, no matter how much her reflection begged her to.

Outside, Mae and Maureen were giggling over a joke in the latest *Reader's Digest*. Delia forced herself to walk over to them and smile.

She told herself that all the Norman Rockwells wouldn't lie.

NINETEEN

They came out of the doctor's office and walked into a cluster of gnats buzzing around the doorway. Mae shook her head frantically, blowing the bugs away.

"Grandma, you're spitting at me!" Maureen snapped, wiping her cheek with the back of her hand. Delia stared at her, surprised.

"I'm not 'spitting' at you, Maureen," Mae said, angrily walking ahead of them, starting to cross the street.

Maureen looked at Delia. "Well?" she asked.

Don't think about it: Delia said that five times to herself. She touched Maureen's shoulder lightly, and they crossed the street, trying to keep up with Mae. "What did the doctor say, Ma?" Maureen wanted to know. Mae stood perfectly still, trying to listen.

"Oh, everything's okay," Delia said, not looking at either of them.

"When do we have to come back?"

"Um . . . tomorrow morning."

"Tomorrow?" Mae turned to face Delia, stopping dead in the middle of the gutter.

"Come on, Mama, we got the light," Delia said, tugging at Mae's elbow.

"Who cares about the light?" Mae blinked rapidly. "I want to know why you got to come back tomorrow."

"I care about the light," Delia said. "You want to get hit by a car?" She kept walking, trying to pass her mother, but Mae wouldn't let her move a step, grabbing her by the collar. When Mae stood on the curb, she was taller than Delia. She jumped up and stared into Delia's face.

"Now you listen to me, miss. I been alive for over sixty years now, crossing streets and everything else without you or anyone else looking out for me, and God willing, I'll be around for sixty more. Don't you be tellin' me to watch out for cars or when I should cross the street. I'm not a crazy old lady yet."

Delia shrugged and looked at Maureen.

"Why do you have to go back so soon, Ma?" Maureen persisted, hovering behind Mae.

Delia needed money for the subway; she dug in her purse for change. "Oh," she said vaguely, "I think they always do this when the babies are late. I sort of remember Rosaleen going every day when she was late for Kevin."

"Was I late?" Maureen asked. "Was Patty?"

"No," Delia said. "You were both a week early."

"Now, Delia Mary, don't change the subject," Mae said. "Don't give me that nonsense that Rosaleen went to see her doctor every day with one of them. You stand right there and tell me exactly why you have to go back there again tomorrow." Mae poked her finger into Delia's collarbone.

"I don't know," Delia said, near tears. "Just like I said, Ma, because I'm late! For Christ's sake, why don't you believe me?" If only Mae would stop pushing at her!

"That's what the doctor said to you?" Mae asked, narrowing her eyes.

"Yes, Ma, he said something like that."

"Don't you be answerin' me fresh, miss, and don't be cursing at me either."

"I'm sorry, Ma, but you keep asking me and I keep trying to tell you. It's just because the baby is late."

"You're tellin' me the truth? Don't think you're sparin' me from anything. I can take it, you know."

Maureen had been looking from Delia to Mae and then to Delia again. She rubbed at her forehead. "Ma, I'm going to go on ahead, okay? I'd just like to look in some of the store windows again."

Mae wouldn't step off the curb. She watched Maureen walk away from them.

"Mama, please believe me," Delia pleaded, desperate herself to believe what she was saying. "Everything's fine. Let's stop talking about it! I'll come back tomorrow and every day if Mullaney thinks

I'm supposed to. Now come on and let's get home. I don't want to make Maureen upset."

"Make Maureen upset? If anyone's doing that, Delia, it isn't me; it's you. Your face is all white, and you look terrible. Plenty of women are late; it happens all the time. Your brother Gerald was very late, and I never acted like you're acting. You just have to be patient. I think I had more faith than you do. You don't have enough faith." Mae was breathing very rapidly, the front of her dress heaving up and down.

"Mama." Delia couldn't find the fare; she finally closed her purse and gave up. "I don't think I can walk another step. You want to take a taxi home?"

"Well, we can get a taxicab if that's what you want, but maybe you'd be better off walking. Maybe it'd start the birth."

"Ma, please?"

"Okay, okay," she said defensively. "We'll take a taxicab. I didn't get to buy you lunch, I'll treat for the fare."

"Maureen!" Delia waved at her daughter, staring for the longest time at a stack of paper towels in a grocery store window. "Look, honey," she said, holding on to her shoulder and guiding her into the middle of the street. "Raise up your hand high and try to look at the cabdriver until you get one who stops for you."

She's too young, Delia thought, watching the cab pass her by. Nobody is taking her seriously.

"We got one, Ma." Maureen smiled, moving away from a cab backing up. She opened the door for Delia. The driver put his arm out. "Look, lady," he said, "I'm goin' home in a little while. I hope you girls ain't going to no hospital or nothin'."

Mae bent into the front window. "Listen, you" — she strained to read his name — "Mr. Meyers, you gotta take us where we want to go even if it is the hospital, or I'll report you. You want me to do that?"

"Okay, okay," he said, scribbling on his clipboard.

Delia got in and leaned back, smelling the perspiration on her hair. She needed another shower. She wouldn't say anything to anybody. She wouldn't tell Maurice just yet; he might disappear. Maybe it was nothing, and tomorrow she'd find out the baby was fine.

Why get everyone all upset for nothing?

"Now here you go, Mr. Meyers," Mae said, as they pulled up in front of the building. "Here's the fare plus a little something for being so fine a gentleman." She handed him the fare in one hand and a nickel in the other.

"Jesus Christ, lady! You keep it. You need it worse than me!" He threw the nickel on the street, and it bounced.

"Now," Mae said as he tore away, "maybe he'll take the next expectin' woman without a fuss. Delia, when we get inside, you rest on one of the boys' beds, and I'll fix you your dinner."

"Hi, Ma." Patty opened the door and pulled at her hand. "What'd the doctor say?"

"Everything's fine. Were you good for Eugene?"

"We fed bread to the birds and then we took a walk. He bought me ice cream."

"Oh, that's nice," Delia said, Mae brushing past her to tie her apron before her sweater was off.

"Patty, you leave your mother alone," Mae said sternly. "You go outside and get some fresh air, and take your sister with you."

Delia lay down on Gerald's bed. On Eugene's small table, covered with change, was something new, a frizzy-haired bare-breasted hula doll, with purple nipples.

She heard Mae whispering loudly to Eugene in the kitchen. "She has to go back tomorrow. That don't sound good at all."

How can she not realize I can hear her? Delia wondered.

"Oh, Ma," Eugene said calmly. "Babies are late all the time. Guy I know, the wife was over a month late, and the kid was fine."

"A month? Eugene, not a month!"

"Well, late anyway. The hell's the difference? Late's late."

Delia wrapped the pillow around her head and pushed at her stomach, gentle at first and then rougher, kneading herself as if she were making bread. She thought she felt something and stopped breathing to wait, but it was only the beat of her own heart. The more she pushed at herself, the faster her heart beat. If she kept slapping at herself, she thought, her heart might stop, and it would be an easy way out.

"And the subway door closed on her, Eugene!" Mae said. "Anything might have gone wrong." The phone rang.

"Hey, Delia?" Eugene rapped on the door. "Maurice is on the horn."

"Hi," Maurice said.

"Hi."

"So how'd it go?"

"The doctor? Oh, everything's okay," she said lightly.

"See? What'd I tell you? I knew everything's okay. Did he say why the baby is late?"

"No, no, just one of those things. You know."

"Well, maybe ol' Vinnie the Thumb figured wrong this time."

"Yeah, maybe." She tried to listen for background noise. "It's so quiet there. Where are you?"

"I'm still at work," he said. "Paperwork. It's like I got a whole tree's worth of paper in front of me. Tree times what I usually got, ha ha."

"Ha ha. When you coming home?"

"I don't know when I'll be done. I'll see how it goes," he said. "Why, aren't you feeling okay?"

"No, I'm all right." She tried not to sound scared. "My back's sore, that's all. My mother is fixing dinner."

"So your brother said. How's the girls?"

"Fine. Out playing."

"Then I'll see you later. Give you a call if I'm real late." It was what he always said. Then he never did.

When Delia hung up the phone, Mae turned on the faucet. The silence in the kitchen had been deliberate; even Eugene had been listening, Delia realized, growing angry. She slammed the door of the bedroom and lay back down on Gerald's bed, but after a few minutes she got up. Gerald's mattress was too stiff. She sat in the chair by the window, determined not to think about the baby for the rest of the night. What was the use? She couldn't hear a sound, even if the child were screaming for help.

She thought of calling Rosaleen. Rosaleen never seemed to just let things happen to her.

The phone rang again.

"No," she heard Mae say brusquely. "She's layin' down, and I won't disturb her."

"Who is it?" Delia called out.

"Rosaleen," Eugene answered, before Mae could stop him.

"I'm awake, Ma," Delia called, pulling herself to her feet. "Tell her to hold on."

"Here." Mae pushed the phone into Delia's chest, annoyed. "You don't need to be talkin' to anyone. You need your rest."

"Boy." Rosaleen whistled. "What's the matter with the Queen of Saints?"

"Oh, who knows," Delia said, watching Mae's scowl. "She wants me to rest. I was just about to get up and call you."

"How did you make out?"

Mae left the kitchen and went across into the living room, and Eugene followed.

Delia threw herself into a nearby chair. "Well, I'll tell you — or maybe you can tell me. The baby hasn't moved a bit, not in more than a week, and today I hurt myself on the subway — the door closed on my stomach."

She hadn't wanted to mention that. She was going to be positive. "It hasn't moved at all" — she started to cry — "not a single god-damned time, and now Mullaney wants me to come back tomorrow — on Sunday, can you imagine? He couldn't find a heartbeat. I don't know what to do!"

"Oh, shit," Rosaleen said. Delia began to bawl.

"Now look, Delia," Rosaleen said. "Before you go nuts, think a minute. I was real late with Kevin, don't you remember? He was upside down until nearly the very end, and then he turned himself all around and he was fine." Rosaleen didn't sound very convincing.

"How late?" Delia asked, wiping her nose with a paper napkin on the table. She seemed to have forgotten the real issue, the absent heartbeat.

"I don't remember, really, but real, real late."

"How late?" Delia persisted, but Rosaleen had no answer. "Nobody's ever been as late as me, Rosaleen," Delia said sadly. "Nobody's ever been pregnant as long."

"How do you know?" Rosaleen asked. "Have you done a survey?

Go out and find the Queen of Saints and ask her. Guaranteed that Herself'll tell you she carried your brother Eugene for six years. Go ahead and ask her."

"Gerald," Delia said, tempted to laugh. She hoped she was not becoming hysterical. "He's the one she said was so late."

"Look, Delia, everything's okay," Rosaleen assured her. "Call me tomorrow as soon as you get home, okay?"

She forgot again to ask Rosaleen how she felt.

Standing near the window, watching Mae spear a steak with a fork as she got dinner ready, Delia looked out at the pink city hospital down the block. She was happy she wasn't having the baby there, where a procession of stab wounds and heads wrapped in bloody gauze floated through the emergency room. Thick white smoke pushed through the hospital's chimney, forcing the clouds into clotted new designs.

That must be what California looks like, Delia thought, staring at the pink building and remembering a picture she had seen of the sunset along the shore of the Pacific.

She had to look somewhere other than at Eugene, with his sad and skinny face, the whites of his eyes appearing ready to burst around the irises and his joints barely covered with flesh. She always avoided watching Eugene cut his food or turn the pages of the newspaper with his bony fingers: they reminded her of Patty's science book picture of a compound fracture, the leg bone sticking through the knee.

Eugene was the one person in the Heights who was not unhappy to see Hans's Groceries blow up, not when he owed the grocer nearly a week's pay. Hans had complained to Delia and she apologized over and over again but she certainly couldn't pay her brother's debt . . . how could she when she was often charging milk and bread herself?

"I don't know if Gerald'll be home for supper or not," Mae said, bending to lower the flame underneath the carrots. "The boy doesn't eat a thing that's good for him, only cakes from that bakery, garbage his girlfriend gives him."

"Ma, Gerald's thirty-five years old," Delia said, moving behind Mae, opening the oven to pierce the baked potatoes with Mae's long fork. They were done. She stood up and held her back, and she heard it before she felt it, a popping in her ear as if she were in a falling elevator, and then another pop, lighter and softer than the first, and then the flood of water, hot and bluish and covering the floor. She dropped the fork, with the potato still on it, into the liquid on the floor, where it made a tiny splash. She had to find Maurice. He wasn't around when she started her labor with Maureen, he wasn't around when she started with Patty, nor on the day when Maureen fell on the broken soda bottle and needed ten stitches in her arm. She had to think of Maurice first whenever anything went wrong: he took the longest to find.

The water seemed to be getting hotter as it leaked, as if it were coming from someplace increasingly deeper inside her, water so deep that Delia's tan shoes were in it, water enough to slip across the floor and puddle underneath the table. She didn't know what to touch. Her hand fluttered from her belly to the base of her throat and to her ear; she was either crying or laughing, she wasn't sure which, seeing the amazing amount of liquid moving the potato and the fork.

You should have seen the water, she'd tell her little boy as soon as he was old enough. And they thought your heart had stopped!

"Sacred Heart protect us!" Mae yelped, staring at Delia with her mouth open.

"Jesus Baldheaded Christ!" Eugene cried, clinging to the refrigerator as if a tidal wave were about to sweep him away.

Maureen ran into the kitchen. "What's wrong?" she demanded, out of breath. "I heard Grandma screaming from out on the street!"

"Maureen," Delia said calmly, "you go and get Patty and bring her inside. I think this is it."

"The baby's coming?" she asked, and then she noticed the liquid on the floor, thinking of the lady she had once seen in the car underneath the el, those high-heeled shoes in that puddle of water.

"Then go upstairs and get my suitcase, like a good girl," Delia said, a twinge of pain in her back.

When the flood of water stopped, the kitchen of Mae's apartment seemed unnaturally still. Eugene skirted around the puddle, grimacing in his socks, anxious to find his shoes. "Taxi," he said to Delia breathlessly, "got to get one, take you to the hospital."

She was too nervous to feel any relief. Eugene might panic, his arms and legs flying through the streets at dangerous angles.

Mae held Delia gingerly by the wrist, leading her down the hallway into her own bedroom as if she were in a trance. Patty had come inside the room, standing next to the radiator in the corner. "Patty," Delia said, trying to sound calm, "come over here to me. There's nothing to be scared of," but Patty shook her head no and just watched Delia carefully.

"Never mind about Patty now," Mae said, waving a packet of tissues at Delia, shutting the bedroom door behind them. She walked to the window and drew the shade. Patty opened the door and left. "No sense showin' the whole neighborhood your Kitty Murphy," Mae said, her own phrase for private parts, and Delia suppressed a laugh. Mullaney must have been wrong, she thought, the labor starting to grow. She had heard that the doctor had once done an unnecessary hysterectomy. "Here, Delia Mary, I'm givin' you my best step-ins," Mae said, shaking the underwear for Delia to slip into, her face gleaming with excitement, small thin gray curls springing along her shiny forehead. "Come on," she urged Delia, who was just staring at her, "put these pants on."

Bending over, Delia examined the underpants closely, white satin trimmed in fine ecru lace. "Oh, Ma," she said, holding the garment to her cheek, where it felt cool and welcoming. "I never knew you had something so nice," and then she got a walloping contraction and dropped the step-ins on the floor.

"Careful, Delia," Mae said. "These are my best drawers. Don't be droppin' them on the floor like that. My cousin Alice gave them to me for my birthday a long time ago. Don't be losin' them on me, okay?" She pulled at Delia's soggy dress until Delia pushed her away. "Now get out of those wet things and put these on."

"Ma, I'm not a kid," Delia said. "I'm not sick. I can certainly get dressed by myself."

"Well, sure you can," Mae said agreeably, humoring her. "Did I say you couldn't?"

But when Delia stood up, another sharp pain grabbed at her, and she had to hold on to Mae's tiny shoulders for support. "Tell me something, Ma," she gasped.

"Anythin', darlin'." Mae looked concerned.

"Just where would I lose your underpants?"

"Don't be so smart, miss. You could. You were always losin' my good gloves and my umbrellas, weren't you? Are you wearin' your miraculous medal?" She pulled on the top of Delia's dress, looking down at her bra. "Where is your medal?" she demanded.

"In my pocketbook. In my change purse."

"A fine place for something blessed," Mae muttered, reaching down into the neckline of her own dress, unpinning her own medal from her corset. "Patty," she called into the living room. "Bring me your mother's purse." She found Delia's medal and pinned it and her own on Delia's bra. When Delia moved, the medals made a small loose sound like dimes rattling in a shirt pocket.

"I feel like I'm the general in some weird religious army." Delia laughed, giddy and sore at the same time. She was in labor, after all. Everything had to be good.

"And take my beads too." Mae pressed her white pearl rosary beads into Delia's hand. "I'm goin' outside to call your husband, and then I'm goin' to call your doctor and tell him you're on the way."

When Mae flung open the door, Patty was crouched in front of it, listening. "Come here, Patty." Delia held out her arms. The child was shivering.

"Does it hurt a lot?" Patty asked warily.

"Well, it's starting to." Delia wished she had her broken-band watch. She should be timing the pains. "After I leave, I want you to be good for Grandma, okay?" Patty nodded.

Maureen rushed into the room with the suitcase along the floor, her bare ankles red and sore. Delia wondered how many times she had banged the suitcase against her legs while she ran down the stairs. "You still okay?" Maureen asked, wide-eyed.

"I'm fine, Maureen. It hurts, but I'm glad it's almost over." After this baby, Delia thought, I'm going to change doctors. Her pains were becoming good and strong.

"Maurice left work early." Mae was at the door, her hands on her hips. "And he said he was working? How do you like that?"

"He said he had a lot of paperwork." Delia shook her head.

"Well, they said he left and they don't know where he went. Isn't that typical of Maurice. Whenever you need him, he's never around. Never mind about him, that rummy. You have your brother, thank God, to take you to the hospital. I'll find Maurice. Maureen and me'll find him if it takes us all day."

Outside, on the street, a car horn blew. It was for her, Delia realized, when Eugene appeared, gripping the bedroom doorknob with his eyes closed; he didn't want to embarrass her if she wasn't dressed. Sweat ran past the large pores in Eugene's skin. "If you're decent, Sissy," he said, finally, "the cab's outside."

"Eugene, I'm decent. Look. You just take my bag, okay?" She remembered now how it was, the surging and then the stopping, which made Delia think of high tide out at Rockaway, the pains as predictable and determined as a drumbeat, leaving her breathless, waiting for the next one. Patty had been born in only a few hours, sliding out of her like a slippery eel. Maybe this time she'd be as lucky.

"Ah, my darlin' girl," Mae said. "It's the pain quickest forgot." She rubbed at the small of Delia's back, then reached up and kissed her cheek. "Go ahead, my darlin's, and godspeed," she said, but Eugene had his arm in the doorway, so that none of them could move past him. Delia realized that he was offering her his arm for assistance, and then, grateful, she grabbed on to him. "Let's go," Delia said, shutting her eyes against another pain.

Eugene marched through the rooms first, Delia holding on to his sliver of an arm and Mae holding on to Delia's back. Maureen, taller than Mae, had her hand on Mae's shoulder, and Patty tugged on her sister's blouse. They shuffled in a large, slow mass to the door and down the six steps to the street. When Eugene stopped suddenly, Mae crashed into Delia and stepped on her heel. "Eugene, don't worry," Delia said gently. He was so careful, so deliberate, she thought; he tried so hard.

Outside, on the street, a few old people had clustered against the car fenders at the curb, staring at the taxi and then at the Rooneys' first-floor windows, just waiting. Most of them had been at Delia's wedding so many years before, counting on their fingertips seven months later when Maureen was born. Now they stood perfectly still when Delia passed by, rolling their eyes at each other when Eugene, somewhat panicky, began making big circles in the air, as if he were trying to clear a path through a forest. "Move back, everyone," he bellowed. "Let's give her some air. Everybody back," although nobody was in their way. Delia winced with embarrassment and pain, and the old women patted her arm when she passed, the old men clearing their throats and looking away, some of them turning their backs. They stood aside and made a little path leading directly to old Mrs. Krupp, the oldest person Delia had ever seen, with no teeth and a nose determined to grow into her mouth, who was sitting on a tiny stool near the curb. Delia found it hard to look at Mrs. Krupp even when she was feeling fine, barely able to understand a word she said. She made brown rock candy for Maureen and Patty in her tiny kitchen, packing the crumbling pieces into tiny dirty jewelry boxes from extinct department stores, and Delia wouldn't let them eat any of it. "It's the dinosaur teeth that make it special," Maurice had said to the girls.

Delia ignored her, so Mrs. Krupp motioned to Maureen with a twisted and gnarled finger. Patty hid behind her sister.

"Hi," Delia heard Maureen say. She turned around to see her daughter nervously fingering the hem of her shorts.

"You girls make sure you said good-bye to your mother?" She cackled, and Maureen nodded solemnly. "You know why you should say good-bye to your ma, don't ya?" she asked, a string of saliva hanging from her pointed chin. Delia was halfway into the cab, but she turned her head to listen. It was the first time she had understood what the old woman was saying.

"'Cause she has to go through the Valley of Death, and you may never see her again." Mrs. Krupp propped her cane between her knees and leaned back happily.

"You'll see me again, Maureen and Patty!" Delia shouted, one leg in the cab, one leg on the street. Eugene had his hand on her shoulder, as if he were trying to stuff Delia into a box. "You'll see me when I come home. I promise I'll come home to you!" she shrieked out the window, her cries muffled by the suitcase that Eugene threw in practically on top of her before he climbed in the front with the driver, and then she buried her face in her hands and wept.

The last thing she saw were her two young girls growing smaller and smaller as the taxi pulled away. She squinted her eyes to see them huddled together near the many folds of Mrs. Krupp's black dress, under the frightening gaze of her dripping, rheumy eyes.

TWENTY

Mae had sent Maureen out to look for her father in the neighborhood. It was a little after six, and the subway cars above Maureen's head were going back into the city one after the other, their brakes screeching so loudly they rattled the fillings in her teeth. Her legs were shaking, and she had a sweet, nervous taste in her mouth. Her head pulsed near the temple; she thought she might have to sit down on the street, just for a bit.

Jut for a bit, she repeated to herself. I sound like Grandma!

The idea of her mother going off to the hospital with Eugene was frightening. Maureen thought her uncle might drop Delia off somewhere and forget where he had left her.

People were passing by, saying hello, moving much too slowly, like people in a dream. By the time she got to the window of the Shamrock Inn, sweat was sticking her bangs to her forehead. She took a deep breath and looked inside, and after a few seconds her eyes became adjusted to the darkness. Fearful faces turned around to look back at her, and Maureen was shocked as always by how quickly their fear seemed to turn to rage. Whenever Delia sent Maureen to look for Maurice, strangers seemed to want to kill her; Maureen never got used to it.

He didn't seem to be in the Shamrock, as far as she could see — or as far as she could stand to look. She moved on to Healey's.

Big Mike, the bartender, saw her at the window and smiled. Mike was her father's friend; she always saw him in church. Now she was afraid to look away from his face: sometimes the people sitting at the bar waved at her to come inside, the ones who weren't angry with her. If they came to the door to get her, she would run. But if Maurice was inside, she had to get the courage to walk right in and tug on the back of his coat.

He'd tell her to go and sit at a table, and he'd order her a Shirley Temple, putting the glass in front of her, rubbing the top of her head, and then he'd go back to the bar and never turn around again unless the bartender nudged him, suggesting she might want another soda. Waiting for Maurice, Maureen would sit all by herself at a table in the middle of the floor, slowly stirring the ice in her glass with the skinny red straw, conscious of the cold air on her knees, trying to fix her face into a proper expression, but what was that?

Delia had told her that people who hung around in bars were bums, she'd screamed it at Maurice, and yet here Maureen would be, in a bar, with bums like her father — though he was not one of them, not a bum at all. She would fold her arms and tell herself that she was a good girl and a credit to her mother. People said that to Maureen from time to time, when she held Patty's hand crossing the street, or struggled under a big grocery bag. She liked to hear that, but she wanted to think that she was a credit to her father too, and stood for the best in him.

In the bars where Maurice sat, ladies with lipstick on their teeth kissed Maureen's cheek and hugged her, and the smell of alcohol mixed with the smell of their perfume sucked away her breath. Sitting by herself, at a table in the middle of the barroom floors, Maureen thought that it was her turn to be looked at: the bums were finally getting even.

He wasn't in Healey's either. The only person she recognized besides Big Mike was Johnny Devane, Eugene's friend, a neighborhood man who wore his pants under his armpits and string ties on all his shirts. Johnny didn't see her. Maureen smiled quickly at Big Mike and walked one more block to the window of O'Brien's, hidden on a side street. Maureen didn't think Maurice went to O'Brien's, but she just had to find him. She dreaded going inside, if he was there, having to drink too many Shirley Temples, then having to pee, making her way to the filthy ladies' room, walking past the inquisitive glances of unfamiliar men, watching her own father standing there with the others until he also looked unfamiliar, unsafe and different than he did at home, as if he belonged more to them than to her, her mother, her sister.

There was something about the way the women in the bars used the bathrooms, some vulgarity about their splayed feet on the floors of the stalls, their beaten pocketbooks listing on top of the sink, sagging toward the faucets, falling into the rusted basins. It sickened her to watch the barroom ladies comb their hair, clumsily butting their foreheads with the teeth of the comb, powdering their noses with stiff brownish powder puffs, then pursing their lips for the kiss of worn-down lipsticks. They asked Maureen how her uncles were and called them "the boys," just as Mae often did, even the very old ladies, adding layer upon layer of face powder until their skin looked like old dollar bills.

Maureen always felt guilty, waiting for Maurice, worrying that he was wasting his hard-earned money on her, that she drank so many sodas, but what else was there for her to do, just sitting there waiting? When they got home, Delia counted her father's salary expertly, like a teller in a bank, and there was always a horrible moment when she looked up, staring at Maurice incredulously, and asked, "Is this it?" and Maureen would hope he hadn't wasted most of his pay on her.

It was in O'Brien's that Maureen found herself staring at the back of Maurice's strong, square head, watching him throw back and swallow a mouthful of whiskey, all at once, and then down a glass of beer in three gulps, and then, while she was standing there, start the whole process again. She wished she could stay at the window forever, watching his beautiful head and his good square hands, and maybe point him out to people passing by, anything rather than actually go inside to get him.

If the truth were known, Maureen grew afraid of her father when he drank and became progressively unfocused, and sometimes she thought that he'd forgotten not only where she was — sitting behind him, behind the empty glasses, waiting — but also who she was. When they left the bar, finally, he might throw his arm around her shoulder or, worse, around her waist, and she was so aware of the two of them bumping hipbones that she could barely stand it, hugging the storefronts along the avenue, hoping not to fall into the glass like her uncle Eugene. This is okay, she said to herself, desperately needing to believe it, thinking of all the fathers and daughters she had ever known, from Jim Anderson on television, hugging and kissing his girls, to her friend Marie Colletti, from school, whose father once walked up to her in the middle of the street and gave her a big kiss. Maybe he's only kidding, Maureen thought, making believe he's my boyfriend instead of my father. In the storefronts, she watched her own expression while they were walking home and her father told her dirty jokes she pretended not to understand. One time, on the street, he rubbed her backside.

On a Saturday, Delia sent Maureen and her father to the A & P and to the dry cleaners and then to the bakery, but they never got to any of the stores and, instead, just sat in the Shamrock Inn all afternoon, Maurice telling her not to tell Delia that they had stopped off, it would be their little secret. When they finally came home, Delia shut Maureen's bedroom door and demanded to know exactly where her father had been with her all day long, until Maureen felt sick, repeating "Nowhere" again and again until she confessed and then, outside, her father had glared at her, muttering, "Thanks, Moodles," and she couldn't look him in the eye, she had felt so guilty betraying him and was so ashamed.

Bars were for bums. Delia had said it often enough, yet, from the window, Maureen watched Maurice enjoying himself in their company, like Gulliver among the Lilliputians in the book she'd read for school last year.

What did the bums have that Delia and Maureen and Patty couldn't give him? Maureen couldn't figure it out.

She took a deep breath and opened the door, looking only at Maurice, but she felt her face flush anyway as the others held their drinks in midair and watched her. Maurice was the only person sitting at the bar who didn't turn around. "Dad?" she said, her hand on his back. He didn't seem to hear her, so she moved over to his other side and looked up at his profile. His elbow slipped off the edge of the bar, and he dropped his cigarettes, coughing when he bent down to pick them up.

"Dad?" she asked again.

"Hey, Moodles!" He blinked his eyes. "Your mother send you out to find me?"

"No, not really."

"Well, here I am," he said, shoving his cigarettes in his shirt pocket.

"Maureen, how is your mother?" A dark-haired woman with a soiled hair bow was looking closely at her. Maureen stepped back: she had never seen the woman before.

"Um, she's okay," she said politely. "Thank you."

"Nothing yet with the baby?"

Maureen shrugged.

"Answer Dorothy, goddamn it!" Maurice said harshly. "Don't stand there gawking!"

"Um, well, she's probably going to have the baby soon," she said, thinking she sounded like an idiot. "At least we think so."

"Yeah," Dorothy said. "Takin' a long time, huh? Well, any day now."

"Yeah." Maurice laughed and coughed. "We been saying that for a month now. The woman just don't want to let go."

"Daddy, c'mon," Maureen whispered. "Mom wants you home."

"Go 'head, Delaney. The old ball and chain," a fat man in a plaid shirt kidded, tapping the long ash of a cigarette into an empty glass.

"Yeah, yeah," Maurice said, "in a little while. Moodles, you have a Shirley Temple."

"No, Dad, really. Let's just go home now, okay?"

"Yeah, yeah. Few minutes. I'll be ready in a few seconds. You go over to an empty table and have a Shirley Temple and wait for me."

"Yeah, what's the big rush?" Dorothy asked, patting Maurice on the shoulder. "Your dad here works hard—why you draggin' him home already, huh? You tryin' to ruin his fun?"

All the people at the bar, except Maurice, looked at Maureen as if they knew that Delia was on her way to the hospital and were wondering why she was finding it so hard to tell Maurice and get him home. If they would just turn around and mind their own business, she could tell her father, and then he'd have to come with her. If she wasn't back soon, then Mae would start to worry and she'd come after Maureen, just like she did when Maureen went by herself to the Chinese laundry to get the sheets. She hated when the bums asked for her mother. She wanted to cover their mouths whenever they dared mention Delia's name. "Let's just go, Dad, okay?" she said.

Maurice turned around and handed her a glass with a red straw held in place by crushed ice. "I said to go and sit down!"

"Tell Frank about the guy you found dead in the mink stole," Dorothy said to Maurice, her head tilted toward the fat man in the plaid shirt, her fingers resting on Maurice's wrist.

"Yeah, yeah," Maurice said, but he began to cough again, and it took him a few minutes to catch his breath. Maureen smiled and nodded, just in case anyone looked at her, as if she knew the story of the man in the mink stole, had heard it, in fact, a million times at the supper table. The only way to know her father seemed to be through someone else.

"Maureen, goddamn it, I told you to go and sit down. Now do what I say!" he barked, and Maureen started to tremble. On her way to the empty table, Maureen remembered that Delia had given her half of Maurice's name so they'd be close, but it seemed the only way to get close to Maurice was to go to a bar, and doing that always made Delia wild with anger. She always wanted to know why Maureen couldn't manage to make her father come right home, and Maureen didn't know why it was so hard herself.

She couldn't hear the story her father was telling, but Dorothy and the fat man were laughing heartily. Maureen was too far away to make out a word. She was so worried about her mother that her stomach was doing flips, and after an hour she had a pile of red straws in front of her and there was nothing for her to do but pick one up and pretend to write on top of the greasy table and wait.

TWENTY-ONE

The first thing Delia noticed when she got out of the taxi was that the air had finally turned cool.

Cooler in some spots than in others, she thought, running her hand over the heart-shaped wet stain on the back of her dress. She wondered how much water could possibly remain. Eugene noticed the stain, taking off his jacket and handing it to her, but she couldn't wrap the jacket around her middle, so he simply draped it over his arm and put his hand in the small of her back, steering her into everyone who passed them in the hospital corridor. With his other hand, he held her suitcase so tightly that his jaw was clenched, his skin mottled with red blotches.

When they got upstairs, Eugene paced outside the door while the nurse helped Delia take everything off (looking strangely at the pair of miraculous medals), and she weighed her on an ice-cold scale in her bare feet, Delia shaking so much it was hard to read her weight. She was still losing water.

A dry birth, Delia thought. Mae once told her that old Mrs. Krupp's son Raymond was a dry birth and he was never "quite right," they had had to put him away.

An orderly brought a wheelchair for her: Delia tried to pull the hospital gown around her rear end, stretching the fabric to fit. The pains were getting stronger and closer together. The nurse helped Delia into the chair and then pushed her down the hall, where she saw Eugene at the admitting desk. The clerk was asking him if he was the father. "Oh, no," Eugene said, looking stricken. "I'm only the uncle!" The woman looked at him.

"The baby's uncle," Delia explained. "My brother."

He hung his head as if he hadn't gotten the right answer. When the nurse handed him a brown paper bag filled with Delia's clothes, he scratched his hand. "Her ring too," the nurse added, dropping Delia's thin gold band (she had shoved it on her pinkie at the last minute) into his open hand. "And the rosary beads," the nurse added, extracting them from Delia, smiling indulgently.

"Give everything to Ma, Eugene," Delia said gently. "She'll know what to do with it." The elevator opened, and a group of people looked out at them. "Going up?" someone asked, from the rear of the car. "That's us," Delia's nurse said cheerily, backing Delia, in her wheelchair, into the elevator. Just before the door closed, Eugene leaned into the car to kiss Delia's cheek. The last she saw of him was his long mournful face and a flash of silver as the door shut.

She wondered if Mae had sent Maureen to find her father. She was glad that this was one time when she didn't have to face that terrible moment when nobody in the bar knew where he was.

She didn't realize how cold she was until her bare toes brushed against the cool gabardine slacks of the man now standing in front of her. Her water was trickling steadily onto the floor, nobody in the elevator saying a word. She tried to stop trembling, and her neck ached with the effort. She stared at the floor, trying to think of something else, but she couldn't: there was too much of a draft near her backside.

She considered being the last person to get on a crowded elevator, the only one present in a backless dress, a big gap between the wheelchair seat and the wheelchair back, and it occurred to her that she was no doubt, at that very minute, showing what Mae would have referred to as her fine Irish asshole to the immediate world. She tried to think about her baby, and yet at the same time she tried not to laugh. She wished they had let her keep her miraculous medals.

When they got off at the top floor (how strange that the delivery room was just below the roof), the nurse wheeled her down a corridor to a pair of double doors at the end, instantly familiar, leading to the room where both Maureen and Patty had been born. The top half of the door was glass, thick and dull as a plastic punch bowl, and the bottom was heavily polished wood. From her wheelchair seat, Delia saw shadows passing through the misty glass, women in silhouette, their noses curved like beaks, their chins somewhat rounded like umbrella handles.

On top of the doors, "Delivery" was halved into two words: "deli" and "very." Delia pointed at "deli"—and a giant pain walloped her. "Pastrami on rye," she shouted, laughing hysterically and gripping the black plastic arms of the wheelchair. "Very lean," and she pointed to the other door until tears ran down her cheeks.

"What's that, dear?" the nurse asked, looking alarmed. "What on earth is so funny?" But Delia couldn't tell her; she couldn't get hold of herself long enough to speak.

Later, whenever she thought about it, she stopped right there, in front of the double doors, and went no further. In September and the months that followed, when she tried to sleep, some nights next to Maurice, some nights on the couch by herself, she'd only let herself get to the part about the pastrami and the nurse's serious, concerned expression, and then she pulled down something from somewhere inside her head like a giant projector screen.

She found herself desperate to get her old life back, sprinkling scouring powder into the toilet bowl, where it turned the water blue, or scrubbing the bathtub, the warm water running over her fingers, and she thought of that afternoon in her mother's kitchen, her own water in a pool around her feet.

She found that she could barely listen to the theme songs of certain television shows or even some music on the girls' hi-fi, especially if a piano was involved, or a flute, for those instruments filled her with both hope and dread and made her inexpressibly sad.

A six-pound eye round at Empire Meats was the same size as her dead baby girl, and Delia tried to force herself to drop the roast in her shopping cart and not cradle it in her arms. When the butcher plopped the meat on the counter in front of her, she stared at it and thought she'd faint, a piece of string tied tightly around the meat like her baby girl strangled by the cord, and she ran outside, leaving her cart and her order behind, making her way home holding on to the subway pillars, trying not to scream.

For a long while, she had to stay far away from Empire (where she thought of all meat as flesh), and she found she needed to stay away from the A & P, with the fat babies sitting in their strollers, and the boxes of baby foods with Humphrey Bogart baby faces on their labels in Aisle Four.

Then she stayed away from church, where they disregarded Sherry Delaney and buried the stillborn as a stranger, for it was their custom, lacking a saint's name, to call a female child Mary.

Delia spent a long time lying on the couch, underneath the open living room windows, letting the sheer white curtains lick her head and puddle on her chest, and she found that if she positioned herself a certain way, she had a clear view of the sky, with none of the other apartments or the fire escapes to obstruct her view.

It had been very late when it was all over, or maybe it was early in the morning: Delia wasn't sure.

The hallways were dark and cool, and clusters of nurses stared at her as the stretcher passed by, the lights throwing weird oblong shadows across their white uniforms and across Delia's sheet. A Negro nurse helped her into her bed, in a room by herself, at the far end of the hall. The nurse bent over Delia to smooth the sheets, and Delia glanced up at her firm and shiny cheeks, breathing in her soapy scent. (I can't be dead, Delia thought, if I still have my sense of smell.) The Negro woman wore a group of thin silver bracelets that snapped together at her wrists, a comforting metallic tingle. "You doin' okay?" she asked Delia. "Your husband's comin' soon and your mama."

When Delia opened her eyes, Maurice was standing at the foot of the bed. He needed a shave, she thought, and his mouth was quivering.

Don't cry, she said to herself, and shut her eyes, feeling his eyes on her face. He touched her foot through the sheet and held on to her toes. She rubbed her hands across her middle, which was hollowed out like an empty ice cream cone.

She tried to feel something, but nothing would come.

"Delia," Dr. Mullaney had said sadly, using her first name finally, "your little girl didn't make it." She remembered that she had nodded emphatically, not wanting him to think he was to blame. She felt nothing, not grief or even sadness. Surprise, maybe; the wrong word but the right feeling. She hadn't been carrying a son, after all.

Nothing would change now for Maurice — somehow she thought she had let him down.

When she opened her eyes again, Maurice was sitting by her side in an old red chair that had appeared from somewhere. She turned her head and saw an empty bed behind him, and then she looked down and saw that he was stroking her forearm. Mae was standing at the foot of the bed, where Maurice had been, and she was crying. "God has His reasons for things," she whispered, "and ours is not to question."

Then they were all gone.

When she woke, it was daylight, and her room was bright. A different nurse was opening the blinds. Delia saw that she had a sink in her room, with a mirror above it. Someone had brought her flowers, red roses and baby's breath in a vase next to her bed. She sat up, carefully touching her knees and feeling her elbows and wiggling her fingers. She shuddered.

"How are you feeling?" The nurse turned around. She was middle-aged and plain.

Delia struggled to her feet. The nurse grabbed for her arm. "I'd like to use the bathroom," Delia said.

"Okay, but take it real easy now. The bathroom is right outside your door."

Delia walked slowly past the sink and felt as if it were a great accomplishment. As she passed the mirror, she glanced at herself over the top of the nurse's head and tried to feel something again, tried to cry, but no sound came out.

A few hours after Maureen had been born, two nurses helped Delia to the bathroom, just like this, and in that mirror she had looked different to herself, as if she were starting life again as someone else. "I'm somebody," she had whispered to her reflection when she was finally alone. "You're a mother," she had said, pressing her face flush against the glass. "You're nineteen years old, and you're a mother."

It had seemed too wonderful to be true. She might as well have been telling herself that she was now President.

"We're right out here if you need us, Mrs. Delaney," someone had said through the bathroom door, alarmed no doubt by Delia's talking to herself. "You've only to press the red button on the wall."

Mom, she had thought. Mommy.

Then she had said it out loud:

"Mother. Mama. Ma." She had liked the last one least.

"Hey, Mom?" she had asked herself, to see if somehow her voice had changed, and then she had whined: "Mom-me-e-e!"

"My mother says . . ." Delia had rolled her eyes at herself and laughed. "This is my mother." She pointed at herself, watching her reflection in the glass.

"You okay in there, Mrs. Delaney?" a voice had asked.

"Oh, yes, I'm fine," Delia had said, overcome with joy.

"My daughter," she had said to herself, looking into her own eyes. "My daughter, my beautiful Maureen."

But this time was different than the first, different from Patty's birth, which was simple and quick.

This time she used the bathroom while the nurse waited outside and helped her back to bed (carefully, as if Delia had been broken in half), where she lay just as still as a stone, listening to Dr. Mullaney, who had suddenly appeared, telling her that these things happened sometimes and he didn't always know why. There was nothing wrong with her, with Sherry, he said, straining to remember the baby's name. It was the cord, he said. It was either too short or too long or too thin or too thick; Delia didn't remember, just remembered that there was something wrong with it.

Mae had warned her not to raise her arms above her head.

(Delia tried to remember when she might have done that.)

"As soon as you're feeling better," Dr. Mullaney said, "you can go home. You seem to be doing fine. You're a healthy woman, Mrs. Delaney," he said, shaking his head, and then he left.

Later, in the afternoon, Maurice popped his head in Delia's room and then out again. Delia stared at the door, thinking she might have imagined him. He came in, finally, and sat down warily in the red chair. He had a bunch of daisies behind his back; he plopped them in her lap.

"Who gave me the roses?" she asked.

"Me," he said. "Roses yesterday, daisies today."

"What's tomorrow?" she asked. Better to keep things light. Her throat was sore; it would hurt both of them to cry.

"Tomorrow I'm bringing you the botanical gardens," he said, smiling, starting to crack his knuckles.

"My throat is killing me," Delia said suddenly.

"How do you feel besides your throat?"

"Better, I guess," she answered, although her cheeks felt as if they were full of cotton, her jaw aching.

"Yeah, you look okay," he said, rubbing his eyes.

She wanted him to collapse and throw himself across her lap and cry, right on top of the daisies. She wanted him to do that for her, because she couldn't.

"Yeah," he said, into the quiet room. "You look real good."

How are we going to get through this? she wanted to scream at him. How can we do this, bury a baby and go on?

"You remember John McGarry?" he suddenly asked.

Cops don't throw themselves over laps, she reminded herself.

"Um, I think I remember him. What about him?"

"Curly red hair?" he asked, making circles on top of his own head. "At a picnic a few years back?"

Of course Delia remembered. He had two little girls. Delia had held the baby on her lap, the infant's hair so pale it was nearly transparent; her skin had the waxy feel of another woman's child. "Yes, Maurice, I remember him. What about him?" she asked impatiently.

"In the hospital. Got hit with a Chesterfield chair. Some stupid bastard threw it out a window yesterday. Landed right on top of his head."

"Is he all right?" She felt safe, somehow, with this new bit of information, wondering exactly what she would do if he did throw himself across her lap. Better to be strong, she told herself.

"Yeah, he's okay. Take a lot to kill that fathead," Maurice said, sitting back in the red chair, exhaling loudly.

Finally, he stood up and put both his hands on her shoulders. "I just came from Holy Sepulchre," he said softly. "It's all over."

"What's all over?" she cried.

"The baby. I had her buried at Holy Sepulchre. My brothers are over there, my father and yours too. Father Sullivan came with me."

She put her head back on the pillow, breathing in tears, feeling as if she were drowning.

"Aw, Delia." He moved closer to her, pressing her head to his shoulder. "Go ahead, cry. Best thing for you to do. I'm sorry," he whispered, "I'm so sorry." He patted her hair. "I know how much you wanted her."

"You don't know," she blurted. "No, you don't!"

"But I do," he said, surprised, rubbing his cheek as if she had slapped him. "I wanted her too."

"You said you didn't care if we had another 'kid.' 'Kid,' you said, just 'kid,' as if another baby didn't matter at all, as if she was just a . . . thing!"

"All right!" he screamed. "Goddamn it, all right! I'm sorry— didn't you hear me the first time? I call the other two 'kids' all the time. So do you!"

"We shouldn't have tried again," she sobbed. "We should have left well enough alone. It was just tempting fate!"

"I know, I know," Maurice said quietly, holding tightly to Delia's wrists. His eyes were red. "We shouldn't have, but we did, and now it's over and done with, and we gotta go on."

"What did you have them put on her?" Delia asked, rubbing her eyes.

"Her christening dress. The dress Maureen and Patty wore. That what you wanted?"

She nodded. "Did you see her?" Delia asked, hiccuping. "Why couldn't I see her, Maurice, why not?"

"Last night, as soon as Mullaney called me, he asked. I didn't know what to do. I asked your mother, and she told me to ask one of the parish priests, and he said seeing her would be too hard on you.

He came with me over to Conlon's, and we brought her over to the cemetery. He prayed a long time for her, Delia. And she was baptized."

"What did she look like?" Delia begged him, now holding his wrists. "Please tell me, what did she look like?"

"She was blond," he whispered, as if he were strangling, "and she looked big — six pounds, they told me, but she looked more like eight or nine. She had just a little bit of blond hair on top, and she looked like she was sleeping, like a beautiful doll, not a mark on her. She was perfect."

"Well, then, why did she *die*?" Delia asked loudly. "If she looked so terribly *perfect* and she looked so beautiful, like a *doll*, why did she die?"

"But you know already why she died, Delia. She was strangled by the cord. Isn't that what Mullaney told you, just like he told me — that it happens sometimes toward the end, that it just happens sometimes?"

"You know," Delia said, not listening to him, "I got pregnant with Maureen the first time and I always expected something bad to happen to her, but she seemed to be fine, and then I expected something bad to happen to Patty just because Maureen was okay. But not now, not to this baby. Why did God — goddamn Him anyway — why did He take her, a little baby like that?" She began sobbing all over again.

"I don't know, Delia. I swear to Christ, if I knew I'd tell you. Even the priest," Maurice said sadly, "didn't know what to say to me."

"The *priest*," Delia spat. "Don't tell me about any priests or any goddamn Church or the goddamn sacraments or even goddamn God. Don't hand me any of that shit! They better not come in here with their hands over their hearts. I'll throw them out the door, and I won't even look in their goddamn faces! I want them to give me a reason, a goddamn good reason why it happened. Can you do me one favor, Maurice? Will you see to it that the holy priests stay the hell out of this room and away from me? Would you tell that goddamn Father Sullivan for me to drop dead?" she cried, throwing herself back against the pillows.

"Ah, Delia, sweetheart, it isn't good for you to say these things. It doesn't do any good, can't you see!" Maurice wiped his index finger rapidly across his upper lip.

"What is good for me, then? You tell me what's good for me! Is it good for me to lose my baby, Maurice? Look at how swollen my breasts are!"

"I don't know anything anymore," he cried. "Jesus, I've just about worn myself out asking why. The kids want to know what happened, and I don't know what to tell them." He buried his face in his hands. "Jesus Christ, first my brothers, and now this. . . ." He shook his head and banged his fists on his knees. "Goddamn unfair," he said. "I can't take this, Delia. I'll come back later on." He walked toward the door, and Delia hated him then as she never had before, leaving her in her bed in misery, and it wasn't only him. She hated her girls, who had led her to believe that having babies was a simple thing to do, and she hated her mother, who had never taught her how to fight. She hoped that Maurice would die.

He turned at the door and looked back over his shoulder.

"I kissed her, Delia," he said, his voice cracking. "Once for me and once for you."

TWENTY-TWO

On her second night in the hospital, nobody came to see Delia.

Maurice had to work. Mae couldn't come because she had a cold, and Patty and Maureen weren't old enough to be allowed up to see their mother. She had hoped that Rosaleen might drop by, but then Rosaleen was due to give birth any day herself.

Delia turned her light off, listening to the excited hum of the visitors in the halls. She had to stay in the hospital at least four days, according to Dr. Mullaney. She was going to make use of the time, going back to the beginning of her life, as far as she could remember, to try to figure out if a mistake she'd made had caused this awful thing to happen to her.

She had been consecrated to the Blessed Mother as a very little girl, and while she didn't remember any ceremony, she remembered the dresses she had worn, hanging in the closet, white and light-blue organdy.

She had liked to sit in the middle of the living room and watch bits of dust floating through the thin stream of sunlight that fell across the faded rug, and sometimes she tried to catch them, but when she did that, grabbing at the air, Mae looked worried and made her go inside her room to read a book. (Her father's mother, for whom she had been named, was a dreamy, sensitive woman given to long walks, entire days walking from one Irish village to the next, leaving behind twelve wild children.)

Delia was fond of fabrics, tracing the threads in the curtains and the towels with her fingers (Mae forever pulling Delia's face out of cloth then, sending her to her room again to read a book). She would examine the sofa closely, amazed to see the fabric turn to strings and the strings to tiny segments and the segments to bits and the bits to nothing, and it was scary and exciting to the young Delia that every-thing familiar was ultimately made up of nothing at all, the world itself as loose and unfettered as a child's lost balloon.

When she was old enough to go to school, the sisters told her that she was dust underneath it all, and she thought of the dust at home scampering through the sunbeam and she was worried: who had that dust been?

After a long time remembering her childhood, she decided she needed to go back further than herself to figure things out. How had Mae, who always knew how to make things safe for her children, failed her?

"Don't wear your rubbers in the house," she had warned them, "or you'll go blind," and they didn't, and not a single one of them needed a pair of glasses (although Delia tested Mae once by closing her bedroom door and stomping around in her red rubbers, then trying to read the fine print in her missal). Sometimes people Delia passed on the street wore thick glasses and heavy rubbers, and she wondered who had raised them.

Mae had never let them open a present with a knife, so as not to cause bad feelings between giver and receiver, and she had never allowed them to give anything sharp as gifts. They had learned to cut ribbon and even thin twine with their teeth, and none of them had cavities.

They were never, ever, to open an umbrella in the house unless they wanted pain to fall upon their whole family. (Gerald had proved this one to be true: while Delia was clomping around her room in her red rubbers, she tripped and sprained her ankle, but it was Gerald's fault for sneaking into her bedroom. Openly defying his mother one day, he had accidentally jabbed his brother Eugene in the eyebrow with an umbrella's sharp metal tip, which caused Denis to rise from the sofa where he had been napping and beat his three children about their heads with a rolled-up *Daily News*.)

No shoes on the table, Mae had said, no hats on the bed. Spill salt and you'll have to throw some over your shoulder: not the right shoul-der, the left one, or you'll have to spill more, and salt is dear.

Knock wood, she often said, rapping the top of her head with her work-hardened knuckles.

Mae was energetic, rapping her head and tossing her salt and grabbing hats from the bed and ripping string with her teeth and throwing the shoes from the table. Maybe, Delia thought, that was why they had so little company; their rare guests tended to hug the walls, watching little Mae carefully.

On New Year's Day, Mae always insisted that a man be the first to cross their threshold, to assure a full year of luck. One New Year's Eve, her father never came home at all, and at dawn Mae woke Gerald, who was six at the time, and made him walk through the doorway three times (six times three equaling manhood), for the last thing Mae wanted to see on New Year's Day, she said, was a pair of cops dragging Denis into the apartment. She didn't know exactly what that might portend for the coming year, but she wasn't taking any chances.

It was as if the past were covered up with glue, or mucilage, as her mother called it, a word that made Delia gag. She stared at the ceiling. When a nurse peeked into her room and asked if she wanted something to help her sleep, Delia swallowed the red pill and the paper cup of water so quickly that she nearly choked, and the nurse looked fearful, as if she was wondering how she might get help, in a room so far from the others.

There was a double-sized wooden chest in the room, and an old silver radiator stashed in the tiny closet, and a bent, rusted pipe on the empty closet shelf. That morning, when she couldn't sleep, Delia had looked through the bottom drawers of the wooden chest and counted seven worn blankets that smelled of lemon, like nuns' habits, and some extra sets of brown-print draperies, the same as the faded ones on her dirty window, and a dozen boxes of white Kleenex, and it made Delia sad to think of herself mixed in with the hospital's supplies.

She was convinced that the sleeping pill wouldn't work; it was the first one she had ever taken. Her feet were chilly; she stared at the dresser drawers, thinking that she really should get up and unfold one of the blankets, and the next thing she knew, it was morning. She had the distinct impression that she had slept with her eyes open, as if they had locked on the dresser drawer pulls.

228

That afternoon, Mae came to see her; she was feeling better. Mae had brought the girls into the lobby to wait, writing little notes to Delia on slivers of pink stationery that Delia recognized as her mother's, so old that the edges were feathered and gave Delia chills to touch.

"Dear Mommy," Patty wrote. "I miss you and please come home."

"Dear Mom," Maureen wrote. "We are fine and don't worry about us. I am helping Grandma take care of Patty. We are sorry about the baby and all. We love you, I love you."

"Dear Patty," Delia wrote back on a crumpled envelope from the bottom of Mae's pocketbook. "You are a fine and good girl and I will come home soon." "Dear Maureen," she printed on the other side, around Mae's address. "I am so proud of you and I am sorry too. And I love you."

Mae brought Delia a present, a soft pink bed jacket, in case company came to see her. She powdered Delia's back, and she tied her hair with pastel ribbon she had brought, and she made Delia smile, complaining how hard it had been to keep the ribbon out of Patty's curious hands. She sat behind Delia on the hospital bed, brushing her hair, holding the ribbon in her mouth, until she had every strand in her fist, just as Delia did with Patty, and she asked Delia where the years had gone. "To me," Mae said, "you look exactly the same as you did when you were three."

Then, on the afternoon of the third day, Mae told Delia that Rosaleen had given birth that morning to another son and called him Edward. Delia stared straight ahead, grabbing on to her knees through the sheet. Mae caught a knot in Delia's hair and tears came to Delia's eyes. "Oh, but the children get a real kick out of sending you those notes," Mae said quickly.

Don't hear, Delia told herself, don't feel. "And I love to get them," she said, "those notes."

Mae straightened the shoulders of the pink bed jacket, hugged Delia, and left. Delia stood up and walked to the window to watch her daughters, her living children, leave the hospital with their grandmother and walk toward the bus. What if the bus goes out of control and kills them? she asked herself. What's to say it won't happen? She waved at Maureen, a tiny speck five floors below, and she blew a kiss to Patty, although Delia knew by the way the children blindly scanned the windows that they couldn't see her at all.

Maurice called. He wouldn't be able to come back; he was on a special detail. "Let me know when they'll let you go," he said. "I'll come and get you. Only a few more days, right?" Well, as long as she was doing fine. Yes, yes, she assured him, she was doing splendidly.

Then Rosaleen called the next afternoon, before Mae showed up, before Delia had a chance to slip into her bed jacket.

"Hey, Delia," Rosaleen said, in a weary voice. "How are you?"

"Okay, I guess." Delia rubbed at her eyes and sat up. "How are you? Congratulations," she said. Don't be a sore loser, she told herself.

"I never thought this would happen, Delia," Rosaleen began. "I mean, it's just such a shock."

"Well, I knew it. I knew there was something wrong," she said. "The — *she* didn't move like she should have. I was so sure it was a boy," she said, and then tried to stop herself. She, Delia thought. Sherry. My baby.

"But didn't Mullaney know?" Rosaleen asked.

"No, not until the end," she said, remembering that the doctor had been sitting by her feet, nervously dropping things. She couldn't see his whole face, only his sweaty pale forehead and his green cap popping up like a buoy between her knees, and afterward the room was so quiet, an orderly next to her mopping the floor. There was drool on her chin. She had tried to wipe her face with her hand, but she was still in the restraints.

"Did you have an easy time, Rosaleen?" Delia asked. Suddenly she felt dizzy, light enough to float. What should she call her experience, she wondered, a birth or a death?

"Oh, yeah, I had an easy time," Rosaleen said. "I saw the girls coming out of Cohen's with your mother. Patty showed me the new crayons your mother bought her. They're awful good kids, you know?"

"I know they are. They won't let them up to see me. You have to be sixteen."

"Well, your mother said you'd be home in another day or so."

"That's what they're telling me." Delia couldn't wait to leave her depressing, lonely room. "What hospital are you at?"

"I'm at Saint Claire's again. They should give me a discount, don't you think?"

"I guess."

"Don't worry, Delia. Once you get your kids back up to your own place and you come home, everything'll get back to normal. You'll see."

The kids. Delia was starting to forget what they looked like.

"How's Maurice?" Rosaleen asked. How's he taking it? That was what Rosaleen was asking. As if Delia had any idea.

"He's had to work," Delia said. "He hasn't been here very much."

"Danny saw him yesterday, on the train. He didn't say too much."

"He said he's on a special detail." Delia tried to sit up straight. Her mouth tasted terrible. Her hands were dry and felt shrunken and tense, like hands kept too long in water. Suddenly Delia began to cry.

"Aw, Delia," Rosaleen said. "They aren't as strong as us, you know that. Don't cry, please don't. Lookit, I called to ask you a favor anyway."

Delia wiped her eyes with the sheet. "What favor?" she asked, rubbing her cheek.

"Would you be Edward's godmother? We want to ask you and Maurice to stand up for him."

Delia shook her head; she couldn't answer.

"Oh, you don't have to let me know right now," Rosaleen said, in the bleak silence. "Soon you'll be home and feeling fine, and then you can decide. You two can always try again, you know."

"No," Delia said. She didn't even want a boy anymore; she just wanted Sherry. She'd never try again, she was sure of it. "Never, never again," she said.

"Well, that's what you say now. I said it myself, after the hard time I had with the third one."

"Yeah, Rosaleen," Delia said, growing impatient. "But there's a real difference between you and me."

"What?"

"Your child didn't die." Delia felt her face distort as if she were having a stroke, her lower lip flattening, a tightness in the base of her throat.

Rosaleen was quiet. "No, Delia," she said finally. "I guess he didn't. Look, I'll call you when you get home. Let me say good-bye before your mother appears. The two of you should visit alone," and she hung up.

As soon as she put down the phone, Delia tried to go back to the beginning with Rosaleen, but she forgot what sort of child Rosaleen had been, only that she had worn her house key on a dirty string around her neck. Mae never forgot that. When Rosaleen first came to Delia's house, Mae sat on the windowsill and asked her about her parents. Delia remembered her shame: Mae's shoes barely touched the floor.

Unlike Delia, Rosaleen sometimes skipped Mass altogether. She had waited (unlike Delia) so long to be churched after Kevin's birth that her son was old enough to crawl down the aisle after her. Where was Rosaleen's punishment? She had even waited until the third one was six months old before she had him christened, his tiny christening cap, with its earflaps turned up, so tight he looked like a miniature aviator.

Mae had said it was bad luck for the baby not to be christened as soon as possible; bad luck if the mother put off being churched.

Just then Mae burst into her room and, before she said a word, cradled Delia's head underneath her own chin, a long silver hair brushing Delia's forehead. She smelled, as she always had, of soap detergent, starch, and bleach.

Somebody had to have sent Kathleen Delaney to Delia's bedside; there was no other way she'd have shown up. It couldn't have been Maurice; he knew that Delia just didn't like her. She was too cold and unfeeling, Delia had said; she didn't take an interest in the girls.

It was Mae, Delia thought; Mae had probably put her up to it. "Oh, Delia could certainly use some company," Mae might have said. "She's over there all by herself," and Delia pictured the way Kathleen might have adjusted her summer straw hat in her hallway mirror, lacing her nurse's square shoes, setting out intently in the summer's heat to do her Good Deed.

Kathleen Delaney was often praised in the neighborhood, tucking the shriveled, clawlike hands of terribly old people underneath her strong elbow and directing them out into the sunshine and fresh air. Even when she wasn't working at her own hospital nursing job, she was careful to learn who might be sick in St. Immaculata's parish, setting out for the nearby hospitals on the hot buses and clattering trains, just to visit.

If Kathleen happened to meet anybody on the street who knew her today, Delia thought she'd manage to look pale and wan but not complain; she'd be stoic in the face of such a misfortune: her poor daughter-in-law, and her poor son, and that poor child.

"I was just taking a nap," Delia said when Kathleen stepped into her room, handing Delia a bunch of white carnations. "Oh, carnations," Delia said, feeling guilty. "They're my favorite." She buried her face in the flowers, which smelled of disinfectant.

"I remembered that." Kathleen smiled. "Just something I thought you'd like. But you go ahead and rest, Delia. I can entertain myself. First I'd like to find a vase," she said, squatting down, rummaging through the nightstand. Delia knew that all she would find in there were extra bars of soap for the entire maternity ward and tightly rolled white facecloths. "They usually have vases in here," Kathleen said. "At least they do in all the hospitals I'm familiar with. Ah," she said, pulling out a cardboard container. "Here's one. You shut your eyes, Delia; you need your rest. Don't think of me as a guest. We can visit when you wake up. I'm going outside to find some water. I hope this vase doesn't leak. Be back in a bit."

Her eyes closed, Delia nodded. She didn't know if she had the strength for this visit. When Kathleen was nervous, she talked non-stop. Take your time, she thought.

After Maureen had been born, Kathleen did not show up until the fourth day. Neither Mae nor Delia could understand it, Maurice handing out cigars in the hospital waiting room and his mother nowhere in sight. "She's rejecting this child just as she rejected Maurice," Mae said, staring at Maureen through the nursery window. Delia wondered how her mother came up with these things, unasked

233

and usually wrong, her tight-lipped judgments. Somehow, even at that early stage, Mae had to be the better grandmother, pulling Delia aside at Maureen's christening to say that Kathleen, holding the baby, hadn't washed her hands.

When Patty was born, Kathleen didn't come to the hospital at all, merely showing up at the apartment with a big walking doll for Maureen, staying only a few minutes. Mae pulled Delia into the kitchen and said that Kathleen was trying to buy a clean conscience.

Kathleen had little to do with the girls, never staying with them when they were infants. Delia had asked her only a few times, and then she gave up. Kathleen had seemed so reluctant, as if her visits to her newborn grandchildren were only obligations: a pat on the babies' heads, and she was gone. She had even had to ask Kathleen to dinner. She never just showed up like Mae was always doing.

"You're lucky, Delia," Rosaleen had told her. "You should never complain. Danny's parents fight a lot and then his mother comes over to sleep on the couch. Count your blessings."

Now, Delia thought, with everything that's happened, she hands me flowers, accusing me, somehow, of failing her son. She never showed up when I did it right.

Delia turned to face the wall, hoping that Kathleen would meet someone she knew out in the hall, lose track of the time, until visiting hours were over.

"Here we go," Kathleen murmured, putting the vase on the nightstand and throwing out the rotted daisies standing in a tumbler. (Mae had taken the roses home for the girls.) She sat down in the red chair, falling into the dents left by a thousand behinds. She got up again, restless, and closed the curtains against the bright and sunny day. It was hard for Delia to believe that things were going on outside just as before, with traffic and hot weather and mornings. When she thought about it, she wished there had been a moment of universal silence for her baby. ("It's damn, *damn* hot," someone had said that morning, passing her door, and then laughed, and Delia was furious that anyone had the peace of mind to do that.)

Good old Kathleen Delaney, Delia thought, staring at the green wall. The woman had suffered in the stifling August steam, trudging through the smoke that rose from the manhole covers, walking underneath apartment windows where thin slivers of curtains were knotted together above the windowsill in hopes of a breeze, all just to minister to Delia, who was now one of her needy. She heard Kathleen open her purse, the rattle of cellophane, and she smelled peppermint. It was too difficult to feign sleep. Delia rolled over and sat up.

"Oh," Kathleen said gaily. "You're awake now."

"Can I have a peppermint?"

"Why, certainly, dear. Can I help you sit up?"

"No, I can do it," Delia said, suddenly strong enough to run around the block five times. She pushed her shoulders against the headboard.

"How do you feel, Delia?" Kathleen asked, pushing her tortoiseshell eyeglasses onto the bridge of her nose. She had strong, square hands like Patty's, with neat short fingernails.

"I'm okay," Delia said for what felt like the millionth time.

"I spoke with Mae. She said the girls were fine. I offered to take them back to my place, but Mae wouldn't hear of it. She said you're coming home tomorrow, and I have to work early anyway."

Delia was grateful for that; she couldn't imagine her girls sitting quietly in the middle of all those dusty pictures of Maurice. She looked at Kathleen and shrugged. It was something new she had learned, easier than thinking, easier than speaking. Shrugging and closing her eyes. She had never realized how simple it was.

"I'm awful sorry about the baby," Kathleen said, her eyes filling up. "A terrible thing that's happened to the both of you."

"I just want to get out of here," Delia blurted. "I'm so tired of just sitting here, thinking about it. I've got to get my mind off it."

Kathleen smiled gently. "You won't get your mind off it for a long time, dear, a very long time. Don't expect it of yourself. Allow yourself to think about it as much as you want to."

"But that's what I've been doing, and I think I'm going crazy! It's almost like I'm never going to get away from it, never going to forget."

"Oh, you will. Eventually. And you won't go crazy, although sometimes you'd like to. After my babies died, I wanted to go crazy. I wanted my husband to lock me up and throw away the key, I really did." She sighed and closed her eyes. "I wanted to die myself, just so I wouldn't be able to think about it another second."

"How long? How long does it take to get over it, at least just a little bit?" She wanted a time frame, some structure. Six months, she wanted Kathleen to say knowledgeably, a year. Delia, when she was younger, had worried that Kathleen might want to talk about her other sons and Delia wouldn't know what to say.

"It was more than forty years ago, and I don't think I'm over it yet," Kathleen said softly. "Not a day goes by that I don't think of them, such little boys, Terence and William. I might be washing dishes in the sink or sitting on a bench in the park or even at work, and I suddenly feel I'm still on that trolley car, on my way to the hospital, the baby Terence on my lap, barely breathing from the influenza, and the other, William, almost as sick, with a woman across the hall. I was frantic to get that baby to the hospital; in those days, very few came out alive. Everyone around me was so scared of that influenza that they wouldn't dare peek into the blanket. That baby laid in my arms like a stone, but I had to take him; I was too frightened to wait until Sean came home from work. I took him myself, and I had to stand on the trolley it was so crowded, and when I looked up, at the trolley coming back, wasn't Sean right there, reaching out at me and I couldn't do a thing but cry. And when I got there, the baby was gone, and then the next morning I lost William. I buried them together, in the same casket."

"Oh, my God." Delia shook her head, as if to push Kathleen's words away.

"But then I had Maurice." Kathleen touched her glasses and smiled faintly.

"But not me. I won't have any more."

"No," Kathleen said, as if it were already decided, and Delia felt grateful. She didn't say she had two healthy children she should be thankful for, surely she was young and could try again. Kathleen added nothing, just sat quietly, looking at Delia.

"You know, Delia," she said finally, "it's still so hard for me to look at any infant or any very young child and not see one of my boys' faces. Even my own grandchildren—especially my own grandchildren—reminded me so much of my own. They looked just like mine. Such beautiful infants they were, mine and yours."

"I never saw her at all." And Delia began to cry. She could never cry enough, it seemed, from that first day in the hospital. Her throat was always sore from the dry sobbing. "I don't even know what she looked like."

"She looked like an angel. Maurice told me."

"I just wish I had seen her for myself."

"I know you do, Delia, I know." Kathleen stood up and hugged her. Her chest felt dense and soft under Delia's head, surprisingly so for someone so thin. Delia let herself sag on Kathleen's shoulder.

"What you will have to do, love, is what I did. I had so much feeling left for those boys after they'd gone that I had to put it somewhere; it was too much for me to hold inside. I tried to put everything I had into Maurice, caring for him as if he were three boys rather than the one, and I think he resented it. All those feelings of mine weren't doing either one of us any good. It was too much love, if there is such a thing, and I had to force myself to hold back my feelings and let him go his own way, so scared that he'd be taken from me as well. I don't think it made him strong, Delia. I think it made him weak.

"I tried to spread my feelings around, working and church and just helping people, and I began to release those feelings, and the sadness just got less. Not gone but less. You'll have to look hard and find something else that you can love."

The trouble with that, Delia thought, looking into Kathleen's sincere face, is that children are all I have ever really loved, and soon my children will be grown up and gone. I wouldn't know where to start.

Late in the afternoon of her last full day in the hospital, right before dinnertime, Delia fell asleep and dreamed that her father was next to her, rubbing her cheek softly with his index finger, which was no longer callused and dirty, as in life, but part of a clean, trustworthy hand, pink and strong. She felt as if she had just met him, so grateful to start again that she moved her cheek against his hand like a puppy. Her smile was a warm, sweet feeling spreading across her face. This father wore a gold wedding band, cold along her cheek, although in life Denis Rooney hadn't owned one.

"Why are you here?" she asked him.

"Why, I've come to take you home," he said, stepping back to straighten his gray flannel blazer, another thing he had never owned, and his bright-red tie.

"Why are you dressed up?" she asked.

"I'm meeting my new granddaughter," he replied, walking to her nightstand and smelling her flowers. She stared at him in amazement. He seemed to be waiting for something. What did he want her to do? She tried to think. It had to be important. When she looked down, she saw a lacy cloth like the train of a wedding gown draped around his bare feet. The cloth reached across the floor of her room and out into the corridor.

"I can't go with you," she said, staring at her father as he walked over to her window. "What would happen to my girls?"

"Take my hand," her father said, smiling happily. "Hold on to me and follow that cloth, and I'll bring you to your baby."

Delia woke with a start, her heart racing in her chest. She hurried into the hall, sweating and out of breath. Dr. Mullaney, standing at the nurses' station, waved. She nodded, came back inside, sat on the edge of the bed, and drank a glass of water. Her dinner, under its silver dome, was on the dresser. She looked at her white carnations, then down at the floor, where the lacy train had been. A piece of tissue lay there.

She wondered if she would ever be normal again, cooking dinner or tucking the girls into bed. She wasn't sure if she could just shut off the light and walk outside. She wanted to go home, to sleep next to Maurice in their sagging bed; she wanted to put on shoes and walk on pavement, although she felt raw and transparent. Maybe she'd have to work up to that part.

A short nurse with a rounded back and thick legs walked past her door, her elbows turned out like a longshoreman's. When the janitor passed by, he pulled his mop and pail to the other side of the hall and looked in at her.

Delia turned her elbows out and swung her legs from the side of the bed. She had to practice being tough. She had heard the babies being wheeled down the hall from the nursery, and her breasts hurt. She tried to read a magazine Maureen had sent up to her. "Jackie's

Tragedy," the cover read, but Delia couldn't get interested. She thought the First Lady should have been left alone.

A young couple passed by her door, holding hands. She looked up, and they discreetly turned away. The boy's hair was greasy, and his pants were too tight; the girl's robe was flowery and faded, with welting on the shoulders like worn slipcovers. She pressed her head against the boy's upper arm.

Maurice is at work, Delia thought, suddenly missing the young Maurice terribly, his sweet-smelling breath and the way the side of his face looked when he smiled.

The last day, she thought, today's the last of it.

She was afraid to go home without a plan. She had to think of one, what she would do once she got there. How long, she wondered, would it take to make it up to Maurice and the children? How long would it take until she felt like herself? She had to plan to stop feeling so bad. She forced herself to read about Jackie's tragedy, but she couldn't understand a word, she was so enmeshed in her own.

She thought about getting up to sit on the other bed, just for the exercise. In the daytime, that faraway bed, made up neatly with a high rounded pillow and a yellow spread, looked comfortable and neat, but at night, when Delia couldn't sleep, she looked across the room and could have sworn that the rounded pillow had a face, a nose and a mouth, and knots at the corners like pigtails.

It was eerie to look at and made her feel foolish: a grown woman leery of a made bed; but in fact, as her stay in Queens Hospital drew to a close, that pillow across the room began to seem more real, its little dents not only a nose or a mouth but two slanted eyes. She was so far away from the other women patients that she thought her room might just as well have been on the surface of the moon. That made bed made her feel as if she were laid out at Conlon's, never hearing the elevator opening or closing, her visitors just seeming to appear in her doorway as if she had willed them. The air on her floor smelled like the inside of Empire Meats.

She was always chilly, but when she covered herself, even with a sheet, she began to sweat, and the cooling sponge baths were no help. The nurses kneaded her stomach like dough; their touch made her flesh burn. She listened to their aimless, conspiratorial chatter and felt like a freak. Their passing voices outside in the hall made Delia want to talk to them about her baby, yet when they came into her room they were so obviously strangers that she couldn't say a word.

They must have seen plenty of women who'd had stillborns, she told herself, and they'd see plenty more after she'd gone home. She wondered how she was supposed to feel. She'd thought about praying to Saint Anthony, finder of lost things, but a baby wasn't a thing, nor was her baby really lost. She wished a jury would hear her side. Would God, called to the stand to explain, admit that he'd made a mistake?

Mae had said that God might have been saving her baby from a worse fate, but what could be worse than what had already happened to her? Born dead. The words canceled each other and left nothing behind. Hurry up down. That didn't make any sense at all. Stop going, Patty had once said to Delia when she was a toddler in a snowsuit, having a hard time keeping up, hugging Delia's knees.

She had to stop thinking. She needed a plan to stop thinking. She looked up and saw her brothers hesitating at the door.

Gerald, in brown pants and khaki shirt, looked ready to turn and run back home. He shifted his bulky trunk from one wide leg to the other. His thin hair was the same color as his shirt, and he wore it slicked back, as if it were wet, away from a forehead that had suddenly sprouted wrinkles. Eugene's shirt was red plaid, and his skin was inflamed with livid patches of acne, even the skin on his neck. His skinny arms seemed nearly to reach his knees. He carried a yellow box of candy to Delia's bed, dropping it on her foot. "How you doin'?" he asked loudly, as if she might not have understood.

"All right," she said.

Gerald patted her leg and sat down in the red chair. He swallowed hard, smiled weakly. "Yeah, you look pretty good."

"How's the food?" Eugene wanted to know.

"It's okay if you like cool broth and hard mashed potatoes," Delia said, eager to put them at ease. "Yesterday they brought us some kind of fish with brown gravy. A lot of green Jell-O too." Us. That wasn't quite right. Fish and hard potatoes were what they had brought to her. The other women, down the hall, might have had steak. So far away, how would she know?

"How come they put you down here at the end all by yourself?" Eugene asked, while Gerald watched him, trying hard to avoid Delia's eyes.

"I guess they wanted to keep me on the maternity floor," she said, and shrugged.

"Oh. Well, yeah." Eugene bit his bottom lip.

"Yeah," Delia said, biting her lip in exactly the same way although she wasn't aware of doing so.

Eugene rubbed his hands together, looking at Gerald. "You remember the time Ma made us that cherry Jell-O and I threw a whole bowl of it across the kitchen at you?"

Gerald laughed. "Yeah, Eugene, you threw it at me and I ducked under the table and all that cherry mess just rolled down the kitchen wall. Then Ma came in and beat you with a shoe." Gerald rolled his eyes at Delia. She smiled. Her mother had never hit her, though her father had. Delia never talked back or threw Jell-O. She didn't remember ever being fresh.

Eugene was encouraged by Delia's smile. "Yeah," he said, "she was good for that, Ma was. Gerald, you remember the time she threw the iron at you?"

"Remember? Shit, how could I ever forget? That little old lady almost killed me with that iron. Thank God, I remembered to duck that time."

"Do you remember the night that Daddy threw the toaster through the kitchen window?" Delia asked, anxious to join in. It felt so long since she had smiled.

"Which toaster?" Gerald asked. "Which window? Christ, we must have had a million of 'em, toasters and windows. I don't remember any one night as different than the rest. But I do remember a few times the crazy bastard tried to throw *me* out the window."

"Yeah, but, Gerald, come on." Eugene opened his eyes wide. "We only lived on the first floor. How the hell far could you fall, for Christ's sake, huh?" He made a face and stuck his tongue out at his brother.

Delia felt better just watching them. She had to keep reminding herself of where she was, and why.

"Oh, you'd be surprised, Eugene. Fall out of bed the right way, Jesus, you'd be dead. You could even drown in a cup of tea if you stuck your nose in it."

"A turkey's the only thing dumb enough to do that," Eugene said. "Breathe in water and drown. Anything else, human or animal, has got more sense. Too bad Pop didn't drown in his beer."

Gerald laughed, a harsh bark. "I used to lay awake at night, thinking of ways to kill him. I really did. Imagine a little bit of a kid praying his old man'd die so he wouldn't have to kill him and go to jail."

"I remember," Delia said, and the three of them nodded seriously.

Eugene spoke. "I'd watch him fall asleep with a lit cigarette in his hand, just watch the cigarette burn down to the end, right down to his fingers, and I'd never do a thing."

"Yeah, and while you did that," Gerald said, "I used to hide his glasses and his wallet so's he'd be late for work."

Delia was shocked. "You did that, Gerald? And I had to run around like crazy, looking for them, so he'd go out the door and leave us alone. He used to tear up the living room, screaming like a crazy man, looking for his stuff. . . . Oh, the two of you." Despite herself, she chuckled.

"Well, Jesus, Delia, do you blame me?" Gerald asked. "Look at what he put me through—all of us, but me and Eugene more than you." He rubbed his hands on his knees. "'Fat pansy,' he used to call me whenever he got the chance. 'Scumbag,' he used to call me, told me I wasn't worth shit. Now what kind of a thing's that to say to a kid, over and over again, for his whole life? I used to think 'shithead' was my name, for Christ's sake."

"You?" Eugene asked. "Jesus, he would tell me I was a worthless moron, that I wasn't worth the powder to blow me to hell—and I used to think he was sayin' something nice!"

"Compared to some of the stuff he was calling me, Eugene, he was." Gerald buried his face in his hands. "You remember the night

242

he told Ma to get the hell out of the house, and then he threw all her clothes in the hallway?"

"But that was after Ma chased him with the butcher knife." Eugene laughed. "Give the devil his due."

Her mother? Delia never remembered anything like that.

"Yeah, Eugene, she chased him with the knife, but you're rushing the story. After she chased him around with the knife, he took off for a few days. It was when he came back that he threw her things outside. Anyway, there was Ma, sitting on the stairs crying into her corset, and who should come waltzing through the lobby but old Mrs. Krupp, who was old even then — "

Eugene took up the story. "'Evening, Agnes,' Ma said." He was laughing so hard his thin shoulders shook. "And then she says to Ma, 'Evening, Mae. What're you doing with all your dresses and your private things all over the hall?' And Ma says, 'Agnes, don't tell me you forgot. You're not helpin' out with the Saint Vincent de Paul this year?' Ma said she ran up those stairs so quick it was a wonder she didn't collapse."

Delia grinned, but she felt uncomfortable. Where was she when all this was going on? There seemed to be whole years that Delia had somehow forgotten.

The small room seemed less confining with her brothers there; the pillow on the empty bed no longer had a face. "Gerald, I want you to tell me something," Delia said suddenly, when the laughing had stopped.

"Sure, what?" he said, his back to her, looking out her window.

"When you were in the seminary, how did they explain things like this?"

"Things like what?" Gerald turned from the window and walked to the door, one foot in her room and one foot outside.

"Things like what happened to me," she said petulantly. "Things like innocent babies dying, for example. Why did they say it happened. God's will?"

"Well," he said vaguely, "not so much God's will but something like free will. You know, like human error or something."

"Like it might have been the doctor's fault?"

"No, maybe more like it was just something that happened. It just wasn't meant to be. I don't know; I don't know what to say to you. It wasn't for me, the priesthood, maybe I didn't even stay long enough to give you an answer. I just wasn't sure what I believed. . . . I was there and I felt all mixed up. I didn't know then and I still don't know why terrible stuff happens. Stuff Pop did was awful and I laugh about it, but I never figured out why he was the way he was. I just don't know."

Neither of them knew what more to say, so Delia opened her candy and offered it to her brothers. She hadn't meant to put Gerald on the spot. They ate the candy, and they made her smile with their jokes, and then the longshoreman nurse came in and said that visiting hours were over and they had to leave. They kissed Delia good night, ruffling her hair as if she were a kid again, and left behind little brown candy wrappers scattered in her blanket like some kind of large foreign seeds.

TWENTY-THREE

Delia came home from the hospital on her husband's arm. Stepping into her messy living room, she decided that the next morning, her apartment would be her first back-to-the-world challenge. She told herself sternly that the place was a disaster and needed desperately to be cleaned.

She began by throwing out the perfume and dusting powder that Mae had brought to the hospital. The mere sight of the containers instantly evoked sickness, the smells brought the bile-green hospital walls to mind, the contents of the fancy bottles so sweet and so sugary in such a bitter time of her life that they seemed to ridicule her.

Maurice emptied her hospital things from the suitcase. "It's good to have you home," he said, neatly folding her sticky nightgowns, even though they were on their way to the laundry basket. He pointed to the coffee table. Sally Malloney had sent Delia two books of crossword puzzles. When she first looked at the books, with their bright-red cardboard covers, Delia thought they said "Curseword Puzzles" and for a few minutes wondered if she had undersold Sally Malloney, across the courtyard. She couldn't allow herself time to just sit and think, and so she threw them away too.

She had been pregnant for such a long time, through the hot summer months when she couldn't see past her belly to the round, hairy orange juice spots in the middle of the kitchen linoleum, never noticing the corners in the rest of the rooms, where dust and humidity blended together and met under the radiators in a sort of paste. She also noticed that the white curtains on the living room windows were now gray and had somehow shrunk, becoming not only shorter but thinner, as if the summer heat had stripped them of their swollen chests, their proud bosoms. Summer was a bully, Delia often thought, although it appeared that the curtains had fought back a bit, halfheartedly lapping at the windowsills, which were covered with a fine silt.

While she had been pregnant, Delia couldn't clean the bathroom properly, not being able to bend down to scrub out the tub or wash the tile floor the way she always had, on her hands and knees. She had made the girls take showers, and neither of them had cleaned their long hair from the drain, and what sat there, in the bottom of the tub, looked like an extremely furry mouse. Delia had to clean that tub properly, and the toilet too, she thought, and not as she had while pregnant, when she simply poured bleach into it, not realizing that the strong fumes would burn the girls' tender backsides, reddening their skin as if they were sunburned.

She left the bathroom and walked through the rest of the apartment as if she were taking inventory.

Something had happened to the big silver mirror mounted above her bedroom dresser. The surface was foggy and pitted with black marks, like tarnish, as if the summer's wet, sultry heat had crept inside the bedroom and sneaked behind the mirror. Her white chenille bedspread was rolled up, plopped on top of the silver radiator. Maurice hadn't used a spread while she was gone; the sheets were covered with footprints, and crumbs lay near the headboard.

In the living room, her end tables were thick with dust, and the handle on one drawer was broken, dangling loosely in midair.

The girls' bedroom wasn't too bad, the blinds shut carelessly, the string looped around the yellowed metal blades like a lasso, slanted like a smile of bad teeth. In the corner of the room, where the crib had been, was a pure and shining island, a perfect square of gleaming wood in a sea of dust and some scattered game pieces and a tiny doll. Her heart stopped: she thought she was seeing one of the dolls that Rosaleen had hung from the crib by long yellow ribbons, but no, she saw as she came closer, it was too big to be one of those dolls, and anyway it wasn't a doll at all; it was only a doll's arm. Patty's doll had lost it, and Patty was downstairs, fine and whole, with Mae. (She had to keep telling herself that her other girls were fine.)

How do you make a Venetian blind, Delia asked herself, standing in the doorway. Punch him in the eye. She left the girls' room and decided to begin in the kitchen.

She reached underneath the sink and brought out a basin and two bottles, pine cleaner and ammonia, her cleaning solutions just as she had left them, arranged neatly and ready for battle. Strange, she thought, how bright and busy-looking bottles and sponges and scrub brushes sat placidly underneath the sink, underneath the pipes smudged with old paint, and looked so smug, made her so angry at the unfairness of things outliving people.

There were brown droplets of grease running down the white-enameled wall behind the stove.

The doctor's green coat had been splattered with her blood, even his glasses.

No.

She dunked the bristle scrub brush into the basin, which was empty. She filled the basin with water and a squirt from each bottle and dunked the brush again, stroking the wall vertically at first and then horizontally and then finally any way at all, just to keep moving, the dirty water streaming down behind the stove like yellow-brownish tears on white enamel cheeks. The smell of ammonia made her eyes watery, too close to tears, so she threw the solution down the sink and filled the basin with clear water, wiping her eyes with the shirt she was wearing, Maurice's old softball shirt. Nothing else fit her yet, so she wore her pale-blue maternity slacks, with the expandable belly, and the green Banshees shirt, its stiff white letters half eroded. She couldn't stand her hair, all over the place, so she pulled it back into a tight and painful ponytail, shoving each loose strand away from her face, using black metal bobby pins to keep it as close to her head as she could. As she worked with her hair, she noticed that her wrists were still bruised from the delivery room restraints; she looked down at the same purplish bruises on her ankles. She was somehow gratified to see marks on her body. She wanted to look like the fighter she thought she was — in fact, she wanted to look like a man, a truckdriver or one of the sanitation guys in the street. She didn't want to look like a woman, not at all; that hurt too much. While she was thinking of it, she left the kitchen half-cleaned and went into the bathroom to cut her fingernails, which had grown during her hospital stay, down to the quick with the nail clippers that Maurice used. Putting them back into the medicine chest, she looked up and saw that Maurice had forgotten to get rid of one thing, the yellow hairbrush with the tiny green ducks on the handle. (Patty had drawn a picture of green ducks swimming in a pond; they were going to tape it to the wall next to the crib.)

Delia slammed the medicine chest so hard that the mirror shook.

She went back into the kitchen and finished washing the walls, moving the chairs into the hallway in a straight line, one behind the other, just as airplane seats might look, Delia imagined. Her uterus ached, the strong pull helped only if she sat down hard on the corners of things. The kitchen chairs didn't offer enough resistance, so Delia dropped down on the edge of the kitchen table, but she couldn't afford to sit still, she just wouldn't stop and think, she wasn't getting any work done in *that* position, so she stood up and swept the floor, ignoring the ache for as long as she could, becoming so angry at herself that she considered jabbing her vagina with the broom handle, forcing her fist into herself as she swept, anything to fill the space and stop the pain, but her fist was too small and inadequate, the hole inside her too big, she needed both hands to work. If she refused to acknowledge it, the pain would go away.

A fat nurse with terrible skin like Eugene's had looked at her impassively and held her hand. "Just don't leave me," Delia had begged, as the nurse scratched absentmindedly at her ear.

"I'm not going anywhere," she said, as if she had heard it all a thousand times before.

Stop.

She decided that the kitchen floor was clean enough for now, just swept. She'd return to it when the weather had broken and she was back to herself. She got a cloth and just scrubbed at the spots, then sat in her make-believe airline seat, pretending she was looking down at farms and prairies (how she liked that word!), at the thatched roof of Mae's girlhood home back in Ireland, the Swiss Alps, the river Thames, the vastness and depth of the world beyond the Heights unfolding before her eyes.

Delia realized that Sherry, her baby, had experienced something she had not, like the world she knew she would never get to see.

Dying, Delia believed, was the only way she would ever leave Queens.

When the spots on the floor were dry, she set the chairs around the table again, at a discreet distance from each other, like polite dinner guests. Chairs, she thought, were the saddest things in the world. After her father had died, it was his empty place at the head of the table that had looked the most alone. She stopped herself right there. Maurice was right: he had said she had to get over it.

Okay, she said to herself, chairs are the saddest. So what are the funniest? She opened the broom closet, trying to think of funny things, and she realized that the secondhand high chair that she had bought from a woman at the playground in June was gone: she had propped it alongside the paper grocery bags she saved, next to her dustpan.

That evening, she had asked Maurice to walk over to the woman's apartment and carry it home.

She forced chairs, all types of chairs, out of her head and thought about . . . hats. Hats were the funniest. Hats, Delia thought, pushed people to extremes. There were the pillbox hats that Jackie wore, and then there were the fedoras on old men, too tiny, silly. Hats made people look either wonderful or ridiculous and kept them floating from one category to the next.

Delia had once seen a very fat woman on the street, on a windy March day, completely bald, chasing a blue hat with a red wig tucked inside, but the scene was as elusive to her as the wig had been to the strange lady.

She walked through the apartment, pulled off all the curtains, dusted the windowsills, straightened and raised the blinds, and then she stripped the three beds, throwing the dirty, wadded sheets into the hall, and her bedspread too. Putting the extension cord onto the vacuum cleaner, she went through the whole place, across the bare floors and underneath the beds.

While she was in the children's bedroom, it struck her that their walls were a similar color to her hospital room; she'd have to change that. Right next to where she had struggled in labor, she had seen a thousand impressions of fingernails.

After the house was neat, she scrubbed the tub, picking up the furry mouse, and ran hot water for a bath, although Dr. Mullaney had told her not to bathe for at least six weeks, to take showers until her stitches had healed; but it was he who'd told her she'd have her baby "any day now" when she was so anxious and overdue.

While the tub filled, she dusted the dressers with an old towel that the vacuum had nudged out from underneath Patty's bed. There were smudges of dirt on top of the light switches where she had hung tiny containers of holy water, hammering long and skinny nails into the walls. It was what her mother had done, kept holy water near the doors so they could bless themselves as they went through the apartment, but the empty plastic containers were dry and cracked, and Delia threw them away.

She missed her girls. They were staying with Mae, who had seemed sure that massive doses of television and a constant supply of cupcakes would help them forget. "Ah," she had said, "they'll get over the disappointment, Delia. They'll bounce right back, you'll see. Kids always do. They surprise you, Delia. They're stronger than we give them credit for."

They were sleeping with Mae in her thick feather bed, and the loud ticking of the clock probably kept them awake, her mother's snoring hurting their ears. Whenever she had slept with her mother, that clock and her mother's gasps had made Delia try to listen for her own heartbeat and count her own breaths. She often wondered what time it would be when her heart finally stopped beating, or what if she just stopped breathing? In all that warm smothering softness, she had never slept, terrified at the thought of her vulnerability, every second one less to have.

Delia had phoned downstairs as soon as she came through the door, but Mae had answered and not Maureen, as Delia had hoped. Though Mae covered the phone, Delia had heard her, clear as day: "Leave your mother rest now, girls." Mae was trying to help, but Delia wanted to sit next to her daughters, with their arms pressed against hers on the couch.

She hadn't seen them at all since it had happened, nor had she seen much of Maurice, who was working days, unable to get any time off, sleeping tightly on one side of the bed and seeming polite and businesslike. "No, thank you, hon," he'd said. "I can get coffee downtown. Don't overdo it," and then he was gone. Which was just as well. She didn't want him to have to sit and hold her hand. He was never very good at that sort of thing. He just wasn't as strong as she was; even his mother had admitted it. Delia could get over it alone if she had to. She couldn't very well just march downstairs and demand her children: she couldn't hurt Mae like that.

She lowered herself into the tub.

The nurse had shaved her pubic hair, and what was so energetically growing back reminded Delia of a newly seeded lawn. There had to be some kind of blind stupidity in growing things, she thought, or maybe a stubbornness, a deaf, single-minded determination stronger than she could imagine. When she raised her arms to wash underneath them, a thin stream of greenish milk began to flow from her nipples and down her belly into the bathwater — she imagined a tub of weak tea.

She tried to remember who it was who liked milk baths.

Cleopatra, the great Egyptian beauty. She had seen the movie with her mother.

She leaned her head back against the wall and draped the wet facecloth over her eyes. She tried again to think about the fat lady with the wig, and she tried to look forward to something. She wondered what her mother was bringing for her dinner.

In the hospital, she measured her time in meals, just like a child, though when they brought her the trays she rarely ate any of it. She nearly gasped with pleasure when she saw a bright sprig of parsley hidden in her steamed rice. Now she wondered if Mae would make her some rice pudding and fill her little brown custard cups to the brim.

"How *are* you doin'?" Mae had asked in that first moment home, her voice whispery. Delia couldn't remember, at first, what was supposed to be wrong with her. Headache? Sore throat? She felt fine. There was only all that pulling and the strong urge to push back.

The telephone, on the kitchen wall, was much sturdier than the holy water containers. Delia tugged on it while she talked to Mae, rocking back and forth nervously on the balls of her bare feet, which seemed tiny and disconnected from the rest of her. "And what do you have planned for *today*?" Mae asked, as if Delia were away on vacation. It's me, Mama, she wanted to cry out, still me!

"I've been getting the place into shape," was what she answered.

Mae would like to hear that. Mae would think she was getting better, getting over it. And certainly she was. She was doing fine.

"Not working too hard?"

"No, Mama, just regular cleaning. I didn't do anything in the apartment all summer long."

"But it's been so hot."

"My feet were all swollen. I could barely move."

"Oh, yes, I remember," Mae said breathlessly. "Of course."

Delia was trying to recuperate rapidly for her mother and forget rapidly for Maurice. It was almost as if she had made the whole thing up.

"Has Maurice called?" Mae asked.

He had called twice. Once as soon as he got off the subway and once when he got to work, but both times the connections were poor and she could barely hear him. He had sounded small and tinny, like Patty's favorite cartoon character, Jiminy Cricket.

"Of course he called, Mama," Delia said impatiently. "He called me twice so far today."

"Well, it's nice to know he isn't too busy to at least think about you."

"Mama, please. He has to work. It's not like he has a choice."

"Well, the important thing is not Maurice. The important thing is that you rest and get back on your feet. That you eat and sleep and feel better. Maybe you should go up to the roof and sit for a while in the sun."

"I will, Mama. I will do it all." She had fallen into her mother's lilting brogue, as easy as tripping on the sidewalk. Mae hated to be teased.

"Mama, can I talk to the girls?"

"But not for too long, Delia."

"Hi, Mommy?" Patty asked. "Can we come upstairs soon?"

"Leave your mother *rest* now," Mae shouted in the background.

"You can come upstairs soon, of course. And remind Grandma I'm not resting all the time. Today I cleaned your room."

"Listen, Delia." Mae was back on the line. "Please, Delia Mary, now I'm beggin' you, let me keep these children until you're back on your feet. They aren't a bit of trouble, and you need your rest. Please,

I'm more than askin', I'm beggin' you — leave them down here with me."

Delia said nothing. Mae sighed, relieved at her silence. "Now here's the big girl wantin' to say hello."

"Mom?" Maureen asked in a tremulous voice.

"I'm right here, Maureen. I'll be fine; don't worry. Are you having a nice time with Grandma?"

"Oh, a real good time. Eugene took us for ice cream and Gerald took us to the movies with his girlfriend. You should see her, Ma, she's really nice. She brought us some free cookies from the bakery, and a few times we went to see her just to say hi. We're having lots of fun, really. Are you okay, I mean really?"

"Yes, I am. Really really." She laughed. What girl? she wondered. That same one? What was her name? Delia felt like someone who had had amnesia, unsure of her age or her looks or even her gender, terribly disconnected. She could have been a schoolchild again or a bride or a soldier, or even an old lady sitting on a park bench, feeding pigeons. Or even one of the pigeons.

She wanted the girls upstairs, but if she suggested it, Mae would throw a holy fit. Delia would hate to have that happen. Mae was so good to her.

"Maureen, put Grandma back on now," Delia said, feeling exhausted. "I love you."

"Me too, Ma." And Maureen was gone.

"Mama, I'm going to lay down now for a while," Delia said. "Maybe I'll take a walk downstairs later, just to visit."

"Delia, you'll do no such thing. I don't want you walking up and down those stairs. You'll have a hemorrhage. Now I want you to rest yourself, please, just for a while. Stay up there, and I'll bring up some dinner for you and for Maurice too, I guess. The man has to eat. Just give yourself a few more days."

"Then let the girls come with you," she pleaded.

"No, Delia, that would be just plain foolish. They'll want to stay and they'll be carryin' on about coming back downstairs with me. They won't give you a minute's peace. Please, Delia. I don't want to see you back in no hospital."

"Okay, Mama, okay. Goodbye."

———

253

But she couldn't sleep. She was tired, but she stayed awake; just as she couldn't eat, though she was hungry. She lay down on her bare bed, the blue-and-gray-striped mattress, and felt as if she were floating through pale and gauzy veiling such as postulants wore. She thought of Maureen's white baby shoes, and Patty's, dangling from the rearview mirror of their Plymouth, and, for some reason, the back of Maurice's head, how it had looked when he was a boy.

Patty had had a clear plastic pocketbook one Easter and had hidden some chocolate bunnies inside on her way to church. In the hot April sun, the bunnies melted into a dark gooey wad, and sometimes Delia thought about it. Those anguished chocolate bunnies just wouldn't leave her mind.

She sat up suddenly.

There was a little yellow and white lace coverlet on order in TotsWorld, a new store on the avenue. (She had taken the girls to the grand opening; seeing how pregnant she was, the proprietors gave her a handful of balloons.)

They were waiting for her to call and give them the baby's name; it was all paid for.

She'd get her money back. She'd just have to explain.

Sherry isn't a saint's name, Father Sullivan had explained to Maurice, and Maurice had explained it to Delia, in Father Sullivan's stern pulpit voice. "'This baby must be buried in the church as Mary. Mary Delaney.'"

She stuffed her naked stained pillow right underneath the old Banshee T-shirt, and she cried.

TWENTY-FOUR

Although it was nearly the end of August, summertime held on stubbornly, through the slightly chilly mornings that led to the sultry afternoons, the sun melting the tar on the roof like a griddle melting cheese.

Whenever Delia went for a quart of milk or a loaf of bread at the new Ukrainian grocery store three blocks away, she noticed that bugs seemed to be too close to her face, as if they had become too heavy to go any higher, close enough so that she could see their transparent wings and the place where the shiny green stripes on the backs bled into the black.

She saw no bugs in her top-floor apartment. There were compensations for living so high up. In the evenings, she stood alone on the roof, watching the girls playing on the street, while Maurice, below her, watched television. (She was glad to have her family back together: Mae had released the girls after a week.) She didn't want to see anybody she knew — they wouldn't know what to say to her — but she hungered for fresh air, in the house so much, and she convinced herself that standing on the roof, just watching, was a way to ease back into her life. Besides, the darkness was coming earlier and earlier (the girls were about to start school), and lately she found herself always worried about her children. When she sat in her living room next to Maurice, waiting for the girls to come home, the night seemed too near. She wouldn't even turn on a light in the room, not wanting to acknowledge how dark it really was.

After that burst of cleaning, the second day home, she stopped doing housework.

She would leave the apartment right after dinner, the dinner dishes on the kitchen table, the fat from the meat congealing on the plates, a thick ring of sour milk settling in the bottoms of the girls' glasses. She let the butter pool in the bottom of the butter dish and slide over the table into the crack that opened to admit the leaf. Maurice sat at the table, eating stale bread spread with goopy butter, just watching her. In the beginning, he had seemed anxious to understand her need to run upstairs, and he was the one who scraped the dishes and put them into the sink, where he washed everything in lukewarm water with a steel-wool pad, letting everything dry on a greasy dish towel spread along the drainboard. He never thought to wash the table, leaving crumbs of bread and bits of vegetables and jagged trails of fleshy meat where they stuck when Delia continued to leave the kitchen to go upstairs and breathe (although it was night air she was taking in, and Mae had told her that was dangerous), and soon he merely scraped the dishes clean and piled them on top of each other on the stove, with the pots.

"Life goes on, Delia," was what he continued to say, but she sensed something different in his voice, just as she sensed autumn on those August mornings, a quaver as he blinked his eyes rapidly.

She looked at him blankly and turned to open the door and climb the stairs. Once, she leaned over and looked down into her own kitchen, and she saw Maurice, standing at the sink, cross himself. It seemed he knew her better than she realized, knew how much she wanted to jump.

It would be so easy to throw one leg over the edge and then the other, her cotton shirt ballooning behind her like a parachute, the soft, sweaty fabric pulling away from her back, the cool wet spot between her shoulder blades as itchy as a handful of ants.

She didn't think she had the guts.

Patty had been such a wiggly baby, so active that Delia had been afraid to bathe her, frightened to loosen her grip even for an instant, merely pulling the naked shivering child out of the tub and flat onto her chest, wrapping them both in a big towel, surprised and delighted by the pleasant odd stirrings in her groin. When she laid the baby down to dress her, Delia would be shivering herself, from the wet dress and the rush of feelings.

She would never feel that way again. Why weren't two babies enough?

From her perch, Delia watched the summer flee from the street, and when the streetlamps were turned on, the light reflected off the tops of her neighbors' heads where they stood clustered on car fenders, and she noted with a bitter satisfaction that Bill Malloney was losing his hair. He wasn't the type to look good bald, his face too soft and kindly. With his arms folded across his chest, he seemed to be gaining weight.

Before her baby had died, Delia liked to stand outside in the evenings with the Malloneys and sometimes the other neighbors, laughing and leaning against Maurice, on his way to work or on his way home, standing thigh to thigh, more married sometimes in public than in private, the children, even Maureen, playing tag through the alleys.

She had tried to join her neighbors a few days after she got home, while the children had been with Mae, but she had felt weak with so many people around, and she shivered in her white sweater although it had been warm, perspiration settling on her upper lip. Maurice had kept her clamped under his arm, as if he were insisting, moving his body so that she fit neatly into him, hip to hip, and no matter how she wiggled, he turned his body so that she'd have a soft place to rest, but it was no good, none of them had known what to say and so they'd said nothing, and the children who were there sat quietly on the curb, just staring at her.

Before the darkness was complete, Delia looked down and saw that the tops of the trees had finally surrendered, turning their leaves over to the pale side, a million tiny declarations of defeat, and she wanted to shout out that the summer had finally given up. She began to say a prayer of thanks for autumn and then stopped herself. Down stairs, they must have noticed her; every now and then, someone would look up and wave, and Delia eagerly waved back to spare them both.

Earlier, in the springtime, someone's dog leapt through an open window and caught his paw on a rusted fire escape, but amazingly enough, the animal had survived.

Delia promised herself that if she jumped, she'd go down cannonball style.

The girls left the street to come upstairs, and Delia turned away, walking to the other side of the building, looking down into the apartments across the courtyard. She saw old Mr. Murray, in his sleeveless undershirt, tapping his foot on a dull green rug to the music of Lawrence Welk, the television turned up as loud as it would go, and she smiled to see one of the old Ryerson sisters, in a pink hair net, rinsing her laundry in the bathroom sink, holding up a pair of dripping pink underpants nearly as big as a tent.

She saw big white unfamiliar rumps planted firmly on toilet bowls, and she saw strangers eating dinner in their underwear. What kept them where they were, she wondered, what mucilage kept them marching in place?

She went back downstairs, to the dishes and the humid bedrooms, with Maureen, in her shorty pajamas, out of the shower and Patty on her way in. Delia threw herself on the couch, crossing her feet at the ankle, without the strength to move, the rough material of the uncovered sofa biting into the backs of her calves like a hair shirt. Maurice stared at the ceiling every time a commercial came on, interrupting one of his western shows, and exhaled loudly. Delia thought it was on the tip of his tongue to tell her that life goes on. "Now where did *that* guy come from?" he asked her gaily, jerking his thumb at a character on the screen.

"I don't know. I'm not even watching it," Delia said, turning to face the wall.

"You ever going to stop moping around here, Delia? You ever going to stop standing on the roof and laying on the couch and letting the place here go to hell? Jesus Christ, none of my shirts are pressed, and the dirty laundry's three feet high!" He stomped off into the bedroom, and then he came back.

"You're not the only one's been disappointed, Delia," he said, his chin trembling. "I wanted the baby too, but I got to go to work anyway. I can't afford to just lay around all the time being sad. We gotta eat and pay bills. How sad do you have to get before you finally stop?" He went into the bedroom again.

She counted twelve steps: she liked even numbers. She knew it was silly, a kid's thing to do. She'd listen for her father to come home, counting the footsteps outside her bedroom window. Even numbers meant it could be him, odd numbers, somebody else.

Babies were born (when they were born) and were carried home from the hospital as Maureen and Patty had been, in their mother's arms. They had to be baptized before they were taken outside in their carriages, and Delia had done that, listening to her mother, who'd insisted it was bad luck for the mother to go to the ceremony, and so she'd stayed home and cooked a roast beef for the party, waiting anxiously for the baby to come back, a screaming, red-faced heap of satin and lace in a bonnet. (Rosaleen had been Maureen's godmother, and even she couldn't wait to give the child back.)

She never ate meat on Friday; she wouldn't dare. She knew of the rumors, everyone having heard of at least one person who ate steak for a Friday supper and choked to death.

Suppose a baby hasn't been baptized, Mae had questioned her. What if they were taken out and hit by a truck? There was always that possibility, their tiny souls rumbling through limbo forever. Hadn't Delia, upon her first glance at her newborns' faces, splashed their foreheads with ice water from the pitcher at her hospital bedside?

Try as she might, Delia couldn't figure any of this out. She didn't want a full year of sore throats for herself or her children, so on the feast of Saint Blaise, she always went to church to have their throats blessed.

She had gone to confession every week and knelt down afterward to say her penance.

She had gone to Mass every Sunday and always received Communion, having carefully spit out every bit of toothpaste in her mouth, so as not to break her fast. She waited at the altar rail with the other young mothers to be churched.

She had done her Easter duty; she nagged Maurice to do his.

She had honored her mother all her life, and she had honored her father, hard as that was to do, and she loved her husband and her brothers and her children: good daughter, good wife, good sister, good mother. Good person? Yes, she had to admit, she probably was.

Maurice was up again, standing in the doorway in his baggy boxer shorts. "You coming to bed, Delia, or what?"

"I guess so," she said, and sat up. Maurice walked over and shut the television off. He double-locked the door and turned off the lights. Standing behind Delia, he put his hands on her shoulders and steered her into their bedroom, bouncing her gently against the hall closet. "Oh, no, little girl, you don't want to go in there. That's where we keep the torture equipment," he said, and then pushed her into the doorway of the girls' bedroom, where they were sound asleep. "And not in there either. That's where we keep the midget women spies." He grabbed her elbows, pulling her down onto the bed, and she offered no resistance at all. She was surprised at herself, needing to be brought to bed. If Maurice hadn't come out to the living room, she would have stayed on the couch all night long in her clothes, the same ones she had worn for two days.

When she turned on her side, Maurice pressed himself against her, his face buried in her hair. She knew her hair was sweaty; she pushed his head away, but he stayed awake for a long time, his eyelashes brushing against the back of her neck in the darkness, staring into the black bedroom, trying to breathe the heavy air, and Delia was frightened to think that neither one of them knew what to do next.

TWENTY-FIVE

Maurice thought a trip to the beach might do her good.

"Rockaway?" Delia asked him, one hand on the receiver, one hand near her mouth. She was trying to think. She had grabbed the new bedroom phone on the first ring, dreaming that the hospital had called to say it was all a mistake. When was Delia going to come back and get her baby?

Her mouth was dry, her mind fuzzy. The new telephone on her nightstand made the bedroom smell like plastic.

"Yeah, we'll go out to the beach," he said. "Get the girls ready, and I'll be home for you in a little while. It's a real nice day."

"But aren't you supposed to be at work?" she asked.

"Never mind where I'm supposed to be! I took the day off, all right with you? You want to go to the beach today or not?"

"Of course I do," she said. "Why are you so nasty?"

"Nobody's nasty, Delia," he said wearily. "Just get ready," and he hung up.

She sat on the edge of the bed, staring at her knees. Getting ready would take a lot of effort. There were red slashes on her thighs; she had slept in her old housedress, stained with two oval dots of tomato sauce, which had become twisted around her. The girls must be awake: she heard the television in the living room. It had to be late by the way the sun was forcing itself into her bedroom.

She didn't really want to go to the beach; she wanted to go back to sleep. She was growing used to it, her body as anxious for sleep as if it were a drug. She wasn't sure she could actually get up and get dressed and go out, as the rest of the world was doing. How did Maurice get up and go out every day?

She picked up the clock, blowing the dust away: nearly nine. She stared at the things right next to her as if she had never seen them before. A glass of water filled with tiny bubbles, a spoon, and a box of tissues. Aspirin, cough drops. All the things Maurice associated with sickness were right within her reach, although she needed none of them.

It was her own fault. She hated to admit that she needed him, never called him at work to say she just wanted him home. Instead, at night sometimes, she asked him to rub her back with Musterole, although it didn't hurt, pretended to have a cough so that he'd bring her an endless stream of hot tea, though the sweat was rolling off her stomach.

"Can I get you coffee, Mom?" Maureen asked from the doorway.

"No, sweetie. I'm getting up now. I'll get it." Her lips felt as if they had been taped over.

"Really?" Maureen asked brightly, and Delia felt awful.

"Really," she said. Had she been sleeping that much? "Daddy called. He wants to bring us all to the beach."

"Really?" she said again.

"Yes, really. Really, really, really. Go and tell Patty to get her bathing suit on." Delia lay down again, just for a minute. She told herself that it was easier to get up in stages. She heard some birds screeching outside the window, a summer sound, but she never saw a thing in that brilliant whiteness.

Before she had dreamed that the hospital was calling, she dreamed that she and Sherry had been arguing. "Not now," the child said. "I'm not ready," but when she turned and faced her, it wasn't a child at all but a creature with an old woman's head in a white eyelet bonnet, running around her bedroom on miniature feet and stumpy legs.

Delia felt so hollowed out; lying on her back, it was almost as if her belly button rested on her spine. With the others, she had never noticed that sort of emptiness, and she developed a theory that nature had a way of taking care of emptiness, the mother spending so much time with the child in her arms that she pays little attention to her own body; but with no baby, the hole in Delia seemed so deep that she was afraid to button her shirts or snap the band of her underpants when she got dressed, as if her insides were on the outside, her body turning itself inside out.

And she had never even seen her face.

"Maureen, will you run me a bath?" Delia called.

Patty ran in and sat down heavily on the bed, so close to Delia that their knees met. "You better, Mom?" she asked.

"I'm trying, pumpkin, I really am." Delia pressed the tip of her finger to the tip of Patty's nose.

All through that never-ending August, Delia thought of Maureen and Patty as if they were still toddlers, having their first birthdays, uttering their first words, cutting their first tiny white teeth, trying to walk in their first pairs of white shoes, and when they came in to say something to her, hovering close, the real-life big children, she was surprised to see the size of them and she felt somewhat grateful, as if someone else had raised them. (She nearly jumped when they bent down to look into her face, so great was her shock.)

It seemed as if Patty had been away for a very long time, as if she had somehow survived a long and hazardous journey, to land inexplicably safe and sound on the other side. Patty was such a gift, and Delia had never truly realized it.

"Why are you crying, Ma?" Patty asked carefully when Delia nuzzled her reddish hair.

"I'm just so happy to see you, sweetie."

As she undressed to bathe, she inspected herself with a careful eye. She had been in bed too much. Her legs were not only shaky, but they seemed so much slimmer and more fragile than they had been before, although she knew she had lost a fair amount of weight, the bones in her backside aching when she sat in the tub. She washed herself carefully, as if she might split open, her ribs so close to the surface that they made her skin look bluish. Getting out, she shaved her armpits with Maurice's razor, powdering herself with talcum. She stepped into a cotton dress, clean but wrinkled. Although it was uncomfortable, she tied her waist with the matching belt. Her hair needed to be colored — it was checkered with bits of brown and bits of blond — and so she covered her head with a bright scarf, the way Jackie Kennedy often did, and, like Jackie, put on a pair of sunglasses.

She had a lot in common with Jackie now. How Delia wished she could talk with her. But she couldn't, and there was nobody else to talk to, not even Rosaleen, so busy with her new baby. She tightened the scarf in the back of her neck so that it was snug around her head, and two curls, tight as commas, escaped.

"You okay, Mom?" Maureen stood in front of the bathroom door.

"Yes, Maureen, I'm fine," she said, carefully applying lipstick.

"Well, Daddy's in the living room," Maureen said.

"Okay." Delia blew her nose and wiped most of the lipstick away. "I'll be right out."

"You ready?" Maurice asked anxiously when Delia appeared.

"*I* am, Dad." Patty hopped around the room with her red-and-yellow beach ball, carrying her sneakers rather than wearing them, as if she were already facing the hot sand.

Maureen was by the door, her white sunglasses on top of her head. She carried a large shopping bag full of towels and an old blanket rolled tightly, crammed on top of the suntan oil, and her small transistor radio and her white cotton sailor's hat for Patty, who burned easily. Maureen had four plastic cups and a package of cookies and a dime for the bridge, which she held proudly in her fist. "I thought of everything," she said happily.

"You know, Moodles, I think you did." Maurice smiled, stealing her sunglasses, propping them on his own head.

"I'm hungry, Mommy. What about breakfast?" Patty asked, scratching at an old mosquito bite on her elbow until it bled and she lost interest.

"Let's go, girls." Maurice kept throwing his keys up into the air, growing impatient. "I got the car double parked downstairs."

"We don't have time to eat breakfast, we'll buy some stuff for sandwiches, Patty." Delia redid her braids. "We'll stop and get some ham and make sandwiches at the beach. How's that?"

"Can I get Twinkies too?"

"Twinkies too."

The green Plymouth waited at the curb. The car was ancient, but Maurice had taken good care of it, shining the chrome until it glittered, polishing the windshield. That was one thing about Maurice: when he decided to do something (except for the dishes, Delia reminded herself), he did it perfectly, stripping things to the bone and beginning from there.

Delia turned in time to see Mae pulling her shopping cart along the street, waving forlornly as the car pulled away. Delia waved back, watching her mother grow smaller and smaller. Mae might have liked a trip to the beach herself.

Maurice double parked up on the avenue. Delia got out and walked past the Shamrock Inn, whose front door was open, the floor being waxed. She was surprised, having never seen anyone maintain the place. The wood floor had been so badly scuffed it seemed white. When she passed, she could see a big picture of President Kennedy at the back, above the bowling game. She wondered what he might think if he could see the way money was thrown right under his nose and wasted, more money than a week's worth of red meat or a pair of children's shoes. Rosaleen once knew a woman who had followed her husband around from bar to bar and routinely swept his beer bottles onto the floor.

She went into the expensive German delicatessen right down the street, Braun's, although she rarely shopped there, usually unable to afford it. She didn't like the owner, who peered at Delia over his rimless eyeglasses, his intelligent blue eyes making her feel foolish, as if she were somehow demeaning him by ordering a pound of his potato salad. He had an annoying habit of waiting a second or two before he got her things, as if he hadn't been quite sure of what she had said. His display case sparkled, the rows of hams browned to perfection, the lines of cloves set precisely in the reddish dark meat, scored with a sharp knife. It crossed Delia's mind that Maurice would be happy working at Braun's, nailing tight little cloves into tender willing hams.

When she went inside, she heard water running in the back of the shop, realizing that Mr. Braun had not heard the little bell on top of the door ring. She was happy to have some edge on him, practicing her order, deciding to give it to him fast and not repeat it, just so he might feel foolish for a change. Maurice blew the horn outside; Delia pressed her face to the door and shrugged. It seemed as if the heat had broken. There was a clarity under the el that hadn't been there before, a breeze blowing papers into the street.

"Yes?" Mr. Braun said, surprised, pushing his glasses back.

"A pound of ham and a pound of cheese and a loaf of rye bread and two dill pickles," she said. He didn't intimidate her today; she might shop in Braun's more often. She'd even ask him for a plastic knife and risk his annoyance. It was just a matter of timing.

She stood waiting and found herself shivering, the deli much too cold for her. She hoped that nobody came in while she was there. Getting used to crowds and stores was going to take her some time. Amazing, when she thought of it, how quickly she had lost the skills she had used all her life. She slid her dark glasses on again; it was so hard to be alive.

Jackie Kennedy, Delia thought, wore scarves and glasses to hide in the world and yet be part of it at the same time. She understood Jackie. She couldn't stand feeling so confined, though, and she pulled the scarf from her head and shoved the dark glasses into the pocket of her dress and ran her fingers through her streaked hair.

She had forgotten two things. She realized it when Mr. Braun tried to hand her the bag. ". . . and a tiny jar of mustard and two packages of Twinkies," she said. "Oh, and can I have a small plastic knife?" she asked, purposely not saying "please" or reacting when he slid her package angrily across his marble counter. She threw her money back at him. Something traveled through his stiff face: respect?

She picked up the bag, counted her change, and went outside to the car. When she sat down, the sun spilled across the tops of her thighs, and she began to relax. "I'm really glad we did this today, Maurice."

"Yeah, me too. You have to get out of the house now. You just can't keep moping around like you've been doing. Things have to change, you know?"

"I know." Delia shifted the cold paper bag close to her body, hugging it. It felt so good to have something in front of her, almost a relief.

They passed a worn park, set into a little weedy island in the middle of the street. Nobody sat there but bums, who often could be seen sleeping on the scaly benches, their legs hanging down, longer legs than human beings were intended to have, sleeping soundly while an occasional pigeon splattered the sound sleepers with white-paint droppings.

"I was thinking we could do a lot of different things, Delia, to get out of the house. We could take a ride upstate, to Bear Mountain, or maybe we could go out to Jersey for the day." Maurice looked over at her. "You know, do whatever you like. You just tell me what you'd want to do."

"Okay, I'll think about it." She smiled. "That sounds real nice."

They passed the stores at the farthest end of the neighborhood, grocery stores that were once German or Polish but now had brand-new cardboard displays in their windows, replacing the old cans with the ripped paper labels that had faded, standing on each other's shoulders like gymnasts.

Gersteins's had become Rivera's and, in the window, claimed to sell plaintains.

"Daddy," Patty asked, "what are plaintains?"

"If you're Spanish," he said, seriously, "then you soak your feet in them. They're like Spanish Epsom salts."

The girls laughed, and Maurice grinned, trying to look at them in the mirror, the Plymouth rocking over the holes in the street. Out of habit, Delia held the door handle to avoid being jostled, pushing her back against the back of the seat.

They passed the old Newfield Church, a two-hundred-year-old building with skinny, short doors, an old cemetery in the front yard. One hot day, Delia and the girls had gone for a long walk and wandered inside (they had to go in sideways). The church had hard wooden pews and an American flag on what Delia thought was the altar, although it had looked like a plain stage. But the outside was much more interesting. They had walked through the graveyard, reading aloud the old-fashioned names on the stones: Ebenezer or Sarah buried with children named Micah or Amy or Beth.

A baby daughter named Sherry, all by herself in Holy Sepulchre.

Patty had always been so afraid of the dark. If they turned the car around and drove another five miles or so from where they were, in front of the Newfield Church—that is, if Delia had the heart for it—she would be able to look out her side and see some of the fierce concrete angels on top of the ornate mausoleums. She hadn't been there since her father died. She remembered the headstones with photographs in little heart-shaped stone frames, although most of the people had been old, of another time, the men wearing collars so tight that their eyes had seemed to bulge, the women dressed in brocade, wearing brooches and dangling earrings, with just the suggestion of a mustache, like Mae.

The graves were piled on top of each other in Holy Sepulchre, as crowded as the stores along the avenue, as crowded as the streets and the subway cars. Terence and William were beneath Sherry (there had been room in the Delaneys' plot), and so was her grandfather Sean. Delia wished that some kindly old couple lay with her baby pressed tight between them, the way she and Maurice had slept with the girls when they were infants, on fretful nights.

"Mom, look." Maureen tapped her shoulder. "A Chinese church."

Delia looked closer at the Newfield Church; indeed, it was a Chinese temple now.

"I think that's a good idea." Maurice looked down at Delia. "They're small enough to fit through those doors."

A furniture store, a luncheonette, a hospital, and then a wide expanse of road. Forest Hills Park on their right, trees bigger and heavier than any Delia had ever seen, bigger, she imagined, than the ones she had read about in California, the redwoods. The park was so dense that it seemed covered in fog, as if spiderwebs hung from the trees and climbed across the picnic tables, like the white fuzz growing on ripe fruit.

Past the park were yellowish brick houses with red tile roofs, attached to each other, and a small bridge, and then another cemetery, more headstones, tiny flags swaying in the breeze. Delia had never noticed it before, although she had been making this trip all her life. "Know why that place is so crowded?" Maurice asked, his face close to the steering wheel.

"Why?" Maureen asked carefully.

"'Cause everyone's dying to get in."

The girls giggled despite themselves, but Delia looked away, at some point past Maurice's strong nose and solid chin.

They passed underneath another el and saw people milling around the front of a screaming-yellow drugstore, men in baggy slacks and women in droopy dresses, couples who seemed too overwhelmed to look up, and then there were more houses, wide front porches held together with broad stone pillars, some of the porches with awnings and some with swings, and then kitchen chairs on porches and then no porches at all, only kitchen chairs in the tiny front yards of small frame houses, oddly shaped, closer together than they should be. Boats were tied up in the watery side yards. At the end of a narrow and rickety boardwalk jutting out from the road there was a bar, and before Delia realized what he was doing, Maurice had pulled into the parking lot and turned off the engine. "What are you doing?" she asked him, turning in her seat, but he wouldn't look at her.

"I gotta go to the bathroom," he said, jumping out of the car. "I'll be right back."

They sat quietly, watching him walk jauntily along the planks, and then he disappeared through the back door. Maureen and Patty began to tickle and slap at each other, falling on top of the back seat. Delia tried not to be angry, not to feel anything. She didn't quite trust her emotions yet, stiffening against them, not sure what would be appropriate, and after a while Maurice came back, recharged, skipping toward the car like a kid, and although she wouldn't look at him, Delia listened to his voice. She always heard how much he had had to drink in his voice. He wasn't so bad. Delia was grateful.

"Next stop on the agenda," he said carefully and clearly, "is for the soda and the ice."

"And the beer," Delia said sarcastically, before she could stop herself.

"That's right, Delia," he answered sweetly. "And the beer."

Just ahead, right before the bridge, Arrow Beer and Soda shared a shack with Arrow Bait & Tackle. Two flights of stairs eaten by salty air led to equally eroded screen doors. Delia had been there before, when they were dating. It had been Maurice's idea to go night fishing. Delia merely held the poles, but when they stopped at Arrow, Maurice sent Delia inside to get the bait — which was in a carton like the Chinese food they sometimes brought home from the Hong Kong China Kitchen — and he went next door for the beer. Watching the clerk, a freckled, sunburned boy with the remains of the day's zinc oxide on his nose, force squirming purple bloodworms into the carton, she had made a silent vow never to eat chow mein again. (Denis had said that Chinese food, good as it was, was made from alley cats. "You never see the animals near the place, do you?")

She had come down the stairs holding the carton far away from her body, but just before she opened the car door, she thought one of the worms had pushed his head through the opening, and she screamed and dropped the whole thing into the street, where it popped open, its contents like writhing spaghetti. Instead of fishing, they had drunk the beer in the car and gone to Playland to ride the roller coaster.

They parked in front of the ice machine on the sidewalk. The ice was sold in bags of cubes or in boulders, which practically flew out through the swinging metal slot. While Maurice was getting out of the car, they watched a deeply tanned man in plaid Bermuda shorts catch his ice and buckle at the knees. Maurice got in line, in his slacks and not so neatly ironed shirt (looking, Delia thought, like some government agent, the others, in bathing suits or shorts, pulling empty coolers along the hot street, peering at him suspiciously, fishing poles in hands).

Delia thought that her husband was still a handsome man. When he stood away from her, she still longed for him, although the longing was tempered with anger. There was something about the line of his neck, leading to his perfect delicate ears, that made her feel sorry for him, wanting to fix everything that had ever made him sad. He was hers as much as he could be anybody's. She looked at him in the line and pretended that she had never seen him paring his toenails, or combing his hair in the bathroom mirror, or sick to his stomach.

Without checking with Maurice, she had told Rosaleen that they wouldn't be godparents to her baby. Whenever she thought about it, the relief made her dizzy. Rosaleen had said she understood.

In that line of men waiting for the ice, she asked herself, if she were given another choice, who would it be? She took off her sunglasses and squinted at the other men, trying to picture each one in her bathtub at home. A few of them shifted uncomfortably from one foot to the other; one man, with bits of tackle dangling from his hat like fringe on a lampshade, stared right back and forced her to look away. She really didn't want to see any of them naked.

The girls were arguing in the back seat, Patty whining and Maureen trying to reason with her. They were fighting over the bag Patty had packed for herself. "Just give it to her, Maureen, okay?" Delia asked, surprised to see Maureen angrily toss the bag at Patty's head. She ignored them, staring instead at the children's day camp on the right; nestled at the ocean's edge was a wading pool, a brilliant shade of artificial blue, the tanned and shouting children clustered in it like blackbirds in a birdbath.

Maurice had finally reached the head of the line. He shoved his coins into the slot, and nothing happened. Then he slammed his fist against the side of the machine; still nothing. He kicked the front of it; no ice appeared. He turned to look at Delia, shrugging, and without warning a tremendous slab of cloudy ice flew out and hit him in the backside, so that he fell to his knees, the ice continuing by itself along the pavement, thumping into the door of the car, leaving a large dent in the side. Delia felt a giggling ache in her collarbone, but she couldn't bring it to the surface — it was too early to laugh as hard as she wanted to — but the girls were hysterical, pushing their teary faces into the rough car upholstery. Patty got the hiccups. When Maurice stood up, the color was gone from his face and his knees had been scraped underneath his torn pants.

"Ha ha," he said, wiping his face with his shirt, which he had taken off. "So goddamn funny." Behind him, the men in their shorts and dangling hats had to look away, laughing so hard they could barely breathe, as Maurice tried to pick up the ice, to carry it like a football. It kept sliding away from him, while the girls jumped up and down in the back seat and the fishermen finally had to turn their backs. Finally, Maurice caught the ice in his shirt and carried it to the trunk, where he found a small screwdriver. Furious, he stabbed at the ice and dropped the chunks into the cooler that they kept in the car, and when he had finished, he shook the slivers of ice that had caught in his shirt on top of the bare feet of the men who had laughed at him.

When they got to the beach, the cans were good and cold, and Maurice was sulking.

The napkins they had brought blew away as soon as they got out of the car, just scrambling across the gravel in back of Finnerty's Franks on Beach 110th Street, where they always parked.

The beach was clean and white. They could see it from a block away, looking right underneath the boardwalk, and beyond it an expanse of blue as far as their eyes could travel. Eagerly, they crossed the street and climbed the stairs, careful of splinters so thick they stood up from the wood like cactus. Old people in soft hats and round green sunglasses sat on the benches, looking out at the water, and then they turned their heads to watch the Delaneys.

What a rude audience, Delia thought. They could at least take off their hats.

Maurice was dragging the cooler along the sand by himself; Maureen had dropped her end, not able to keep up, and he was annoyed with her. Delia carried the damp spread and Patty's shoes and Maureen's shopping bag. "Patty, wait. Don't run so far ahead!" she called, but Patty turned and laughed at her, her pretty hair whipping across her face, her skinny feet making delicate tracks in the sand like the fossils of small animals. Delia felt tired; she wanted to stop walking. "Maurice, we can just sit right here, can't we?" she asked. He pulled the cooler backward, stopped, and then sat on the top.

"Maureen, help me with this blanket, okay?" Delia asked, careful not to get any sand on it, knowing how Maurice hated to be uncomfortable. Bad enough his knees were scraped and his pants ripped. Delia put all their shoes on the corners, so their blanket wouldn't blow away. Patty was already in the water, which was swirling around her thighs.

"Maureen, go out there and watch your sister, please," Delia said, and as her daughter passed, she noticed that Maureen's hips were widening and her ankles were starting to thin out, the bathing suit she wore, navy blue with a small white skirt, fit her differently this year than last. The skirt stuck out above the tight crotch like a ballerina's tutu, and Maureen kept tugging to pull it over her backside, which caused the neckline to plunge, her swollen pink nipples pushing at the shiny fabric as if they were trying to escape.

She looked out at her two girls and worried about the undertow. It couldn't be stopped; she wasn't sure it wouldn't snare them, no matter where they stood. She wanted to tell them not to have children.

Patty flapped her arms, jumping until the water foamed around her head. "C'mon," she called to Maureen, ankle-deep in the greenish water.

"No, Patty, you go ahead and swim," Maureen called, tightening her arms around herself, across her breasts. "You be the swimmer, and I'll be the lifeguard."

Delia felt sorry for Maureen and sorry for herself too, at the mercy of things she didn't understand, at the mercy of change. Her girls were little specks of life in such a vast ocean. On the other side of the ocean were England and Ireland and then France and, somewhere even farther away, China and Japan, places Delia could barely believe existed. When she was young, she often sat at the shoreline and wondered what would happen if a boatload of ancient Europeans somehow appeared, sailing right into Beach 110th Street — Columbus, dressed in archaic garments, wading away from his wood vessel with its horizontal sails, jabbering away in a foreign language, unfurling a parchment scroll to show her a map, clearly asking for directions — and then she'd turn around and see her family huddled together under the beach umbrella they had to rent, all of them with their pale skin, her father's feet covered by the white cotton socks her mother insisted on, and she'd wish that she could have been kidnapped.

The water was calm, and Delia noticed that Maureen had actually sat down. She walked to the water's edge and looked along the coastline to where she imagined that Hyannis, Massachusetts, might be. It made Delia happy to think that whole beachfuls of Kennedy children were probably bouncing around in the exact same ocean as the Delaney children. She wished she could see their bare backs, probably freckled like their faces, and their bright white teeth and thick, spunky hair.

Irish hair, Mae had called it proudly, as if she had grown it herself.

There were so many Kennedy children. Delia wished she had one for herself, she thought, the wind forcing her cotton dress against her legs.

She turned to go back to Maurice, who was sitting on the blanket, but she saw him reach into the cooler and grab a beer and she grew angry, watching him wipe the moisture from the top of the can with his palm. He saw her look at him. She kept walking and sat down. "Nice day, hon, isn't it?" he asked, looking up at the sky with his eyes shut against the brightness, and then he screwed the beer into the sand as if it were incidental to him. He took off his undershirt, his skin as pale as Delia's.

An Irish tan, Mae called it, whenever Delia came in from being in the sun, which was now giving her a headache, as usual, although it was nearly the end of summer. They couldn't have rented an umbrella even if they had wanted to. The stands were shuttered closed.

As they watched their daughters frolic in the water, they were both as conscious of the beer can as if it were dynamite. If he had started to drink it and Delia looked at him suddenly, he'd be resentful and angry with her and the outing would be ruined for sure; but if he had started to drink it and she didn't look at him, her anger, an anger she mustn't give in to, would make her pulse race. So much had happened, the baby just gone like that. They needed time to get over it, time as a family, but the beer picked Maurice up and put him in a room of his own, with Delia and the girls waiting for him to come out.

She wouldn't get mad about the beer, she told herself. Not today. She owed them all at least that much. She just wouldn't ruin their nice family time. Maurice had done so much, he really had. The baby had died and he had buried her and then he went off to work the very next day. Every time she had tried to talk about it, Maurice had put his hand up as if he were directing traffic, telling her that life goes on. He bought more aspirin and more cough drops and packed them into the bathroom closet above the towels, like canned food in a bomb shelter.

He looked at Delia, made a pillow of his damp shirt and patted it. "Why don't you lay down here next to me and rest?" he asked.

"But the kids —"

"Don't worry about the kids. I'm here, right? I'll watch them for you."

She turned on her stomach, and it ached. She brushed the sand from her lips, unfolded Maurice's shirt, and put it over her head, her cheek pressed to the hot sand, which felt like Mae's remedy for an earache: heat some salt in a skillet and pour it in a wool sock, then press the sock to the ear. Mae claimed it worked every time.

Maurice leaned over and picked up his beer, rubbing her back. She could almost hear his sigh of relief now that she wasn't looking at him, but he moved suddenly and she sat up, looking for the children, while Maurice shook their towels and shook their shoes and shook the bags the girls had brought. He shook Patty's hat and dropped it; Delia caught it before it blew away. "What's the matter?" she asked. "What are you looking for?"

"You got an opener?"

She poked through the bags and upended them. In Patty's bag, she found the tin of baby powder they had bought for the new baby at the Rexall that hot afternoon. That must have been what they were fighting over back in the car, Delia thought, before we got here. It was just a can of baby powder; Delia didn't have to feel a thing. She pushed the powder to the bottom of the bag. "I don't think we brought one," she said carefully. "I guess I should have checked the bag myself. I didn't even see what they brought and what they didn't. I'm sorry."

"Jesus Christ," he said to her. "Don't you care about anything anymore?" The holes in his pants had begun to droop, like slack toothless mouths.

She knelt down, shielding her eyes to look up at him. "I guess I don't," she said.

"We really didn't bring one?" he asked, not quite believing it, poking through the bag from Braun's and then searching her pocketbook.

"Maurice, I don't carry a beer can opener. What are you doing?"

"You didn't bring a knife for the mustard," he accused her. "You don't have a knife for the sandwiches."

Delia pushed at the containers. "I asked that man for a knife," she said, "and I thought he gave it to me." That bastard, she said to herself. Maybe she had dropped it. She wanted to keep it a nice day, their first family outing since it had happened. "Please," she said to him. "I'm still so raw." She looked up at him again and shook her head, but he hadn't heard her, slapping his legs in anger, stalking to the water's edge.

"*Maureen!*" he screamed, his pants cuffs getting soaked, hanging limply on top of his white feet. The sun was in his eyes; he put the beer can next to his temple. "*Maureen!*" he screamed again, when she didn't answer. "You bring a can opener?" She couldn't hear him and pointed at her ears, staring at Patty, who had waded farther out. "*Maureen, Goddamn it, did you bring a can opener?*" he yelled, his face purple. She ran toward him, looking back at her sister.

"Maureen, for Christ's sake, stop watching your sister! Now did you bring a can opener or not? Answer me!"

"Oh." She pressed her knuckles to her mouth. "I forgot, Dad. I'm sorry, I just forgot."

"Son of a bitch! Now how is your mother supposed to have a soda? Goddamn it!" He shook his head and threw the can of beer into the sand, where it landed with a soft thud.

"I'm sorry." She started to cry.

"Well, sorry doesn't cut it. Look at me when I talk to you, goddamn it. Never mind your sister and your mother — I'm talking to you."

Maureen hung her head; her shoulders slumped.

"Maurice." Delia walked up to him, her temples pulsing. "Maybe you can borrow a can opener from someone here." She put her arm around Maureen's shoulders.

"From *who?*" he asked. "Look around, Delia. You see anybody we could ask?"

"Maybe over there." Delia pointed to the stairs, where a young couple were leaning against each other, reading. "Or over there," she said, pointing to an elderly couple farther along the shore, sitting in webbed chairs underneath small individual umbrellas, the man in huge khaki shorts, the woman in a long, stretched-out bathing suit.

"I'll go ask them," Maureen said nervously, pacing around him. "Please, let me go and ask them right now?"

"Never mind! I swear to Christ, you can't do one goddamn thing right, can you? I'll go and ask them myself. If I have to, I'll go back to the car and open the beer with that screwdriver, just like with the ice." He walked away from them, toward the older couple. The man looked up, alarmed, and Delia couldn't blame him, an angry screaming man with ripped pants appearing from nowhere. They didn't have an opener, and Maurice came back, his wet cuffs gathering a crust of sand so that they made slapping noises against his ankles and he began to trip. He yanked his pants up to his chest, furiously approaching the second couple, leaving not prints in the sand but gouges.

Delia watched the young people shake their heads. Maurice stopped and looked back at her, his face distorted with anger, and then he walked away, up the stairs, across the boardwalk, and was gone. Patty had come out of the water, her lips blue. Delia wrapped her in a towel, and the three of them stared at the boardwalk, the happy family day having disappeared, along with Maurice.

"Come on, girls," Delia said. "Lunch." She fixed them ham-and-cheese sandwiches and broke the pickles in half with her hands, which stung from the juice, and they giggled when she kissed her finger and held it up to God, dunking it in the mustard jar and then making a face. They ate quickly, rubbing the sand from their skinny calves.

"I'm thirsty, Ma," Patty said.

"I know," Delia answered. "So am I."

They finished their lunch and threw the garbage into a wire basket nearby, so many bees inside that it looked like a hive. Delia sat Patty down in front of her and began to brush her hair, the air growing chilly.

Where's Maurice? she kept asking herself, the familiar cold feeling creeping along her legs from her icy feet to her quivering stomach, her teeth, when she got nervous, starting to chatter. "I wonder where your father is," she finally said.

Maureen stood up to look. "I'm really worried about him, Mom. He doesn't have a shirt on, and he's not wearing any shoes. He's been gone a long time."

"We'll wait a few minutes more, and then we'll go and see if we can find him."

"We always have to do this, Ma," Patty said, letting her head loll back against Delia's brush, "always looking for him. He never stays with us."

"I know, Patty. I know." She hated when he disappeared, and she hated when the children talked about it. She kept hoping they wouldn't much notice. Kids'll bounce back from things, that's what Mae had always said.

"It was my fault," Maureen said. "I'm the one who was so stupid and forgot."

"Maureen, do I have to tell you a hundred times not to worry about it?" Delia said wearily.

Please, Maureen thought, tell me a hundred times. "It was my fault, even if you say it wasn't." I never prayed for you the day before you went to the hospital. I never told you, but I forgot. That one day, I forgot. I try so hard to remember everything, and then it's too much, and there's always something I forgot. Something important. The can opener, prayers for you and the baby.

She wanted so badly to make it up to Delia, to see that she got what she deserved and that everyone left her alone. She was scared that her mother might die of grief. People did; that's what Grandma Mae had said. She had told Maureen that she hoped Delia wouldn't die of a broken heart; Grandma Mae was "confidin'" in her, and she wasn't to repeat it, but Maureen couldn't leave her mother alone, she just couldn't go downstairs with the other children and forget about Delia alone in the apartment or up on the roof. Delia thought she was standing up there by herself but Maureen had found a perfect hiding place, on the roof of the apartment house around the block, and she watched her mother the entire time she was supposed to be downstairs, watching her sister, and Patty had covered for her. Every time Delia had called down to ask where Maureen was, Patty had pointed underneath the heavy branches of some trees. Delia never knew Maureen was right in back of her, just watching.

She hated her father for doing this, leaving them like that, dragging his pants. They always started out on their trips so happy, but he always did the same thing, just disappearing, as if he couldn't stand to be with them for too long, even on a beach big enough for a thousand people.

Delia had told Maureen that she was very tiny as a toddler and everyone had thought that she would have blond hair, light like her own, and that Maurice had called her Moodles all the time and not just when he had drink in him, that he used to hold her in his arms and bring her to the kitchen window, looking at her eyes intently, nuzzling her hair. "Then what happened?" Maureen had asked eagerly, as if Delia might utter one word and Maureen would be small and blond again. "Well, your hair just turned dark and you grew," Delia had said, somewhat surprised, as if she didn't understand the real question, but Maureen thought it had to be deeper than that, she probably had done something very wrong to make her father drink like he did, something had to have happened to turn her hair dark, like Pinocchio, who had lied and watched his nose grow away from his face.

She had almost made it, she thought; she came so close to being the daughter her father had always wanted, as if it might have made all the difference.

Patty decided that she didn't want braids, after all. She wanted her hair held back by a pair of barrettes, away from her face. Delia was trying to be patient: Patty had suffered a loss too; she had been through an ordeal.

When she undid Patty's braids, Delia spotted a pair of dark pants coming across the boardwalk. Maureen had spotted them too. Maurice waved down at them, his arms flapping over his head. He smiled, showing too much gum, a crooked smile as if his teeth had shifted suddenly in his head. His pants were still slipping, his belt now underneath his navel, and they blew around his slim legs like sails on masts. The girls drew closer to Delia, who stared at him with the brush in her hand and one of Patty's barrettes in her mouth.

"Please, Mommy," Maureen pleaded, grabbing for Delia's hand. "Please don't fight with him, don't say anything. Let's just go home now."

"Hey, Ma?" Patty laughed. "I got an idea. When Daddy gets down here, just leave the barrettes in your mouth, okay?"

They watched him stumble down the boardwalk steps, his feet splayed out like a duck's. "Hey, m'girls, how you doin'?" he asked, swaying in front of them, his hands in his pockets, rattling change and keys. He squatted down, and the old people at the water's edge, who were packing up to leave, looked over at him. Delia was afraid that the man might ask her if everything was all right. She smiled at them when they passed. Maurice was grinning foolishly.

"Hon, you'll never guess who I met," he said, his breath making her dizzy. She ignored him, kept brushing Patty's hair. "Aw, c'mon, don'tcha wanta know who I met?" he pleaded, his lower lip stuck out like a child's. He steadied himself with one hand planted between his knees.

"You stink." Delia waved him away with the hairbrush. She couldn't breathe near him; the smell of alcohol made her sick.

"Who'd you meet, Daddy?" Maureen pulled on his shoulder, and he nearly fell back onto the sand.

"Hey, Moodles, easy now." He smiled at her; Maureen knelt beside him.

"C'mon, Daddy, who'd you meet?"

"Well, your mother don't wanna know, but *if* she did, *if* she wanted to hear about it, you could tell her that I met up with Kelly the Fireman in the joint across the street."

"Another joint," Delia said, pulling Patty's hair so tightly that the part in her hair seemed to bulge, her skull shiny and white, gleaming through her hair like a path in a forest.

"Mommy!" Maureen shrieked. "Kelly the Fireman! Daddy met him." She ran from her father to her mother, trying to look into Delia's face, but Delia had turned away. "Daddy, please tell her about him anyway. C'mon, tell us about Kelly." Maureen pushed her hair away from her eyes, looking at him pleadingly.

"You got a mother don't want to hear about Kelly. Your mother just wants to be mad at me." He turned around and plopped into the damp sand in front of them, staring morosely at the water.

Kelly the Fireman, according to Maurice, was fat (he weighed at least four hundred pounds) and so short that he looked like a fireplug. He had bright-red hair.

Maureen didn't believe that there was a Kelly, and even Patty was beginning to have her doubts, but Maurice seemed to like the Kelly stories so much that they encouraged him. He just had to mention

Kelly's name, and the girls wouldn't move from their chairs. Yup, he would say solemnly, it's Kelly's hair that gets him in trouble: the other firemen are always trying to put it out. The girls would giggle. Yup, he would say a night or two later, Kelly's got trouble with his hair again. He's so fat he can't fit into the barber's chair, and his wife had to cut his hair with a soup bowl pressed against his forehead. The girls would search Delia's face for a trace of a smile, but they never found one. They would laugh anyway, feeling guilty.

Poor Kelly, he would continue (while Delia stood up to clear the table, starting to wash the dishes, running the water more forcefully than she needed to), poor Kelly, the way he had got stuck sliding down the pole in the firehouse. He had kicked and screamed, he was wedged so tight, but all they could do was starve him, and then he had slid out on his own. "Well, then, Daddy," Patty would ask, "how'd the other firemen get out, if Kelly was stuck right in their way?"

"They had to jump out the windows," Maurice would say, shaking his head regretfully, "and they didn't have time to use the nets. A lot of firemen fell on the street and busted their heads. Word has it that Kelly killed a whole firehouse that way." Then he would sigh and look down at his hands, a signal that once the girls laughed, they were free to go. "Aw, Dad," Maureen would usually say, punching Maurice softly on his shoulder on her way out of the room.

"Poor Kelly," Maurice said, now staring at the ocean, as Patty scrambled away from Delia on her hands and knees, to sit next to him.

"What happened to him, Daddy?" Maureen asked.

"Told me the alarm went off at the firehouse the other day, and ten firemen tried to hang a ladder on Kelly."

Patty giggled, rolling across the blanket. "Patty!" Delia screamed, tugging the blanket, trying to pull it out from underneath her. "Get off this damn thing, will you? I'm trying to fold it up, for God's sake."

"Poor Kelly," Maurice said again, in the same flat tone, as Patty continued to roll and giggle, careful to avoid the blanket. "Kelly couldn't find his feet," Maurice said, "his belly was so big, and instead he wound up sticking one of his boots on his—"

"Maurice!" Delia shrieked, the wind so strong her voice seemed to slap her cheek. "Get up, Patty," she said, pushing the child's sneakers into her hands. "Take your stuff and go and sit on the bench and wait for me. You too, Maureen, let's go." Patty stomped her feet, gathered her things in her arms, and ran off.

"Come on, Dad." Maureen tugged on her father's elbow. "Let's go, and you can tell me the rest about Kelly."

"Maureen." Delia pulled her away from Maurice. "You go up there with your sister and wait for me." She held on to the blanket. "We're leaving, Maurice. You can sit there if you want to. I'll take the girls home on the train or the bus. It's up to you." She turned around and pushed Maureen's back, harder than she had intended to. Maureen stumbled and began to cry. "Oh, for Christ's sake!" Delia shouted. "Stop being such a goddamn baby!"

Maurice turned to watch them go. "Poor Kelly," he cried across the sand.

Patty sat sulking at the top of the stairs, the hardened sand around her bare ankles like gray chains. Delia sat next to her, watching Maurice. His shirt blew away in the wind, right past his grasp, along the shore. "Leave it," Delia barked at Maureen. She didn't even know where the bus stopped, how to get home by train, if she had enough money for the fare. Finally, Maurice stood up, draining the cooler into the sand, his pants clinging to his legs from the dampness. He hoisted the cooler onto his shoulders and climbed the stairs; Delia noticed gray hairs on his chest and sand in his belly, and he was shivering, for clouds were moving in.

At the top of the stairs, he lost his footing and began to fall backward. The cooler rolled down into the sand, but Delia grabbed onto him.

"Maurice!" she cried, holding his elbow with all her strength. "What's wrong?"

"My foot," he gasped. "Splinter."

"Oh, and I've got your shoes," Maureen said, waving them. "I'm sorry, I just picked them up!"

"Ow, ow," he mumbled, leaning on Delia's shoulder. "Shit." Gingerly, he sat down on the bench, Delia kneeling in front of him, poking and prodding at his foot with a tissue Maureen had handed her. The splinter was big, easy to grab.

"It's out," Delia said, shaking the sand from his shoes, sliding them on his feet, tying the laces tightly. Maureen brought her white sweater from one of the bags and tied the arms around her father's neck. He stood, pulling up his pants, tightening his belt, throwing his arm around Delia's shoulder, wearing Maureen's white cardigan like a scarf. He had no socks on, and no one knew where they were. His pearly-white ankles gleamed above his heavy black shoes, round and knobby at the toes like the shoes of circus clowns. "Troops!" he yelled triumphantly, pointing in the general direction of the Heights. "Carry on!"

Delia admitted, on the drive home, that Maurice would never change, that all their outings, prepared for or spur-of-the-moment, would probably turn out the same way. It was almost as if the beer he had to have was an uninvited guest, someone she hated. She was tired of looking for reasons why Maurice drank so much. Yearning to blame the latest incident on the baby, as if somehow she were responsible, Delia sadly realized finally that nothing would ever have changed, even if the baby had survived.

She thought about all this as Maurice drove them home, so slowly, his eyes shutting over the steering wheel, that other cars passed them at a frightening speed, blowing their horns ferociously.

Why had she ever thought he might change?

I was a different person then, she understood.

Well, of course she was. But that was frightening: she hadn't wanted to change. Things had changed her while she was thinking everything was fine. All her life, it seemed, it had been Maurice and the babies and the house. That clean, vacuumed brown rug. On the rainy days, in the apartment all day long, when the children were sick, nothing gave her as much pleasure as her cleanly vacuumed brown rug. At times, it was the only thing in her world that made perfect, utter sense.

She thought about a church service for Sherry and then discounted it almost immediately. She was angry at God still, looking for an answer but receiving only silence.

The girls seemed to be asleep in the back seat. Maurice kept stopping the car fifty feet before the intersections. She hoped that they would make it home; she was anxious to see the baby's grave, although she would have to work up to it. She had gone too soon to see her father's, the oblong spot free of grass, but once she looked closer, she saw that the grass had begun to grow in, right on top of him, without a sound, so much life and miniature growth on top of nothing, as if Denis might just have raised his hand and grabbed at some of it to continue.

She thought she would be ready to go in a month.

They turned down their block and parked in front of the building, Maurice shutting his eyes and throwing his head back, the car keys dangling near his knee. "Tired," he said petulantly.

"Come on, girls." Delia turned around to shake their legs. "Wake up. We're home."

TWENTY-SIX

Soon after the trip to Rockaway, Delia stopped doing two things.

The first thing was praying. No more quick ejaculations when Maurice walked out the door on his way to work; no more chill of the door's chain across her lips as she waited at the top of the stairs for him to come home, scarcely daring to breathe, scared she wouldn't hear his footsteps four flights below. All the prayers she had poured into her own father, she had been pouring into Maurice — even using the very same words. It just wouldn't do any good. Her father had kept on drinking although they had begged him to stop, and Maurice would do the same. It seemed that the man Delia had married was now only a sliver, hidden deep inside the man he had become, such hard work to keep searching!

Maurice loved her, that she knew, as much as he could love anyone, but he just couldn't be any different. For now, the baby's death would tide them over, buy them a little more time; nobody would say that he wasn't suffering. As for Delia, she thought she was learning how to handle things. She considered giving up cosmetics and nice clothes, so that no one would think her unfeeling. She might buy mature dresses and long skirts, and when she had to leave the house, she'd walk through the streets with sober purpose, more mother than wife, more mother than woman. Such a loss was sure to give Delia a visible depth; as with Maurice's mother, Kathleen, people might poke each other when Delia passed by: she's the one, you know, the one I was telling you about.

Although the girls had gone back to school, she had stopped saying a decade of the rosary for their safe return. Praying felt juvenile and foolish. (She had read somewhere that ancient Chinese people had given their children terrible names in hopes that the gods might spare them; maybe she should have done that.)

People Delia had known since her own childhood were bound to see her on the streets, sober purpose or not, and she knew they would stare into her face, trying to figure out what exactly had gone wrong, and once she realized that, she stopped doing the second thing: going out of the house. Delia just couldn't bear to see anyone, not even her only friend, Rosaleen (who was too busy anyway). She had one close call; she ran down to Mae's apartment to borrow a tin of pepper, was squeezing through Mae's door when she caught a glimpse of Sally's pert, bouncy hairdo by the mailboxes.

People selling diaper services began to call her on the phone. The first time it happened, Delia had to sit down, and after that it became easy just to slam down the phone before she had heard more than five words. She slammed the phone on a dozen baby photographers and a company that delivered milk and slammed the phone on a handful of women who called to ask if Delia was in the market for a new crib.

She called TotsWorld and told the saleslady that her baby had died. The shocked silence gave Delia a sense of revenge. "The cord was around the baby's throat," she continued, almost unable to stop herself. She wouldn't need a name on the yellow lace pillow, she didn't need the yellow lace coverlet.

The saleslady promised to refund her money, and Delia began to cry.

She didn't know how long she would want to stay in the house. Technically, she told herself, she did go out, back to her old habit of hanging her wet clothes out to dry in good weather. She had been so happy in those early days, the taste of the wooden clothespins in her mouth sweet as her mother's puddings. The roof was one place she'd be sure to be alone: her neighbors were all risking their leases by buying electric clothes dryers, sneaking them into the building under old bedspreads.

She sat by herself with the blinds closed against the autumn, although it used to be her favorite season, the chill in the air like breathing in the vapor from ice cubes in a glass. She didn't want to face any of it, sitting in her apartment in the false dark, thinking of her life as one long unbroken string, not knowing how to make the string continue to grow so she might see this awful thing as a knot she had left behind.

Was it possible to forget how to live?

She kept losing her timing or missing her step, walking into doorways, pressing her fingers into the bruises she never remembered getting. She hadn't brought Sherry full circle: she still hadn't visited the grave. "I was already there, Delia," Maurice had told her. "You don't have to be there. It's over and done with. A year from now, you'll be ready, and we'll go together. We'll get her a stone. Would you like that?"

"We'll put 'Sherry' on it?"

"Hon, we'll put anything you want on it."

After a long time in the house, Delia found that everything was too tall for her. Patty and Maureen were too tall now, or Delia was too short. Maurice had said it was because she never went out, never wore her shoes. "Of course things are taller to you when you're barefoot," he'd said, quite reasonably.

She got out of bed early and sat in the dark living room, watching the sky turn from black to green to gray and then pink. The only time during the day that she opened her blinds was at dawn, when the rosy glow outside made every apartment window seem anxious to please her, as if they were all her friends and wished her well. But when the other blinds went up, the tenants ripped away the pink glass, filling the windows with music from the radio and the windowsills with freshly polished shoes, the stuff of ordinary apartment house lives.

Maureen had learned to press her school blouses, and she did Patty's too, just as Mae had taught her. (Mae called them "waists"; Maureen thought her waist was somewhere between her armpits and her belly button, and ironing her blouse somehow made her real waist itch and burn.)

First she pressed the shoulders, waking up the rest of the blouse, and then she pressed the sleeves, flat to the pointy tip of the ironing board, and if she saw even a tiny wrinkle, she made herself start over.

Somebody had to iron, and her mother didn't do it anymore, didn't do much of anything anymore, just sat around the apartment with the blinds down. The house was always a mess. Whenever they opened the front door, balls of dust skipped down the bare wood of the hallway.

On the day before school started, their uniforms came by mail from a company in Saint Louis, Missouri. Delia ripped open the box and then the plastic bags, hanging the blouses on the bathroom shower rod, telling the girls that the steam from their baths would iron out the wrinkles. But the next morning, Maureen's sleeve was so dented that it chafed her arm, and Patty's collar wouldn't stay down, flipping up and brushing against her ear. They forgot all about the blouses when everyone crowded around them in the schoolyard, teachers and children, to ask if it was a boy or a girl, Patty letting go of Maureen's hand to run into the church.

Maureen wasn't prepared for them.

She wanted everybody to forget, right away, as she had been trying to do, but it seemed that everything brought it back: the new display of baby sweaters in the window at TotsWorld on her way to school, the same place where she had gone with her mother to order the yellow pillow and the lace coverlet for the carriage; the powder-blue and pink letters spelling out "Winter Layettes" in the window of the five-and-ten, the soft, warm comforters and the tiny long-sleeved undershirts spread on top of the plaid woolen blankets, together with diapers and diaper pins, just like the ones they had bought in the summer, the ones her father had made her find and throw out.

He went through the apartment like a wild man the night they found out that her sister had died, and it didn't seem to take too long from the time she was finally able to get him to leave the bar (by staring at him, and weaving back and forth behind him) to the time that the doctor had called. She just couldn't stay at that little table one more minute, not with her mother on her way to the hospital, suffering like that. Outside, on the street, Maureen had told her father that Delia had gone with Eugene, that she had broken her water, and they practically ran back to Mae's house together, but by that time Eugene was home again and told them that they couldn't do anything but wait. Maurice had called the hospital, and the nurses promised that Dr. Mullaney would call Mac's house the second there was any news.

Eugene had gone out for beer so they could all celebrate, and in the meantime Gerald had come home, sitting down with them to try to watch television and not the clock above it, the picture so bad that the screen seemed covered in cloth. "Big Ben," the clock said, in fine print on the bottom, and Maureen had tried to make different words out of the letters in her grandmother's hot living room, the smell of her father and her uncle sitting in their undershirts, their shirts hanging on the doorknobs, reminding Maureen to sit like a lady. When the phone rang, Eugene had just come in the door, gone into the kitchen for glasses; Maurice winked at Maureen and ran inside, into the crook of Mae's bedroom wall, where the phone sat on a wobbly table, only he didn't come out right away, talking too much, Maureen had thought, for good news. When she got up and peered inside, he was sitting on the edge of Mae's bed, holding his head, the phone in his lap. Eugene had walked behind her; he tapped her on the shoulder and handed her a tiny glass of beer, and Maureen looked past him and saw that Patty had a glass too, and had drained it in one gulp, shuddering. "Hey, Patty," Eugene was saying. "Don't drink so fast, kiddo. Let's see first if it's a brother or a sister," but when Maurice wouldn't come out of the bedroom, Mae had gone inside to get him, and Patty pulled all the cushions from Mae's couch in her excitement and jumped up and down on them, and nobody had tried to stop her, not even Maureen, who peeked in the bedroom door and sipped at the beer and finally put the glass down. When Mae and Maurice came outside, Maureen was amazed to see her grandmother's tiny arm around her father's waist and his hand on her shoulder. Maureen had had to brace herself, holding on to the wing of the red brocade chair in the corner. "Jesus Christ, what?" Eugene asked frantically, sitting in the skeleton of the couch, his feet on the pillows, his hands gripping his skinny knees.

"Delia's fine," Mae had said quietly, "but the baby didn't live. A girl . . . The cord . . . Now you girls have your own baby angel up in heaven, and aren't you lucky."

Maureen remembered exactly how Mae had sounded, as if she

were hearing it again and again, and she thought of how her grand-mother had smelled while she hugged her and cried, of soap deter-gent and onions, but Patty wouldn't let Mae near her, squirming away, back to jumping on the sofa cushions, nobody saying anything for the longest time. They watched Mae walking out of the room, and Maureen couldn't forget how she had looked from the back, wringing her hands as she went into the kitchen.

There was nothing to say.

Maureen sat with her stunned father and her stunned uncles, watching Patty jump on the cushions, again and again, a fixed stare on her face, as if she were in a trance.

All Maureen could think about were the dolls dangling from the slots of the empty crib upstairs in her bedroom. Maurice finally stood up and said he was going to go to the hospital but first Maureen should come with him, he needed her help upstairs, and that Patty should stay where she was, and when they got into the apartment, he had walked straight to the silverware drawer and got the scissors. Maureen had followed him inside to her bedroom, watching him walk around the crib, grabbing a handful of yellow ribbons, a clump of them at a time, cutting them so that the baby dolls fell to the floor, some of them losing arms and legs, and they didn't seem cute any-more, but hateful, like insects, Maureen picking them up from the floor by the bits of ribbon, throwing them into the garbage bag so hard that the dolls bounced on the bottom of the bag.

Something happened to Maurice as he worked, and by the time he came back around the crib to where he had started, he was breath-ing hard, staring at the stubs of yellow ribbons sticking out like a blond giant's beard, throwing the scissors clear across the bedroom floor, yanking the mattress out of the crib, hardly able to grip it, throwing the mattress down too, and then he tore at the springs, huffing and puffing, demanding to know where the baby's clothes were. Maureen gave him everything that she had squirreled away in her bottom drawer, the kimonos and the receiving blankets, and she watched him throw them into the garbage bag, and then they went through all the cabinets and all the closets and all the drawers and dumped the baby's fine-tooth comb, the diaper pins with the ducks on the ends. He had forgotten the baby's brush, but Maureen couldn't bear to see it go and so she had said nothing when he cleared an entire shelf, the bottom one, of the medicine chest with his hand, just sweeping everything into the sink. A bottle of Delia's liquid makeup fell and broke, splattering his shirt and the wall and the backs of his hands, and when he was finished in the medicine chest and rubbed at his forehead, a smear of makeup whitened the front of his hair.

He went into the kitchen for another bag, and he spotted the old high chair in the broom closet, exactly where he had left it, yanking it out, the brown paper bags sliding onto the floor underneath his feet, and he opened the front door in a rage and threw the high chair down the marble stairs, making a terrible clattering noise that caused doors to open, alarmed faces to appear. When he had finished, he dismantled the crib and brought it down to the curb. When he came upstairs, he went into the shower and stayed there for a long, long time.

Maureen had sat quietly in the living room, waiting for him. She had left a book on the table that morning; she wished she could open it up to her old place and be who she was then.

Maurice had never said anything about how he had acted that day, the day her sister had been born, or the day she had died, or however Maureen should think of it now. She had wanted to tell Delia what he had done to the baby's things, but she never did. Someday she would. Maureen had been angry with the baby in the very beginning, and she felt guilty because of it: what kind of girl is mad at a little baby for ruining her life?

She couldn't wait to get away from it all and start school, but that first day brought her no relief.

Not when Steven Quigley's mother brought her seven children to school, the eighth one in the stroller. Maureen's new teacher, Sister Stella, touched the baby's hat and looked anxiously at Maureen, who couldn't believe that Steven's mother wasn't sick of seeing mashed Quigley faces, that she would have another Quigley on purpose. They never would have missed it if the baby had been born to the Delaneys instead.

That first day, she must have said a million times that the baby had died. Was it a boy or a girl, they had all wanted to know, as if that would have made a difference, all the small white faces pressing down on hers, and she had to say it was a girl, and then that thing about the cord, and some of the kids wanted to know what cord, so after the first million times, when they asked why the baby had died, Maureen just said she didn't know.

On the second day of school, Maureen concentrated on the heady aroma of shiny new book pages and fresh chalk and forced herself to forget about the baby, but then Sister Stella asked her to stay behind for a few minutes after class, and when the last boy in his rumpled white shirt had slammed the classroom door, Sister Stella asked her how she was doing.

Maureen's face grew hot. Fine, she had stammered.

"And how is your mother, Maureen?"

"Oh, she's fine too."

"Good. And your dad?"

Maureen choked up when Sister Stella called him that, Dad, as if she might have known how much Maureen loved him anyway. She always had to add that, words like "anyway" or the phrase she sometimes thought of when it came to her father: in spite of it all. She knew how wrong he was to drink, and every time he was drunk it was terrible, but she loved him, and "anyway" gave her the freedom to admit it. She needed that word: she would never turn from him.

"And your sister?" Sister Stella asked, when Maureen couldn't say a word about Maurice. "I hear she's got Sister Thomas this year."

"She's fine too," and Maureen nodded.

"Good," Sister Stella said, and then she hesitated, looking down at her. "You know, Maureen, when I was a young lady like you, my grandmother died, and I loved her very much. I felt just awful. When I found out, I just cried and cried, and I couldn't understand why this had happened to someone I loved so very much, and when one of my aunts came over, do you know what she said to me? She said, 'Elaine, God wanted her more than you did.'" Sister Stella paused and stared at her.

Elaine, Maureen thought, her real name is Elaine. Why did the church do that, take away real names and then give back fake ones?

Elaine, she thought again, folding her hands across her chest as if Sister Stella had given her something delicate to hold. "Thank you, Sister," Maureen said, and left the room. She didn't think about what Sister had said until she was nearly home, something about God wanting Sherry more than they did. She didn't know if that was possible.

TWENTY-SEVEN

All through the crisp, brilliant fall, Maurice was working days.

After the girls came home from school, Delia smelled the chill from the top of their heads when she kissed their shiny hair. While they began their homework, Delia fixed dinner, hamburgers or frankfurters with fried potatoes and beans, easy to cook and hard to clean up, leaving streaks of grease on the stove and on the table, but she didn't do the dishes after dinner anyway, she just left them for the next morning, clearing the table just enough for the textbooks and the notebooks. (Sometimes their arithmetic homework was hard to read, the paper so greasy in spots it was nearly transparent.)

In the morning, after everyone had left, Delia promised herself that they'd have a long talk about the baby that evening, but when they came back, brimming with the smell and feel of the outside world, none of her carefully rehearsed words would emerge. She told herself to be happy that all of them had come home to her.

She owed it to them not to make the whole thing worse. Not to keep the whole thing so alive. She owed it to her fresh-faced, pretty daughters and her sober, handsome husband (who was trying so hard for her). After dinner, while Delia poured fruit cocktail into the small white dishes with the gold trim flecked away, counting out the red cherries so the girls wouldn't fight, she swore she'd try harder to forget and go on. Tomorrow, she told herself, that was when she'd really start.

Rosaleen stopped calling when Delia confessed that she didn't have the energy for a chat.

Mae climbed the stairs a few times a week to drink tea in Delia's dark and dirty kitchen. She had tried to clean up only once. Delia had turned furious, white-faced and trembling, and Mae put the dishcloth back in the sink and sat down. She didn't say much, only sat watching Delia. In the beginning, when Delia first came home, Mae had told her that she had to be a soldier. "If I was a goddamn soldier, Ma," Delia had said, "I wouldn't be in this goddamn mess."

Mae brought Delia the newspapers and the church bulletin and new women's magazines from Cohen's, which were usually left on the table until her next visit, spotted with circles of coffee and milk.

"When I was in the hospital," Delia said one night at the dinner table, but the children stared at their plates, lowering their heads, and so she stopped. Maurice swore to the girls after dinner that he was meeting Kelly all the time lately, when he brought out the garbage at night, and by now Kelly was so fat that he cracked the pavement whenever he walked and he wore only bedsheets and wouldn't go out in the daytime. Of course the girls never saw him.

Delia smiled at them. They had probably forgotten all about the baby, and it was just as well to leave the subject alone. Mae was right: they had bounced back.

Still, she wanted to make sure. She pulled Patty close and held her, swaying back and forth. "Do you want to talk?" she asked, but Patty giggled and shook her head no and squirmed away. She approached Maureen, but Maureen just shrugged.

After Maurice had left the table one evening, with Patty following behind, Maureen sat with Delia and, her hands on her cheeks, talked about her eighth-grade class, which boys liked which girls and who Maureen thought might like her, though she didn't like any of them (not even John Fallon, whom everyone else had a crush on). She said that her teacher Sister Stella's real name was Elaine. "Sometimes, Sister Stella said, when someone you love dies, it's because God wants them more than you do. Do you think that's right, Mom?" Maureen asked, and then, without waiting for an answer, she ran inside with the others to watch television. Delia sat at the table for a long time, staring at the dirty dishes.

God wanting her baby more than she did.

Just like Maureen, Delia wondered if that was possible. The thought did comfort her: a big sculpted hand, the palm made of white pillows, and her baby, making cooing sounds, lying on her back, kicking her feet in the air, pink-flushed and healthy-looking. Happy. She had never once considered the baby as being happy. She only thought of the way she might have struggled to breathe, her hands plucking ferociously at the cord around her neck. Maybe she hadn't tried hard enough. Maybe she had inherited some weakness, some lack of character or strength, from one of her parents.

She imagined Sherry floating on top of the cotton-candy clouds she remembered from sunny days, and she began to open her blinds in the late afternoons, just out of curiosity, when she thought the clouds might be full and soft-looking, passing over the chimney stacks above her head, and she pretended her baby was right smack in their center. For no discernible reason, she was not as angry with God as she had been.

For a few weeks, Maurice was home when he was supposed to be there and at work the rest of the time. He ate dinner with them at night and talked a lot about his work, watching her face intently as he oversalted his food. Afterward, he fixed her a cup of tea and one for himself and sat across the table, trying hard to be pleasant. How were her brothers doing, had Mae been up to see her? How is Danny, have you heard from Rosaleen? So many questions all in a row that her head ached. Maurice nodded his head patiently when she said she didn't know a thing. He brightened considerably when she said that she had gone down to the lobby to get the mail from the mailbox herself rather than wait for one of the kids. It made her sorry for herself to see the intensity of his smile.

At night, before they fell asleep, he told her that he loved her, sleeping with his hand on her hipbone. She had wriggled away from him the first time he had done that, misunderstanding. No, no, he had said, not that, we have time, whenever you're ready, and she had relaxed. She wasn't sure when she could get back to that. She loved him for his patience. He was trying so hard.

And then he went to a retirement dinner, came home in a taxi, and somewhere along the way lost his wallet. He had been sick all over himself and slept in the bathtub, and when he began to cry, she simply shut the bathroom door and went back to bed, thinking herself too sore inside to go through it all again. She wasn't shocked by Maurice's behavior, realizing that it had been somewhat expected. She knew she could live through it. Compared to losing her baby,

Delia thought, she could live through anything. Losing Sherry had given her strength. Maybe, she began to think, she was starting to develop character.

In the mornings, as soon as she opened her eyes, waiting for the murky furniture to become familiar, she said simple prayers for her baby, and then she felt better.

She began to crave the smell and sight of the candles at church, flickering in front of the Our Lady statue, and she began to crave the smell of the peppery incense at the benediction service after the last Mass.

She was hungry for food and for light and for people, wondering how many pink sunrises had happened beyond her kitchen window, all those years when she stood squeezing oranges for the morning juice, and to her surprise, she found she wanted to go to the movies.

"Well," Mae said, the morning she walked into Delia's clean apartment, the windows all opened up, and the fall air smelling of apples and soap. "You got the blinds up finally, I see," and Delia realized by the way her mother's mouth trembled that she was about to cry. Delia turned to fill the kettle, giving Mae time to compose herself. "I got up early today, Ma. I just straightened up a bit."

"Looks real nice, Delia. Real nice. I just come from church. I wanted to talk to you, but you got me all surprised. I thought you'd be sittin' here still in the dark."

"What is it, Ma?"

"Okay," Mae said, taking a deep breath. "It's that, Delia Mary, I think we should have a Mass said for the baby." Mae sat back, pressing her lips together. "A proper funeral Mass. Delia, she never had one."

"No," Delia said quietly, "not with them standing on the altar saying 'Mary Delaney.' 'Mary Delaney' never existed, Ma. They'd print 'Mary' in the church bulletin, not 'Sherry.' They wouldn't use her right name at all. They'd call her by that name, and then it's like they won."

"Who's 'they,' Delia? And what is it exactly that they're winnin'?" Mae couldn't understand her daughter. She kept staring at Delia's lips as if the shape of her words might make more sense than the content.

"I don't know, Ma. It's like I have to somehow pay for the Mass by giving up my own idea of my baby."

"What's the difference what they call her, Delia?" Mae said, exasperated. "We know who she was, don't we? They could call her Rice Krispies, and it wouldn't matter a bit, would it? It's the same baby, the same soul, and if we don't give her a Mass, a proper Mass, then she'll wander around limbo for all eternity. Is that what you want? Remember what you used to say to me, that your father had all these principles too and nobody listened to him and nobody cared. Remember how he sat in his chair and hated everyone? He was all alone doing that, Delia. You want the poor soul of your child wandering around limbo all alone?"

"She was baptized already, Ma, right after she was born. She isn't in limbo. That's only for babies who were never baptized."

"Well, an extra bit of blessing, then, some way to give her something from us. We need a way to say good-bye."

"Not their way, Ma. I just couldn't bear it if they called her Mary. I don't want to be like Daddy, but I just know I'd walk out. I'm sorry, Ma, but no."

"Just think about it, Delia," Mae said, putting her hand on Delia's shoulder. "That's all I'm asking you to do."

"No, Ma." Delia walked away to set up the ironing board. "Just no."

The new restaurant, finally built, had a white brick front—how stupid, Mae said, with all that dirty soot always falling down from the el—and baby-blue drapes tied back from the big window facing the street. Its menu was taped on the glass by the door. "The Savoia" was ornately scripted over the door in gold, underneath a golden awning, taut enough to bounce a dime on.

Delia, beginning to embrace her old life, thought the restaurant looked nice, a new white building, so different from those around it, which were coated with gray dust and grime. She especially liked the drapes—baby blue was her favorite color now—and the blue letters on the white menu, the lettering so fancy that one word ran onto the next, although the closer she stood, the harder the menu was to read, blue ink drizzled across the shiny white cardboard.

Everybody in the Heights seemed to be afraid to look in at the place, glancing up at the menu when they passed by and then scurrying away, all except Delia, who stopped dead underneath the gold awning, shielding her eyes, and, standing her shopping cart off to the side, stared inside. She looked at the floor for something Hans might have forgotten: his cornhusk broom, with the bristles mashed in all directions like an old-fashioned handlebar mustache, or even one of the black waxy pencils he always kept tucked behind his ear. She didn't care who saw her, she wanted something of Hans's to keep for herself. Whatever was inside the place, whoever might be passing by, didn't matter a bit, and although Delia had always been afraid of things before, the pregnancy, if nothing else, had left her with something like courage. She went downstairs by herself at night, to drop the garbage into the cellar, stepping neatly over frantic clusters of mice running between the silver pails. Late at night, not even looking for Maurice, she sat by herself on the roof, watching the subway cars going into and out of the station, and she hadn't a twinge of apprehension, as if someone foolish enough to grab for her shoulder would find himself tossed to the pavement below.

She saw nothing but shiny floors in the Savoia, and after a week or so, she found it hard to look inside the place anyway, for it seemed that whenever she passed by, the sidewalk in front was crowded with silver-haired men in gray iridescent suits that glinted in the bits of light the el couldn't swallow. (Delia called them the Metal Men and made herself chuckle: they reminded her of the huge shiny flies she used to see pushing themselves into and out of the holes in the screen door of the Clancys' bar.)

Delia strained to hear the Metal Men speak when she passed by on her way to meet the children after school, glancing up at their gleaming gray hair, slicked straight back from their bumpy foreheads, but all she ever seemed to hear were references to someone named Nunzio, and she finally realized, by the way they turned simultaneously one afternoon to face a long and skinny man climbing out of a silver Cadillac, that he was Nunzio, the owner of the place, who had the longest and skinniest feet that Delia had ever seen. The alligator shoes he wore in a soft tan color made him look as if he were walking around on two fresh loaves of long pointy bread.

In the mornings, when the front of the Savoia was empty and the light underneath the el the brightest, Delia might run out to get the newspaper and see Nunzio already there, looking around him before he opened the door. He smiled at her, raising his dark eyebrows ever so slightly, and she thought he was handsome, with blue-gray eyes in a deeply tanned face. He put his hand on the fancy gold doorknob of the restaurant, and Delia saw his white-gold ring, set with a giant blue stone that matched his eyes. After he went inside, the Metal Men began to show up, one by one, as if they didn't want to seem too anxious to follow. They smoked filter cigarettes, held so that the burning end faced the palm of their hands, smoke drifting through the knuckles. Sometimes they smoked the cigarettes with their index finger and thumb enclosing their noses, and Delia thought of the Altar Society ladies, her mother's friends from church, who once sipped tea in Mae's kitchen with their pinkies extended into the air.

The Metal Men seemed proud of the Savoia, walking up and down in front as if they were rehearsing going inside, their chests puffed up in their foil suits. Nobody ever stood outside the Emerald Inn or the Shamrock like that, Delia thought; they leapt for the doors, staying as far away from the windows as they could, as if swallowing whiskey were an unpleasant chore, like secretly running into Murphy's Pawn-brokers to trade rings for cash.

After a while, other Cadillacs parked right behind Nunzio's in front of the place. They were driven by Metal Men whose jobs, it seemed, were to push thin dimes into the parking meters and nod at the policemen strolling along under the el.

Delia wondered if any of the Metal Men had wives, and then she went to Cohen's one night for a bottle of cream soda and saw a handful of women with enormous beehive hairdos wearing tight dark sheath dresses climb out of a cavalcade of fancy cars, one spike-heeled shoe at a time, and the few people on the street, herself included, stopped dead in their tracks. Delia had never seen stockings as sheer as the ones those women wore, as if they were bare-legged; their slender legs seemed to have no bones and promised they could be bent in a hundred directions. When the women stood and arranged them-selves, their shoes forced their tiny bellies to stick out a little, their backs arched so their tight rear ends had a bit of a curl.

When the door of the Savoia opened, thick, strong music belted Delia in the face like a slap, and when finally she had room enough to see inside, the red cigarette tips were glowing like the eyes of the devil.

Eugene and Delia sat with Mae in the kitchen, discussing the Savoia.

Eugene said he had been inside already, at the bar. "Christ," he said. "I never seen such women or such dancin' in my life. Floors shiny as a skatin' rink, like ice. The women's shoes are like stilettos."

"But what's it like inside?" Delia wanted to know more than those shiny floors.

"Red wallpaper, the kind you could feel." Eugene shut his eyes, remembering. "Every kind of Eyetalian food you could want, though I didn't eat any of it. I just watched the others. We only stood at the bar, me and Johnny Devane, with two bottles of beer, right at the end, and all them shady-looking guys at the other. Johnny seen one of the guys, told me the guy was in jail, he pointed the guy out."

Delia sat forward. "What'd he look like?"

"Some guy with gray hair. Gray suit."

Delia rolled her eyes. "Well, that makes it clear to me."

"Well, what d'ya want? I didn't go up and ask the guy his name. Me and Johnny, we took some of the match boxes off the bar." He reached into his shirt pocket and threw two tiny white boxes with the familiar blurred printing onto the table, like a pair of dice.

Delia picked one box up. "'Nunzio D'Amato,'" she read carefully, "'your host.'"

"Yeah," Eugene said, smiling. "Christ, what a name, huh? That Nunzio guy, he come over and shook our hands. Over the bar, they got a couple pictures with lights on the bottom, real fancy. The place with all the canals over in Italy and some guy in a helmet, some Eyetalian guy, I think. They think they're too good for pictures of flowers, I guess. It ain't the Shamrock Inn, that's for sure."

"The nerve of them," Mae said, "bringin' the criminal element into the Heights."

"What 'criminal element,' Ma?" Eugene stared at Mae. "One guy who was in jail?"

"It only takes one bad apple, Eugene," she said primly.

Eugene shot his mother a look of disgust and turned to Delia. "Next week, when I get paid, I'm askin' you all to be my guests around there, the kids and Maurice and Gerald. I got some money saved, and I want to treat everybody to dinner." Proud of himself, Eugene sat back in his chair and folded his hands on top of his head.

"What for?" Mae asked incredulously. "Eugene, you don't have the money for that. What're you, crazy?"

"Who says, Ma?" He threw his hands on the table. "I got the money! And what I don't have"—he paused, for the front door had opened—"Gerald'll give me."

"Huh?" Gerald came in, throwing his keys on the table. "Sure, Eugene — how much you need now?" he asked.

"Gerald, wait now, d'ya know what you're promisin'?" Mae asked. "You're promisin' to take us all to dinner, you and your brother, at that new Eyetalian place around the corner."

Gerald rubbed his upper lip. "So? Sure, I'll go. I got someone I want you all to meet anyway," he said quietly, staring at his hands.

"Who?" Mae asked, leaning over the stove, her sweater too close to the gas jets.

"Aw, Christ," Gerald said, jolting his head a bit. "You know who, Ma. Berni!"

"And who the hell is Berni?" she asked.

"That girl in the bakery. We been going out. You know that, Ma," he said sadly.

"Well, this is a fine way to be meetin' some girlfriend of yours, not even in my own home. In a restaurant, no less. In a foreign restaurant, a criminal place!" Mae scratched at her cheek until it was red. "A foreign girl in a foreign place — well, that figures."

"What's the difference, Ma?" Delia asked quickly, resting her hand on Gerald's arm, hoping he'd stay. "Gerald, that's just fine. I'd like to meet this Berni. We'd all like to. You go ahead and bring her."

Mae, her back to them, threw four tea bags into cups.

Delia watched her mother. "You know, maybe it's time we got an interesting place around here.,Some fancy place where there's dancing, nice food. When I go, I'm going to try some ravioli; I heard that's really good."

"You'd be better off seein' what you're eatin', miss. You don't want to be sick, you get a piece of meat, maybe a potato. If I can't get that, then I'm not going." Mae sat down.

"Well, Berni's Italian," Gerald said happily. "Maybe she could tell us what to order."

"Is this her idea to go there, or yours?" Mae snapped. "Are some of them hoodlums around there her family?"

"It's my idea, Ma, not his," Eugene cried. "Remember?"

"Yeah, it's Eugene's idea to begin with, Ma!" Gerald pointed at his brother, letting out a sharp sigh of relief.

"We could even try some lasagna." Delia smiled. Patty came in from the living room and snuggled against her. "I know that Rosaleen makes lasagna all the time."

"And I bet she don't even wash her hands," Mae sniffed.

"Oh, Ma . . ." Delia laughed.

"Meatballs and spaghetti," Patty offered.

"Do they have any hamburgers?" Maureen asked, suddenly appearing in the doorway, frowning. "Any roast beef?"

"There's my girl," Mae cried, opening her arms to hug Maureen.

"Well, if they don't have any meat, Ma, or potatoes," Eugene whispered, "then we'll order you both, you and Maureen, a big bowl of meatballs, and we'll wash them off in the glasses of water on the table, and then I'll smash 'em down with a saucer and put the whole mess on a hunk of bread. How's that?"

"Good." Maureen giggled. "Then they'll throw you and the meatballs out on the street!"

"But don't worry, Ma," Gerald said. "We'll go and bring him back. We could even order a bottle of wine, like we're celebrating, and you kids can have a taste, okay?"

"No they won't, Gerald," Delia said, seriously. "They'll have soda."

"Aw, Ma," Patty whined, chewing on a strand of hair.

"Can we get a fancy dessert?" Maureen asked Eugene, who was unsettled by the new responsibility. He stared at the table, trying to concentrate. "As I remember," he said solemnly, "they got a whole glass case full of fancy desserts. They got all kinds of cakes and pastries with whipped cream, and I think I seen some puddings too. Only thing is" — he stopped and stared at them — "you can't go askin' for ice cream."

"Why not?" Maureen asked him.

He looked around the table to make sure everyone was listening. "They call it spumoni. Not ice cream. Order ice cream, they won't know what you're askin' for."

The children nodded slowly and seriously, as if they were trying to memorize the new word.

"How come you know so much about this place?" Mae asked Eugene, her hands on her hips. "Seems like you know an awful lot for just bein' there the once."

"Ma, I was standing right next to the menu, and I seen the case full of desserts right next to me. They got a beautiful bar, anything you could think of, and I seen that just by lookin' too."

"Do her people come from the Heights?" Mae asked Gerald.

"I told you, Ma, no. I keep tellin' you she's from Forest Hills."

"Forest Hills! Why, that's so far away!"

"Ma," Delia said, a daughter leaning on either shoulder, "it's fifteen minutes on the train."

"Was I speakin' to you, Delia?"

"No, Ma, but—"

"Well, don't be answerin' for someone else." Mae stomped out of the kitchen, while the others—even, after a while, Delia—muffled their mouths, trying not to laugh.

Mae gone, Eugene's puny chest quivered with excitement, and he cracked his knuckles. Gerald pretended to arm-wrestle Patty. Maureen had her arms wrapped around Eugene's shoulders now, and he sat turned toward her a bit, the way a straggly plant turns to the sun.

Delia, watching them, was struck by their terrible smallness, as if someone had taken away the four floors of apartments above them and exposed them to the elements. She thought of Patty, who pulled the roof of her dollhouse away to look down into the sheet-metal kitchen with its red plastic table and the hooked rug painted on the metal floor. Delia felt at a great distance from her brothers and her daughters, almost as if she were the new baby starting to take shape in a pile of clouds somewhere, liking the view from wherever she was, the whole picture of selves appearing and selves growing older and selves changing.

They would probably never go together to the Savoia, unless there was some momentous event or other, for despite Eugene's good intentions, he'd never have the money. He'd have a bet to pay, or a bill he'd forgotten all about, or an old loan still outstanding, or maybe he'd need shoes.

It was fun to plan, but she couldn't imagine that their trip to the Savoia would ever come true. When she looked down, she saw the ripped linoleum on Mae's kitchen floor, which would have to be replaced soon, and then she noticed, when Gerald stood up, the hardened pieces of a million old suppers stuck to the rungs of the chairs.

"Delia, I know how we can do it," Mae said on the telephone a few days later.

"Do what?" Delia asked. She was pulling wet shirts out of the washing machine, trying to untangle the stringy sleeves. Already she was losing patience again with household tasks. They were all too much.

"Have the Mass said for the baby."

"I told you, Ma—"

"Now don't you go gettin' on your high horse, Delia. Look, I've been thinkin'. We go to the last Mass on Sunday, all of us, you and your family, me and the boys. God knows when either of them was in church last. We go to the Mass early and make sure we get to sit down together, and when the priest comes out on the altar—you know, when they announce the name of the person the Mass is for—well, we say her name to ourselves. 'For Sherry Delaney,' we say. We don't even have to stay for the benediction service at the end; we'll leave right away, as soon as the Mass is over. What do you think, huh?"

"Well, I don't know," Delia said, although the idea made something inside her tremble. "I'll think about it, and then I'll call you back, okay?"

"Okay," Mae said. "God bless," and she hung up.

Immediately, Delia wanted to call her mother back and say yes, just like that, but she was still angry, not so much with God anymore but with the Church. She was angry for the guilt she had felt on her wedding day, pregnant with Maureen, a guilt that had never left her, so that she had lived with a daily expectation of retribution—and yet their baby needed something. Delia wanted something else for her, and what else was there?

What would Maurice say? Delia didn't want to dwell on it, keep pushing the baby in his face. Life goes on, true, but whose life was it he kept talking about? Certainly not Delia's. Hers wasn't going anywhere.

This might be the right thing to do, she thought, the ending she had been searching for. The idea of being back in church gave her a sense of solace, the angels wriggling their bare toes on the domed ceiling, the purple velvet curtains of the confessional so heavy while her own skirts, made of thin fabrics, kept her aware of how she stood in the sun.

If the first child were stillborn, she thought for the hundredth time and then stopped herself. . . .

The Mass, she finally decided, was a good idea, something that fit. She felt a warmth inside her when she considered it, a sort of glow. Things sometimes fit together for the strangest reasons. A Mass for her baby, but on Delia's own terms. And then, just like after a real funeral Mass, they'd all go to the grave. She called Mae.

"Ma, I'll see what Maurice says when he comes home, but I think a Mass like that would be a real good idea."

"Oh, Delia Mary," Mae said, "I'm so happy for that. My prayers are answered."

She brought it up at dinnertime.

"On Sunday," she said, waiting for them to look up, "would you like to go to Mass at church, the last Mass, all of us, just for your sister?"

Your sister. It was so easy to say.

"Like a funeral Mass?" Maureen asked.

"Something like that. Only we aren't going to say anything about it being a funeral Mass. We're just going to go to church and pray for Sherry ourselves, all of us, Grandma and the boys too. What do you think?"

"Well, we go to Mass anyway on Sunday with Grandma." Maureen looked at her thoughtfully. "Yeah, I think that's good."

"And then to the cemetery," Delia said, looking at Maurice, who was fidgeting with his fork.

"Aw, Delia," he said. "Why now? I told you we'd go in a few months." He shifted in his chair. "Why now?"

"I don't know," she said. "It's just something I want to do. I feel like I can't do anything else until there's some kind of ending, you know? I have to see where she's buried."

She wanted to add: It might make me feel better, but she wasn't sure it would, and somehow that didn't matter.

"Can we bring flowers," Patty asked, "me and Maureen? A bouquet, like for my Communion? Just leave them for her, our sister?"

The baby had become more real than ever.

"Sure, Patty." Delia smiled. "That'll be just fine."

TWENTY-NINE

Late that night, Eugene called.

"Hello?" he asked, speaking so loudly that the receiver vibrated in Delia's hand. She walked the length of the hallway outside the kitchen, stretching the cord to its full length as if walking away from the base of the telephone might make him lower his voice. Shhh, she wanted to say, the girls are asleep.

Maurice sat up on the couch, looking at her quizzically. Nobody ever called them so late.

"Listen, Delia," Eugene said, in a rush. "Can't talk long—I'm at work—but I need you to do me a favor."

"What is it?"

"On Sunday? After the baby's Mass? I'd be pleased and honored if you'd let me take all of us out to eat." He sounded out of breath, as if someone were chasing him.

"Aw, Eugene." Delia was touched. "You don't have to do that."

She listened to his silence and knew that his feelings had been hurt. Delia could just see him, staring at the dial of the phone.

Let him be a part of this, she thought. He's part of so little else. "Where would you like to take us?" she asked.

"Where?" The receiver vibrated some more. He might have been ready to hang up. "Oh," he said, "around to the Savoia. As my guests. I want to do this for the family and for the baby. Ma says we should call her Sherry, that you'd like it better."

"Yeah, Eugene, I think I would." Delia wanted the name used as much as possible, dreading the next week, the next month, the next year, when they'd hardly say it at all.

"Can I do it, then, Delia? Can I make a reservation?"

"Eugene, you don't need a reservation there."

"But I want it," he said anxiously. "Just so's there's no mix-up, you know?"

"Okay, okay. Then you'd better make it. That'd be really nice."

"What time should I tell them?"

After the grave, she thought. They'd leave the church and go to Holy Sepulchre, say a prayer, and leave. It was what they'd done when her father died, the same sequence of events. The funeral Mass, which Delia had left feeling positively glowing, as if she were lit from within and happy for Denis, and then the cemetery, the harsh reality of wood and ground, the fleeting worries of her father's chill in winter, the summer sky above his head, which he would never see, and the horror of insects. She shuddered to remember it. The party back at Mae's house, for that was what it had been. Jimmy Conklin, a skinny kid with a crew cut, was the altar boy, and he had waltzed through Mae's kitchen carrying a jelly glass full of ice cubes and her father's rye. Denis's eyeglasses were on the kitchen table, where he had left them, magnifying the blue flower sprigs on the tablecloth until Delia was sure his eyes had looked exactly like that. She kept looking through the crowd for her father. Every closed door had its possibilities, and every ring of the doorbell made her heart jump. She had been so pregnant with Maureen, she kept bumping against the men who lined the wall in the living room, jostling their arms and spilling their drinks, forcing them to blot the whiskey spots from their ties with their handkerchiefs. "It was the baby did that," she'd joked. "It's taken the pledge," and the men had laughed and looked away.

"Well, what time?" Eugene asked. "I gotta make the reservation." Reservation. She could almost hear the word whistling through his head, over and over again, like a train. "Four o'clock," she said. "Make it for four."

"My pleasure," he answered, deepening his voice. Briefly, fleetingly, her brother had such possibilities. "Eugene?" she asked, when he didn't say another word. It'd be just like him to simply hang up.

"Yeah?"

"Thanks."

"Yeah," he said, and then he did hang up.

She could do it, she told herself, go to the grave, if she thought about the restaurant or the next morning. Even at Holy Sepulchre, she could think her twenty-four-hour thoughts.

In twenty-four hours, she had always told herself, when she was sick or in labor or having a tooth pulled, she'd be all over it, and she usually was, thinking of what Mae had always said:

"Ah, this time tomorrow, and you'll be walkin' inside a new day."

"Wait till you get a load of this." Mae phoned early the next morning, right after she waved good-bye to Maureen and Patty on their way to school.

"What, Ma?" Delia had been standing in front of her closet, wondering what to wear on Sunday. She didn't know what she could fit into. She hadn't looked at her clothes in months.

"It's your brother Gerald. He's takin' that woman he's runnin' around with, that one from the bakery, that Eyetalian one he's with when he's never home here. He's bringin' *her* to the Mass, the one for our baby, and then he's bringin' her to that restaurant around the corner too. How do you like that one, Delia?"

"Well, um, is she Catholic?"

"Is she *Catholic?* Delia Mary, what kind of a question is that? Yes, she's Catholic—most of them people are, aren't they? It's not the point, her bein' Catholic or not! The point is that this is personal family time for us, and a stranger is interferin'. It isn't right, is all I'm sayin'."

"Well, I don't know, Ma. If he's with her all the time and he wants to take her to meet us, maybe it's serious. Maybe he's finally going to get married, Ma."

"I think he should stick with his own kind, Delia."

"Oh, Ma . . . now it's your turn to sound just like Daddy. Remember when Bridget got married to Henry Goldblum? How Daddy wouldn't go, and it was just you and me?"

"You really surprise me, Delia. I thought you'd have more feeling for your own child's memory," and she hung up, leaving Delia standing with her mouth open. If she could have laughed, she would have.

Delia wore a blue skirt and a white blouse with small pink flowers on the collar. The clothes were old, but they were soft against her flesh. She didn't want anything tight, no mean-spirited fabrics to gnaw her skin. The girls wore cotton jumpers, a year old and a bit short. Maurice was back working night tour, and he was coming straight from work to walk with Delia and the others to church.

Straight from work, Delia kept assuring herself, hoping with all her heart that he wouldn't just disappear.

Early Sunday morning, she was fully dressed before the sun was up, wondering why Sundays had a different feel about them than the rest of the week. She looked out the window at the pink windows across the courtyard. Her hands were ice cold, and so were her feet; the coffee she was drinking made her tremble and caused her kidneys to burn. Every time she ran into the bathroom, she combed her hair, and then she looked in at the girls, hoping they'd get up. She called Mae well before seven. "Mama, I'm so scared," she said.

"Darlin' girl," Mae said hoarsely. "You'll do just fine."

She was determined to act calm for her girls.

When they got up, she followed them into the bathroom, carrying their underwear. She tried to help Patty with her hair, but Patty managed fine by herself and, lately, had learned to make tighter, neater braids than Delia ever could. She gave Maureen one of her lipsticks, the lightest shade she had, and watched her pout in the mirror just as she herself had always done. She wanted to tell Maureen that she was afraid. Though she didn't, Maureen, walking past Delia, patted her mother's hand. They waited in the living room for as long as they could, listening to the other apartment doors slam as the neighbors left for church, and then they went downstairs to wait on the street for Maurice. There Mae stood, wearing a white sweater over a dark dress, and Eugene, who had bought an unflattering gold-colored suit that was too big.

"Where's Maurice?" Mae asked, her eyes narrowing.

"Well, where's Gerald?" Delia asked. "Maurice isn't home from work yet, but we're going anyway. He'll come over to the church. He knows where we are." I hope, she thought.

"Your brother went off to get that woman. He said he'd meet us over there, at church, in front. He had to go all the way to Forest Hills, just wouldn't listen to reason," Mae said bitterly, shaking her head. "Some family we got."

"Mama, please."

"Okay, okay. Let's go."

Delia walked between the girls, knowing that if she didn't, Eugene would take her arm and march her through the church and everyone would know that for the Delaneys, the Mass was special. She hadn't seen many people since the baby had died; she didn't want to make such an arrival. Her daughters seemed somehow to hide her. They made her feel anonymous.

At the corner, they heard a yell, a name and then maybe not. Everyone turned around except Eugene, who hadn't heard a thing. They saw Maurice running up the block toward them, a white paper bag in each hand. His clothes were rumpled and sweaty, he had a vague stubble on his cheeks. His eyes were bloodshot, and his hair fell across his forehead. He held the bags out to them, so out of breath he nearly fell across the hood of a nearby car. They stared at him.

"Maureen," he wheezed, "take this. One's for you, one's for Patty."

Maureen reached inside and pulled out the most exquisite nosegay that Delia had ever seen, tiny white tea roses in a nest of pure white baby's breath. Long white curling ribbons scattered across Maureen's wrist. Patty's nosegay was miniature pink carnations, the pink ribbons long enough to brush against her knees. "For our sister." Maureen started to cry.

Her father nodded. "It's why I'm late," he said, pressing his fingers to his chest.

Increasingly, as they made their way to church, Delia wished she hadn't agreed to the idea.

Alice Branigan was right ahead of them, supporting the withered figure of Mrs. Krupp. It was so unfair, Delia thought, that she should live on and on, while Sherry . . .

Rather than have to greet the two women, Delia crossed the street, and her family followed, overtaking Anna Curley at the corner. The old busybody turned and smiled, looking at the flowers in

313

the children's hands, and Delia could have punched her. Maurice, sensing her agitation, grabbed for her hand.

They spotted Gerald's plaid sports coat in front of the church. He had his arm around the shoulder of a plump woman in a black skirt.

"Look at the lard of her," Mae said of Bernadetta LaBriola, a pretty woman with a round face and reddish hair, big legs but no ankles, and a full figure. She wore too much jewelry, a matching set of blue stone earrings, a necklace, and a bracelet, with blue stones set in a circle pin on the shoulder of her black blouse. As soon as Gerald introduced them (pulling his hand away from her shoulder and shoving it in his pocket), right after Delia said hello, Berni stepped forward and kissed Delia's cheek. She tried to kiss Mae, but Mae was too quick, pulling Patty in front of her so that Berni stepped down hard on Patty's toe. "Oh, I'm just so sorry," were the first words she said to the child, bending down, looking into Patty's face, desperate to accommodate.

They went into the church, Delia dunking her fingers into the holy water font by the front door, the water yellowish and somewhat oily.

"Just a minute," an usher said to Delia, blocking the pews. "What are those children doing here? Don't you know the children's Mass is at nine o'clock and not twelve?"

Surprised, Delia looked down at him. He was Maura O'Reilly's father. Maura had been in Delia's class at St. Immaculata's, the oldest of six daughters, all now as full-breasted and ungainly as a flock of pigeons. "Why weren't those children at this morning's Mass?" he persisted, as if he had any right to ask, looking curiously at the nosegays, Patty's face buried deep in hers, the reddish hair spilling over the edges of the pink. Delia was seized with the urge to turn right around and run home.

"They weren't at this morning's Mass, Mr. O'Reilly," she said, advancing toward him, half a head taller than he was, "because they're here now with me." She looked from his loose jowls to the tarnished Holy Ghost pin in his worn green lapel.

"Now, miss." Mae had squeezed next to her, taking her arm. "There's no need to go bein' fresh to this man."

"Mama," Delia said, loud enough for everyone to hear, "there's no need for you to talk to me like a child!"

Insulted, Mae stalked away from them, down to the first pew, to sit by herself. Delia blinked, amazed at herself. "Well, the next time," Mr. O'Reilly grumbled.

"Don't worry, Mr. O'Reilly," Delia said, loudly again. "There won't be a next time. I'm not coming back."

Berni LaBriola stood next to an empty pew, just waiting for them, an unfamiliar face to the congregation, but she didn't seem to mind at all, smiling at Delia and rolling her eyes at Mr. O'Reilly's back. There was a fussiness about her that Delia instantly liked, her small pink fingernails and her small round hands, a way of showering attention on things, touching Delia's arm when she passed, gently touching Gerald's back.

Thomas Hanratty, who lived around the block, was in the pew across the aisle. His mother had recently died, at ninety, and he had married a dark-skinned woman with two teenage daughters. The four bored faces looked up at them, and Delia grabbed Patty and made her go in first. Patty had been stroking her cheeks with the bouquet: Delia was afraid that if she stopped looking at her, Patty might begin to eat it.

The Delaneys, with Gerald and Berni, sat together in the middle of the church, shoulder to shoulder, pressed together. Mae was somewhere in the front, and Eugene stood in the side aisle, next to Patty. Delia knew he couldn't allow himself to be cornered. He would sooner run out the door. Gerald pulled Berni's arm through his, and Delia slid her arm through Maurice's. Gratefully, he smiled at her. Mr. O'Reilly, Delia thought, was a prime example of what was wrong with the Church. Those ridiculous rules and regulations. Delia was restless for the Mass to begin, shuffling her feet back and forth, sliding her shoes off, sighing and looking nervously around her. She didn't even care that her mother was mad at her.

Kathleen Delaney had called Delia a few days earlier. She would have liked to come to the baby's Mass, she explained, but she had to work. Delia had said she understood, and then Kathleen had said, "I love you, you know," and was gone, leaving Delia to stare at the telephone for a very long time.

Delia shifted in the pew, lifting one buttock at a time and moving backward and forward, folding and unfolding her hands. She dug through her pocketbook for change for the collection and dropped a dime, which nobody could find. She picked at the lint on Maurice's sleeve. Berni smiled at her, leaning sideways over Gerald's knees, and Delia noticed how strong and white her teeth were.

The baby, the flowers, the grave: she did not want to think about it.

She was doing this, she decided, for her family. She still believed in God, but little Mr. O'Reilly was the last straw. She would worship God in her own way, without any foolish rules, at home in the living room. When the priest came out on the altar and the congregation stood to welcome him, Delia remained in her seat. Maurice looked down at her questioningly and shrugged. She breathed in the perfume around her, so sweet, but insufficient against the blanket of breath in the church, sour and bitter in her nostrils, cloying and warm around her face. Delia wouldn't kneel when the others did, staying where she was, listening to the shuffle of feet and the blowing of noses, the rattling of coins falling on the floor. Eugene leaned down and tugged on Patty's hair. She giggled and clamped her hand over her mouth.

Suddenly, from the back of the church, there was a sharp, shrill scream.

People began to turn around, stunned to silence, and Delia heard a second scream and then the sound of running and scuffling on the marble floor.

Mr. O'Reilly ran down the center aisle, and two cadaverous men in mismatched pants and jackets ran along the side aisles, one of them tripping over Eugene's feet.

Before Delia had turned in her seat, a woman ran by, a flash of dots and gold and long blond hair, and she turned at the altar to face the congregation, swaying back and forth. Mr. O'Reilly grabbed her, and she threw him off, onto the floor, while the cadaverous men tried to pinion her, but she broke away from their matchstick arms and ran to the center of the church. Her blond hair fell into her eyes, and the crowd gasped. A leopardskin coat gaped open over a black slip, so tight they could clearly see a slim garter belt, thinner than Maureen's, pressing into her flesh, holding up black stockings that descended into backless gold shoes. "Are there any single women here?" she asked, in a husky, tobacco-drenched voice, while Mr. O'Reilly, who was on his feet behind her, planned his attack. "I'd like to address the single women of the parish"—she had begun to slur her words—"the goddamn fucking old maids. I can save you plenty of heartache."

Now Mr. O'Reilly took her by surprise, grabbing her around the waist and tugging, trying to pull her toward the main portal, but the woman struggled, slamming her shoe into his instep, and she slipped, landing on her knees. Her bare breasts fell out of her slip and everyone gasped again, but she threw her head back haughtily. "Never love a goddamn man," she sang out, sitting back on her haunches. "They aren't worth the goddamn trouble!" And then Mr. O'Reilly pulled her to her feet, trying to close the leopardskin coat, while the skinny men fumbled with her legs, and together they dragged her down the aisle and across the front of the altar and out the side door. "Ayeeee," the woman screamed, kicking her legs and swinging her arms, her brownish nipples bubbling around the white-ness of her arms like tiny buoys. One gold shoe fell off and spun across the floor, clanging against the iron altar gates. There were more mud-dled screams, bodies thudding against the closed door, and then it was quiet.

Father Sullivan opened his arms to the parish. "Let us pray," he said quietly, "for the sick and the sad."

Stunned, shocked, Delia and Maurice stared at each other. Mr. O'Reilly came back inside, mopping his fat face, the knot in his tie pulled off to the side, the Holy Ghost pin dangling loose, the lapel of his green jacket wrinkled and crushed. Delia tried to see Mae, but she couldn't find her, and she looked incredulously at her girls, who were grinning, and at Berni, who was smiling and had the fattest knees that Delia had ever seen, and Delia began to laugh, finally, until the tears streamed down her cheeks, and then she couldn't help herself, she stood up and applauded.

To Delia's great surprise, the screaming woman hadn't been struck dead after her outburst. Somehow, she gave Delia the courage to stand in front of Father Sullivan and feel she had nothing to hide. It surprised Delia afterward to realize how much it had mattered to her.

Rules didn't make the Church. The lady in the leopardskin coat, as imperfect as she was, dragged out the door by people just as imperfect, who dumped her on the street like that—it was just something that had happened, as Gerald had said to Delia in the hospital.

She was glad that the fuss had happened at Sherry's Mass. It was fitting somehow; her daughter would have been as light and as bubbly as her name.

Years later, after Maurice had died and the girls had grown up and gone (Patty an actress in California, Maureen the mother of Terence William Daly), when a woman in flannel pajamas and a green velvet bonnet poked a hand covered with a cotton gardening glove into Delia's chest in the ShopSmart and told her to hurry and buy light-bulb stocks, she thought of her Sherry as if the baby had planned it all.

She wouldn't have been as serious as Maureen (it had always amazed Delia, how Maureen had started her periods on the same day that President Kennedy had been shot; so much blood, as if it were her responsibility, along with the country, to finally grow up) or as flighty as Patty. Sherry (Delia just knew it) would have been carefree, the type to laugh easily, in some way the type Delia felt herself becoming, sitting in that church, free, as if lightheartedness and appetite might have been passed backward from her infant daughter, a sort of reverse inheritance. Any baby might remind her of Sherry, especially if it smiled at Delia, especially if it winked.

There was no stone at all on the grave at Holy Sepulchre.

None for Sean Delaney or his baby sons, none for Sherry Mary, which was what Delia decided to call her after all. Two names together. Why not, she had asked herself, the same as my middle name, the same as the girls' and Mae's. It sounded nice.

The grave site wasn't barren, as she had feared, but was a fat square of thick grass in the midst of stone angels, their arms flung wide open, beseeching, so many angels and lambs and crosses in so many different sizes, right across the street from Arthur's Discounts, that Delia could barely see the sky. Maureen knelt down and blessed herself, her long dark hair spilling over her shoulders, her back straight, looking exactly like one of the statues nearby, the one of Saint Bernadette holding a calf.

Maureen left the flowers on top of the grave, and after some urging, Patty did the same.

Berni stayed on the path by herself, underneath a tree that was dropping dry brown leaves around her at a great rate. "I'm so sorry about your baby," she had said to Delia after the Mass, and "Pleased to meet you" to Mae, who simply looked right through her, turning to Delia.

"Did you hear the crazy one who *clapped* when they threw the madwoman out?" Mae had asked, amazed, as if she suddenly remembered it.

"No," Delia said. "Really?" and Maurice laughed.

"Angels cry when fools laugh," Mae said loudly. "D'ya know that, Maurice?" and when he laughed even harder, Mae had stomped off and sat in the back seat of the car.

Delia knelt with Maurice, and they prayed, the girls and Mae waiting for them, and after a while Berni made her way up toward them, holding on to Gerald's hand. Eugene had been walking through the cemetery by himself, but just as they were ready to leave, he appeared, blessing himself and clasping his hands in front of him, leaning on the full stone skirt of an angel right in back of him.

Delia wondered what she felt: calm, peaceful.

Maurice hugged her close and kissed her forehead. "You ready?" he asked after a while, and she was, whispering good-bye to the bubbly, budding Sherry Mary, the thick grass and the pretty flowers, knowing full well that she hadn't left her there at all but was carrying her inside, back home to the Heights.

THIRTY

The day outside was bright, and when they walked into the restaurant, Delia couldn't see a thing.

They went on their way into the dining room, but to get there they had to walk through the front of the Savoia, where the bar was. Someone called out to Eugene. "Hey, how you doin'?"

"Hiya," Eugene answered, looking around in the darkness.

Delia felt too white and too bright in such a black place. Her whole family, with their Irish complexions, looked eerie in the darkness, with sudden dark, deep circles underneath their eyes. She felt as if she radiated a glow, the hair on her forearms downy and golden.

All along the avenue, Mae had stared at Berni's backside, which was large and round, and when she walked ahead with Gerald, her dangling blue stone earrings made small clicking sounds like chewing. Mae had stared pointedly at Delia, as if Delia should recognize at once that being full-hipped and wearing dangling earrings were serious character flaws.

"So nice to meet you," the woman had said again, trying to get it out of the way, and all Mae had said was "Huh," standing with her hands on Patty's shoulder. Delia was embarrassed for her.

Maurice was so careful of Delia outside, tugging on her elbow when they came to the curbs, as if she couldn't see very well or the baby had died the day before and she hadn't had the time to get over it a bit, all that time when he was at work, when the girls were with Mae or at school. There was something about Maurice, Delia thought, how he ran off somewhere when she needed him, as if he knew what had happened and didn't want to know at the same time, yet when he finally came back to her, back home, he acted as if time had stood still, as if he were unable to understand that things never stayed the same. He couldn't face change. If Delia were still wondering why he drank, she would say that was the reason.

But the truth was, she had given up wondering why he drank.

Whenever he became sober, things seemed over and done with for him. But situations were never really resolved. That was what Delia couldn't understand about life. Things were never truly over with; they just became other things. Even if you sat in your house, even if you spent your life in the very bed you were born in, things wouldn't stay the same. You would age, events would occur that you could never control. A plane might crash into your roof, a fire might cook you in your bed, your pillows scorched and melting like marshmallows.

She thought she might have asked Sherry Mary to accomplish too much. She was supposed to be a boy, first of all, for Maurice, and then she was supposed to give Delia a new beginning, or maybe it was an ending she was looking for, the last pregnancy, the one she had saved for the end, like a tiny package left behind underneath the Christmas tree. The baby might have been overwhelmed and just given up. Delia shouldn't have asked this much from her.

They had to wait to be seated. Although the Savoia wasn't very crowded, a velvet rope was drawn across the dining room.

"I think this is just about where Hans stacked the crackers," Delia said to Maurice. "I think that right now we're standing in the aisle where"—she tilted her head—"he kept those little cans of peas."

"I was just thinking that we were standing in the freezer case with the ice cream."

She smiled; there was such joy when they connected.

A tall woman in a black dress walked toward them, her blond hair piled elaborately on top of her head, the heavy white menus underneath her arm. "Hello, Delia," she said. "Hello, Mae."

Delia stared at her. "Mavourneen!" she said in surprise, then poked Mae in the arm. "You remember Mavourneen Curley, Ma, don't you? Anna's daughter?"

"Oh, yes, of course I do. How are you, dear?" Mae asked, tilting her head so far back she might have been studying Mount Rushmore. "I thought you'd moved far away."

"I did." Mavourneen shifted the menus. "I got married, and then I got divorced, and now I'm home."

"Oh, my dear." Mae squeezed Delia's hand. "What a shame."

"No, not at all." Mavourneen pointed at the longest table, smoothing her hand over the slender back of her neck. "Really for the best. Come this way, please."

Before they had sat down, Maurice asked Mavourneen for a beer.

"I'm not your waitress, sir," she said icily, "but I'll send her over right away. Delia and Mae, enjoy your meal." She smiled, not recognizing Maurice, not recognizing Mae's sons.

Mavourneen Curley had been so anxious to leave the Heights, Delia thought, saving every cent she made, her mother had said, working the cash register at Hans's store in the summer and after school. She had been a fashion model, according to Anna, and she had lived in New York and eaten dinner at the Plaza. Anna had said that she had been to Paris, and yet here she was (Delia had to smile to herself), right where she had been at seventeen. All the way around and now back in the Heights.

Delia wondered if anyone ever really left the place where they were born. If Mavourneen Curley had come back, then maybe the Heights wasn't such a terrible place to be.

"Ah, poor Anna," Mae whispered, sliding into the chair against the wall. "A divorce in her family; what a shame."

"Minestrone," Berni said brightly, reading from the menu, looking down the table at them all. "My mother used to make that for us all the time. I love it."

"Is that full of tomatoes?" Mae asked. It was the first time she had looked directly at the woman.

"Well, yes, there usually are tomatoes in it," Berni said apologetically.

"Those Eyetalian people," Mae sighed. "I'm surprised they don't throw tomatoes on top of ice cream like chocolate syrup."

"Spumoni, Ma." Eugene looked across at Mae. "They call it spumoni, remember?"

"Okay, *spumoni*, then. Sounds like spaghetti to me anyway. It all sounds the same."

Berni looked at Gerald. "I'll take some of that soup too, Berni," he said, ignoring Mae's withering glance. "Sounds pretty good to me."

Mae closed the menu and dropped it onto the table. "I'll eat when I get home. Nothing here looks good."

When the waitress came to their table, Eugene ordered a boilermaker for himself and one for Maurice. "Order anything you want," he said to his guests, "it's all on me," but all the rest of them wanted seemed to be Cokes with cherries bobbing around the ice cubes.

Nunzio, the owner, passed by, and Eugene plucked at the hem of his jacket. "Hey, Nunz, how you doin'?" Eugene smiled so broadly his gums glistened. "Brought my family around." He pointed quickly at each of them. "Oh, yeah, and down there? That's my brother's girl sittin' at the end."

"How you doin'?" Nunzio asked, smiling at everyone. Delia was sitting closest to him; he bent down and kissed her hand. Something started inside her; she shifted in her chair and pulled her hand away. "I'm so sorry," Nunzio said to Eugene. "I'm real bad with names."

"Rooney," Eugene said petulantly. "Eugene Rooney. Been in this place a good coupla times now."

"Oh, I know your face," Nunzio said, shaking his head. "I'm just awful with names. Please forgive me, Eugene. I'll send the waitress over with another round. Enjoy yourselves. Charmed to meet you," he said to Delia.

The waitress set down second drinks for everyone, although the first ones were still full, and though she wasn't very hungry, Delia had a sudden urge to order two dinners just for symmetry.

The jukebox in the bar began playing. She recognized Bobby Darin singing "Mack the Knife" and started tapping her foot, the unfamiliar motion making her shinbone twitch. She used to love to dance, although Maurice danced only to please her. The music kept playing, switching from one song to the other, some that she recognized and some that she didn't, the slow romantic ones making her lonely for her younger self. She looked over at Maurice, but he was draining his second glass of beer in a few gulps and didn't notice her.

Nunzio came out of the darkness, starting toward their table, his long black shoes gleaming, his black hair shining underneath the dim lights. He held his hand out to Delia. "Dance?" he asked, and her cheeks flushed, she felt a burning at the base of her throat. She looked around frantically for someone to tell her what to do. "Yes, you," Nunzio laughed. "Who else do you think I'm asking?"

She looked at Maurice, but he was turned in his chair, trying to get the waitress's attention, his finger in the air, the glasses in front of him empty.

"Yes," Delia said, just like that, and put her hand in his, soft and heavy. Another man's hand, she said to herself as she stood up, watching Maurice writhe in his chair, his head bobbing up and down as he focused on the swinging doors, paying no attention to Mae, her tiny fingers fluttering in his direction, who stared at Delia with her mouth open.

Maureen grinned at her mother.

Delia folded herself into Nunzio's arms, and she watched her family at the table grow smaller and smaller as she sailed across the room, their tablecloth pitched like the sail of a ship, her family floating away from her, or she away from them, across the shiny, slippery wooden floor, unsure who had let go of whom. She danced in the arms of a strange man, past where Hans had had his paper goods, down the bread aisle and over to the milk case.

She had survived, it was all that mattered, to survive and endure and let go. She had lost her baby, her child, and she was still here, as if the child had died in order that Delia might live, almost as if Sherry had given birth to her.

She could never go back to that other self. Nothing broken ever mended the same. She had labored over enough broken teacups, the tiny curved handle in one hand and the thin silver tube of cement in the other, trying to force the handle to the cup, but it had never worked out quite right, there was always the hairline mark, and she never treated it the same way, always wary of a spill or a burn.

She always ended up buying a bigger, stronger cup.

She felt as tall as Maurice in Nunzio's arms, maybe even a bit taller, smelling his strong exotic aftershave, dancing as she had once danced with Maurice but hardly the same person as she was at all. She had endured. The future, despite Maurice, despite her mother, despite Sherry Mary, belonged to her. She had come through it, prevailed over the thing she had most feared, and she laughed for the second time that day, her shoulders convulsing with something like joy, and she had forgotten how good that felt, like being rocked again in her mother's arms.

She'd never know how she had done it.

Right where Hans's soaps had been, Nunzio dipped her. She threw her head back, and she laughed again, just for the exercise. Looking at the ceiling, she thought she heard soft applause, the sound of baby hands clapping.